The Candle Maker's Assistant

A TALE FROM THE MIDDLE AGES

BY

PATRICK J. SIMONS

Green Ivy Publishing
1 Lincoln Centre
18W140 Butterfield Road
Suite 1500
Oakbrook Terrace IL 60181-4843
www.greenivybooks.com

ISBN: 978-1-945650-54-3

Ebook: 978-1-945650-55-0

Also by Patrick J. Simons

Zebediah

The harrowing tale of a young man's journey through life,
with multiple five-star reviews on Amazon.com.

sric was a foundling who grew up in the harsh conditions of a church-run orphanage. It was long suspected that his parents abandoned him because he was a dwarf, though nothing is known of them. His spine was misshapen and his face was populated with dark warts. As if he needed additional separation from humanity his nose was much too large for his face, and his feet were those of a man half again his height. Osric's spindly legs could do little more than support his body, and he could not walk any great distance without resting. His legs may have been weak, but his arms, chest, and neck were massively strong. Osric's natural arm strength had been enhanced by the countless hours he spent pumping the bellows for the candle maker and ringing the massive bells in the cathedral.

The story that has been handed down through the generations depicts Osric's employer, the candle maker, as a plump but not quite fat man, whose large head gave the appearance of having been pinched from the sides. In modern times, the candle maker is always portrayed in drawings as mostly bald with a fringe of dark curly hair circling the back of his head, extending down past his ears, and around his chin. His face is accented by bulging eyes, and by overly thick, and overly pink lips which appear locked in a permanent pout. Though it may have been added to the story of Osric long after his death; Osric is supposed to have compared the vast expanse of the candle maker's fleshy face to "an arsehole giving birth to a kidney."

Osric hated the candle maker, and he hated pumping the bellows, but it was the only employment he could secure; as a penniless dwarf, he would never be admitted to a guild in any capacity. In spite of his many physical limitations, Osric was a proud man who had sworn to starve before begging in the square. He pumped the bellows and performed other work for the candle maker from sun up to sun down, five days a week. In exchange for his labors, he was given a few coppers, a bit of food, and a drafty, rat-infested, garret above the candle shop to lay his head.

Chapter One

The Garret

Hot pain shot down Osric's spine, running to his feet then back up to his neck, echoing back and forth through his twisted frame until coming to rest, just below his shoulders. When the pain subsided to a point he could breathe again, he swung his thin legs over the side of his pallet and, with the aid of his walking stick, stood and stretched to the extent his crooked back would allow. An ordinary man would have been reduced to tears, but Osric gritted his teeth and waited for the pain to ease. He slept on a pallet softened only by a rough mattress filled with straw, and it was a rare morning he did not greet the day with pain. His unhappy life revolved around the twin certainties of pain and hate. Osric lived in pain, and he hated the hand he had been dealt in life, and everyone who had ever added to his misery. In addition to the candle maker, he hated the man's wife even more than the man himself because she was the one who fed him. He hated the black robes in the cathedral who had raised him in the orphanage, and who mistreated him still. Osric hated the children who tormented him on those rare occasions he was allowed to venture out in public, and he had come to hate children, generally.

It would not be fair to say Osric hated everything, for there was one thing he did not hate at all. When it came to brown ale, he experienced something that went beyond ordinary love. He would permit himself to be laughed at, and be subjected to humiliation if doing so resulted in enough brown ale to drown his demons, if only for a while. When Osric allowed himself to daydream, his dreams always centered around possessing all the brown ale he could ever drink. He would sometimes imagine himself as young, fit, and handsome with barrel upon barrel of brown ale at his disposal. In his dream, he began, and ended, each day with a stein of ale with many, many steins in between. Alas, as the candle maker's assistant, the reality of his meager wage allowed him no more than four steins of ale in a good week; even fewer if he did something to upset the candle maker, and he saw his wages docked.

When the pain eased to the point he could walk, Osric laid his stick aside then hobbled across the dimly lit room and opened the door. There, at his feet lay a tray, containing a bowl holding a small loaf, and a pitcher of water. He could see the bread was hard and dry, but that was not unusual. The only time he saw fresh bread in the garret was on Christmas, and not always then. There had been more than a few times he discovered his bread had been chewed upon, or even stolen by rats. Osric gathered up his meager ration then shuffled back to his rude table, and sat down to eat. "Bloody hell! Another day and this excrement would have gone all to mold." The candle maker was a prosperous merchant and Osric knew the man and his wife ate well, enjoying meat at their table at least three times a week. Knowing how well they lived made the near-to-rotting bread taste all the worse. "They probably couldn't get their stinking cat to eat this spew." Osric hated the candle maker's cat nearly as much as he hated the man himself and had sworn to throw the little beast into the melting oven, if he could ever manage to catch it.

Osric attempted to soften the dry bread with sips of water between bites, and the water proved to be no more palatable than the bread. "The foul wench must have dipped the pitcher into the god-rotting gutter! Fresh water is free for the taking in the square and yet, she gives me this!" After Osric had eaten the last of his breakfast, he considered returning to his pallet. It was market Thursday, the one day he did not work, and he was forbidden to leave the garret. "The one day I could get some bloody rest and my god-rotting back won't let me." His garret had a small window but the candle maker had long since nailed the shutter closed leaving the slats pointed upward, as to allow in a bit of light but preventing Osric from seeing anything beyond a small patch of sky and a corner of the bell tower. He spent several minutes stewing in his misery, thinking of how he might fill his day, then he brightened! There was to be a public flogging at midday! It had been announced from the pulpit the previous Sunday! Upon remembering the flogging, Osric became a new man. The thought of a flogging brought him about as near to happiness as he ever came. Even better than a mere flogging, it was a woman who was to be flogged! "The wench is an adulteress," thought Osric, hugging himself with glee. "In the old days they would have burned her, and that's what they bloody well should be doin' today! Sod the candle maker. I'm not his bloody slave!" He resolved to find a way to watch the flogging.

The cathedral clock struck eleven, and then it struck the half hour. The cathedral held its own dark place in Osric's heart, but on this day he found knowing the time to be useful. He carried his walking stick, lest its tapping betray his movement to the candle maker and his wife in the shop below. Osric gained the door then eased his way down the steep stairs to the melting room. Out of long habit he opened the oven door and checked the fire. The fire had been reduced to coals, so he added a few pieces of wood and positioned them with the poker. In his heart of hearts, Osric would have been happy to see the candle shop burn to the ground, but having the fire die completely could cost him a full day of employment, and a stein of ale as well. After closing the oven door, Osric listened for the candle maker's approach. If the man only found his assistant tending the fire, he might not be chastised. Hearing nothing untoward, Osric hung the key to the back door around his neck, then let himself out and made his way out into the alley.

The narrow, foul-smelling alleyway was a wretched mixture of mud, garbage, and excrement. Pigs, cats, chickens, and other fowl roamed freely. Osric always hoped one of the beasts might venture near enough that he could smash its skull with his stick. He expected to find the ally deserted as the people of the town were now congregating in the square to view the flogging, and this proved to be correct. There were never many people who used the alley, but it was a familiar place to Osric as it was his route to the back door of The Dancing Pig, and its treasure trove of brown ale. He picked his way through the muck and garbage to a point he judged to be nearest the whipping post. He knew of a gap between two shops he thought might be wide enough to allow him entry. He found the gap and saw its far end was closed off from the square with boards. "If I can make it through to the end, there should be space enough between the boards to let me see the square, and if I can't see through the cracks, I'll just break the bloody boards with me fists."

The gap between the buildings was narrow, and Osric had a trembling fear of confining spaces. He suffered from recurring nightmares of the many times in the orphanage when Brother Benedict locked him inside a child's coffin as punishment. He looked up and down the alley and saw no other way of getting close to the square. Going around the row of shops and entering the square would mean exposing himself to the public, and being seen in public carried many risks. There was the likelihood he would be tormented by children, and there was little doubt he would be reported to the candle maker. Osric pondered his situation, knowing he had little time to make a decision. At last, his fear of tight spaces was overridden by his desire to see the flogging, and he began squeezing between the buildings. He worked his way through the narrow gap until he reached the wooden planking that closed off the gap from the square, and just as he hoped, there were cracks large enough to see through. His joy was short lived because when he put his eye to a crack, he saw nothing but wicker. A mound of baskets had been stacked against the boards, and not only was his view of the square being blocked, he found the boards were far too thick for him to break with his fists. "Oh, bloody hell!" cried Osric, aloud. "Oh bloody, bloody hell!"

He had maneuvered himself into a difficult spot, and when he attempted to make his retreat he discovered, to his horror, he could not turn around! He looked up at the planking and saw the tops of the boards were far beyond his reach, and he would never be able to climb over them. He would have to make his exit by walking backward. Walking a few paces backward is of no concern for the able bodied, but Osric had difficulty walking forward, and it was a serious matter indeed. He closed his eyes and fought to control his rising panic. This was not the first predicament he had found himself in, and he knew his very survival depended on calming himself. He closed his eyes until his pulse and breathing returned to normal, then worked his stick around to his side nearest the alley. By leaning against the stick and riding up on it, he was able to begin inching his way out of the trap. The distance Osric had to cover was less than twenty feet but, at the rate of an inch or less per effort, he was facing an immense challenge.

He was half way back to the alley when he heard a roar go up from the square. The flogging had begun and he was missing it! Osric was well accustomed to dealing with his physical pain, but the thought of missing the flogging through his own misadventure resulted in a tear of anger forming in the corner of his eye. "Bloody hell!" muttered Osric, with rising bitterness. "Bloody, bloody hell!" Now the roar from the square became a rhythmic chant as the lashes were laid on, one following the other. "I'm going to miss all of it!" He put forth a great effort, pouring all his rage into his walking stick. It fueled his anger that the hard work increased his pace only a little, and his legs were growing weaker by the second. "My bloody, god-rotting legs!" Osric realized he was now sobbing, so great was his sorrow at having caused himself to miss the flogging. He had not sobbed since the childhood beatings he had suffered in the orphanage. He was now just over an arm's length from the alleyway, but could go no farther. His burning legs were near exhaustion, and he knew if they collapsed he would find himself wedged between the buildings and unable to move. Fighting for control, Osric leaned on his stick, closed his eyes, and rested as long as he dared. He then spent the last of his strength on one mighty effort and escaped the trap.

When Osric burst through to the alley, his momentum carried him onward. His weakened legs could no longer hold him up, and he went sprawling backward into some of the worst muck in the alley. He was filled with rage and revulsion, and desperate to be out of the filth, but so complete was his exhaustion, he could do nothing but endure the situation until he felt some strength return. The chanting from the square had ended now, and all Osric heard was a general murmur coming from the dispersing crowd. The certain knowledge he had missed the flogging only deepened his despair. As Osric lay in the filth, waiting for his legs to recover, his disgust flashed to white hot anger when he realized a cat was urinating on his trousers. He swung his stick in blind rage, missing the cat, but making perfect contact with his foot. The cat evaded Osric's stick and danced away a few paces, where it sat down just beyond his reach as if to mock him. The pain in his foot was now equal to the pain in his back that announced the beginning of each new day. Knowing he had done it to himself took him to a new level of impotent rage.

When he could regain his feet at last, Osric began hobbling back to the candle shop. The throbbing in his foot was now added to all the other pains that plagued his body, and his slow pace was further reduced. Both he and his clothing were soiled and reeking of the alley's filth. Then, as if he needed additional misery, Osric remembered he was two full weeks away from the single time per month he was allowed to bathe and clean his clothes. "Oh, bloody hell," cried Osric, in despair, "what will I do?"

'Oh bloody hell,' was an expression that had crossed Osric's mind and lips so many times it had ceased to exist as individual words and had morphed into the single thought that symbolized the misery that was his life. "Maybe the bastard will take pity on me and let me bathe." He did not think the prospect likely. He unlocked the melting room door and eased it open, hoping the candle maker and his wife would be engaged in the front of the shop. His hopes were dashed when he heard the roar of his master's voice the moment the door began to open.

"Where have you been Wretch?" shouted the candle maker. "You went to the flogging didn't you?" Osric had experienced the man's wrath countless times, but this was unlike anything he had ever seen.

Osric did not answer. He only lowered his head and stared at the floor.

"I should bloody well thrash you!" snarled the candle maker, taking a step toward Osric.

When the candle maker uttered the threat, Osric tensed and brought his stick up in front of him. The ferocity in Osric's eyes stopped the man in his tracks. Though he was much taller than Osric, the candle maker was well aware of Osric's strength, and he thought better of striking his assistant. He knew Osric would defend himself at all costs, before allowing himself to be beaten. If the threat of a physical attack passed quickly, the verbal harangue had only begun. "You're a filthy, stinking mess Osric!" bellowed the candle maker, with renewed venom. "You know you are forbidden to leave the shop on market days! So what in bloody hell were you doing outside?"

Osric's eyes burned into the angry man, but he remained silent.

"You have been asked a question by your master you little beast, now answer or find yourself without a roof!"

Feeling trapped and hopeless, Osric replied in a pleading voice, "I only went for a stein of ale, Master. I lost my footing, and I fell into the muck."

The candle maker's wife had joined her husband upon hearing the loud voices coming from the melting room. The woman's empty gray eyes focused on Osric, "You horrid little monster," shrieked the pale woman upon seeing and smelling Osric. "You leave when forbidden, then you bring your filth and stench back into the shop!"

"I didn't mean to fall in the muck, Mistress," Though he hoped the woman might take a bit of pity on him, he had no real expectation of her doing so, as she tended to be even more foul tempered than her husband.

"If you hadn't gone out, you never would have fallen into the muck at all, would you?" screeched the woman, bending down and looking Osric directly in the face.

"Come closer, wench," thought Osric. "Come one finger width closer, and you'll meet your bloody maker."

As it had with her husband, the ferocity in Osric's eyes quieted the woman. The couple hated their employee as much as he hated them, but their mutual hate did not outweigh their mutual dependence. Osric needed work and a place to live, while the candle maker knew he would struggle to find another assistant willing to suffer the abuse and meager wages Osric tolerated. The tense standoff lasted until the venomous woman broke the silence. "I suppose we have no choice but to allow you to bathe, you filthy beast, but this will be your new bath day from now on!"

"Yes Mistress, I understand." Osric only wanted the encounter to be over and spoke in a subdued tone that hid the rage boiling inside him.

"You disgust me," said the candle maker's wife.

"Come within the reach of my stick and say that, you god-rotting wench," thought Osric. He said nothing aloud, and lowered his head in submission, hoping the man and his wife would now go away and let him bathe.

The candle maker departed, then returned a minute later with a wooden tub he rudely dropped at Osric's feet. "Heat some water on the melting oven if you're not manly enough to bathe in cold water." The candle maker spoke with heavy sarcasm.

"Thank you, Master," said Osric, "God bless you, sir." He would indeed heat water. He had experienced quite enough of cold baths in the orphanage. The mere thought of being immersed in cold water caused him to recoil in pain.

As the candle maker and his wife were leaving, the man paused then turned back to his assistant. "Due to your disobedience, there will be no wages for you this week, Osric. I've no doubt the guild will support me in this matter should you dare to challenge it."

"Yes, Master," said Osric, again hanging his head. His defeat was complete. He had missed the flogging, he had fallen into the filth, injured his own foot, and now he would go a week without ale. Had Osric been given the option, he would relive the humiliation of falling into the muck a hundred times over in exchange for brown ale.

As the candle maker was leaving, Osric asked in a humble voice, "Master, am I allowed to fetch water from the square?"

"Damn you to hell, Osric!" bellowed the candle maker, only just remembering the need to fetch water. "No! You are bloody *not* allowed to fetch water from the square! As if I've not enough to do, tending to business, now I must take the time to fetch your dammed water, and all because of your disobedience!" The man's face was red, and his voice was cracking with rage.

Though the candle maker's reaction filled Osric with joy, he did not betray himself. He lowered his head again, and said, "Thank you, Master. May all God's blessings be upon you, Sir."

As he often was, the candle maker was nonplussed any time his assistant wished God's blessings upon him. He had long suspected Osric of blasphemy but had never been able to prove it. Was he being sincere, or was he taunting his master, and mocking God at the same time? The candle maker was at a complete loss for words and could only stand and stare at his assistant. At last, unable to respond, the man seized a pair of oaken buckets and went to fetch the water.

Osric kept his eyes fixed on the floor until the door closed behind the candle maker. Not daring to laugh out loud, lest the foul wench hear him, Osric allowed himself only a small, sly, smile at having flummoxed his master once again. There would be time for laughter when he had rid himself and his clothing of the muck, and he was back in the solitude of his garret.

In the candle maker's absence Osric hobbled up the stairs, then returned with the nightshirt he would wear while his clothing dried. Upon his return to the melting room, he took a large iron pot down from the wall and placed it beside the oven. He shuffled around to the oven door and inspected the fire, poking the embers expertly, then adding more wood. He picked up the bellows to fan the flames, and for some reason, squeezed the handles a bit before inserting it into the opening on the oven. Something, perhaps a wad of cobweb, shot out of the end of the nose with an audible pop, startling Osric. When he realized what had happened, Osric had a moment of silent laughter over having alarmed himself.

The candle maker returned in a few minutes and placed two buckets of water in front of Osric. "Now, get thy bloody bath taken then get thee to the garret and do not let me see your vile face again today, Osric!" The candle maker's cold sarcasm radiated his loathing for his assistant.

Osric gave the candle maker a humble bow, and said, "Thank you, Master. May God bless and keep you, Sir."

The candle maker was not mistaken in his view that Osric was taunting him, and being blasphemous at the same time. He was desperate to do, or say, something in response, but as he always did, the man found himself paralyzed in the face of his assistant's subtle provocation. At last he could do no more than snarl, "Just get your bloody bath taken and do not take all day about it, Wretch!"

Osric decided not to press his luck and refrained from again asking God to bless his master. "Yes, Master. I shall be quick about it."

The candle maker returned to the shop, slamming the door as he left. Now, Osric allowed himself a small, but silent, laugh. He knew that neither his master nor his scrawny wife would dare risk seeing him in a state of undress. Osric emptied the contents of one of the buckets into the iron pot, and placed it on the melting oven, then emptied the other bucket into the wooden tub. Taking up the bellows again, he got the fire roaring, and the water in the iron pot was soon heated. Osric mixed the hot water with the cold, undressed, then settled himself in the tub. The warm water felt wonderful, but he did not linger in the bath. Bathing was held in deep suspicion by the common people, and it was believed one should only bathe when faced with no alternative. Osric did not know what to think. He only knew the warm water eased the pain in his legs, and he felt better after bathing. Osric dried himself with a piece of sacking, then donned his night shirt and set about the task of cleaning his clothing. He scrubbed his trousers and his jersey, then using all his strength, wrung out all the water possible.

When the tub had been emptied and put away, Osric climbed back to the garret and hung his damp clothing on a piece of twine, draped across the room for the purpose. He sat down to rest his aching, legs and spent several minutes gazing at the window. All he could see were slivers of light between the upturned shutter slats, and a bit of sky. Though he cared little for his work, Osric found being imprisoned in the garret with nothing to do even worse than his duties in the melting room. He considered it to be a good market-day if his tortured body allowed him a bit of extra sleep during his long hours of confinement.

The passing of time was marked by the cathedral's clock tower, and the cathedral was another place he had no love for. On Sunday mornings, well before daybreak, he was ushered into the bell tower on the side of the cathedral opposite the clock tower. It was his other job to ring the bells on Sundays, and he was only allowed to view the services through a small window that could only be seen from the altar. He was never allowed to be seen in the sanctuary. Though he had been given no say in the matter, Osric had been handed a life-long obligation to ring the cathedral bells on Sundays, as repayment to the church for the expense of raising him.

Even with levers to aid him, pulling the bell ropes was brutal work. Harder by far than any task he performed for the candle maker, and it was one more thing that had built his strength over the years. Osric performed his duties while giving them little thought. His only goal as a bell ringer was to avoid mistakes, and, in turn, the wrath of Brother Benedict. After the last service of the morning, a priest would bring him holy communion, blessing him and always dispensing with the task in as little time as possible. Osric was not allowed to leave the bell tower until after sundown. His only compensation for bell ringing, and day-long confinement in the bell tower, was a good meal at midday. If the weather allowed, he also had the small pleasure of spending the afternoon gazing at the countryside from on high.

Osric sat, swimming in his misery, longing for enough brown ale to obliterate his pain. Then in an instant, he was startled from his stupor when he saw a small crescent of light appear on the outside wall! How could it be he never seen it before? Then, as quickly as it had appeared, the sliver of light was gone. He stared at the wall for a long time, waiting for the crescent of light to return. When it did not reappear, he began questioning himself. "Mayhaps me eyes were tricking me. It's been a bloody awful day, and I'm all muddled, I am." As the afternoon wore on, he decided to take a closer look at the place where he had seen the light. He sat down on the floor and studied the wall but he could see nothing in the dim light. The candle maker allowed Osric only a few candles a year, and he used them sparingly. Lighting his candle would also require a trip back down to the melting room, and Osric had seen quite enough of his master for one day.

Another hour passed and Osric's boredom overcame his desire to avoid the candle maker. Leaving his walking stick behind, Osric picked up his candle in its holder, then crept down to the melting room, making as little noise as possible. He reached into the oven with a pair of tongs, retrieved a glowing coal, then used it to light the wick. Once the candle was burning, he closed the oven door and hurried back up to the garret. He was still dealing with the effects of the morning's misadventure, and his legs had yet to recover. Osric collapsed on his stool and remained sitting until he felt strong enough to hobble to where he thought he had seen the sliver of light. He sat on the floor and held the candle in front of him as he began giving close attention to the wall. Then, he found the source of the light. A knot in the wall board had become partially loosened. The garret was always so dark, small details easily escaped his notice. It became evident why the light had appeared and disappeared so quickly. Light would only make its way through the sliver of an opening when the sun was at the proper angle.

Osric had long pondered the movement of the sun during the hours he spent confined in the bell tower. Where did it come from each morning and where did it go at night? Why did it have to come and go at all? He asked himself, "Why couldn't it just stop, and put the bloody candle maker out of business?" Osric thought about these and many other things but did not pose his questions to anyone. He had learned early in his life to be very careful about what he asked a black robe, because asking the wrong question might well result in a beating. He would never consider asking the candle maker or his foul wench anything, as he thought them to be quite stupid. The one person he ever dared discuss his questions with was Kurtz, the publican. The alehouse keeper was one of the few people who had ever shown him any kindness, although it did not escape his notice, Kurtz was kind to everyone with coppers to spend in his tavern.

He put his musings on the nature of the sun aside and returned his attention to the knothole. He began probing the knot, and with a bit of wiggling worked it completely loose. He discovered the small end of the knot was on the outside, and it could not be pushed out through the wall board. Osric began slowly working the knot out of its hole with his fingernails. When the knot was free, he put his eye to the opening, and what he saw amazed him. He had before him, a fine view of the entire square! "I could have watched the bloody flogging from the garret had I only known!" muttered Osric, in dismay. "I'll never miss another one, I won't." He sat, mesmerized with joy, observing the square as the market day activities were winding down. Finding himself in the position of being able to observe the square, while remaining unseen, left Osric almost as happy as did thoughts of a flogging.

Osric did not leave his observation post until darkness was falling, and he heard the rap on his door announcing the arrival of his supper. He hurried to get his food, lest a rat get there first, but left the knothole open. Once he had his supper dish where he could keep an eye on it, he began inspecting his blanket, and when he found a loose thread, he carefully stripped a few inches away from the cloth. He tied the thread around the knot, then pushed the knot back into its hole. He had a broad smile on his face when he pulled on the string, and the knot came out easily. Even better, the dark string was all but invisible against the wall. Though the candle maker rarely visited the garret, he would take no chances with his wonderful secret.

When he sat down to his evening meal, he found his supper to be no better than his breakfast. Although his bread was just as dry, and his water equally rank, he took no notice. He was filled with a joy that allowed him to transcend what had otherwise been a dreadful day, and all because he had discovered something as simple as a knothole. When he finished eating, Osric snuffed the candle and settled himself on his pallet. He had burned far more candle on this day than he would have normally allowed himself to do, but it had been well worth it, and he had no regrets. He now possessed a view of the square, and he would no longer feel quite so trapped and alone on market days. When Morpheus took Osric into his arms that night, he took a contented man.

Chapter Two

Osric Prays for the Candle Maker

As if the universe had at last decided to smile upon him, the candle maker's assistant awoke on the morning after discovering the knothole not to wrenching pain in his back, but to the rap on his door announcing the arrival of his breakfast. Mornings like this were very rare, and Osric was moved to hug himself with joy. He hurried to the door and retrieved his meal. After placing his bowl and pitcher on the table, Osric removed his clothes from the line, then dressed. He hung his blanket over the line where his clothes had been drying, then sat down to eat. His breakfast proved to be no better than most of his meals, but such was his state of happiness, he did not care. He had discovered a way to observe the square, and then he had awakened without pain.

Not even the thought of a week without ale could undo Osric's good mood. When he took up his duties in the melting room that morning, the candle maker found the smile on his assistant's normally dour face, to be more than a little unsettling. All through the morning's work, Osric responded without complaint to the candle maker's orders, while occasionally adding to his employer's confusion by pausing to extend his master a sly grin. At mid-morning, two apprentices from the butcher's guild arrived at the back door of the candle shop with large wheelbarrows heaped with tallow. Scooping tallow into buckets, and then lugging them into the melting room was a task Osric had always approached with disgust, but on this morning, he performed the job without complaint, thus further unsettling the candle maker.

The effect his good behavior was having on his master did not escape Osric's notice, and he chided himself for not having thought of it sooner. A plan began forming in his agile mind. A few days of good behavior, so that the candle maker might come to expect it, then back to his old self! Oh, what fun! It then occurred to him, he might even mix up his behavior over the course of a day, so that his master would never know what to expect. Mixed behavior was what he opted to try first, but the possibilities were endless. He smiled to himself and muttered, "I'll have the bastard pissin' himself before I'm done with him, I will."

Shortly after the clock tower announced midday, the candle maker's wife brought Osric his dinner. The candle maker only fed his assistant a midday meal on the days Osric worked and did not feed him at all on Sunday, leaving that responsibility to the cathedral. Osric carried his bread up to the garret and closed the door behind him. He hurried through his meal, then sat down on the floor, and felt about for the string. He pulled the knot free then put his eye to the hole, and gazed at the square. Below him, he saw people going about their daily business. There were women drawing water, people conversing, and carts piled high with goods moving about. Most people would have found the activities in the square quite unremarkable, but Osric was viewing what he had only seen on rare occasions. For the most part, activities in the square were things known to him only by the sounds they made; so determined was his master to keep him hidden from the public. When it was time for Osric to return to work, he closed his small window to the world with reluctance and made his way back down to the melting room.

Having been put off his guard by Osric's good behavior over the course of the morning, the candle maker issued a friendly hello to his assistant upon his return to work. Osric responded with icy silence. He gritted his teeth while his eyes burned into the candle maker. Osric held his bewildered master in his angry stare, until he thought he might explode with laughter, then turned and stomped his way to the oven. The candle maker was left to stare as his assistant threw wood on the fire, then slammed the oven door closed.

Osric was pumping the bellows with intensity, when the candle maker managed to stammer, "I-is something troubling you, Osric?"

Osric acted surprised by the question, and returned his master a pleasant smile, "Oh, everything is quite alright, Master. Couldn't be better. Why do you ask?"

"I-it's, just that you seemed upset about something, Osric."

"Me, sir? I'm quite alright, I am."

The candle maker paused a moment and eyed Osric warily. "Very well then. We should get back to making wick."

"Yes, of course, Master. God bless you, Sir." The perplexity on his master's face left Osric near-to-bursting with happiness. He said nothing, however, and his face betrayed not a trace of emotion. Osric returned to tying stones to the ends of long strands of yarn and then dropping them into the melting vat. Once a length of yarn had become saturated with the clarified tallow, the candle maker would fish it out of the vat with a metal hook, then hang the length of yarn from its center, over pegs in a rafter overhead. The stones allowed the wicks to stretch and straighten as they dried. As the candle maker was retrieving a length of yarn, he glanced up to see his assistant facing him with his eyes closed, and moving his lips in silence. The candle maker found the sight so startling, he dropped the yarn back into the melting vat.

"O-Osric! What are you doing?"

. . . "I'm praying for you, Master."

"P-praying for me?"

"Yes, Master." Osric closed his eyes again, then continued to move his lips silently for a few more seconds. He opened his eyes again, blessed himself, then returned the candle maker a wistful smile. "God bless you, Sir." Osric nodded to the candle maker, then returned again to the business of preparing wick, leaving his bewildered master to stare at him in silence.

A pause of several seconds ensued before the candle maker could manage, "Osric? . . . Why were you praying for me?"

Osric looked up at the candle maker and eyed him thoughtfully. After a moment, he said in a soft voice, "I've been taken by an awful feeling, I have, Master. I fear something dreadful is about to happen to you, and I felt I should say a prayer for you." Osric said no more. He put his head down and continued with his work. It took all of Osric's considerable willpower to contain his laughter. The immobilized candle maker stood, and continued to stare at his assistant for several additional seconds. Osric did not look up again, and said little to the candle maker, for the remainder of the day. His communication with his master that afternoon consisted of little more than a few sad smiles.

After the close of business that evening, the candle maker's wife found herself deeply perplexed by her husband's faraway look and lack of appetite. "You only picked at your mutton, and you've barely touched your tart, Dear. You've always loved my tarts. Do you find your supper lacking?"

The candle maker emerged from his stupor long enough to look up at his wife, and respond in a weak voice, "No, my Dear. Nothing is wrong with your cooking, or your tart. I'm just not very hungry, this evening." The candle maker turned his head away and appeared to take himself to a distant place.

The thin, pale, woman was left feeling very helpless as she continued to observe her husband. Her man had always devoured his food, and she found the detachment she was witnessing more than a little frightening. She was taken with the growing fear her husband might be losing his health, or even worse, had been the victim of a witch. Throughout the course of their supper, and on through bedtime, nothing she said could rouse him from the depths of his detachment.

While the candle maker's wife struggled to understand her husband's behavior, Osric, in his dark, lonely garret, hugged himself as he dissolved into repeated bouts of silent, hysterical, laughter.

The second morning after discovering the knothole was not as pleasant as the first. Saturday was usually the best day of the week for Osric, as it was a shorter workday, and the day he was paid his wages, then allowed out of the candle shop to visit The Dancing Pig for a few hours. On this Saturday, however, he woke to greater than normal pain, and the knowledge there would be no wages, or brown ale, this week. Then, the arrival of his breakfast was announced by a hard pounding on his door, rather than the light rap he was accustomed to. The startling knock was followed by the sounds of someone stomping their way back down the stairs to the melting room. "That's bloody odd," muttered Osric. "The foul wench is usually quiet as a mouse, she is." Forgoing the usual morning stretching of his aching back, Osric hurried to the door and caught just a glimpse of the candle maker's wife as she disappeared into the hallway leading to the couple's residence. "Bloody odd, this is," he thought, as he struggled to understand the woman's behavior.

Enough time had elapsed since his discovery of the knothole to allow him to again pay attention to the poor quality of his meals. "This god-rotting swill is worse than ever!" mumbled Osric, just above a whisper. He tore off the mold he found growing on one end of the loaf and struggled to eat what remained. "Bloody hell!" snarled Osric in disgust, and rather too loudly. He slammed his water pitcher down on the table top in frustration, then regretted it. He had made more noise than he normally allowed himself, and he hoped no one was yet present in the melting room, who might have overheard him.

When the clock tower announced the beginning of his work day, Osric picked up his stick and made his way down to the melting room. On an ordinary morning, the candle maker would be there waiting for him, but on this day he found himself alone, leading him to mutter, "This is bloody odd." Osric glanced around for a few minutes, wondering what he should do, then decided to go ahead and begin the day's work without his master. He added wood to the embers, then pumped the bellows, and carefully brought the congealed tallow up to dipping consistency. He skimmed the surface of the melting vat, and drew off the contaminates, leaving only the clarified tallow.

Osric had never actually made candles before but had observed the candle maker do it countless times. He began by cutting the wick they had prepared the previous day into lengths and then attaching the lengths of wick to the dipping rack. When a hundred wicks had been connected, he attached the rack itself to the dipping mechanism, then swung the rack over the melting vat. As he had seen the candle maker do thousands of times before, Osric used the large lever to lower the wicks into the melted tallow, then he raised them out again a moment later. He held the rack above the vat until the newly coated wicks cooled, then repeated the process. Again and again, he lowered the growing candles into the melting vat. The rack of candles was half way to completion when the candle maker's wife burst into the melting room, shrieking, "What are you doing?"

The woman's grating voice startled Osric, but he caught himself in time and did not lose control of the candles. He moved the lever into the notch that the held rack of candles away from the vat, then answered, "I've begun making a rack of candles, Mistress."

She had expected Osric to recoil in fright at the sound of her harsh words, but his calm response left her searching for something to say. Gathering herself again, she shrieked, "Who told you to do that, you little wretch?"

Osric paused before answering the woman, "No one, Mistress. This is what we do every morning, except on Friday when we make wick." The woman teetered back and forth and seemed to be on the verge of falling down as she struggled to think of something else to say. Osric interrupted her search for words by asking, "Where is my master, Mistress? Has he taken ill?"

"He has taken to his bed. I finally got him to tell me, that he caught you praying for him!"

"Oh, bloody hell," thought Osric, suddenly concerned by what he might have set in motion.

"What have you done to him, you little monster? You have bewitched him!" The woman was doing all she could to maintain her anger as she struggled to focus her empty eyes on Osric. She soon found herself to be no match for Osric, who returned her gaze with unflinching intensity. She looked up at the ceiling and clasped her hands in front of her chest.

Osric waited until the woman lowered her eyes to look at him again, then said, in an even tone, "I've done naught but say a prayer for my master, Mistress."

"Why were you praying for him?" The woman's voice was weakening, and her resolve was fading fast in the face of Osric's simple statement.

"I felt a bit of worry for my master, Mistress, and I wanted to say a small prayer for him, I did." The wide-eyed stare Osric was receiving from the woman, nearly resulted in his exploding into laughter, when he thought, "Her eyes are the very color of old pigeon shit!" Fortunately, his long years spent keeping himself under tight control in the presence of his employers, prevented him from exhibiting even a trace of a smile. At last he said, in a placating, voice, "I had no idea that sayin' a prayer for someone could ever be a bad thing, Mistress. I did not mean to cause my master distress,

I didn't." What Osric was telling the candle maker's wife bore no resemblance to the joy he felt in the distress he was causing her.

The woman continued to stare at Osric for a few more seconds, and when she could no longer endure the sight of him, turned and fled from the melting room. Osric thought it very strange the woman did not go to the front, and open the shop for the day's business, but instead, left through the hallway door leading to the square. "I wonder where she's bloody going," he muttered. Osric waited a short while, anticipating the woman's return. When she failed to reappear after a few minutes, he returned to dipping candles.

When the candles were nearing completion, Osric began testing their size with the guild ring before each new dipping. The wooden ring determined the minimum legal size of candles, and when the ring would no longer fit around the candles, he applied his master's, *one more for good measure* rule, and dipped the candles a final time. He swung the candle rack away from the melting oven and secured the lever in its notch. The candles would now be allowed to cool thoroughly before he cut them from the rack.

Osric added more tallow from the storage vat, then tended to the fire. He pumped the bellows to restore the consistency of the tallow and strained the surface again. He was standing back, admiring the first rack of candles he had ever made, when the candle maker's wife returned to the melting room, accompanied by an elderly priest. It took Osric a moment, but his mind flashed back to the orphanage, and he recognized Father Gregory.

"This is him, Father! He's the blasphemer who bewitched me husband, he is!" The woman's thin, nasal voice had regained all of its anger and was now ragged with hysteria.

The aged priest advanced into the melting room and said, mildly, "Hello, Osric. What mischief have you been up to?"

Before Osric could answer, the woman shrieked again, "The blasphemous little monster bewitched me husband, he did!"

Father Gregory turned to the candle maker's wife, and said in a calm voice, "I do not take accusations of witchcraft and blasphemy lightly, Missus. Now, please go to your husband and allow me to speak with Osric."

"You know this little beast?" cried the distraught woman.

"I've known him since he arrived on our doorstep, when he was but a few days old. I named him when I baptized him."

The woman glared at the old priest, wide eyed in disbelief, struggling for something to say. At last, she spat out, in a frantic wail, "He's a blasphemous little beast, and he's bewitched me husband, he has! You must have him burned!"

"No one is going to be burned," said Father Gregory, in a firm tone. "I must insist that you go now, and be with your husband. I must speak with Osric in private." The candle maker's wife wavered a moment, then spun around, and hurried back to the residence.

The old priest turned to Osric but said nothing. He seated himself on a stool, then folded his hands in his lap. His cool eyes rested on Osric for what became a very uncomfortable interval. Osric's tension was reaching the breaking point when the priest asked, "Well, Osric, what do you have to say for yourself?"

Osric had a long history of verbally and mentally jousting with the nuns and brothers in the cathedral, and even some of the younger priests. Father Gregory however, was a different matter altogether. He was the nearest thing Osric ever had to a parent, and he found himself powerless in the man's presence. Osric thought God himself must look a lot like Father Gregory. As frightening as he found the man, in the back of his mind, Osric was grateful not to be facing any other priest.

Osric remained stuck in his trance long enough for the priest to demand, "I'm waiting for your explanation, Osric. I have never known you to be at a loss for words, so let me hear them."

"A-all I did was say a prayer for me master, and wish God's blessings upon him, Father Gregory." He looked into the old priest's piercing blue eyes, while feeling as helpless as a condemned criminal moments from hanging. "I ne'er thought there was anything wrong with prayin' for someone, I didn't."

The priest continued to stare at Osric, knowing full well how uncomfortable he was making him. He knew Osric, and understood perfectly well what he had done, and why. He asked in a very serious tone, "Osric, the questions before us are what moved you to pray for your master, and were you being sincere?"

Osric could lie easily, and without remorse to almost anyone. He did not consider it wrong to lie if his survival was in question, and he enjoyed lying to people, generally. However, in the face of Father Gregory's withering gaze, he felt his legs melting like tallow. He struggled to speak, but the words would not come. What Osric would never know, was that Father Gregory thought Osric's prayer for his master bordered on genius, and the old priest was struggling to maintain his own composure. Father Gregory was well acquainted with the candle maker and the man's family. He considered the whole clan to be God's test of his Christian charity, and he understood Osric's motives perfectly. Though he had always been careful never to let Osric know his true feelings, the priest had long had a soft spot for Osric's mischievous, obstinate, intelligence, and had often enjoyed a private laugh over the difficulties he had presented the nuns and brothers in the orphanage.

"Must I repeat my question, Osric?" Father Gregory, spoke firmly and continued to hold Osric frozen in fear.

Osric struggled to speak, but could only return the priest a lost and helpless expression.

With exquisite timing, honed over a lifetime, Father Gregory softened his expression, lifted his hand, and bade Osric come to him. "Please kneel, Osric." Father Gregory made the sign of the cross over Osric, then placed his hand on his shoulder. He asked, quietly, "Osric, were you truly praying for your master, or were you merely trying to vex him?"

"I-I was trying to vex him, Father Gregory." Osric spoke in a weak and trembling voice, that seemed to come from someone other than himself.

The priest caught himself before he laughed, then asked in a gentle voice, "Do you know, what you did was wrong, Osric?"

"Yes, Father."

Father Gregory paused, letting the tension in the room rise once more. "Osric, if you do this again, I will be left with little choice but to have you removed to a cell below the cathedral and order an exorcism be performed on you. Do you know what that means?"

"Nay, Father."

"It means the exorcist will be called to come and cast the demons out of you. Do you think you are being possessed by a demon, Osric?"

Osric was so distraught, it was now far beyond his comprehension that the old priest might be manipulating him. He tried to calm himself, then answered with grave sincerity, "Brother Benedict has accused me o' bein' full of the devil many times, he has, Father."

The mention of Brother Benedict drew a spontaneous cough from the priest. He took a moment to control himself, then said, "That is not what I'm asking, Osric. The question is; are you in control of your behavior, or are you being controlled by a demon?" Osric struggled to answer, and after a moment the priest added, "I'm simply asking if you can behave yourself of your own free will, Osric."

"Yes, Father. I think I can."

"You had better be able to do more than you think you can, Osric." Father Gregory spoke with just enough sharpness to send a new wave of fear running through the penitent. "An exorcism may very well end with you at the flogging post, or worse. Now, do you understand the importance of what I'm telling you?" Inwardly, Father Gregory disliked everything he was saying to Osric, as he had no intention of carrying out any of his threats. However, if a healthy dose of fear kept Osric from robbing the candle maker and his wife of their reason, then his small deception would benefit everyone.

Osric knelt with his head bowed, deep in regret over his false prayer. At last, Father Gregory said, "Look at me, Osric." Osric reluctantly lifted his eyes to meet the priest's. "Osric, no one is telling you not to pray for your master, or anyone else. Everyone needs to be prayed for. But, by saying a false prayer, meant only to vex your master, you have committed a grave sin. Osric, you must promise, before God, to complete the penance I will give you, and never to commit this sin again."

"I promise, Father."

"Very well then, I absolve you of your sin, Osric. Say your penance sincerely. Go forth and do not commit this sin again." Father Gregory could see the immense relief on Osric's face. He waited a moment, then continued, just above a whisper, "Do you have any idea how fortunate you are that I was the one your mistress happened to speak to when she came pounding on the rectory door, Osric?"

He had a very good idea, and responded, humbly, "Yes, Father Gregory."

"Had your mistress spoken to nearly any other priest in the cathedral, you would likely be in chains at this very moment, and facing a very bleak future. It is very wrong to try and deprive another person of their reason, Osric." The old priest paused, and eyed Osric, before continuing, "I am well acquainted with the candle maker and his family, and I know they can be difficult. They have not made life easy for you, but you must always consider how your actions might come back to you. Good day to you, Osric. You are in my prayers."

"Good day, Father Gregory. God bless you, Sir." Though Osric often called upon God to bless others, he seldom meant it. This time, however, he spoke with total sincerity. A very subdued and chastened Osric watched as Father Gregory entered the hallway, and then knock on the door of the candle maker's residence.

The old priest was admitted to the residence and then ushered in to see the distraught candle maker. He blessed, and prayed for the man, then assured him that his assistant was not possessed by a demon. "After having spoken at length with Osric, it is my considered opinion he was being entirely sincere, and meant you no harm."

The candle maker responded in a trembling voice, "B-but why would he have a feeling something dreadful is going to happen to me?"

The priest was far too shrewd to tell the candle maker his current state was the result of being a gullible fool who had been manipulated through the power of suggestion by someone a great deal smarter than the man he worked for. Instead, Father Gregory smiled, and said in a kind voice, "It is not for me to speculate on the nature of the apprehension Osric felt for you. The Holy Spirit is a mystery and was perhaps speaking through Osric. Be in peace now." Father Gregory blessed the candle maker again, and the man's wife showed him out of the house.

The priest left the residence, certain in the knowledge he had just planted another powerful suggestion in the candle maker's mind. One that was likely to keep the man in a state of distress for days to come. Father Gregory had no qualms about what he had just done and considered it just payment for the aggravation the candle maker's family had caused him over the years. The priest also felt very good about having directed attention away from Osric. Even though it was not yet noon, Father Gregory resolved to lock the door to his study and enjoy a brandy while having a quiet laugh over Osric's prayer for his master.

With no one to direct him, Osric returned to making candles and completed two more racks by the end of the day. Osric's candle making was a matter that would only add to the candle maker's perplexity upon his return to the melting room, as he believed his assistant incapable of accomplishing such a feat. This would, in turn, lead to the candle maker's renewed suspicions of Osric being possessed by a demon.

Chapter Three

The Harvest Festival

For the most part, summer was the season enjoyed best by the people of Osric's time. Food was more plentiful in summer, and hunger rare. The green of summer did much to mask the ugliness that marked so much of the people's lives, and the sun's warmth dried up the muck and stench of winter. While there was no season Osric liked particularly, it was summer he disliked most. In summer, the garret became an oven, and even gazing through his knothole lost its appeal. If there was any advantage to living in the candle maker's garret it came during the winter when some of the warmth from the melting oven found its way up to Osric's room, leaving him a bit more comfortable than many of his countrymen. Unfortunately, what lent comfort to Osric's life in winter, only compounded his misery in summer.

The fire in the melting oven was allowed to die only four times a year; at the turning of each new season. After allowing the fire to die, and once the contents of the oven were cold, it became Osric's arduous and dirty task to clear out all the ash accumulated during the previous three months. The periodic clearing of the ash was one reason the candle maker always employed a dwarf if possible, as a normal sized man was far too large to fit through the oven door. He could employ a boy for the job, but boys outgrew the oven and came to demand higher wages than Osric, whose opportunities were very limited. Should Osric leave his employ, the candle maker would search out another dwarf to fill the position. It took a long day, to complete the grimy, unpleasant, job of cleaning the oven. As miserly as the candle maker tended to be, Osric always received a few additional coppers, and an extra bath, when the cleaning was complete. More coppers meant more ale, and more ale went a long way toward enabling Osric to overcome his fear of confining spaces.

The ash Osric removed from the oven was not discarded. Oven cleaning time marked the beginning of a week dedicated to manufacturing the candle shop's other product; soap. Water was heated to boiling on the melting oven then poured into a box filled with the packed ash, in order to extract the lye. The hot water filtered through the ash and was then collected in buckets below the box. The water was then reheated and the process repeated several times in order to concentrate the lye. Next, the lye water would be allowed to simmer and thicken in the melting vat, and when it reached the proper consistency, tallow would be stirred in. After additional cooking and stirring, and after all excess water had been drawn off, the resulting mixture was poured into wooden molds and allowed to cool and harden. After the soap was added to the shop's inventory, the candle maker and his assistant returned to the business of candle making.

The season of warm weather saw the town square play host to three festivals. For reasons no one could explain, Mayfair was held in mid-April to mark the arrival of the planting season. Mid Summer's Eve, at the solstice, marked the time when the young men and women of the town, who had turned sixteen during the previous year, officially became adults. The candle maker forbade Osric from attending either of these festivals, and he had to content himself with viewing them through his knothole. The Harvest Festival, however, was a different matter. The candle maker did allow Osric to attend Harvest Festival in no small part because of the King's decree ordering all masters and nobles in the realm to allow their employees and servants to do so.

The Harvest Festival began on the third Thursday in September when casks of ale and cider were wheeled into the square. The Count himself would come down from the manor house, and when the clock struck ten, he would ceremonially tap the first cask, officially marking the beginning of three days of feasting, drinking, dancing, games, and the judging of livestock. Osric grew giddy with the approach of the festival. The happiness he and the other working people felt was not shared by those in the cathedral who seethed in silence, knowing full well, that all of the festivals were but adaptations of ancient pagan rites the church had never been able to fully suppress. The church had used every means at its disposal to end the festivals until at last, under pressure from the King, the names of obscure saints were bestowed upon the gatherings, thus giving them a thin veneer of Christianity and the church's grudging endorsement.

Osric loved the Harvest Festival more than all the other days of the year combined. In addition to being able to drink all the brown ale he could hold, the royal decree gave Osric free access to the square. Aside from the festival, he was allowed only a quick scuttle across to the cathedral and back on Sundays, and then only under the cover of darkness. Osric was otherwise denied access to the public space. Though the candle maker made no secret of his loathing for his assistant, and did so to Osric's face, the man did take a certain self-serving interest in Osric's safety. He did not want ruffians injuring his employee, and thus force him to find a new assistant. The candle maker's fears for Osric's safety were outweighed by his fears of what the muscle-bound dwarf might do to a tormentor if he ever got hold of one. Thoughts of a drunken, enraged Osric, rampaging in the square, filled the candle maker with dread.

During the Harvest Festival, Osric took up his station near the ale wagon under the protective eye of Kurtz, the alehouse keeper.

Kurtz was as heavily muscled as Osric in addition to being two feet taller and much swifter afoot. Kurtz could be relied upon to put a quick end to any harassment of the dwarf, who left undisturbed was content to sit quietly, and drink himself into a stupor. Unknown to Osric, the candle maker had a standing arrangement with Kurtz whereby the publican kept track of what Osric drank during the festival. After the close of the festival, Kurtz would present the candle maker with a bill that included a tip for himself as payment for keeping an eye on Osric. Osric never thought much about who was paying for all the ale he drank as he was usually too inebriated to think about much of anything. The candle maker never questioned the bills presented by Kurtz. He considered it to be a good investment as the publican kept his assistant out of mischief, and the often troublesome Osric could be counted upon to be on his best behavior for at least a month leading up to the festival.

The early years of Osric's attendance at the festival would find him completely besotted and passed out beneath the ale wagon before the clock struck noon. Typically, Osric would rouse from his stupor by mid-afternoon then return to the cask and repeat the process, occasionally passing out three times over the course of a single day. As he grew older, he learned to pace himself. Now, in his early middle age, he sipped his ale at a slow and steady pace throughout the day. Osric chatted with Kurtz and enjoyed the spectacle around him. Each evening of the festival, the lighting of the torches, and the arrival of the musicians, signaled it was time for the dancing to begin. The torch lighting was also Osric's signal to ramp up his rate of ale consumption. He had perfected a formula that left him just sober enough to find his way back to the garret at the end of the evening.

As one of the festival's officials lit the torches on Saturday evening, the final day of the Festival, Osric found himself filled with melancholy. Kurtz refilled Osric's stein, and as he handed it back, they exchanged wistful smiles. "Almost over for another year, eh' my friend?"

Though the publican spoke with a trace of sadness, Osric doubted the man's sincerity. What was a time of celebration for others was three days of hard work for Kurtz. "Aye, Kurtz, that it is." Osric spoke in the same sad tone, but he had no need to act sad because he was sad, though not quite so sad that he would fail to consume at least three more steins of ale before the festival drew to a close.

"T'was, a grand festival, though, don't you think, Osric? Not a spot of rain all three days, and I've never seen such food." The publican paused a moment then smiled and slapped the side of a cask. "I think this year's run of ale was right good too, if I may say so myself." The publican took obvious pride in his handiwork.

Osric lifted his stein to Kurtz in a toast. "There is no such thing as a poor run of your brown ale my good Kurtz, and I'll fight the man who says there is!"

Kurtz's great shoulders shook with laughter, and though the publican drank little during the festival, he poured himself a stein and returned Osric's toast. "To brown ale, Sir. The very stuff of life!"

"To brown ale, Sir!"

On the other nights of the festival, the lighting of the torches hastened Osric's drinking pace. However on this, the final night, such was his melancholy, he began slowing down. He sipped more slowly, savoring each swallow as he watched the dancers and wondered what it would be like to dance. Later in the evening, as the festivities were winding down, Kurtz began disassembling the apparatus that allowed him to link the ale casks together. He laid a length of wood down near Osric, and when his curiosity got the better of him, Osric picked it up and began inspecting it. He saw, to his surprise, that the wooden rod was hollow. He immediately chided himself, thinking, "Stupid Osric, did you think the ale flowed through solid wood?" Kurtz appeared to be preparing to throw the wooden pipes away, moving Osric to ask, "What do you do with all this, Kurtz?"

"It's of no further use," said the publican, with a shrug. "Don't ask me why it is, but if I were to try using them again, the ale would most likely go bad and turn to vinegar. Just like the brewing casks. I use them but once, then sell them to anyone who can use them."

"Will you be selling this, Kurtz?" asked Osric, holding up the wooden tube.

Kurtz looked at the tube Osric was holding, shrugged his shoulders again, and said, "I've never found anyone who wanted any of the tubes so they usually wind up on my fire. The tubes cost but four pence a foot. They're not a big expense. Do you want it Osric?"

He did want it. He wanted it very much, although he couldn't have said why. Osric thought the wooden tube to be a wondrous thing, much too precious to burn. "If you've no use for it, Kurtz," he said in a hopeful tone.

"Well then, by all means, my friend, consider it yours. It's just one less thing I have to haul back to The Dancing Pig."

Osric thanked the publican for the tube, and when the lute player sounded the final note, Osric drained the last of his ale, bade Kurtz goodnight, and began hobbling back to the garret. His mind was muddled as he made his way to the candle shop. On one hand, he was gloriously tipsy from brown ale, but, on the other hand, the festival was now a full year away. Adding to his confusion was the wonderful wooden tube Kurtz had given him. If backed against a wall with a sword to his throat, Osric would have been unable to explain why he thought the tube a wonderful thing, he simply knew it was. The happiness he felt by possessing the wooden tube was elbowed aside when he remembered it was Saturday, and the dawn would bring another visit to the bell tower. Back inside the garret, Osric donned his night shirt in the dark, then settled himself on his pallet. After lying down, he mourned the end of the Harvest Festival for a few minutes, but sleep soon took him.

It seemed no more than an hour had elapsed when the great pain in his back, the candle maker rapping on his door, and the clock tower striking five, hit him simultaneously. Few of his mornings were good ones, but this one was a good deal worse than most. He was dealing with a brutal hangover, with the pain in his head exceeding the pain in his back. Osric was ravenously hungry yet he knew that he must fast until after he had received holy communion. "Oh bloody hell," muttered Osric as he drew himself to his feet, and stretched. He could hear his stomach grow, and it deepened his hunger. He knew he was forbidden to even drink water before receiving communion, but so great was his thirst, he put his immortal soul at risk and drained what remained in his water pitcher. He donned the trousers and jersey that would become his everyday clothing at the turning of the new year. It was a by-law of all the guilds that masters must provide their employees and apprentices with a new set of clothing at the new year. For the first year he owned them, Osric wore his new clothes only to church.

As Osric was preparing to leave for the cathedral, it occurred to him to take the wooden tube with him. As it was with wanting the tube in the first place, he could not explain why he thought taking the tube to church was a good idea. He made his way down to the melting room, then hobbled to the hallway leading to the candle maker's residence. Osric put the key around his neck, then let himself out through the hallway door. He shuffled in near total darkness towards the only light he could see: the twin candle lanterns hanging outside the cathedral. They were bee's wax candles that burn brighter and cleaner than common tallow candles. The candle maker only made bee's wax candles once a year, just ahead of Christmas, and all of them went either to the church or the Count.

Osric was grateful for the darkness, as no one could see him carrying the wooden tube. He thought it unlikely Brother Benedict would give him much notice when he knocked on the vestibule door, as the man could not abide looking at him. Even at his slow pace it took Osric less than two minutes to reach his destination. He was far too short to lift the knocker with his hands so he reached up with his stick, raised the heavy knocker to maximum height, then let it fall with a crash. He knew this was something Brother Benedict hated, which was the very reason he always did it. The horrifying memories of his childhood and Brother Benedict were not separate things in Osric's mind, and he would never have anything but a burning hatred for the man.

The vestibule door jerked open, and Osric was greeted by a man who closely resembled the candle maker, which was unsurprising given that Brother Benedict was the candle maker's older brother. "Wretch!" hissed Brother Benedict, standing aside and allowing Osric entry.

"Good morning Brother Benedict. Wonderful weather for the festival don't you think?" Osric spoke in a pleasant voice, knowing full well how much Brother Benedict, like all the denizens of the cathedral, hated the festival. He held the wooden tube alongside his walking stick in hopes it would not be noticed.

Brother Benedict glared at Osric for a brief moment, then as if he found the experience painful, looked away. "One day you'll push my patience too far, Osric."

"And, one day you'll try layin' a hand on me again, you god-rotting swine, and I'll cave your bloody skull in," thought Osric, as he followed Brother Benedict to the bell tower door.

Brother Benedict unlocked the heavy door, then stepped aside. "Get thy conscience in order Osric. Father Stephan will be up directly to hear your confession."

"I will, Brother Benedict. May all God's blessings be upon you, on this the Lord's day." Osric was hidden from everyone but Brother Benedict and proceeded to extend the Brother a sly grin.

Brother Benedict possessed a mind even slower than that of the candle maker. He struggled to speak but had no response to the subtle taunt. After a long pause, Benedict said, "Father Stephan should order you to be whipped as penance, Osric."

"Whip me?" cried Osric in alarm. "I'm but a poor workin' man who has ne'er harmed anyone! Why on earth should I be whipped?" Osric's voice was pleading and plaintive, and he did his best to look frightened while betraying none of his insincerity.

Brother Benedict had no answer. Any outsider overhearing their conversation would not have thought Osric guilty of anything. With this in mind, and thinking that he had perhaps gone too far, Brother Benedict replied in a more conciliatory tone, "Perhaps I overstated my case, Osric. Now get thee up to the bells and await the signals."

"Yes, Brother Benedict, and may God bless you." Osric began climbing the long, steep, flight of stairs leading up to the bell ropes. He had to stop and rest his weak legs twice before completing the climb, and it took him a good deal longer to ascend the stairs than an able-bodied man.

When Osric reached the room below the bells, or his 'other prison' as he called it, the first thing he did after closing the trap door was hide the wooden tube behind the only furniture in the room, a small, pew-like bench where he rested between services. Osric sat down and massaged his aching legs. Fifteen minutes later a young priest, fresh faced and earnest, pushed open the trap door. "Good morning. I'm Father Stephan, and I've come to hear your confession." The young cleric was startled by Osric's appearance and Osric could see the man was having difficulty looking at him.

"Good morning Father Stephan, I'm Osric, the bell-ringing dwarf." Osric spoke in a bright tone, in hope of further disturbing the priest, and was pleased by what he saw. Most people meeting him for the first time found his appearance unsettling, and this young priest was clearly more disturbed than most, leaving the situation ripe with possibilities.

Osric had met a great many priests in the course of his bell ringing duties, as no priest had ever volunteered to hear his confession twice. If they tended to find Osric's appearance unsettling, many of them found his determination to test the seal of the confessional to its limits, positively unnerving. It was Osric's long-standing practice to continue confessing until ordered to stop. In the course of his rambling confessions, he would admit his desire to kill the candle maker, the man's wife, and their cat as well if he could only catch the satanic little beast. Osric confessed that once the candle maker had been dispatched, it was his fond desire to then burn the candle shop to the ground. Depending upon his mood, he would on occasion go into excruciating detail, describing what he would like to do to his master, once, going so far as to express a desire to cook and eat the man's liver. On this morning, Osric told Father Stephan, that in addition to his feelings for the candle maker, he had no great love for Brother Benedict either, and would very much enjoy seeing the man flogged, or even better, burned alive. "I believe I would even piss on his grave if e'er I got the chance, I would," said Osric, smiling happily, at his horrified confessor.

After listening to Osric's confession for as long as he could endure it, and when it appeared the sinner had no intention stopping of his own accord, the shaken priest raised his hand brought matters to an end. Father Stephan assigned Osric a penance that would take several hours to complete, if he said all the prayers. As the priest was beating a hasty retreat, Osric called after him, "God bless you, Father Stephan, I do hope to see you again next Sunday." With the trap door closed, Osric collapsed on the floor in silent laughter, rolling about and hugging himself with malicious glee. "Give me all the prayers in the stinkin' world, you galloping fool, but I'll see you in hell before I bloody say 'em!"

Osric's joy was brought to a sudden, shuddering, halt when the bells in the clock tower began chiming. The clock tower was more than a hundred feet from the bell tower, but Osric was more than four stories above ground, and the heavy shutters designed to keep out the sound of the bells, had been left open. The noise was deafening. Had he been less absorbed in the effect his confession was having on Father Stephan, he would have heard the clock mechanism preparing to strike the hour, and would have closed the shutters and prepared himself. Osric began a frantic effort to stuff balls of wool in his ears. He never left for the cathedral without making certain that he had balls of wool in his purse. He stuffed the wool in his ears then clapped his hands to the sides of his head as additional protection. Osric had begun the day with a pounding headache brought on by three days of heavy drinking, and now the bells were raising the pain in his head to the level of torture. As the last reverberations of the clock tower were dying away, Osric was on the floor, writhing in agony. So great was his pain, he had thoughts of climbing out the window, and throwing himself off.

Osric could endure pain as well as any man, but what he was experiencing now brought him close to paralysis. His eyes felt as if they might explode out of his skull, and waves of nausea swept over him. It took several agonizing minutes to regain control of himself. It was not until Brother Benedict pushed his head through the trap door, angrily demanding an explanation for his failure to ring the bells on time, that Osric was able to stagger to his feet.

Such was Osric's appearance, that even the hostile Brother Benedict was moved to ask, in alarm, "Osric, are you unwell?"

Osric teetered on his feet, returning Brother Benedict a blank stare. He tried to mouth words, but could produce no sound. When he found his voice at last, he stammered, "T-the clock tower. C-caught me unaware. H-head hurts bloody awful." Osric wobbled on his feet, and only his stick prevented him from falling.

"You weren't up with the bells were you? If you were inside where you belong, the bells should not cause you harm."

Osric continued to wobble as his head begin to clear. "The shutters were left open."

The little compassion Brother Benedict had shown Osric evaporated, and he sniffed, "You're suffering from too much ale, Osric. This is a result of your own sinful debauchery, and you're getting exactly what you deserve! Now, get thee to your post, Wretch, and if you fail again, you'll get no dinner!"

Humbled, and beaten into submission by the brutal pain in his head, Osric replied in a weak voice, "Yes Brother Benedict." He cared not one whit for Brother Benedict, the bells, or anything having to do with the cathedral, but he cared very much about his dinner. He closed the heavy shutters on the clock tower side of the room, then shuffled to his station near the bell rope levers, and slid back the panel that allowed him to see the altar. When the acolyte lit a particular candle, it was his signal to begin the first toll. The first signal candle was already burning, which explained Brother Benedict's anger, and now the second signal candle was being lit. Four pulls on the bell rope, well spaced, followed by a pause equal to the time the bells had rung, and then four more pulls on the rope. Osric had been apprenticed as a bell ringer before he was strong enough to pull the levers. His predecessor had been another unfortunate dwarf whom the church officials would not allow to be seen in the sanctuary. Godfrey was a dull-witted man of few words, and Osric did not find a kindred spirit in his fellow dwarf. A dull wit was not something to be found in the list of Osric's infirmities.

The rest of the morning passed without incident. With the heavy shutters closed and wool stuffed in his ears, the clock tower bells were muted to a fraction of their full volume, as were the great bells above his head. Four services and only one missed toll on Osric's part. When he rang the bells to mark the end of the last service of the morning, his work was finished until Vespers. With his morning duties completed, Osric began anticipating the arrival of Sister Adele, and his dinner. His dinner was his only compensation for ringing the bells, and it almost made the job worthwhile. It was his only meal of the week that included meat of any kind. It would not be accurate to say Osric loved Sister Adele, though he hated her a great deal less than Brother Benedict. Of all the people he had ever known, she came the closest to ever having offered him a degree of affection. Affection, she would withdraw from him without explanation or warning, leaving him hurt and confused. Osric had built his barriers against her, as well. At the end of the last pull on the bell rope lever, he hobbled to the trap door, then left it open for the sister.

Before Sister Adele arrived with his dinner, Father Stephan returned with a chalice. The priest blessed Osric, then asked if he had completed his penance. Osric assured him that he had, then went on to add that he was well and truly sorry for his multitude of sins, and would lead a better life from this day forward. The priest could not hide his skepticism, but gave Osric communion, and asked God's blessing upon him.

"Thank you, Father. May all God's blessings be upon you as well." Father Stephan had far too little experience with Osric to realize the bell ringer tended to say the very opposite of what he meant. Father Stephan left the room with the misapprehension that he had, perhaps, effected a bit of good in the poor and unfortunate child of God whose duty it was to ring the bells on Sunday.

A few minutes after the priest departed, a plump, middle-aged woman with a rather cheery face, poked her head through the trap door. "Hello, Osric. Could you be kind enough to take the tray from me?" I'm afraid I'll spill it."

Osric hurried to her aid and took the tray. He scuttled back across the room, then placed his dinner on the bench, and sat down to wait for the sister. "I'm getting old Osric. These ridiculous stairs are closer to being a ladder, and I can't manage them as well as I once could, especially when I have a tray in my hands." They sat on opposite ends of the bench. She folded her hands in her lap and gave him a kind smile. "How are you Osric?"

"Oh, I'm well enough, I expect," Osric was ever on guard for the Sister's mercurial mood swings, and chose his words with care.

"Did you misbehave at the festival?" The Sister asked the question with arched eyes, and a mischievous smile.

He made a display of surprise at her question and responded, "Now what, exactly, would you call misbehavin' Sister Adele? I wasn't carted off by the Bailiff, and I didn't thrash anyone." Osric paused a moment then added, in the same mischievous tone, "Not that I can remember at least."

Sister Adele threw up her hands in mock exasperation, shook her head, and laughed at Osric's joke. She continued in a more serious tone, "I worry about you, Osric. Yours is not an easy life, and you've seen more than your share of suffering." She paused, not taking her eyes off his face. Out of everyone he had ever known, Sister Adele was the only person who had never seemed to find his appearance disturbing. "Take care of yourself, Osric. I'll leave you to your dinner. You are always in my prayers. God bless you."

"And may God bless you, Sister." There was some genuine sincerity in his voice. As she made her way down the stairs, he wondered what she would be like the next time he saw her. Kind and almost motherly as she was today, or as snarling mean as Brother Benedict. He never knew with the Sister, and he had learned to guard his feelings lest she turn on him. Osric sat down and removed the cloth covering his dinner tray. He found, to his delight, a roasted breast of chicken, a nice loaf of fresh bread, a pitcher of milk, vegetables, and a baked apple, as well. Though he would never have done so in the garret, Osric said a blessing over his meal. He would take no chances with his Sunday dinner.

When he finished eating, Osric sat the tray aside, then curled up on the bench. He was soon asleep and enjoyed two hours of solid rest. He awoke, well fed and much refreshed. He stood and stretched then hobbled over to the window, opened the heavy shutter, and looked across to the clock tower. "Ah, a good half hour before the bloody bells ring again. It's a beautiful day. I shall go up for a look-see, I will." The bell tower windows afforded fine views of the town, but the view from the belfry was much better, at least on a nice day. Osric learned, long ago, the open belfry was no place to be in a thunderstorm, or on a cold winter's day. No one had ever forbidden him to go up to the bells, and Osric considered that to be as good as having received actual permission.

His weak legs were of little use when scaling the long ladder so he tucked the wooden tube under his chin, and scaled the ladder using little more than his arms. When he reached the top, he slid back the bolt, then pushed the trap door open as dozens of pigeons erupted from the belfry. The length of time he could spend in the belfry depended on the clock tower, and how recently the pigeon droppings had been cleared. On this particular Sunday, he was pleased to find the belfry relatively clean. The friars used the pigeon dung to fertilize their kitchen garden, and they assigned the unpleasant job of collecting the droppings to the novitiates. "Cleanin' up stinkin' bird shit is about the only god-rotting job the poxy bastards have never stuck me with," muttered Osric, with a sense of relief. "They must not think I can climb up here." He stood between the two great bells, and surveyed the countryside for a few minutes, marveling at the autumn colors that were beginning to paint the land. Then, he made a circuit around the perimeter of the belfry using the bells to steady himself. A person could see a long way in all directions from the belfry. Osric had often wondered what life might be like in the distant mountains. Never, had he traveled beyond sight of the place where he was standing.

When he tired of looking at the countryside, Osric turned to the stone bench that ringed the inside of the belfry. He brushed off a spot then sat down where he could see the clock, and began inspecting the wooden tube. "Oh, what a lovely, perfect, thing this is." Osric spoke out loud, knowing there was no one within earshot. Unlike an ordinary piece of wood, this was perfectly round on the outside with a perfectly round hole running through its center. "How ever do they make such a thing?" Other than soap and candles, Osric had very little knowledge of how anything was made. "There must be ways of doing these things, or I suspect they would have never stopped burnin' witches."

He held the tube up to his eye and sighted through it, finding it strange and amusing to see the world through a small hole. Never having owned a toy of any kind, his delight was that of a small child. He tried holding it up to his lips and blowing through it. He held it to his nose, and could detect the scent of brown ale, which he thought wonderful as well. Osric blew through the tube again. This time, without intending to, his lips were pursed, and the resulting sound astonished him. "It's like breakin' wind!" exclaimed Osric, his eyes wide with wonder. He immediately put the tube back to his mouth, pursed his lips a bit more and blew much harder. The result left Osric with tears of hysterical joy streaming down his face. He could not see the two friars walking in meditation in the garden below the bell tower as they paused, and eyed each other with suspicion.

When he had his laughter under control Osric looked to the clock tower, and saw that he must soon get back indoors or risk having his eardrums blown out. He started down the ladder, but just before he was to pull the trap door closed, something moved him to point the wooden tube directly into the underside of the largest bell. Osric took a deep breath, pursed his lips, then blew into the tube with all his might, thus producing his finest imitation of flatulence yet. The great bell amplified his efforts, and it was as if God himself had broken wind from the heavens. The sound that went rolling across the town caused every jaw within earshot to drop in astonishment. It was a bright and sunny day without a cloud in sight, and everyone knew it could not have been thunder. All those enjoying a Sunday stroll in the square were awestruck by what they heard. When the moment passed there was much laughter, scratching of heads, and many accusations leveled. Osric lost himself in hysterical laughter, and had he not managed to catch himself at the last possible moment, would have lost his grip and gone crashing to the floor, far below.

Osric calmed himself just enough to close the door to the belfry, only moments ahead of the clock striking four. Once he was back at the bottom of the ladder, Osric hid the wooden tube behind the bench again, then sat down with his face buried in his hands, still struggling to control his laughter. His glee came to an abrupt halt when he heard heavy footsteps on the stairs, which could only mean the approach of Brother Benedict. Osric curled up on the bench and was feigning sleep when the trap door burst open, followed a moment later by the irate brother.

Brother Benedict's bald head was red with anger as he rose through the door, bellowing, "Osric!"

Osric did his best imitation of a man suddenly roused from a sound sleep. "Brother Benedict?" he asked while scratching his head and doing his best to sound confused.

"What did you do, Wretch?" Brother Benedict was quaking with rage, pointed an accusing finger at Osric.

Osric responded with perfect innocence. "Do, Brother Benedict? . . . I've been sleeping, is all I've been doing, it is."

"You didn't hear anything a few minutes ago?" shouted Brother Benedict.

"Hear what, Sir?" Osric did his best to appear very interested in the brother's question.

"A loud, blasphemous, sound from the bell tower!"

Osric paused as if deep in thought, then replied with false sincerity, "I've been told that I snores a bit when I sleep, but I've ne'er been accused of blasphemy because of it, Brother Benedict. What e'er you heard wasn't enough to wake me, I'm afraid." Osric continued to present the Brother a confused expression.

Having no idea how Osric might have produced such a sound left the slow-witted Brother unable to respond. He stared at Osric until he could endure the sight of the misshapen dwarf no longer, then said, "No more sleeping this afternoon Osric! Be alert if the sound comes again. If you hear it, report to me at once! Vespers begins in an hour, be at your station, and no more mistakes."

"Yes Brother Benedict, I'll be keepin' my ears open, I will." Unable to resist, Osric then presented Benedict with a curious expression, and asked in an earnest tone, "This sound you heard Brother Benedict, what was it like, so I knows what to listen for?"

"Flatulence, Osric. The sound was like very loud flatulence."

"Flatulence, Brother Benedict? I'm afraid I don't know what that word means, Sir." Osric continued to feign innocence and sincerity.

To his joy, Osric could see Brother Benedict's bald head turning red again, making the man appear to have been boiled. At last the brother stammered, "Breaking wind, Osric! The sound was like a great, thundering, breaking of wind!!"

"Oh, I'm sure I would have noticed that, if I'd heard it," said Osric, shaking his head.

Brother Benedict could think of nothing else to say, and, after giving Osric another hard stare, turned and made his way down the steps. Osric shuffled over and closed the trapdoor, then once again dissolved into silent, convulsing laughter. When the moment passed, he hobbled to his bell-ringing station and slid the panel open. As he watched the altar and waited for his cue to begin ringing the bells, it occurred to him that taking the wooden tube with him when he left might prove very dangerous. "Brother Benedict's a fool but he's not a complete fool. He'll have his eye on me for sure when I leave." The problem he now faced was, where could he hide the tube? Aside from the single bench, and the box he stood on to ring the bells, the room was bare. He could put the tube in the belfry but he knew of no good place to conceal it, and it would surely be discovered by anyone visiting there over the next week. Novitiates rang the bells during the week, and Osric had no idea if they ever visited the belfry but could only assume they did.

He stood at his station waiting to ring the bells. Now, the situation was not quite as funny as it had been. He would not bet against Brother Benedict searching the room, and the belfry as well, after he departed for the day. If Brother Benedict found the wooden tube, Osric knew he might very well find himself at the whipping post, and he would be shown no mercy. He became very subdued as he watched the altar and waited for the signals. What could he do? Take the tube back up to the belfry and throw it off, and hope no one found it? Osric's mind raced as he considered his few options. Then, when he was on the brink of despair, he noticed a small ledge on the other side of the sliding panel. How had he not seen it before? He pushed the box closer to the panel, then reached his arm through the opening and felt the ledge. It was just wide enough for the tube, and if he wedged his balls of wool next to it, the tube would not roll off.

His wonderful wooden tube would rest there on the ledge, as far from the sliding panel as Osric could reach, for many weeks. Not until he was convinced Brother Benedict had forgotten the incident, and winter was nearing spring, was he able to return the tube to the garret by hiding it under his shabby cloak.

Chapter Four

Osric Makes A Friend

Another market-Thursday was winding down, and once again, Osric found himself wallowing in misery. His back was aching, and the novelty of observing the square through his knothole was beginning to wear off. It all left him as bored and unhappy as he had ever been. Earlier in the day he had placed his wooden tube up to the knothole and sent the sounds of flatulence floating out over the square. He only did it a few well-spaced times, being careful not to overexpose himself. The last time Osric looked out to check on the effects of his labor, he saw a man staring back at him. He found the man's stare disconcerting, and decided to abandon the practice, at least for a while. The man was some distance away and Osric had no idea if he could actually see the knothole or if he was merely looking in the direction from which he thought the noise had come. In either case, he decided not to press his luck. "I've not hurt anyone, but the bloody candle maker would nail a board over the knothole if he found out about it. The spiteful, god-rotting, swine!" The injustice of it all only compounded his misery.

Osric considered lying down on his pallet but dismissed the idea. Not getting a noontime meal on market-Thursdays always left him very hungry by evening. He could not take the chance of sleeping through the rap on his door, and losing his supper to the rats. In any event, he doubted his weariness could overcome his discomfort. He sat on his stool, idly drumming his fingers on the table top. The shadows crossing his shuttered window told him it was now late afternoon. "If I only had something to do, it wouldn't be so bloody bad. I've darned my stockings and patched me trousers, and now I've naught to do but sit! I don't know why that bloody, puking, god-rotting, sod of a candle maker won't let me spend my Thursdays in The Dancing Pig. It's not as if that would be hurtin' him in any way." The more he thought about his life, the more enraged he became. Osric stewed in his anger, for a few more minutes, then an idea popped into his mind that made him smile. "I should climb up to the bloody belfry, then hide and throw stones at people! I could heave a stone, then be well hidden before it landed! I might even crack a stinkin' skull or two! I'd do it too, by God, if I could only find a way to steal Brother Benedict's keys to the bleedin' bell tower." Osric slammed his fist on his table with too much force, and he hoped the candle maker would not come to investigate.

As it always did when thoughts of Brother Benedict intruded, Osric found himself consumed with anger. Memories of his childhood flooded his mind displacing everything within range of his senses. Memories of learning to walk long after other children his age. Memories of constant belittling and taunting at the hands of the clergy; Brother Benedict in particular. Memories of being beaten with a wooden rod when he was young, and with a leather strap when he was older. Worst of all were the terrifying memories of being pursued by Brother Benedict as he tried to flee a whipping then being caught, whipped, and slammed into the small coffin where he would be left for hours, knowing additional punishment awaited him if he soiled himself. He remembered every beating, every whipping, all the hunger, and every minute of his confinement in the small black coffin. Osric's anger multiplied in later years when he came to realize the source of so much of his childhood misery was but a few years older than himself, and at the time Brother Benedict could have been little older than the apprentice boys who delivered tallow to the melting room.

In the course of his life in the candle shop, Osric had overheard many conversations between the candle maker and his wife. He had been shocked to learn Brother Benedict was actually the elder brother and had been given over to the church because his father considered him too dim to become a candle maker. Following one's father into a guild was most often regarded as the birthright of the eldest son, but in this case the candle shop had passed to the second son. "Too dim to be a sodding candle maker?" muttered Osric, upon learning this information. "Makin' candles is about as bloody difficult as breakin' wind, and if you can empty a stinkin' chamber pot, you can make soap!"

It took several angry minutes to calm himself enough to return to thoughts of wreaking havoc on the square, but when it did return, his mind went racing. "Oh, it would such bloody good fun!" muttered Osric, with rising malevolence. "What if I startled a horse or an ass, and it trampled someone, or even better, trampled a whole bleedin' mob of people? It would be bloody wonderful, it would!" Osric hugged himself, as he always did on those occasions when he was joyful. "I'd wait for the stinkin' candle maker to come outside, and then I'd bounce the biggest stone I could throw off his fat, poxy skull! I'd put him flat on his thunderin' arse, I would!" Once these thoughts began entering his mind, Osric's considerable imagination was unstoppable. He imagined several possible scenarios for the mayhem he could cause with each new plan being a bit more extreme than the previous one. It all left him feeling very happy. This reverie continued for the better part an hour until the bleak reality of his life began reasserting itself. "It will never happen. . . . I only fool myself. I'm a poor wretch of a dwarf, trapped in the bloody candle maker's attic because I'm too ugly to be seen in public, and that will never change."

Osric was in a sour frame of mind when the rap on his door announced the arrival of his supper. He shuffled over and retrieved his meal as quickly as his weak legs allowed. His food was poor stuff, but it was all he had, and he would, 'Kiss Brother Benedict's rosy red arse,' before he shared it with the rats. As he had done countless times before, he chewed the stale bread and sipped the rank water while cursing the candle maker and his foul wench in silence. After eating, the fantasy of assaulting the square from the belfry returned, causing him to smile in spite of the general state of his misery. Then, a memory of a different sort intruded upon his thoughts. He remembered the time when he pumped the bellows without having inserted its nose into the opening on the melting oven, and something had gone shooting out the end, and his mind sped up. "What would happen if you shot something out of the bellows on purpose?" He resolved to find out.

It was market-Thursday, and as usual he was forbidden to leave the garret. After considering the matter for a few minutes he decided his curiosity regarding the bellows did not rise to the importance of a flogging and did not outweigh his reluctance to have an encounter with the candle maker. He could, perhaps, sneak down to the melting room after the candle maker had locked the shop and retired to his residence, but this too carried risks. He knew the candle maker always returned to the melting oven to stoke the fire sufficiently to carry it through the night, and he wouldn't want to be surprised by his master. After pondering the situation, Osric decided he would just have to wait for an opportunity to test his idea during working hours. "Shouldn't be too difficult, really. The sod often disappears long enough during the day to try it, and the foul wench spends no more time in the melting room than e'er she must."

Osric removed the wooden tube from its hiding place beneath his pallet and began playing with it. He amused himself and laughed in silence as he produced sounds of flatulence, too soft to travel beyond the walls of the garret. Over the course of his difficult life, Osric had mastered the art of silent laughter for his own survival. It was during such a moment, another idea popped into his mind. His arms were not long enough to allow him to hold the tube to his lips and test for air movement with his fingers, so he removed one of his boots and placed the end of the tube near his toes. He blew through the tube, and when he felt the air rushing from the end, Osric wondered why he had never thought of trying to do so before. "If I can shoot something out of the bellows, why couldn't I shoot something out of my bleedin' tube?" Osric began scouring the garret for something that would fit inside the tube. Darkness was falling and he wondered if it was worth lighting his candle. Then, when he thought of the candle another inspiration struck him. "Tallow! Tallow will work!" Osric began shaving the sides of his candle with his fingernail. When he had an appropriate amount, he rolled the tallow into a ball.

After a few false starts, Osric succeeded in forming a ball that fit inside the wooden tube. He struggled to contain his excitement as he placed the ball in one end of the tube then blew through the other. The ball of tallow came out of the tube a short distance, then fell to the floor. Osric was disappointed. "I thought it would go farther than that," he muttered. He rolled the tallow between his fingers again to restore its roundness then, placed it back in the tube and made a second attempt. This time Osric blew as hard as he could, and though the ball of tallow traveled farther than his first attempt, it fell well short of his expectations. He reshaped the ball once again, and placed it back in the tube, but before he could test it a third time, he heard a commotion coming from outside. He hurried to his knothole and looked down at the square. Below him, he saw a man struggling to control an unruly cart horse, in the midst of much shouting from the few remaining market goers. The man was able to calm the horse after a minute, and he muttered, "Too bad the stinkin' beast didn't trample someone." He replaced the knot in its hole, then returned to his table. He put the tube to his mouth again and pointed it towards his window. What happened next, stunned him.

The ball of tallow shot out of the tube with an audible pop, then splattered against the window an instant later. "What in bloody hell just happened?" Osric chastised himself for being too loud and risking an altercation with the candle maker. He scuttled over to the window and began scraping the tallow from the glass. As he scraped the splattered tallow from the window, his mind raced.

He had twice tried blowing through the tube with little success. What had happened with the third attempt to make the outcome so different? Then it occurred to him that he had, perhaps, blown from the opposite end. "Is it that simple? Does the ball need to be on the end nearest my lips?" Osric began reassembling his ball of tallow only to discover what he was able to salvage from the window was insufficient, forcing him to reclaim more tallow from his candle. When he again had a ball of the proper size, he pushed it inside the tube, then gave a gentle puff from the same end. "That's it!"

Osric was beside himself with joy. He hugged himself and came the nearest he ever had to dancing. "Sod the bleedin' belfry! I'll shoot stinkin' balls of tallow out my knothole and no one will e'er see me do it! I'll have no trouble pilfering a bit of tallow, I won't!" Osric returned the ball of tallow to the tube several times and continued experimenting with it until it became too dark to see. After he had hidden the tube and donned his nightshirt, he settled himself on the pallet and was soon asleep.

Friday morning's rap on the door found Osric in some of the worst pain he had ever experienced. Though he greeted most days with pain, what he was feeling on this morning exceeded anything in recent memory. When he was able to stand at last, Osric had to lean on his stick much more than usual as he tried to stretch his back. He was having difficulty breathing, and his eyes were refusing to focus. As the time ticked away, he knew he was taking a chance of losing his breakfast to the rats, but he could not make himself move. With agonizing slowness, the pain began to ease, and he made his way to the door. Osric left his stick behind when fetching his food on most mornings, but today he suspected he might need it to fend off the rats, and his suspicions proved to be correct. As he opened the door, a large black rat was preparing to run away with his bread. With stunning swiftness, Osric brought the end of his stick down on the rat, killing it instantly. "BLOODY GOD-ROTTING RATS!"

When Osric sat down to his breakfast, he was still fighting nausea from the pain in his back, and seething with rage. "Every other merchant on the square hires the bloody rat catcher, but not the miserable, ill-bred, god-rotting, swine of a candle maker! I don't care if they bloody hang me, I'm going to kill that bucket of pig shit if I ever have to share my bread with another god-rotting rat!" Osric picked away that part of his bread where it appeared the rat had bitten. He ate in silence, trying with little success to calm himself. His pain was so intense it took all his willpower just to keep from regurgitating his food. Osric was only able to regain his mental equilibrium by thinking through, in exquisite detail, how he would go about killing the candle maker. When he finished eating, he dressed and made his way down to the melting room, pausing on the way to pick up the dead rat by its tail.

When the candle maker entered the melting room that morning he was taken aback by the foul look on Osric's face. He started to ask about the smell coming from the melting oven but stopped in mid-sentence. Osric, however, preceded to answer the man's question anyway. "It's a rat. A bloody, god-rotting rat got into the oven."

"But how could a rat . . . ?" The candle maker halted in mid-question. The burning anger in Osric's eyes told him exactly how the rat had gotten into the oven. For the first time in their association, the master found himself in genuine fear of his assistant. He looked at Osric, then after a tense silence, said, "I'm thinking of hiring the rat catcher, Osric."

"I think that's a bloody wonderful idea, Master," Osric responded in an even, but intense, voice. He kept his eyes locked on the candle maker, driving his master's level of fear even higher. "No one should have to share their food with stinkin' rats."

"Qu-quite right," stammered the candle maker. "Should have done it long ago. I will have my missus contact him this very morning."

"May God bless and keep you, Sir." Osric's words were heavy with sarcasm.

The few words that passed between the candle maker and his assistant were not a measure of the communication that had taken place. Without having made an actual statement, Osric informed his master he would be pushed no further, and having to share his food with the rats again would not end well for the candle maker. His master acknowledged a line had been crossed, and if the rat infestation was not addressed, his assistant would take his revenge regardless of the consequences. They stood for several more seconds, each locked in the intense stare of the other.

It was the candle maker who blinked first. "Well, what say, old man, why don't you add some wood to the fire and get it pumped up a bit? The apprentice boys will be along soon, and we should be ready for them."

The candle maker's use of a familiar and friendly form of address startled Osric, causing him to release a small gasp. His given name and variations of 'Wretch,' 'Beast,' and 'Monster,' were the only things his master, or the foul wench, ever called him. "I would have challenged the miserable sod a long time ago if I had any idea I could actually frighten the bastard," thought Osric, in amazement.

"Yes, Master." Osric scuttled around to the oven door and assessed the fire. He added the amount of wood he judged appropriate for the morning's work, then set about pumping the bellows. The candle maker disappeared into the front of the shop, and Osric hoped the man had gone to tell his wife to go and search out the rat catcher. His master had no more than left the room when Osric tore off a bit of sacking and stuffed it into the end of the bellows. The wad of cloth was fitted quite snugly in the opening, and Osric did not expect it to fly far when he closed the handles. He gave the bellows a hard squeeze and was stunned when the cloth shot clear across the room with a loud pop. "FOR THE LOVE OF SATAN'S HAIRY BALLS!" Osric had been much too loud, and his elation was brought to a sudden end when the candle maker returned to the melting room.

"Were you calling for me, Osric?"

His quick-witted assistant seized upon the opportunity, and said, "Yes Master, I had a question but I answered it myself."

"What was your question?"

"It's of no importance." Osric returned the candle maker a sly smile.

The candle maker looked at Osric in confusion and was about to speak again when there came a knocking on the back door of the candle shop.

"It's the tallow, I expect. I'll tend to it, Master." Osric used the opportunity to turn away from the candle maker. The most miserable of mornings had just taken an unexpected turn for the better. He unbolted the door and greeted the apprentices from the butchers guild.

When the two young men, scarcely more than boys, were greeted by a dwarf they were at once tempted to begin taunting Osric, as had so many others. However, one look at Osric's bulging arms and neck, and the oaken stick in his hands, made them quick to reconsider. This pair of boys was unfamiliar to Osric. Unknown to him, Clive and Anir the two young men who had made the deliveries for the past several months had been promoted, and delivering tallow now fell to these lads. Osric had liked Clive and Anir about as much as he liked anyone. They too had once been tempted to taunt him, but as they came to know him, the two boys had grown quite friendly. The three of them shared a bond borne of the unpleasant chore of hauling the smelly tallow into the candle shop in buckets. Osric had even come to tease the two boys a bit by demonstrating his ability to hold up full buckets of tallow, with his arms extended straight out from his sides. He challenged the boys to do the same, but they could not come close to matching his strength. After issuing a challenge of arm strength, Osric always added, with a wry smile, "I shan't be challenging you lads to a foot race, though."

After the apprentice boys had gone on their way, Osric was ladling tallow from the storage vat, into the melting vat when, it suddenly occurred to him to ask the candle maker, "Master? . . . Do you think one of the lads delivering tallow this morning seemed a bit off?"

"Off? . . . What do you mean, 'off', Osric?"

Osric eyed the candle maker as if in deep in thought for a few seconds, then shrugged his shoulders. "Oh, it's probably nothing, Sir. Forget I mentioned it."

"Osric! What do you bloody mean by 'off', and which boy were you referring to?" The candle maker spoke with rising anxiety, as memories of Osric's prayer came flooding back.

Osric said nothing aloud. He continued to eye his master with a mild expression, while thinking, "That worked bloody well!"

"Osric! I'm waiting for your explanation!"

"As I said Sir, I'm sure it's nothing to worry about. I should never have said anything. The lad is one of God's children, too, and I wouldn't want to cause problems for him. I'm sure everything will be alright." Osric had by now discarded Father Gregory's admonishments and was jubilant he had asked the question, though, as usual, no observer would have detected his joy. He made a mental note to ask the candle maker a similar question at some point in the future. "The fire's down a bit, Sir. I had best attend to the bellows." Osric turned his back to the candle maker and scuttled around the side of the melting oven. For the next few minutes, he pumped the bellows while the baffled candle maker struggled to get on with his work.

As they proceeded with their normal Friday task of making wick, Osric would pause from time to time and eye his master with a thoughtful expression, thus adding to the candle maker's unease and confusion. Osric decided the next time the candle maker spoke to him he would face down the man with all the ferocity he could muster. "He'll be drinkin' from the bloody chamber pot before the day's over, he will! Serves the bastard right. Bloody, god-rotting rats."

The candle maker, however, said nothing to Osric over the remainder of the morning, thus depriving his assistant of the opportunity to again frighten his master. Osric climbed back up to the garret and ate his noon-time meal, seething with renewed anger over the rat he had been forced to share his breakfast with. His dinner was interrupted by an unexpected knock at his door. "That's bloody odd. No one ever comes here." As a precaution, Osric carried his stick with him when he went to answer the knock. "Who is it?"

"Fendrel, the rat catcher!"

Osric was too surprised to speak and opened the door at once. The man standing before him was a few years younger, and though not a dwarf, looked quite similar to Osric. He was much taller, but barrel chested, and thin of leg. The rat catcher's clothing had not been new for some time and sported many patches. A shapeless hat rested upon the man's head and emphasized a nose as prominent as Osric's. The rat catcher was carrying a large leather bag by a strap that went over his shoulder. For reasons he could not explain, Osric felt an immediate kinship with the man standing before him. "I'm Osric."

"Aye, Osric. I've seen you at the festival, drinkin' with Kurtz, I have. I've been of a mind to talk to you any number of times, but Kurtz always chases me away, he does. I don't know why he does that but, still and all, I like Kurtz well enough, I do. The man makes a fine brown ale, he does, by God!" The rat catcher's rapid speech carried a lilt of laughter, and the man returned Osric a broad smile.

"You like brown ale?" asked Osric.

"Oh, bloody hell yes, I like brown ale, I do," boomed the rat catcher, in a jovial voice that contrasted the poor state of his appearance. "I more than like it. I think I'd just pitch it all, and jump in the bleedin' river if I had to live without brown ale, I would."

Osric had only shaken hands a few times in his life, but he extended his hand to the rat catcher, "Welcome to my home, Fendrel, shabby and miserable though it is."

"Do not beset yourself with worry, Osric. Your lodgings are not far different than my own. Now tell me, where do you most often see rats?"

Osric pointed out the places frequented by rats. He told Fendrel he also often spotted them at the top of the stairway, and they were always a menace to his meals when the foul wench brought them.

"Aye, aye," said the rat catcher with each place Osric pointed out.

"I've seen them everywhere," said Osric, "but those are the places I see them most often."

"Aye, aye," repeated the rat catcher. "Much as I would expect, aye, aye. I'll soon set it right, I will. May I use your table, Osric?"

"Yes, of course."

Fendrel placed his leather bag down on the table, then withdrew two wooden boxes. "These are the traps I use the most, Osric. If they don't clear the little beasts out then I've got some others we can try." The rat catcher placed one of the boxes where he thought the rats were most likely to visit, then reached inside and poured a handful of grain on a tray. The trap's door was connected to a counterweight that would cause the door to fall if a rat touched the bait tray. "I'll be back, morning, noon, and night, to check the traps, Osric. In the meantime, can you abide a cat?"

No, he couldn't abide cats. Especially so, after his unfortunate experience in the alley on the day of the flogging. However, such was his growing sense of kinship with Fendrel, he was compelled to ask, "Abide a cat? What do you mean, Fendrel?"

"Well, some folks likes em' and some don't, but if you can stand the little beasts then there's nothing better for keeping rats down, than a cat."

Osric had led a very sheltered existence and had no idea cats were used to control rats and mice. "Cats kill rats, Fendrel?"

"Oh, bloody hell yes they do. Why do you think there's no rats in your master's house?" Fendrel seemed surprised by Osric's ignorance of cats, but there was nothing accusatory or condescending in his tone of voice. "I'm sure I could get a cat for you, if you're of a mind to try one."

Osric was embarrassed by his ignorance. "Let me think about it Fendrel. I've spent near all my life locked up in this stinkin' garret or the bloody bell tower. Before that, it was the orphanage. I'm only let out for a bit on Saturday evening when I visit The Dancing Pig. I'm afraid there is much I do not know of the world."

Upon Osric's mention of the bell tower and the orphanage, the rat catcher lowered his voice, and asked in a conspiratorial tone, "I expect you're fast friends with Brother Benedict, then?"

At the mention of Brother Benedict, Osric flashed anger and then dissolved into silent laughter when he saw the rat catcher grinning at him, and he realized he was the recipient of the man's joke.

Fendrel leaned close to Osric, and whispered, "I'd turn all the bleedin' rats I catch loose in the bastard's trousers if I could find a way of doin' it. I hate the stinkin' sod." The rat catcher went on to explain how he too had spent his early years in the foundling home and had come to know Brother Benedict far better than he had ever wished to. "I expect I was a bit more fortunate than many, because I got adopted out to a decent enough couple while I was young, and me old pa taught me the rat catchin' trade. Catchin' rats doesn't cover a man with glory, but it keeps a roof over me head and food in me belly." Fendrel gave Osric a sly wink. "Not to mention a stein or two of Kurtz's ale now and again." The rat catcher smiled, then stood and surveyed the garret. "I'll be back this evenin' when I'm makin' me rounds, Osric. Good day to you, now."

"Good day to you Fendrel," said Osric, as he again shook the rat catcher's hand. Osric knew sharing his feelings toward Brother Benedict was something that could land the rat catcher in serious trouble, and that meant Fendrel was a man he could trust.

"What a day this is turnin' into! I'm mighty pleased to have met this Fendrel chap, I am." Osric's afternoon was uneventful. He ladled tallow, pumped the bellows, and tied stones to the end of the wicks. When the candle maker's wife arrived with his supper, his work day was over, and he climbed the stairs back to the garret.

He was eating his bread when there came another knock at his door followed by, "Fendrel here, Osric."

"Come in, Fendrel, come in," called Osric, not bothering to get up to admit the rat catcher.

"Good evenin' to you, Osric. I thought I'd just call out me name so you wouldn't have to get up. I expected you might be eatin' your supper." The rat catcher walked over to one of the traps and asked, "So, have me traps done any good this afternoon, Osric?"

"Well, I don't know, Fendrel," laughed Osric, a little embarrassed. "I'm not used to havin' them here, and I forgot all about them."

"Do not worry, I'll check them straight away." The rat catcher picked up the first trap and said, "Aye, caught you, ya poxy, bastard!" He held up the trap and showed Osric the dark gray rat, behind the metal grating.

"I hope it's the bleedin' brother of the filthy devil I killed this morning!"

"Aye, aye, could be, could be," laughed the rat catcher as he removed a cage from his leather bag. Fendrel held the rat trap up to a door in the cage, opened the trap, and shook it until the rat fell into the cage. He repeated the process when the other trap also proved to contain a rat. After Fendrel reset the traps, Osric was expecting the rat catcher to be off, but instead of leaving, Fendrel sat down on the floor beside Osric's table, shook his head, and said, "That's not the finest lookin' loaf I ever laid me eyes on, it ain't." Osric was surprised by the rat catcher's remark, but before he could respond Fendrel reached back into his leather bag and produced a cloth pouch, saying, "Try a taste of this Osric, I expect you may find it a bit more pleasin'." The rat catcher laid two beautiful loaves of dark bread on the table. Osric found himself speechless.

When he recovered from the shock, he asked, "What's this?"

"It's fresh bread ya' blinkin' fool!" laughed the rat catcher. "Baked this mornin' and I bought it not two hours ago. It isn't every day I gets the chance to share me supper with a friend, it ain't."

"But I've no money to pay you. Not until tomorrow, at least."

Fendrel was a man who lived nearly as close to the edge of society as did Osric, and he too was a master of silent laughter. When his laughter subsided, the rat catcher leaned close, and said just above a whisper, "Your bleedin' master's payin' for this, Osric. The damned fool just doesn't know it. The pleasure of your company is payment enough me friend." Being provided with fresh bread would have been astonishment enough for Osric, but Fendrel wasn't finished. He reached into his bag again and produced a stone jug with a wooden stopper. Next, he placed two pewter mugs on the table, then filled them with brown ale from the jug. "No better way to wash down fresh bread than brown ale, Osric. That's what I always say, it is. To your health Sir," said Fendrel, raising his mug to Osric.

After taking a moment to recover from this additional shock, Osric raised his mug to the rat catcher and exclaimed, "And to yours, Fendrel!"

The new friends shared their meal, and they both grew quite mellow after the rat catcher produced a second jug of ale. "Bloody hell!" cried Osric, in amazement, upon seeing the second jug.

The rat catcher laughed, and said, "I keeps the rats out of The Dancing Pig, and Kurtz pays me by fillin' me jugs for just three pence each!"

Osric and the rat catcher discussed their mutual loathing for Brother Benedict and other subjects as they sipped their ale. So confident did Osric become in Fendrel's company, he ventured to tell the rat catcher about his wonderful wooden tube, even going so far as to admit his guilt in the matter of the bell tower breaking wind.

"That was you, Osric?" whispered the wide-eyed rat catcher. Fendrel kept his voice down but, his mouth hung open in awe. "I was walkin' in the square, and I came near to wettin' meself, I did! You're a bleedin' hero, Osric, that's what you are!"

Osric told Fendrel of his exchange with Brother Benedict following the event, and this too convulsed the rat catcher. Then Fendrel told Osric of the day of his adoption, when he waited until Brother Benedict was in his bath, then crept into his cell and liberally dusted the inside of the man's codpiece with the mustard powder he had stolen from the kitchen.

"The bishop himself was sayin' high mass that mornin', Osric, and the miserable sod had to sit through it all with his bleedin' balls on fire!" Tears were streaming down Fendrel's cheeks. "You should have seen his face! I was singin' in the boys' choir that mornin', and lookin' straight at the bastard! I've ne'er seen anything like it, before or since! I think he came near to pissin' himself, he did! I'll wager that was the last time the bastard e'er let his codpiece out of his sight!" The rat catcher paused and took a large swallow of ale to calm himself then continued, in a more thoughtful tone, "I went home with my new ma and pa that very afternoon. I ne'er found out if anyone got a beatin' over it because I never went near the bloody orphanage again."

They continued to laugh in silence for a time, only pausing to toast the heroism of each other. When they recovered from their laughter, Osric told Fendrel of his experiments with shooting tallow out of the wooden tube, then mentioned shooting the wad of cloth out of the bellows. "I think it would be bloody good fun to shoot someone with a wad of tallow on market day!" said Osric, in an excited whisper.

The rat catcher gave his hearty assent then paused for a moment, deep in thought. Fendrel asked, "Osric, I wonder what would happen if we married up your tube to the bellows and shot a nice round pebble out of it?"

Osric was thunderstruck. "Oh bloody hell, Fendrel!"

"If you was to compare the size of the bellows to your finger, Osric, how big would it be?"

Osric thought about it for a moment, then held up his hand and said, "A bit larger, I think."

"Your finger won't fit inside the tube will it?"

Osric tried sticking his finger in the tube, then said, "Nay, Fendrel. The hole's a bit small for me finger to fit in."

"Aye, aye," said Fendrel, "I thought as much. . . .Osric, if you've a mind to trust me with your tube, I have tools me old pa left to me. I use them to make me traps. I'm thinkin' I could easy open up one end of the tube so's that the nose of the bellows would fit inside, all snug-like. I'm thinkin' we could hit the far side of the square with a pebble, if we use the bellows."

Fendrel had shown himself to be a man willing to share his love of brown ale as freely as his hatred for Brother Benedict. The rat catcher could have no higher recommendation in Osric's eyes, and he agreed without hesitation. "Yes, of course, Fendrel."

"I'll treat it with great care, I will," said the rat catcher, as he slipped the tube into his leather bag. "I best be on my way now, Osric. I've two more stops to make before I rests me weary bones."

"I'll pilfer some tallow when the candle maker is out of the room Fendrel."

"Aye, aye, that would be good, Osric, that would be good. We can't go usin' up all your candle. I'll be seein' you in the mornin', me friend."

Osric accompanied Fendrel down the stairs to let the rat catcher out the back door of the candle shop. Before leaving, Fendrel held his finger up to the nose of the bellows to gauge its size. It took some time for Osric to fall asleep after he returned to the garret, so alive was his mind with the possibility of actually creating havoc in the square.

The next few days saw Osric's difficult life take a small turn for the better. He collected the droplets of spilled tallow he would have otherwise returned to the melting vat and cached them in a hidden nook. Fendrel returned to the garret three times a day and left each time with two rats in his cage, a pattern that continued for four consecutive days. On the morning of the fifth day, only one trap held a rat, and on the evening of the fifth day, neither trap was sprung. "I believe we're gainin' the upper hand on the bastards, Osric, but I'll leave them set for a few more days." Fendrel spoke with a satisfied smile that turned to a mischievous grin. "I've somethin' to show ya." Fendrel withdrew the wooden tube from his bag and presented it to Osric.

Osric inspected the tube and found that one end of the hole had been carefully enlarged and now had a tapered opening that easily admitted his finger, then got progressively smaller. Amazed by what he saw, Osric asked, "However did you manage such a thing, Fendrel?"

The rat catcher engaged in another round of silent laughter. "I used a rat-tailed file, Osric! A hell of a thing for a rat catcher to own, eh?" Fendrel had another silent laugh, then responded to the puzzled look on his friend's face, adding, "Tis just a round file Osric. One o' the tools me old pa left to me. I just started careful like, workin' me way around the hole, keepin' the end o' the file pointed in towards the middle o' the hole. I worked on it when I had time, but I don't think it took me more than two hours, all told, to finish it."

"It's near full dark or I'd say we try it right now Fendrel," said Osric, grinning.

"Aye, aye, Osric. I'm eager to see how it works meself but, tomorrow's market-day and I'm thinkin' it's worth the wait." The rat catcher paused, giving Osric another sly smile, then reached in his bag again. "Feast your eyes on this, Osric." Fendrel held up an almost perfectly round pebble. The rat catcher took the tube from Osric and demonstrated how well the pebble rolled through it. "I must have looked at every bleedin' pebble within half a league before I found this beauty," beamed Fendrel.

Osric inserted the pebble in the tube and gave a gentle puff, sending the pebble halfway across the garret. "I think I could hit the middle of the square just by blowin' into it, Fendrel!"

"Maybe we could break one of the big windows in the cathedral with the bellows, Osric!"

Osric's eyes were wide with wonder as he responded, "Oh, wouldn't that be bloody grand! With a bit o' luck, it would fall on Brother Benedict, and ship the bastard off to hell!" Osric grew quiet, then said in a more somber tone, "The popping sound it makes is a worry, Fendrel. We don't need anyone lookin' in our direction because o' the noise it makes."

"Aye, Osric. Aye, aye." The rat catcher thought about the situation for several seconds then broke the silence, asking. "What, do you suppose, would happen if we wrapped your blanket around the end o' the tube Osric? Leave a hand's width of blanket stickin' out past the end?"

Osric retrieved his blanket from the line and folded it over until its width was roughly equal to that of the tube. Next, he rolled the tube inside the blanket, leaving the cloth extending past the end of the tube by the width of his hand. Fendrel held the tube while

Osric blew into its end, and the result was nearly silent while the pebble again flew across the room. They knew they had made an important discovery, and engaged in another extended round of silent laughter.

Osric's excitement made it difficult for him to sleep that night, and when morning came, he took little notice of the pain in his back. He ate his morning meal, then waited for the rat catcher with rising anticipation. Fendrel arrived, and after he checked the traps, the conspirators began shaping balls of tallow from the lump Osric had pilfered from the melting room. They waited impatiently for mid-morning, when they knew the crowd in the square would be at its largest. When the cathedral bell struck ten, the moment had arrived for a test. Osric wrapped his blanket around the tube and Fendrel steadied its end, a finger's width away from the knothole. Osric inserted a ball of tallow into the tube, took a deep breath, and blew with all his might. They took turns surveying the square for anything they may have hit but were disappointed to discover the balls of tallow had missed everything. The dwarf and the rat catcher continued to experience disappointment until their fifth attempt. When Fendrel looked out through the knothole, he cried, "By Satan's tail, Osric! You hit Badric, the smithy, smack in the side of his head!"

Osric looked out the knothole and saw a very large bald man wearing a bearskin vest, storming about the square shaking his fists and bellowing at the crowd around him. The enraged man's arms were massive, and the glee Osric felt at the wad of tallow finding its mark was tempered by the fearsome appearance of the man he'd hit. Osric turned to Fendrel and said, "I'll fight almost any man, but I wouldn't try that bastard. He makes three o' me!" Osric replaced the knot in its hole, and as the pair waited for the noise in the square to abate, Osric turned to Fendrel and said, with a malevolent grin, "Too bad I didn't hit the bastard in the eye, eh Fendrel!"

On market-Thursdays, the candle maker closed the candle shop for a half hour, beginning at three o'clock. This was the time the man and his wife made their own tour around the square, visiting the stalls of the sellers in order to purchase the goods they needed for the coming week, often paying for their purchases with candles and soap. Osric and the rat catcher agreed this would be the ideal time to steal the bellows, and shoot the pebble from the tube. When the clock tower announced three o'clock, Osric had his eye pressed to the knothole. When he saw the candle maker and his wife cross the street to the square, he said, "Now Fendrel! Hurry down and get the bellows!"

The rat catcher was down the stairs and back in the time it would have taken Osric to reach the doorway. They could hardly contain their excitement as they loaded the pebble into the tube then mated the nose of the bellows into the tapered opening. Scarcely more than a minute after going to fetch the bellows, Fendrel had the end of the tube centered over the knothole, the width of his finger away from the wall. As the rat catcher steadied the tube, Osric opened the bellows as far as it would go. They both took a deep breath, and Fendrel said, "No second chance this time, my friend. You either hit something or we have to wait until next week."

Osric nodded to Fendrel but said nothing. He calmed himself, focusing all his hatred for the candle maker and Brother Benedict into the handles of the bellows. When the hate in Osric's mind grew until it could grow no more, he used every ounce of his great strength to slam the bellows closed. So mighty was the blast of air exiting the tube, not even several layers of blanket could completely muffle the noise it made. Fendrel, being closest to the knothole looked out at the square and what he saw, struck him dumb. Before the rat catcher could speak, Osric heard the roar rising from the square. "What is it Fendrel? Did we hit something?"

"For the love of Satan's tail!" muttered the rat catcher as he continued to watch the events unfolding below him.

When it did not appear Fendrel was going to move, Osric elbowed the rat catcher aside and looked at the square.

Pandemonium was reigning below him. A huge draft horse, attached to a heavy wagon, was rampaging through the square. A streak of blood ran down the side of the enraged beast's hind leg. The horse's owner was engaged in a futile attempt to bring the animal under control as it rampaged around the square destroying everything in its path. Hundreds of people were running in mad panic in a desperate attempt to escape the mayhem. Osric pulled away from the knothole and stared at the rat catcher. Their eyes locked upon one another, both of them unable speak. When he found his voice, Osric said, "Fendrel! Get the bellows back to the melting room, then throw the tube into the oven! Make haste Fendrel! Make haste!"

"Aye, Osric! Aye!" The rat catcher grabbed the bellows and wooden tube then flew down the stairs to the melting room. He returned the bellows to its rack, then opened the oven door and committed the wooden tube to the flames. Fendrel was back in the garret less than a half minute after leaving it. When he returned, the rat catcher said, "Osric, mayhaps you should remove the string from around the knot. Just to be safe."

Osric saw the wisdom in doing so, and hurried to remove the string, then inserted the knot back in the wall, trying to make it look as natural and undisturbed as possible. They moved to Osric's table then sat a long while, shocked by what they had done, as the roar coming from the square slowly died away. Fendrel broke the heavy silence at last, saying, "I need some bleedin' ale Osric." The rat catcher retrieved one of his stone jugs from the leather bag and filled their mugs. They downed the ale in a single pull, and Fendrel refilled them just as quickly. It was not until they were well into the second jug, they began to speak.

"Did you ever see such a sight, Osric?"

"Nay Fendrel! Never!" Though he had often dreamed of inflicting chaos on the square, Osric found himself stunned by the reality of it all, which is not to say he was filled with regret. His only regret came later, when he learned the candle maker and the foul wench had managed to escape injury. It would be a long time before Osric and the rat catcher could freely discuss the event and laugh about it between themselves.

No one in the town would ever cast suspicion upon either of the culprits, and the candle maker never searched the garret. In time, their fears of being found out began to ease, and the candle maker's assistant and his friend the rat catcher shared a great quantity of brown ale in fond remembrance of the madness they had unleashed in the square.

The wound to the horse proved to be superficial and the animal made a rapid recovery. The citizens present that day, advanced many theories regarding the cause of the mad event. In time, the people of the town reached the general consensus it had probably been an act of witchcraft: an opinion strongly endorsed in the cathedral.

Chapter Five

The King's Visit

sric spent his morning making wick, as was normal for a Friday. What was different about this particular Friday however, was the absence of the candle maker who had been summoned away early in the day by a messenger from the manor house. "What ever can this mean?" wondered Osric. "I've ne'er seen anything like this before, I haven't. The only time the miserable sod ever visits the manor house is to deliver the beeswax candles, a week ahead of Christmas. It's all very strange, it is. If I see Fendrel today I'll ask him if he knows anything about it, I will." Osric's curiosity only increased when the candle maker's wife brought his midday meal. Though, as usual, she said nothing to him, he could not help noticing the woman seemed even more vacant and detached than usual. It was obvious something was bothering her. "Maybe the foul wench found out her poxy, god-rotting, husband is next in line for a flogging," mused Osric. "Oh, wouldn't that be bloody grand!"

Osric took his meal up to the garret, and was pondering the candle maker's absence, when a knock came at his door, followed immediately by Fendrel's voice, "Tis only I, Osric!"

"Come in Fendrel, come in."

The rat catcher was beaming with excitement as he seated himself on the floor alongside Osric's table, and whispered, "Did you hear the news Osric?"

"My bloody master has been gone all mornin' to the manner house is the only news I know of Fendrel."

"Aye, Osric. He's up at the manner house along with the other guild masters. *All the guilds*," added Fendrel for emphasis. "The word 'round the square is, the King is comin' for a visit! The smithy's helper heard it from one of the Count's servants who was in town for market day!"

"Bloody old Urloch himself?" asked Osric, wide eyed and much too loud.

Fendrel glanced around out of pure reflex. "Please be careful who hears you say that me friend. Don't be sayin' anything like that outside this garret. There's already strangers around the square," whispered Fendrel, who was ill at ease. "Everyone I talks to thinks they're the King's men, scoutin' the territory, so to speak. So, be very careful what you say about the King, Osric." Fendrel paused, then added with a smile, "You're safe with me though, my friend."

Osric acknowledged Fendrel's advice with gratitude, saying in a quiet voice, "I won't be sayin' anything about the bloody King to anyone but you Fendrel. I've even less love for the floggin' post than I do for kings and noblemen."

"I'm glad I had the chance to forewarn you, lest you misspeak on accident, and find yourself in trouble at The Dancing Pig, Osric."

"When does the miserable sod arrive?"

"Friday next is what I heard, a week from today. No one I've talked to seems to know if he'll be stayin' on for a bit or if he's just passin' through. I'll be lettin' you know if I hear anything I think might be true."

"Thank you, Fendrel. I'm sure I won't be hearing anything from the bleedin' candle maker. He likes keepin' me in the dark, he does."

"Well, I must be off Osric, I just wanted to give you the news. I've got traps to be checkin'. Be sure you tell me straight away if you've any more trouble with rats."

"I've not seen any of late Fendrel, and with little to eat, they may stay away."

After Fendrel departed, Osric finished his dinner while many thoughts swirled in his mind. The King's visit explained the candle maker's absence well enough, but it didn't explain why the foul wench was so worried about it. Was a visit from the King something to fear? He had no idea, but he admitted to himself, the idea of seeing the King was rather exciting, even if he couldn't understand why. While it was easy for him to make disparaging remarks about his monarch to Fendrel, in the privacy of the garret, Osric had never seen a King before and had only seen the Count a few times. "The only way I'll see bloody old Urloch is through the knothole," sighed Osric. "The swine of a candle maker will ne'er let me near the square."

When the clock tower announced one o'clock, Osric returned to the melting room and resumed his wick making. It was nearing three when the candle maker joined him. Osric gave his master an inquisitive look in hope of an explanation for the man's absence, but the candle maker said nothing of his visit to the manor house. To Osric's surprise, however, the candle maker came as near to offering him a compliment as he ever had when he said, "You've done well this morning, Osric. We're not far behind where we would be, had we both been making wick."

"Thank you, Sir." Osric was more than a little surprised by his master's words. He gave the candle maker another inquisitive look, and again, received no response. Osric's curiosity was driven to new heights when the foul wench appeared in the melting room and whispered something in her husband's ear, whereupon they both left the room, closing the door behind them. Osric cupped his ear toward the door and listened carefully. He did not dare go and place his ear to the door, as he would never be able to move away fast enough if he heard the candle maker returning. Osric heard only the muffled and agitated voices of the man and his wife coming from the shop and was unable to make out any of what was said. "This is bloody strange, it is," thought Osric. "Bloody, bloody strange."

It was only after Fendrel returned to the garret that evening that Osric began understanding the candle maker's agitation. "I've more news, Osric," whispered the rat catcher, grinning.

"I'm eager to hear it, Fendrel!"

"I heard from one of me customers the King has decreed that all subjects, regardless of station, are to be present in the square to greet him when he arrives, Friday next. That's what the big meeting at the manor house was all about. Or so I heard."

"What does this mean, Fendrel?"

"If what I heard is true, then I think it means that even poor knaves like us will have to be there to greet the bloody King. Not just the guild masters."

Osric was stunned. He pondered the question for a moment, then shook his head. "The god-rotting candle maker will never let me leave the garret and be seen in the square."

"From what the baker's helper told me, your master will be riskin' a trip to the floggin' post if he doesn't let you go," said Fendrel, grinning from ear-to-ear. "Much like the Harvest Festival."

Osric extended the rat catcher a sly grin. "Maybe I should just stay away then."

"Oh, that would be grand indeed if it got your master flogged, but if you are found out, you could be the one gettin' whipped, Osric."

"The risk might be worth it."

"Nay. I think not. I couldn't bear the thought of seein' you whipped, me friend."

Osric released a deep sigh. "You're right Fendrel. I can't say that I've any love for the floggin' post, if I'm the one to be whipped."

"You've made a good decision, Osric. Well, I must be off. I've two more stops to make yet today. Good night to you, Osric. I'll see ya tomorrow at The Dancing Pig.

Osric bade the rat catcher good night and changed into his nightshirt. As he settled himself for sleep, he wondered what might be in store when the King came calling.

Market-Thursday was normally the busiest day of the week in the candle shop. However, the Saturday ahead of the King's visit was proving to be even busier than a market day. The candle maker and his assistant found their work interrupted time and again by men Osric recognized as guild masters, from the chains of office they wore around their necks. The candle maker was summoned to the front of the shop for closed-door conversations several times over the course of the morning. Osric struggled to overhear, without success.

When the bell tower announced four o'clock on Saturday afternoon, it also signaled the end of the work-week in the candle shop. This was the time the candle maker paid Osric his wages and released him to spend a few hours in the ale house. Osric returned his master a questioning look as the man counted coppers into his hand, but there was no response from the candle maker. His master said only, "The interruptions have caused us to fall well behind today, Osric, and we may need to work a bit longer on Monday to catch up." Then, as if driven by some inner demon that forbade his ever having a civil discussion with his assistant, the candle maker added, "See to it that you do not make a fool of yourself in the ale house, Wretch."

Osric accepted the coins, smiled, and replied in a mild tone, "Thank you, Master. May God bless and keep you, Sir."

The candle maker inhaled sharply, wanting to respond to Osric's subtle blasphemy, but as usual found himself unable to speak as memories of his helper's prayer left him paralyzed.

"Good night, Sir." Osric continued to extend the candle maker a pleasant smile.

"Do not forget that your day starts early tomorrow, Osric!"

"How could I bloody forget it?" thought Osric as he turned and made his way to the back door. As he hung the cord holding the key to the melting room around his neck, Osric once again wished all God's blessings upon his master.

No one watching him make his way to The Dancing Pig could have detected Osric's glee at having driven the candle maker to anger, but it was there all the same. Osric never cracked a smile and resisted every temptation to hug himself as he hobbled toward the ale house. It was a pleasant spring evening and he was as happy to find the winter muck disappearing from the alley, as he was with the candle maker's impotent anger. Upon reaching the back door of The Dancing Pig, Osric reached up and tapped on the knocker with his stick. A moment later the door swung open and Kurtz extended his welcome.

"Hello Osric, old man! Just like clockwork on Saturday, you are!" The publican shook Osric's hand and ushered him into the ale house.

"A man needs a reason to live, Kurtz, and your brown ale is mine."

The publican laughed at Osric's joke, but he knew his words were the product of an unhappy life and carried more than a little truth.

"Has Fendrel arrived yet, Kurtz?"

"I've not seen him yet this evening, Osric, but I expect he will be along soon." Osric paid for a stein of ale then claimed his stool in a small alcove just beyond the bar. Kurtz kept a dwarf-sized stool in the alcove just for Osric, where he could sit and remain largely out of the sight of other patrons. The arrangement gave the publican the ability to keep an eye on Osric in the event an unruly customer began taunting him. The candle maker was not the only man who feared what an enraged Osric might do if pushed too far. Kurtz was pleased Osric had made a friend and regretted having kept him apart from the rat catcher during the Harvest Festival and in the ale house. After Fendrel came into Osric's life, Kurtz added another stool and a small table in the alcove for the rat catcher.

Osric leaned back against the wall, savoring his ale as he awaited Fendrel's arrival. In the adjoining room a musician began strumming a gypsy harp, and the patrons of The Dancing Pig were soon joining in ballads ranging from sad to bawdy. Osric had to content himself with listening to the singing at a distance, however. He had once made the poor decision to join the singers, only to have a group of patrons decide it would be a fine time to enjoy a round of dwarf tossing. The resulting melee left several would-be dwarf tossers bruised and bleeding, and Osric banished from the ale house for two months and a fortnight. His exile from The Dancing Pig marked a period of Osric's life only slightly less sad than his years in the orphanage. It was only after giving Kurtz his solemn promise to use only the back door, and restrict himself to the alcove, that he was allowed back inside the alehouse.

Fendrel joined Osric a half-hour later and the two friends spent their evening eating, drinking, and laughing at the song verses that grew increasingly ribald as the evening progressed. It was nearing midnight when Osric bade Fendrel and Kurtz a good night and began making his way back to the garret. One of the changes that had come to Osric's life since becoming friends with the rat catcher was that he now enjoyed at least two more steins of ale on a Saturday night than before. He felt bad because he could not afford to repay Fendrel's generosity, but the rat catcher was emphatic when telling Osric not worry himself, as he was greatly pleased to have a friend to drink with. "Meetin' Fendrel was the best day of me life, it was," thought Osric, as he shuffled homeward.

When the candle maker rapped on the garret door early the next morning, Osric greeted the day with his usual back pain, plus a hangover. It was not the debilitating variety of hangover he experienced during the Harvest Festival, but it was still considerable. Osric drank all the water in his pitcher in an attempt to quench his thirst, though he knew the church forbade it. He had first drunk water on a Sunday morning when in the throes of a wrenching, Harvest Festival hangover, and his thirst was unbearable. When no change resulted in his life, he decided to ignore the church and drink all the water he pleased. "The bastards would have me believe I'm bound for damnation because I take a drink of water on Sunday mornin' while Brother Benedict is bound for paradise because he whips children and locks 'em in coffins?" Nothing roused bitterness in Osric quite like memories of his childhood. Though Osric had no great love for children, he hated Brother Benedict far more.

Osric dressed in his new clothes, then made his way out of the candle shop, and to the cathedral. On Saturday evenings and Sunday mornings, the candle maker allowed Osric to take a key to the melting room with him. The predawn light was more than adequate for him to see his way, and someone, Brother Benedict probably, had already extinguished the candle lanterns outside the vestibule. "Why," Osric wondered, "are the lengths of the days always changin'? But a month ago it was dark as midnight when I left for church, and now there's light enough to see. It's a mystery to me, it is." When he reached the cathedral door, Osric was an instant away from letting the heavy knocker come crashing down when he had an idea. He slowly lowered the knocker arm, then used his stick to gently tap on it. A moment later, Brother Benedict swung the door open, smiling, and expecting someone other than Osric. When he was greeted by Osric's lop-sided grin, the brother flashed red with anger.

"Wretch!"

Osric responded with a hurt and confused look. "You chastise me when I knock too hard, and now you chastise me for doing as you ask. It's all very confusin', it is, Brother Benedict."

Brother Benedict was beside himself, but unable to respond to Osric's subtle mockery. At last he sputtered, "Get thee to the belfry, Wretch, and examine thy conscience!"

"May all God's blessing be upon you, Sir." Osric's voice carried the faintest trace of sarcasm. He continued to leer up at the Brother while holding his stick in front of him in fighting position. He hoped the man would lose control one day and attempt to strike him, whereupon he would make him pay a heavy price, regardless of the consequences. After a few tense seconds, Brother Benedict turned and marched to the belfry door, unlocked it, then stood aside for Osric. After climbing the first few steps, Osric turned back and asked, "Brother Benedict? I've been meanin' to ask if you ever heard that wind breakin' noise comin' from the bells again? That was a real puzzlement, it was."

For a second, Brother Benedict appeared to be choking then, managed to stammer, "N-no Osric, I've heard no more of it." It had been two-and-a-half years since the incident and Benedict had forgotten it until the memory came rushing back on the wings of Osric's mocking grin. He now knew, beyond doubt who had been responsible, but having no idea how Osric might have accomplished such a thing, left him unable to do more than fume.

Osric shrugged, "I just happened to think of it, Brother Benedict, and I thought I would ask. May God bless you, Sir."

For a moment, Brother Benedict teetered like a man on the verge of falling off a ledge, then he slammed the door. Osric had to contend with his silent laughter as he completed the arduous climb up to the bell ropes. Upon reaching the room below the bells, he went to the window and looked across to the clock tower. He had nearly an hour before the first round of bell ringing. He made sure the shutters were closed, then he inserted wool in his ears. Being caught unprepared for the bells was a mistake he had never repeated.

Osric sat down on the bench and began massaging his aching legs, and wondering who might be coming to hear his confession. A few minutes later, he heard footsteps on the stairs, and when he saw his confessor's head rise through the trap door, Osric said, "Father Stephan! How nice to see you! I've not seen you in quite some time now."

The young priest completed his climb into the room and regarded Osric warily for a moment before speaking. "Good morning, Osric. Have you examined your conscience?

"Aye, Father Stephan, I have indeed."

Father Stephan appeared to brace himself as he made the sign of the cross over Osric. "Very well, then. Please begin."

Osric gave the priest an earnest look and said, "After thinkin' long and hard about it Father Stephan, I can think of no sins I've committed in the past week."

"W-what . . . ? Not a single sin?"

"Nay, Father Stephan," said Osric, shaking his head. "Not to the best of my recollection, I haven't."

"You've not wished your master harm?"

"Nay Father! Certainly not!" Osric appeared shocked by the question and stared at the priest before continuing in a quiet, plaintive voice. "I've come to see just how wrong I was in the past, and I've come to love me master for all the kindness he's shown me, Father. I'm most terrible sorry for ever wishin' to see my master harmed, I am. I'm really a most fortunate man, Father Stephan. I know that now, even if I didn't before." Osric looked away as if deep in thought and gazed at some distant place for a few seconds before shaking his head as if disgusted with himself. When he turned back to the priest, Osric appeared to be on the verge of tears. "I only hope Brother Benedict can find it in his heart to forgive me one day for the many unkind things I've felt about him, as well." Osric spoke with sadness, his voice trailing away.

Father Stephan, lost and helpless, fixed his eyes on Osric until he could no longer bear the sight of the dwarf's face, then turned away. As if forcing himself out of a trance, the priest turned back to Osric and asked, aggressively, "You've not even used the Lord's name in vain?"

Osric returned the priest a horrified look and cried, "Nay again, Father!" He continued staring, wide eyed, at Father Stephan as the situation grew ever more uncomfortable for the bewildered priest. At last, Osric asked, with a trace of sarcasm, "Use the Lord's name in vain, and have eternal hell-fire for my reward? I'd sooner be led to the whippin' post every day o' the week, Father Stephan!"

When the priest was able to break free of his mental paralysis, he made the sign of the cross over Osric and assigned him a penance in spite of his not having confessed any sins.

"Thank you, Father Stephan, I shall say double the penance you gave me, I will. May God bless and keep you, Sir."

Father Stephan struggled to respond but could only stare at the Osric. At last, he turned away and fled down the steep stairs as if escaping an encounter with the devil himself.

Osric gave no outward sign of having done, or said, anything to upset the priest. He crossed the room and lowered the trap door. Only with the door securely closed did he sink to his knees in silent hysteria. "I thought he might piss himself, I did!" Osric hugged himself and reveled in the discomfort he had inflicted upon the priest. "I'm just damned glad Father Gregory is too bleedin' old to climb up here," muttered Osric as he continued to laugh in silence.

When the laughter passed, Osric got back to his feet and shuffled over to the bell ringing station. He stood on his box then slid back the panel that allowed him to see the altar. Opening the panel always brought back fond memories of his wonderful wooden tube. "I'd ask Kurtz for another tube but I'm afraid he'd want to know what I did with the last one, and I'd be afraid to tell him," sighed Osric, fighting back more laughter. He leaned against the wall for support and waited for the acolyte to light the candle that was his signal. Though Osric was illiterate, there was always a schedule posted, that employed a series of dots to indicate the day's bell ringing pattern. "This is bloody odd! . . . I've ne'er seen anything like this before!" Osric counted the dots then said, aloud, "Eight, eight, eight, eight? I've ne'er had an eight bell pull before, let alone repeated four times! Is this a bloody joke? Is god-rotting Brother Benedict trying to get me whipped?"

Osric thought about it and decided he had no alternative but to comply with what was posted. He would take the posting with him when he left, and if anyone accused him of wrongdoing, he would have it to point to. He was not about to make the difficult trek back down the stairs just to ask Brother Benedict for clarification. Before he had time to consider the situation further, the first signal candle was lit. "This is bloody early. It must be because I've so bleedin' many pulls this mornin'." Osric performed the eight bell pull, alternating between the two great bells. He did so again and again, as the signal candles were lit. Brother Benedict never rushed to the bell room to chastise him, and his fears of punishment eased. The great bells above Osric's head each weighed as much as six horses, and by the time the fourth service of the morning had concluded, Osric had pulled the bell rope levers a staggering one hundred and twenty-eight times, leaving him exhausted and in pain.

When Father Stephan returned to give him holy communion, he was too spent to ask about the extraordinary number of pulls that had been required of him. The priest blessed him, then hurried back down the stairs. Father Stephan did not bother to close the trap door behind him and Osric left it open for Sister Adele. He sat on the bench, massaging his aching muscles while he waited for the nun to arrive with his dinner. If she was in an approachable mood, he would ask her about all the bells. Thoughts of his dinner revived him a bit. "I hope she brings me something good!" Osric rubbed his hand together in anticipation. "I'm bloody starvin'."

When Sister Adele's head rose out of the opening, she did not finish climbing into the room. She placed Osric's tray on the floor, then said in a sharp voice, "Here is your meal, Osric. Brother Benedict said you have been disgracefully disrespectful this morning, and this is your reward for impertinence! You should be deeply ashamed of yourself! I hope, for once, you can be properly thankful for being fed at all! This is far more than you deserve!" Sister Adele said no more. She turned and made her way back down the stairs.

"Oh bloody hell, she's in another of her moods, she is. There won't be any talkin' to her today." He hobbled across the room, and picked up his tray, and was not encouraged by the lightness of it. When Osric removed the cover, he found only a small bowl of thin oat gruel, that had gone cold, a sliver of bread, and a small pitcher of water. The sight of the miserable food before him left him stunned. He sat down on the bench and tasted the gruel and found it contained neither salt nor honey. In spite of his burning hunger, Osric was unable to even force it down. "Dog's vomit!" Osric's voice was loud enough to be heard in the sanctuary. The bread was as hard and stale as anything the candle maker's wife had ever put before him. He broke off the mold that was beginning to grow on one end of the small loaf and managed to swallow the bread only by consuming all of the water. He had just been served the most miserable meal he had ever experienced during his time as a bell ringer, and on the day an unprecedented number of pulls had left him exhausted. The meager meal only increased the intensity of his hunger, and he still had thirty-two more pulls ahead of him at vespers.

The afternoon turned cold and stormy, and the weather was a perfect reflection of Osric's mood. Bone tired, hungover, and too hungry for sleep, Osric passed the afternoon in a nightmarish state where his pain, hate, and hunger fused into a single, stone-hard, thing. He remained tethered to reality only by his twin dreams of brown ale, and killing Brother Benedict. Even with the heavy shutters closed, Osric could hear the wind howling, and the rain pelting against the stone walls of the bell tower. Fortunately, no one disturbed him during that long, miserable, afternoon as it might well have proven fatal for the visitor. Using the last reserves of his great strength, Osric managed to complete his duties at Vespers. He eased his way down the stairs the moment he thought it dark enough for him to leave. He was so weakened, he did not think he could defend himself if it came to a fight, and for the first time since leaving the orphanage he found himself in fear of Brother Benedict. To his relief, the vestibule was deserted when he arrived at the bottom of the stairway, and he did not wait for Brother Benedict to let him out. He unlatched the heavy door and pushed his way out into the storm.

It had been a mild spring morning when he left for the cathedral, but it now felt like the return of winter. Osric kept one hand on his hat and bent low against the wind as he struggled back to the candle shop in near total darkness. His floppy hat did little to prevent the cold rain from stinging his face. Osric had made the foolish mistake of not wearing his cloak, and his woolen clothing was soon soaked through. His weak legs were beginning to fail when he caught his toe on a raised cobblestone, and went crashing to the ground. He fell elbow-first and an instant later, his head made solid contact with the paving stones. Hot pain flashed up his arm leaving his left side momentarily paralyzed. The blow to his head, combined with his weakened condition, left him dazed and unable to move. As the storm raged around him, Osric began preparing himself to die where he had fallen. Then, as his consciousness was beginning to fade, he felt strong hands lifting him to his feet, accompanied by Fendrel's voice over the roar of the storm.

"Osric! Osric! You must get to your feet man! Let me help you inside!"

Osric could only stare in the direction of Fendrel's voice. At last he managed a weak, "Fendrel?" Suddenly, Fendrel's face appeared out of the stormy darkness as the rat catcher lifted a candle lantern.

"I don't think I can walk any farther, Fendrel," cried Osric, his voice barely audible above the storm.

"Grab hold of your stick, Osric! I'll do the walkin' for the both of us!" The rat catcher scooped Osric into his arms and carried him as one might carry a baby. Other than the odd handshake, Osric allowed no one to touch him, but on this night, he was far too weak to protest.

When Fendrel gained the shelter the passageway connecting the melting room to the candle maker's residence, Osric said in a weak voice, "Fendrel, the key to the door is on a cord 'round me neck."

Fendrel found the key and unlocked the door. Once inside, the rat catcher sat Osric down on a stool near the melting oven. He draped his own cloak over Osric's shoulders then hurried to add wood to the oven, and began pumping the bellows to get the fire roaring. Next, Fendrel hurried up to the garret and returned with Osric's night shirt and blanket. "This is no time for pride, old man," said Fendrel, as he began stripping Osric of his sodden clothing.

Osric was helpless to resist, but his loss of dignity was soon replaced by gratitude as the warmth of the melting oven, his dry nightshirt, and blanket began pulling him back to the realm of the living. It took some time for Osric's teeth to stop chattering, but he was eventually able to murmur, "You saved me miserable life, Fendrel. How ever did you happen to be there in the square?"

"There's a helluva storm goin' on, in case you didn't notice, ya blinkin' fool," said the rat catcher, with an impish grin. "I thought mayhaps ya could use a helpin' hand gettin' back to the candle shop, so I was bringin' me pa's old storm lantern. I didn't expect to find you half-dead, I didn't. What happened to you, Osric? Why are you so bloody weak?"

It took Osric a moment to summon the strength to respond. "Did you notice all the bleedin' bells I had to ring today Fendrel?"

"Aye, the priest announced from the pulpit that the great number of bells was in honor of the King's visit, Osric."

Osric managed the weakest of smiles. "Maybe I should pay attention. I only try to ring the bells on time. There's no one lookin' over me shoulder so, I pay no mind to the rest of it unless Father Gregory is sayin' mass." Osric paused as a shooting pain caused him to grimace. He was filled with a mixture of gratitude for his rescue and the misery of his pain-wracked body. He looked up at Fendrel and said in a pleading voice, "They didn't bloody feed me, Fendrel! The hardest work I e'er done as a god-rotting bell ringer, and they didn't bloody feed me! I've had but a tiny scrap of rotten bread since midday yesterday. Sister Adele said it was Brother Benedict's punishment upon me."

"Bastards! Let's get you up to the garret then I'll run fetch food from my lodgings." Osric put forward a weak protest, saying the rat catcher had done more than enough, but Fendrel brushed the words aside. Once Osric was settled on his pallet, Fendrel hung his wet clothing on the line. "Sleep if you can, Osric. I'll wake you when I return."

Osric must have slipped into a shallow sleep, for it seemed that no more than a minute had passed when Fendrel was shaking his shoulder saying, "Sit up, old man. I've food and drink for ya." Fendrel helped Osric to his stool, then laid a loaf of dark bread on the table. He removed a glass flask from his leather bag and poured a measure of brandy into a pewter mug. Fendrel handed the mug to Osric, saying, "Toss this over your chest, Osric, you'll feel better for it."

Osric had only rarely tasted spirits, and he let go an involuntary gasp, as the brandy spread its warmth. In spite of his miserable state, Osric managed a small, wide-eyed smile and said, "Bloody hell, Fendrel! Where ever did you get brandy?"

"Let's just say I found it layin' about, and not put too fine a point on it, me friend. One more for good measure." After Osric had his second brandy, Fendrel said, "Now then Osric, let's be gettin' some food into ya."

It took Osric some time, but he ate the entire loaf and washed it down with brown ale from Fendrel's jug, then finished with another brandy. As the rat catcher was helping him get resettled on his pallet, Osric was overcome with emotion, and could no longer hold back his feelings. "Fendrel, you've saved me worthless life, you have. No man ever had a better friend . . ." Osric's voice was thick and tears were spilling down his cheeks. He struggled to continue, "I don't know how I can e'er repay ya, Fendrel, but if e'er I can, I will."

"I've done no more for you than you would do for me Osric. Think naught of it, me friend."

As Fendrel was preparing to leave, the garret door burst open, and the candle maker stormed into the room, bellowing and quaking with rage. "What is all this bloody coming and going? What are you doing here rat catcher?"

If Fendrel was startled by the candle maker's outburst, he did not show it. Instead of recoiling in the face of the man's anger, Fendrel advanced straight to the candle maker, jabbed the man in the chest with his forefinger, and snarled, "Your god-rotting excuse for a brother came near to killin' this man today by not feeding him, you thunderin' arsehole!"

Until this moment, Osric had not realized the rat catcher was a good deal larger than the candle maker. Osric also saw the flash of fear in the candle maker's eyes and realized his master was as big a coward as his brother in the cathedral. The candle maker tried to speak but Fendrel's finger interrupted the man's sputtering with another sharp jab to the chest.

Fendrel's face was only inches from the candle maker's. "Now you listen to me you miserable, swine! I'm a free yeoman and no man's servant! I have station to swear out a complaint with the bailiff, and if any harm befalls this man, then by God I will be doin' just that! If the bailiff doesn't deal with you, then be prepared to spend the rest of your stinkin' life lookin' over your shoulder! You are not worthy of this man, Candle Maker, and you've abused him for the last time! Now, swear on your life, that you will treat this man decently, or I shall take him to my own lodgings this very night!"

The candle maker had not been prepared for Fendrel's response and had gone from angry red dawn to pale moonlight in the little time it had taken Fendrel to bark out the words, and he had gone from strutting ass to a quivering glob of tallow, just as quickly.

The candle maker recoiled in the face of the unexpected assault from the rat catcher and struggled to speak. "I-I was only trying to learn the source of all the noise coming from the garret."

"You're the only one who believes that, Candle Maker!" Fendrel spoke with quiet ferocity, never taking his eyes off the candle maker. "Now, do you swear or do I take Osric home with me?"

"I-I, swear. . ."

"What's more, Candle Maker, you will feed this man properly, and do so three times a day, every day, or find yourself in more trouble with your guild than you can ever bloody hope to deal with."

"Y-yes, of course," sputtered the candle maker, cowering before the rat catcher.

"See to it that you do, Candle Maker, and be aware that from this day forward there will be many eyes upon you. If ever you backslide on your promise you will pay dearly for it! Now, be gone so I can say goodnight to me friend!"

The candle maker tried to speak but could only sputter. He turned on his heel and fled the garret. Fendrel listened at the top of the stair until he heard the door to the candle maker's residence close, then turned back to Osric, convulsing with silent laughter.

"Bloody hell, Fendrel!" exclaimed Osric, just above a whisper. "You put the fear o' God into him, you did! Other people watchin' him? What does that mean, Fendrel?"

When the rat catcher's laughter subsided, he bent low and whispered in Osric's ear, "I just bloody made that up, Osric, and he's a big enough fool to believe it! I thought the miserable sod might piss himself, I did!" Fendrel paused to calm himself again then continued in a quiet voice, "I meant what I said about takin' you out of this place, Osric. I'll find work for ya if things get too bad here."

Now it was Osric's turn to stammer. Fendrel held up his hand to silence his friend and said with a smile, "Don't be arguin' with me, ya damn fool. I think I can bloody well take ya in a fight, I do." Fendrel paused a moment, then added with a sly wink, "At least tonight, I think I could."

Osric felt the tears welling up again and could only manage, "Fendrel. . ."

"Enough talkin' from you, now. Be gettin' some sleep. You're needin' it bad. I'll check on you tomorrow."

Osric greeted Monday morning with his usual assortment of pains, but felt better, generally, than he had expected to given the ordeal of the previous day. When he retrieved his breakfast, he was astonished to find fresh bread and a small pitcher of milk as well as fresh water. "Fendrel worked a bloody miracle, he did!" whispered Osric, wide eyed. After eating, he dressed for the day and made his way down to the melting room. Though he had enjoyed his much-improved breakfast, Osric was on guard against any retaliatory measure the candle maker might take. For once it was the master's turn to flummox his assistant as the candle maker gave no sign anything out of the ordinary had happened. By the time his midday meal arrived, Osric was distracted and on edge. His found his dinner to be as improved as was his breakfast, and this raised his anxiety level still higher.

Throughout the morning, the candle maker said nothing to Osric beyond what was necessary to accomplish their work. When Osric returned to the melting room after eating his dinner, the candle maker looked to his assistant and said in a pleasant voice, "Osric, you've been with me these many years with no increase in wages. I've given it some thought, and have decided to increase your wages by six coppers a week, beginning Saturday."

"Oh, my word sir . . . !" Osric was stunned to disbelief. Though Osric's grasp of mathematics did not extend beyond counting to twenty, he immediately understood six more coppers equaled two more steins of brown ale.

"You do your work well Osric, and there is no need for there to be all this unpleasantness between us."

Years of hate and resentment were suddenly butting up against a new reality, and it was leaving Osric utterly baffled. At last he managed to stammer, "G-God bless you, sir," and for the first time in his many years with the candle maker, Osric came near to actually meaning what he said.

"You've, no doubt, heard that the King will be passing through the town on Friday?"

"Yes, Master. Fendrel told me, and it was all the talk in The Dancing Pig."

"All the shops on the square will be closed Friday morning during the King's visit. You are to dress in your best clothing and make yourself presentable. I will give you leave to visit the barber so that your hair and beard can be trimmed. You are to have a bath after the shop closes on Thursday."

"Yes, Master." A nervous, electrical, energy permeated every part of his body, leaving Osric feeling very strange. He had never visited a barber and had only ever cut his own hair and beard when they became too long to manage.

"I shall accompany you to the barber to ensure no harm befalls you, Osric."

"Yes, Master."

The remainder of the week was a whirlwind of activity for everyone in the town as the King's visit drew near. The Count sent men to assist in making the square as attractive as possible. Both the candle maker and his assistant visited the barber, and upon their return, were pronounced presentable by the foul wench. The candle maker's wife even complimented Osric on the cut of his beard, and her solicitous remark drove his angst to a new height. "What is she bloody up to?" Osric was wary, and his nerves were being stretched to the breaking point.

Little actual business was transacted on market-Thursday as excitement filled the square and the market goers could do little but talk of the King's coming visit. Osric was not the only citizen who had never seen his monarch. He was not, of course, allowed to visit the square on market-day, and had to content himself with viewing preparations for the King's visit through his knothole. Fendrel arrived in the garret late Thursday afternoon displaying a rather sheepish grin as he was wearing a new set of clothing, acquired for the King's visit.

"Bloody hell!" laughed Osric. "Are you on your way to court some fair wench, Fendrel?"

The rat catcher accepted Osric's gibe with the humor it had been delivered. "Little danger of that, me friend," laughed Fendrel. "Wenches, fair and otherwise, have always found me to be someone they can easy enough do without. Rat catchin' is a fair and honest trade, but it does not seem to be a thing that warms the hearts of women, Osric." Fendrel laughed with the air of a man who had long since become reconciled to his station in life. "Your hair and beard are lookin' right smart, Osric. Me thinks it likely you might be catchin' the eye of a handsome wench your own self." The two friends laughed at the absurdity of their lives while Fendrel filled his pewter mugs with brown ale. As they lifted their mugs, Fendrel toasted, "To all the wenches, fair and otherwise, who know not what they're missin'!"

On Friday morning Osric awoke to a level of excitement he had not experienced since the day he and Fendrel employed their weapon to unleash mayhem in the square. He sat down to another fine breakfast, muttering, "I believe the miserable sod took Fendrel's warnin' to heart, I do." After he finished eating, he dressed in his new clothes. Osric had neither comb nor brush so he used his hands to smooth his unruly hair and beard as best he could. Although he thought the candle maker might be calling on him at any moment, Osric took a chance and peeked at the square through the knothole.

Even at this early hour there were almost as many people milling about as one might see at midday on a market-Thursday. When he heard the candle maker's footsteps on the wooden stairway, Osric replaced the knot and scuttled to his table.

The candle maker stuck his head inside the door without knocking. "Come down and wait in the shop, Osric. We may have little warning when the King approaches, and we must be ready." Osric gathered up his stick and followed the candle maker down to the melting room and then into the shop, itself. Osric had been in the employ of the candle maker since failing as a grave digger a few days after being declared an adult. So determined was his master to keep him from public view, Osric, now in his early middle age, was visiting the front of the candle shop for only the third time. The candle maker pointed Osric to a tall stool and told him to wait there.

It took some effort to climb up on the stool, but he settled himself and sat swinging his legs as he observed the square through the many panes of candle shop's large windows. The candle maker stepped outside and began arranging a stack of large wicker baskets in front of the shop. "That's bloody odd," thought Osric, "I wonder why he's doing that?"

A man, unknown to Osric, strode up to the candle maker, spoke a few words, then moved on to speak to another merchant. The candle maker returned inside then hurried out the back, returning less than a minute later with his wife. The woman was dressed in what must have been her best gown, though Osric thought it added little to her attractiveness, which led him to think, "I've seen people three days dead with more life in their eyes than the foul wench."

The man Osric had seen speaking to the candle maker returned and tapped on the window as he pointed to the west entrance of the square with his free hand. "It's time," said the candle maker. "Come along Osric."

He followed the candle maker outside and was directed to the stack of baskets he had seen his master arranging earlier. "These baskets will keep you largely out of sight, Osric, and prevent people from taunting you."

He told Osric to stand on the board he had placed across the bottoms of two large, overturned, baskets. He complied with some difficulty, as the baskets came up above his waist. With the candle maker's assistance he was at last able to get to his feet and found he was just able to see over the tops of the baskets in front him. "This is bloody odd, it is. None too steady, this." He felt very insecure, having only the wobbly stack of baskets in front to help him maintain his balance, so he positioned one end of his stick on the cobblestones behind him. His stick steadied his perch to a degree, but Osric still felt as if he was walking on ice.

"Just stand steady, Osric. The King is not stopping, and it should not take him long to pass through the square on his way to the manor house. After he dines with the Count, he will be continuing on to the capital."

"Yes, Master."

Osric waited on, and mostly hidden by the baskets, flanked by the candle maker and his wife. It proved to be a short wait for no more than a minute later there came a loud fanfare of horns followed by a roar from the crowd. Osric had never heard horns before and their sound startled him, nearly causing him to lose his footing. The first riders of the Household Guard entered the square from the west. He steadied himself then watched in awe as row upon row of men in armor rode past, mounted on the most magnificent horses he had ever seen. The outriders were followed by a large company of foot soldiers, marching in unison to a drummer's beat. As the first of the mounted men were reaching the far end of the square, the King's carriage pulled into view, and the roar of the crowd reached a new level. All around Osric, people were cheering and waving their arms in welcome.

The people amassed in the square were carried away by the spectacle unfolding before them, and Osric, too, became caught up in the moment. He began waving his arms and cheering the King, and this proved to be a bad decision as his perch began deserting him. All at once, instead of waving to the King, Osric's arms were flailing about in all directions in a futile attempt to remain upright. He tipped backward and caught himself with his stick, then over corrected and leaned too far forward as the mound of baskets disintegrated beneath him. All at once, Osric found himself on the cobblestones and rolling in the direction of the King's carriage. He struggled back to his feet then lost his footing again when he stepped into a basket and went sprawling backward.

Over the roar of the crowd, came the voice of the King himself. "A DWARF! A DWARF! SEIZE THE DWARF! I MUST HAVE THE DWARF! SEIZE HIM!"

In an instant, Osric found himself caught up in a madness that went far beyond what he and Fendrel had unleashed in the square. There were hands reaching for him from all directions. He swung his stick in a savage arc, and someone screamed in pain. He turned in what he thought was the direction of the candle shop and began battling his way to the door. As Osric fought his way toward the candle shop he felt a hand on his shoulder, and he drove the end of his stick back into the midsection of his attacker. He turned and swung at his pursuers, making solid contact with a skull. He struggled free of a pair of grasping hands and was within an arm's length of the candle shop when a horse's legs appeared in front of him. Osric did not hesitate, and swung his stick with all his strength, shattering the horse's lower leg on contact. The enraged beast reared high and rolled backward, dropping, then nearly crushing, its rider. Before Osric could reach the door, the pain-maddened horse struggled back to its feet then charged through the candle shop's window. Trapped in the shop, the horse thrashed wildly in all directions, destroying everything in the room.

As suddenly as the horse had leapt through the window, Osric found himself smothered under a mass of bodies. Several hard blows were delivered to his face and torso, adding to his rage. In spite of his burning anger, not even Osric's great strength was enough to overcome the half dozen soldiers, holding him down. He was rudely jerked into a sitting position, and an instant later, a rope went around his chest as other hands bound his feet and arms. For one brief, lucid, moment, Osric realized the crowd in the square had grown very quiet. All he could hear was the injured horse as it continued to rampage inside the candle shop and the roar of the King's laughter. Osric struggled to see, and just for an instant, there was Fendrel looking on helplessly. Before he had time to consider his predicament, Osric found himself being borne away on the shoulders of the King's men. He was carried to a heavy cart well behind the King's carriage, then heaved into the back.

By the time Osric had been deposited in the baggage train, the front of the procession had begun moving again. Battered and bruised, he felt every cobblestone as the cart made its way across the square, and out of the town. He was wedged face down between sacks of grain, and unable to roll over. Osric managed to turn his head just enough to see the bell tower disappearing over the sides of the cart. He would never see the cathedral, or the town, again.

Chapter Six

Osric Meets the King

The cart bearing Osric away from the only place he had ever known, began to sway and bounce even more after it passed beyond the cobblestones of the town, and onto the rutted track leading up to the manor house. The journey between the town and manor house lasted no more than a half hour, but to the bruised and tightly bound prisoner, it seemed an eternity. Every bump caused his bruised ribs new pain, and his back was aching terribly, though Osric was grateful to be lying on bags of grain instead of something harder. He was relieved when the cart came to a halt at last. He was still very uncomfortable and unable to move, but at least the bouncing and jostling had stopped. Osric continued to lay face down, wedged between two large bags of grain for additional minutes, growing ever more unhappy.

Then, a not unfriendly voice asked, "What ho, Dwarf, are ya alright?"

After the initial shock of the question passed, Osric responded in a sharp tone, "Does it bloody look like I'm alright?" Osric knew the voice was close at hand, but he could not tell exactly where it was coming from.

The friendly voice responded with more laughter, "Aye, I expect that was a foolish question, it was. Are ya' needin' to relieve yourself, Dwarf? Could you do with somethin' to eat?"

After having been beaten, bound, and heaved into the back of the cart, Osric was more than surprised by the questions. "Aye, I could well stand to do both, I could."

"If I was to unbind you, would you go to fightin' with me, Dwarf?" The voice paused a moment then added, with a laugh, "Hell of a fighter, you are, by God!" The voice then continued in a more serious tone, "I'll be needin' your solemn promise Dwarf, and just so you know, the guards are near at hand should you decide to try runnin' away."

"I can barely bleedin' walk, ya damned fool, and I canna' run at all! Where is my bloody stick? I canna' walk far without it." Osric spoke with rising anger.

"I'm thinkin' His Majesty himself has your stick, Dwarf. He was bloody well impressed at the way you used it, he was."

"Will he give it back?"

"That is between you and His Majesty, Dwarf. This poor carter ain't about to go before the King, askin' to get your stick back, he ain't. . . . So, do I have your solemn promise, or do I need to be callin' some guards to watch over you while you go to relieve yourself?"

"You have my promise."

"Aye then, you're making a good decision, Dwarf. The King is right particular about how his dwarfs are treated, he is. If you behave yourself, no harm will befall you. I'd caution you not to go causin' any more of the King's horses to be killed, though. Oh, what a helluva sight that was!" The voice continued to laugh as Osric heard the end gate of the cart fall open.

The husky red-haired man he saw out of the corner of his eye appeared younger than what the sound of his voice had led Osric to expect. The man turned his back to the open end, put his hands on the floor then lifted himself, rump first, into the cart. He swung his legs inside then crawled the short distance to Osric and set to work untying the bindings. "Do ya have a name, Dwarf?"

"Of course I have a bloody name. Doesn't everyone?" The prospect of being untied had done little to diminish Osric's anger.

The man laughed again, "Aye, another foolish question, it was. All right then, what *is* your name, Dwarf?"

"Osric."

"Osric. . . a fine name, that. I've ne'er known anyone named Osric, I haven't." The man was quiet as he continued to untie Osric's bindings, taking care not to cause him any additional pain. "Jarin, here. Jarin the carter. There we go, Man. See if you can roll over. If you can scoot to the back I'll give ya a hand gettin' to the ground."

Much as it had been when he first met Fendrel, Osric's instincts were telling him he could trust the cart driver. Though the man held every advantage over him, he had made no attempt to exploit the situation. Thus far, at least, he had shown him only kindness. When Osric tried to roll over he was gripped by an intense pain in his back that went well beyond what he was accustomed to. He stopped, winced, held his breath, and waited for the pain to pass. When the pain eased, Osric finished rolling over then drew himself into a sitting position and began scooting to the edge of the cart bed. When he dropped his legs over the edge of the cart, to Osric's astonishment, Jarin simply picked him up under the arms, then gently sat him on the ground. Under normal circumstances, such behavior would have drawn a violent response from Osric, but he found himself standing on the ground before he could react.

"There ya' go, Man. Yon woods will allow you to relieve yourself with a bit of privacy," said Jarin pointing to his right.

"I canna' walk that far without me stick."

Jarin seemed perplexed by the situation. A strapping young man such as himself could walk to the woods in short order. It had not occurred to the cart driver the distance involved would present a serious obstacle for Osric. Jarin thought for a moment then asked, "Would you like me to carry ya, Osric?"

"No! I don't want you to bloody carry me!" He regretted his tone of voice at once, as it was clear the carter was only trying to be helpful. "I did not mean to sound harsh, Jarin. I do not relish being touched, is all."

"Aye, aye, I can understand that well enough, I can." Jarin continued to ponder the situation, then clapped the palm of his hand to the side of his head, "Bloody hell, Osric. I'm lookin' right at the answer, I am. How do ya' fancy a ride in a wheelbarrow?"

"Ride in a bloody wheelbarrow?" Osric's only exposure to wheelbarrows involved the smelly vehicles used by the apprentices from the butchers guild to deliver tallow to the candle shop.

"Why not, Man? I have one right here. I use it to tote grain 'round to all the horses when we makes bivouac for the night. I've given rides in me wheelbarrow to more than a few children, I have."

After considering it for a moment, the prospect of riding in a wheelbarrow began to strike Osric as rather humorous. The distance to the trees was too far to walk, he needed to relieve himself, so he agreed to the ride. Jarin went around the far side of the cart, then returned a moment later pushing a wheelbarrow that was a good deal smaller than the ones employed by the apprentice boys from the butcher's guild. Osric arched his eyes in surprise. "This is not what I was expectin', Jarin. The barrows they use to deliver tallow to the candle shop are much larger." Osric paused a moment, screwed up his nose, and added with a grimace, "And, they smell bloody awful, too."

Jarin laughed and said, "This barrow has seen nothin' but oats and barley. Here ya' go man, just sit down, then scoot to the front and we'll be off." Osric did as he was asked, then Jarin picked up the handles, and began wheeling him in the direction of the trees. Osric was soon enjoying the ride a great deal, and Jarin asked, "So Osric, you're a candle maker, then?"

Osric returned Jarin a wry smile, "Nay, Jarin. I was just the bloody candle maker's helper, I was. I made some candles once, and me master thought I was possessed by a demon."

Jarin laughed, "Masters can be an odd lot sometimes, they can. The carter paused a moment, then continued, "A fine trade, though, candle makin' is."

He had never thought of his trade as 'fine', but after he considered it a moment, Osric replied, "There's worse things, for sure. Candle makin' is done indoors, and not out muckin' about in the rain." Osric then added with a grin, "And, I'm thinkin' it's a wee step up from grave diggin', it is."

Jarin laughed again, "An honest grave digger is never out of work, though."

"Aye, unless we learn to live forever." He paused a moment, then continued, "Brother Benedict tried makin' a grave digger out of me before I left the orphanage. I found out diggin' graves is done with your legs as much as your arms, and me god-rotting legs just ain't equal to pushin' a spade into the ground. I can't say that failin' as a grave digger broke me heart, though."

As Jarin and his passenger were nearing the edge of the woods a knight galloped up and halted, lance-in-hand, between them and the trees, demanding, "You there, Carter! Where are you going with the King's dwarf?" The armored man sent a shiver of cold of fear running through Osric, as the knight pointed his lance at Jarin's chest.

Jarin too was unnerved by the experience and stuttered as he responded, "T-this poor man canna' walk very well, Sir Brom. I-I'm just helpin' him to get to the woods for a call of nature, Sir."

The knight seemed to accept Jarin's explanation, then lifted his lance and tipped his head in the direction of the trees. "I'll accompany you."

"Yes, Sir Brom." Jarin resumed wheeling Osric into the trees, and when a sufficient degree of privacy had been achieved, sat the wheelbarrow down. "This should do, Osric. We'll do our business, then get back to camp."

Osric shuffled behind a shrub and began relieving himself. He completed the task with considerable difficulty, as the knight kept the point of his lance inches from his back. When he finished, Osric climbed back aboard the wheelbarrow, and Jarin started back to the encampment. The knight seemed to lose interest in them after they emerged from the trees and cantered his horse back to where the rest of the cavalry had established a defensive line. The King's foot soldiers were maintaining an outer perimeter with the cavalry positioned behind them. Together, they formed a semi-circle in front of the manor house, that left the King's troupe inside a protective arch behind the soldiers.

As he watched the knight ride away, Osric said in a low voice, "Bloody hell, Jarin! Makin' water is bleedin' difficult when there's a god-rotting lance pointed at your back."

Jarin glanced around to ensure he was out of earshot, then spoke with caution. "Nay, Osric, it isn't. Sir Brom's one of the better ones, though. Some of the bloody knights will run a man through without botherin' to ask any questions. I've seen it happen, I have. You're likely safe, though. The King is right partial to his dwarfs, he is."

Osric was struggling to understand the carter's continuing references to 'the King's dwarfs', and when he could no longer contain his curiosity, he asked, "His dwarfs, Jarin? The King keeps dwarfs? How many dwarfs does he have?"

"The King collects fine horses the way kings do, but he also collects dwarfs, Osric. There were over forty, last I counted. They come and go. He sends the dull witted ones away, and some pass on of course. Others have been with the King from birth, and there's even dwarf married couples, livin' in the castle with their families."

The thought of the King 'collecting' dwarfs horrified Osric. He was a man, and not a thing to be collected! Osric glanced about, seeking any possibility of escape, but saw no chance of success. His captors were many, and he was much too slow afoot. At that moment, Osric was prepared to give up a year of his life, foreswear brown ale, and grovel at the feet of Brother Benedict, if he could only be back in his garret. He was so preoccupied with thoughts of the King and his collection of dwarfs, he remembered nothing of the ride back to Jarin's cart. Only when the carter sat the handles of the wheelbarrow down, was he jolted back to the moment.

"Here we are, Man."

As if waking from an unpleasant dream, Osric lifted his chin and looked around. He blinked his eyes, then said, "Oh, yes. Thank you Jarin. I could never have walked that far, and I'm not fond of pissin' meself, I'm not."

"Think naught' of it Osric. Watchin' after you will be my lookout until we're back at the castle. Disappointin' the King can get a man whipped or worse, and I've no love for gettin' whipped, I don't." Jarin paused a moment and eyed Osric, "Now Osric, if I was to leave you sittin' here whilst I go fetch our dinner, will I find you waitin' for me when I get back, or do I need to bind you?"

"I canna' outpace a small child, Jarin. There's little chance of me runnin' away."

"Your solemn promise before God, then?"

"Aye, Jarin, you have my promise."

"Alright then, just put your foot in me hands." The carter laced his fingers together to form a stirrup. Osric did as he was asked, and Jarin boosted him up to the cart bed. "I shan't be long Osric, just sit here whilst I run to the cook-wagon."

Jarin hurried away while Osric sat on the end of the cart bed, taking in his surroundings. The people making up the King's party was a number far greater than he was capable of counting, and may have exceeded the number of people present in the square on a market-Thursday. Though there were many people around him, unlike being in the square, no one in the King's party made any move to taunt him. A few people cast curious glances in his direction, but nothing more. Though his new situation continued to leave him ill at ease, being left alone in this situation was helping relieve his distress. Jarin returned after a few minutes with a basket in one hand and two steins of ale in the other.

"The bread was baked fresh last night, and the baker does a right fine job of it, too. Do ya' care for brown ale, Osric?"

"You brought brown ale, Jarin?" Osric's eyes were wide. Some brown ale would go a long way toward setting the events of this awful morning to rights.

"Aye, Osric. The King always travels with a bloody great cask of it, and he shares it with everyone."

"I've often told Kurtz, the alehouse keeper, that his brown ale is me reason for livin', Jarin."

The carter smiled as he broke off a large chunk of dark bread, and handed it to Osric. "Aye, aye, there's worse reasons for stayin' alive than brown ale, there is." Jarin handed Osric one of the steins, then joined him on the end of the cart. Jarin lifted his stein and said, "Here's to stayin' alive, Osric."

Osric joined in the toast then lifted the stein to his lips and tasted the ale. It was *not* the brown ale of The Dancing Pig! This ale was both nuttier and more bitter, and did not flow as gently across his tongue. Though his first impulse was to reject the ale, Osric soon thought better of it. Poor ale was far better than no ale at all. The bread, however, was very good. All things considered, Osric had few complaints about his first meal as a captive of the King, even if the brown ale fell well short of the standard set by Kurtz in The Dancing Pig.

After they had eaten their bread and drunk their ale, Jarin returned the steins and basket to the cook-wagon. He rejoined

Osric in the back of the cart upon his return, then settled himself across the bags of grain. He made himself comfortable, and within minutes the carter was snoring. Osric considered trying to sleep a bit himself but decided against it. His ribs were still aching, and everything going on around him on this sparkling spring day made life far too interesting for sleep. He observed the King's soldiers taking turns going to the cook-wagon for their bread and ale while the other men kept the watch. Osric had only ever ventured outside the walls of the town a few times in his life, and then never very far. He had no idea what the soldiers might be guarding against and resolved to ask Jarin about it when the carter woke from his nap.

Jarin was still sleeping when the horns that had startled Osric so badly in the square sounded again. He found them less frightening this time, and he was not trying to maintain a precarious perch on a mound of baskets. Jarin sat up and stretched. "Did ya rest a bit, Osric?"

"Nay, Jarin. I've only been watching what is going on in the camp."

Jarin hopped to the ground and said, "The trumpets mean we will be leavin' soon, and to make ready. Could you do with another trip to the woods Osric? I could, and we'll be off soon. We may not be stoppin' for some time, it's always up to His Majesty."

After consuming the stein of ale, Osric saw the wisdom of revisiting the woods and climbed back aboard the wheelbarrow. On this trip, no knight interfered with their journey and they were able to complete their mission and return to the cart without incident. Jarin closed the end of the cart, then hung his wheelbarrow on the side of the vehicle in a bracket designed for the purpose. "Come 'round to the side Osric, and I'll give you a boost up to the seat. No need for ya' to be ridin' in back." Osric complied, and the carter again made a stirrup by lacing his fingers together, then lifted Osric up to the seat. After Jarin climbed aboard, he took the reins in hand, and said, "Now we wait, Osric. The King tells the Lord Chamberlain he is ready to depart, then the word gets passed on down to the heralds who blow their bleedin' horns to tell the common folk to make ready. Sometimes the King appears posthaste, and we're off in a trice. Other times we wait considerable. There's no tellin' with His Majesty."

Osric took advantage of the wait to question Jarin about the way the soldiers had deployed around the other travelers. "It's just a precaution, Osric. We're not close to the frontier so there is little danger of any enemy appearin', but they always post a guard. There's brigands and vagabonds in the forests, though they would never confront the soldiers. The commander of the guard takes no chance of being caught unawares."

Osric found Jarin's response more than a little confusing, and his first question was, "What is the frontier, Jarin?"

Jarin looked down at his new traveling companion with surprise. "The frontier is where our country meets another country, Osric. The nearest one is at least thirty leagues away."

"There are other countries?"

"Oh my, Osric! You've much to learn, you do!" The carter was surprised by Osric's ignorance of the world, but his tone of voice was never less than friendly. "There are many other countries, and ours is but a small one. Spain and France are much larger and mightier, but lucky for us, they're far away and pay us little attention. Russia is closer, but they've caused no trouble, in my lifetime at least. For the most part, the kings and princes in this corner of Europe engage in petty squabbles that kill few people and do not cost them a lot of money. I think sometimes they fight just for sport, I do. In any event, all the kings are related, by blood or by marriage. I expect killin' too many people might lead to awkward conversation over the Christmas goose." The cart driver laughed at his joke, leaving Osric more baffled than ever. Before he could ask additional questions, there came another blast from the horns, and Jarin said, "We'll be off when it comes our turn to move, Osric."

He watched in amazement as the mounted knights assembled into a formation at the vanguard, with the foot soldiers lining up close behind. As the King's shiny black carriage rolled away from the manor house, all the soldiers stood stiff and straight. The carriage driver took up a position behind the foot soldiers, and once in place, another blast from the horns set the whole procession in motion. When it came their turn, Jarin lightly flicked his whip over the backs of the two large horses, and they too began rolling along. Jarin and Osric fell into the procession well back of the King's carriage with only two baggage carts trailing behind them. Though it was not as comfortable as his stool in the ale house, Osric found riding on the cart's seat to be a great improvement over being wedged face down between sacks of grain, while bound from head-to-toe.

The procession moved away from the manor house and resumed travel on the track leading away from the town. The traveling party soon settled into a rhythm, the pace being governed by the marching soldiers. After they had ridden a few minutes, Jarin said, "If we were closer to the frontier, the commander of the guard would likely split up the troops, and half of them would be marching behind us."

"Do you always travel with the King, Jarin?"

"Most always. As did me father, and his father before him. Between us, my family has seen every corner of the realm, and parts of other countries as well. We served this King's father and grandfather. Destrian VII and Urloch I, as well as the Lord Chamberlain during his time as regent. My family has been most fortunate to retain our positions with the changing of the kings."

"I've known only Urloch II in my lifetime."

"Destrian may well have been King when you were a wee lad, Osric, but it's not surprising you would not remember him. He only reigned as King for a bit over a year before he was struck down by a fever. Right young he was, too. Our Urloch II was but a small boy when he became King and his uncle, the Lord Chamberlain, ruled as regent until Urloch achieved his majority, and took the throne."

"I've ne'er heard of the Lord Chamberlain. It's all very confusin', Jarin"

"Aye, aye, I expect it is Osric," said the carter, smiling down at his passenger. "As I said before, if you behave yourself, no harm will befall you. Our King is right fond of his dwarfs, he is."

They conversed less and less as the procession rolled on through the afternoon. Osric was fascinated by everything around him, having never before ventured more than half a league from his place of birth. At some point it occurred to him he was visiting places he had seen when he stood alongside the great bells. Thoughts of the bell tower brought a smile to his lips as he realized he had gone all day without once thinking of killing Brother Benedict. Osric craned his neck in all directions, in hope of catching a glimpse of the cathedral, but he never spied it. He was experiencing a curious mix of emotions as he was being carried away. On the one hand, he felt exuberant joy at the prospect of being forever free of the candle maker, the bell tower, and Brother Benedict. On the other hand, he was filled with fear and trepidation at having had every familiar thing torn away from him. Most of his thoughts were of The Dancing Pig, and he would have given anything to be there, sharing brown ale with Fendrel.

The traveling party halted at regular intervals over the course of the afternoon to allow the foot soldiers to refresh themselves with water and dried fruit. Jarin explained how the Lord Chamberlain, during his regency, had the tendency to drive the troops to near exhaustion, a practice Urloch II discontinued upon taking the throne. "The men bloody loved him for it, Osric! The King told the troops they were of little value if they were too tired to fight."

The sun was nearing the treetops when Osric heard the herald's trumpets sound again. This time, however, instead of halting on the track the vanguard led the party out into the center of a large meadow. The foot soldiers quickly spread out and formed a protective ring around the travelers with the mounted knights taking up positions behind the infantry. A wagon that had been traveling immediately behind the King's carriage advanced to the center of the circle, and the moment it halted, several men jumped down then set to work erecting a large tent. In far less time than Osric thought possible, the King's standard was hoisted, and Urloch II left his carriage and entered the royal tent.

After halting the cart, Jarin too hopped to the ground. "I have work to be doin' now, Osric. I must be gettin' a ration of grain 'round to all the horses." Jarin removed the wheelbarrow from the side of the cart and began loading it with bags of oats.

"What am I to do, Jarin?"

After a moment's hesitation, the carter shrugged, and said, "I expect you can just sit here, Osric. No harm will befall you. Ye may want to get down and stretch your legs a bit. After I've fed all the horses, I'll fetch our supper from the cook-wagon."

It all seemed too simple to Osric. He was a captive, but unbound and unguarded. If he only had a stick to aid him he could just walk away, then make his way back to the candle shop. He scanned the area in the vicinity of the cart but saw nothing he could use. Then he realized the protective ring of soldiers meant there was little need of his captors to guard him. There was no place to hide, and he could never get past the armed men and cross the open field to the forest. Osric swung his legs around then lowered himself into the back of the cart. He used the seat to help himself stand and stretch. As he was stretching, he saw a tall, silver-haired man dressed all in black, and flanked by two soldiers, striding toward the cart.

When he was still several paces away, the tall man raised his hand, and without breaking stride, pointed a long finger at Osric. "You there! Dwarf!"

Osric turned to the man and said, "Sir?"

"I am Favian, Duke of Bruno, the Lord Chamberlain, and you will address me as, *My Lord!* Is that understood, Dwarf?" The man's voice was deep and sharp, and though the Lord Chamberlain did not appear to be heavily muscled, his countenance terrified Osric.

"Y-yes M'Lord," said Osric, fighting to control his nerves.

"Do not look at me, Dwarf!" shouted the Lord Chamberlain, pointing his finger at Osric like a weapon. "If you fail to bow your head in my presence, Dwarf, you may very well lose it!"

The man's words stung like a whip, and Osric was now trembling. Brother Benedict at his worst had never frightened him the way this man did. He lowered his head and said, "Yes, M'Lord."

"Get thee down from that cart, and be quick about it, Dwarf! You are to meet the King!"

Osric shuffled to the back of the cart then sat down on the floor and rolled onto his stomach. He pushed himself out of the open end of the cart, and lowered himself until his feet touched the ground. Still trembling, Osric hobbled around to where the three men were waiting for him.

"That way, Dwarf!" barked the Lord Chamberlain, pointing to the King's tent.

Without his stick to aid him, Osric's slow pace was reduced even further. He scuttled along, his upper body tipping side to side with each step as he struggled to walk as fast as he could. Suddenly, the blunt end of a lance jabbed him in the back, and he was sent sprawling forward. Osric fought to control his rage, knowing he was unarmed and outnumbered.

"Walk faster, Dwarf!" shouted the Lord Chamberlain.

"Y-yes, M'Lord."

Osric struggled back to his feet and continued toward the King's tent. He was walking as fast as he could, and his ever-weak legs were beginning to fail.

"The next jab of the lance will not be with the butt-end, Dwarf!"

Osric was now in a desperate struggle to stay on his feet as he closed the distance to the King's tent with agonizing slowness. His legs were on fire, and the King's tent was still far away. If jabbed in the back again, he resolved to seize the lance if he could and fight to the death.

Osric was dizzy with pain, and near to collapse when a voice boomed out, "Favian! That is enough! Give the poor fellow a rest!"

"Yes, Sire. I did not want him to keep you waiting."

"We will discuss this later, Favian, now return to your duties. . . . You men! Assist the dwarf into my tent!"

"Yes, Sire."

Osric had kept his eyes on the ground throughout the ordeal, and never actually saw the King. The Lord Chamberlain strode away while the two soldiers advanced, lifted him under the arms, then resumed the march to the King's tent. So spent were Osric's legs, he could do little more than trip his toes along the ground as he was hauled forward. When they arrived at the King's tent, the two guards released Osric who sank to his knees in exhaustion. Two other men, whom Osric would later learn were members of the household guard, lifted him back to his feet and escorted him inside the tent. As they were crossing the threshold, one of the guards rudely snatched Osric's hat from his head and snarled, "It is forbidden for any man to wear a hat inside the King's chamber, Dwarf! Be it here or in the castle!"

The two guards drug Osric the last few paces then released him, whereupon he collapsed again.

The voice Osric now recognized as the King's said, "Help the poor fellow to sit down."

"Yes, Sire."

The men lifted Osric back to his feet, then helped him into a dwarf-sized chair, positioned behind a dwarf-sized table.

"A man is not usually allowed to sit in the King's presence unless he's been given permission to do so, Dwarf. You seem to be having trouble standing, and you have my permission to sit."

"Thank you, Sir," said Osric, in a weak voice.

"You are to address me as *Sire*, or *Your Majesty*, Dwarf. Do not be forgetting that in the future." Although the King spoke with authority, his voice did not carry the implied violence of the Lord Chamberlain's.

"Yes, Your Majesty."

There ensued a heavy silence as the King eyed Osric. When Osric's anxiety was reaching its maximum, the King said, in a mild voice, "You fight very well, Dwarf. I would pay handsomely to have a troop of men who could all fight as well as you." The King paused a moment, then continued, "I do not, however, take kindly to people killing my horses for any reason, and I caution you to never do that again. I certainly did not enjoy paying that wretched candle maker for the damage the horse did to his shop, either."

"Yes, Sire." Although the King's tone was mild, it was doing little to ease Osric's fear.

After another uncomfortable silence, the King asked, "What is your name, Dwarf?"

"Osric, Sire. My name is Osric."

"Are you hungry Osric? Do you thirst?"

The question surprised him, but after a moment's hesitation, he responded, "Aye, Your Majesty. I am hungry, and I do thirst."

The King snapped his fingers and servants hurried away. "Lift your head, Osric. Your King wants a good look at you."

"Yes, Sire." Osric was filled with fear as he lifted his head and faced the King. The man before him was younger than he had expected him to be. He had dark, curly hair and the whitest teeth he had ever seen. Urloch II was the only king Osric could remember, and yet this man appeared to be no older than him.

The King eyed Osric for a moment then said, "You have an awfully big nose, Osric."

Osric recoiled at the sting of the King's remark, then replied, in a humble voice, "Yes, Sire, so I have been told."

"It suits you, though. A smaller nose would make you ordinary, and the ordinary soon becomes boring. You don't strike me as boring, Osric. Are you?"

"I do not try to be boring, but I've had much boredom forced upon me, Sire."

Osric's simple honesty struck the King as quite humorous, and Urloch II erupted with laughter at the comment. "I've never had a subject make such a remark. From where do you get your wit, Osric?"

Osric did not begin to understand the King's question, but answered with all the honesty he could, "I was a foundling, Sire. I grew up in the orphanage. I know not, from where my wit comes." This time the King roared with laughter and slapped one hand against the arm of his chair. Osric had been so overwhelmed at being in Urloch's presence that he had not, until that moment, realized the King was holding his stick between his fingers and slowly drumming the carpet with it.

As the King continued to laugh, two servants entered the tent, carrying trays. One of the servants sat his tray before the King while the other placed his before Osric. The servants took a step back as a priest, whose presence Osric had not noticed, stepped forward from the shadows, and offered a blessing. Following the prayer, one of the servants bent low and whispered, "Thee must always allow the King to begin eating before you do." Not knowing if he should speak, Osric turned his head to the servant and nodded his acknowledgment.

A servant lifted the cover from the King's tray and Urloch II said, "Ah, splendid! Do you like venison, Osric?"

Osric looked down at his tray as a servant removed the cover, then back to the King. "I've ne'er eaten venison before, Sire."

"I hope you enjoy it, Osric." The King said no more and began eating in earnest. The servant standing by his table nodded to Osric to indicate it was now permissible for him to begin eating as well.

Osric tasted the venison. It was unlike anything he had ever eaten. The little meat he had consumed in life had always been some kind of fowl or pork. The venison tasted nothing like bird or pig, and he was not at all sure he cared for its strong flavor. He ate everything on his tray, however, not wishing to do anything that might offend the King, and washed it down with the inferior brown ale. When they finished eating, the servants cleared away the trays but left the ale steins. Moments after the servants departed, musicians entered the tent, carrying lutes, harps, flutes, and other instruments Osric did not recognize.

"Do you care for music, Osric?"

"Oh, indeed I do Sire. I listens to music at The Dancing Pig, I do."

"The Dancing Pig? What on earth is The Dancing Pig, Osric?"

Osric felt a new wave of anxiety surge through his body. Had he said something wrong? How could the King, of all people, not know what The Dancing Pig was? He stuttered as he responded, "Th-The Dancing Pig is an ale house, Sire."

"Oh, I see." To Osric's relief, the King seemed unperturbed once he had been given an explanation. The King appeared rather wistful and far away for a moment, then said, "One of the worst things about being King is that I am not free to visit an ale house at my leisure. You are most fortunate in that regard, Osric." Osric was astonished, because 'fortunate' was never a word he would have used to describe his life.

At a nod from the King, the musicians began playing. They performed songs Osric had never heard. These were not the bawdy ballads honoring wenches of easy virtue he was accustomed to hearing at the ale house. These melodies were much sweeter and told of fair maidens, bold knights, love, and honor. The musicians continued to play for the next hour while servants refilled the steins of both Osric and the King as they emptied them. Another nod from the King ended the evening's entertainment. The musicians executed deep bows to the King, then backed out of the tent. After the musicians had departed, Urloch II turned his attention back to his guest, saying, "We're early on the march in the morning, Osric, we had best be getting some rest. I hope you have enjoyed the evening."

"I've enjoyed it very much, Sire."

Osric grew uncomfortable once again as the King focused his attention on him. At last Urloch spoke. "If I return your stick, do you promise not to kill any more of my horses, or injure any more of my men with it, Osric?"

"You have my promise, Sire."

"Breaking a promise to your King carries the most severe consequences, Osric." There was no malevolence in the King's voice, but Osric was left with no doubt the King was a man who should be taken at his word. Urloch's eyes continued to bore into Osric for a few more uncomfortable seconds, then with a light flick of his wrist, the King tossed the oaken stick across the tent to Osric, who caught it with both hands. Osric realized it took a very strong man to do what the King had just done.

"Return to the carter for the night. He will provide you with a place to sleep. I may send for you in the morning, Osric."

"Yes, Sire."

Chapter Seven

Osric Begins A New Life

As the King rose from his supper, a cadaverous old servant shot Osric an angry glare and indicated with his hands that he must also get to his feet. Thankful to have his stick again, Osric used it to help himself stand, then bowed his head before the King. He was unsure bowing his head was required but felt it to be the safest thing to do. The King said nothing, but simply turned and walked into another room of the large tent. Following the King's departure, the servant preceded to give Osric a lesson in royal protocol.

"Listen to me Dwarf! You must never sit in the King's presence unless given leave to do so! When the King stands, you must stand up at once! If you are ordered to leave the King's presence, you must never turn your back to him, and always exit the room walking backward! Do you understand what I'm telling you, Dwarf?"

The man's voice reminded Osric of a hissing snake. The servant was old, and when the hollow-eyed man pointed his bony finger at him, Osric felt a new wave of fear. He understood what the servant was saying well enough, but when the man mentioned walking backward he could not prevent his mind from flashing back to the awful day he found himself trapped between buildings when he had attempted to view the flogging. As the ancient servant glowered down at him, only his promise to the King prevented him from doing to the man what he had attempted to do to the cat that had urinated on his trousers the last time he had been forced to walk backward.

Osric's flashback lasted long enough for the servant to repeat the question, with increased venom, "Do you understand, or not, Dwarf?" The quaver in the man's voice carried the heavy threat of violence.

"Yes, Sir."

"You do not address me as Sir!" came the hissing response. "You are to address me as Goran! I am the King's butler! All of the King's household staff answer to me!"

"Yes, Goran. I understand." If it came to a fight, Osric knew he could dispatch the King's butler in less time than it took to tell the tale, though he had little doubt guards would soon come to the man's aid. Other than being freed from the child's coffin by Brother Benedict, Osric was never more relieved than when he was finally allowed to leave the King's tent. As he made his way through the dark camp, he soon became confused and began sinking into despair as he reflected on the events of the day. Jarin seemed like a fine fellow, and once he had been untied, he had soon come to enjoy the carter's company. After he overcame his initial fright at being in the royal presence, the King himself had been very gracious to him. The Lord Chamberlain, however, and now the King's butler, made Brother Benedict seem friendly by comparison. Osric was realizing life around the King might be a very complicated business indeed.

As he shuffled on, Osric realized he might not be going in the right direction. He had been walking more than long enough to have reached Jarin's cart, but when he looked around he could no longer even make out the King's tent among the shadows. He stopped and turned in all directions, but could not see a single recognizable thing. It had been daylight when he was hauled before the King, and now the only light came from a few well-spaced candle lanterns. The camp was not large, and an able-bodied man could walk its entire circumference in a matter of minutes, but

Osric was far from able-bodied, and he viewed the world from a perspective two feet lower than most men. His ribs ached, and his legs had yet to recover from the forced march to the King's tent. The mere thought of trudging around the camp in search of Jarin made his pains flare anew. As the night closed in around him, Osric descended into a black pit of despair.

The whole traumatic day began collapsing in on him. Osric felt afraid, sad, bitter, angry, and more alone than he had ever been. Though he had spent the great bulk of his life in isolation, at this moment there was not a single person or familiar thing he could draw comfort from. Gone was his garret, the bell tower, the candle maker, the foul wench, Fendrel, Father Gregory, Brother Benedict, Kurtz, and The Dancing Pig. Not knowing where to turn, he sank to the ground. He was physically and emotionally spent. He stretched his legs and began massaging his aching muscles. The camp was even darker now as the some of the candle lanterns had been snuffed out. He sat for a long while looking at nothing in particular, as a river of misery flowed over him. At last, he curled up on the ground. "This is a bloody poor place to sleep, but I've walked as far as I'm going to for one day. Sod the bloody King, and all the poxy bastards kissin' his royal arse! Sod everybody! I wish I would have killed all of the King's god-rotting horses, and then they could have just killed me right along with them. I don't bloody care if I die right here."

Osric closed his eyes and may have even experienced a few minutes of troubled sleep because the sound of Jarin's voice startled him. "Osric! There you are! What on earth are you doin' sleepin' on the ground?"

It took Osric a moment for his eyes to focus. All he could see was the shadowy outline of the carter, as the man held a candle lantern above his head. "I could not walk another bloody step, Jarin. I left the King's tent, and I got lost tryin' to find you."

"I think you went in the wrong direction, Osric. Here, take the lantern, whilst I run to get me wheelbarrow. It isn't far." Jarin handed the lantern to Osric, then ran back to his cart.

Osric could not help but wonder what it would be like to run the way the Jarin did. He knew it was just one more unanswerable question.

Jarin rolled the wheelbarrow up to Osric, saying, "Here ya go, Man. Climb in and I'll have us back in no time." Osric got into the wheelbarrow then held the lantern above his head as Jarin began hauling his passenger back to the cart. "You had me bloody worried, Osric. I came back from feedin' the horses and you were gone." Jarin glanced around to make sure he was not being overheard, then whispered, "One of the other carters told me you had been marched off by the Lord Chamberlain, and I had no bloody idea what that might have meant. I was glad he only took you to see the King. Then, when you didn't come back after the music ended, I got worried again, so I went in search of you."

Though Osric was somewhat grateful for having been found, he was bone tired, in pain, and filled with new anger at the situation he found himself in. He responded with petulance, "I did not mean to cause you worry, Jarin, but I wasn't having such a bloody grand time my own self."

Had there been more light, Osric would have seen an understanding smile appear on the carter's face. "Aye, Osric, aye. I've no doubt it's been a helluva day for ya."

"I don't suppose you'd be willin' to take me back to the candle shop?"

"And get meself whipped, or maybe even hung?" There was real fear in the carter's voice.

"Nay, I wouldn't ask that of any man, Jarin," sighed Osric, his voice trailing away. He had known a great deal more sadness than joy in his life, but never more sadness than at this moment.

"Here we are, Osric," said the carter, lowering the handles of the wheelbarrow.

Osric looked around but did not recognize Jarin's cart. The cart was nearly hidden by a tarp that had been raised above it to form a crude tent, and the horses were not present. He realized, he may have walked right past without realizing it. "I may have missed the cart in the dark, Jarin."

"Aye, aye, you would not have known what to look for. I may have already gone in search of you and we missed each other. I'm sorry you got lost, Osric. The stable master, who I answers to, brings all the cart horses together for the night, so they weren't here. Let me give you a boost." Once again, Jarin made a stirrup with his hands and lifted Osric into the cart bed. Once Osric was under the tarp, Jarin lifted the lantern and said, "T'isn't a grand palace to be sure Osric, but it keeps me dry if it rains, and it stops the wind on a cool night. There's a blanket there, for ya. I just makes meself comfy on the sacks of grain as best I can. T'isn't the worst bed a man can have, and it's a damn sight better than sleeping on the ground, it is."

"Thank you, Jarin." Osric crawled to one side of the cart and smoothed out a resting place by pounding the sacks of grain with his fists. He wrapped himself in the blanket Jarin provided, and as the carter said, it was indeed better than laying on the ground. Osric was soon overwhelmed by his fatigue and drifted into a fitful sleep just minutes after the carter took the lantern away. Images of Brother Benedict began haunting his dreams until the brother was pushed aside by the candle maker, and visions of the foul wench shrieking at him. Then, he had a terrifying vision of Father Gregory's blue eyes, looking directly into his soul. His tortured sleep gave him little rest, and when he was jolted awake by the sound of Jarin's voice, he was again doing battle with the King's horse.

"Osric! Osric! Are ya alright, Man?"

Had Osric been roused to consciousness after passing out beneath the ale wagon during the Harvest Festival, he would have been no more bewildered than he was at this moment. Where was he, and what was that sound?

Again came Jarin's voice, "Osric, are ya alright, Man? You were thrashin' about like you was in a bleedin' fight."

Osric's mind was very slow to return to his new reality. At last, he remembered he was in the back of Jarin's cart, but what was that noise? . . . "Jarin?"

"Yes, Osric. I'm right here, man. I'm thinkin' you were havin' a bloody bad dream, I am." Jarin's voice was filled with concern.

"Jarin? . . . What is that noise?"

"Oh, that's just a bit of rain, Osric. I'm damned awful glad I found ya when I did, and the Lord Chamberlain never heard about ya bein' missin'. The King would for sure have me whipped for lettin' you sleep in the rain, he would."

Again, as it had been when he met Fendrel, Osric felt a kinship with the carter. Though his minder had his own self-interest to consider, Osric sensed Jarin would be treating him with kindness even without the threat of punishment hanging over him. A great flash of lightening and a resounding clap of thunder startled both the carter and the dwarf. When the moment passed, they shared a small laugh. "I don't think I'll be gettin' any more sleep until the storm passes, Jarin."

"Nor will I, Osric. I don't mind a bit of rain on the tarp. In fact, it can be a right pleasant thing to listen to, but there's no way I can sleep through that kind of thunder." The carter had no more than finished speaking when another clap of thunder, louder than the first, echoed across the camp. Thankful to be under cover, they laughed again and drew their blankets around them as it began to rain much harder. Jarin used the opportunity to speak in a quiet voice, "I was going to wait until we were on the march tomorrow to talk to ya, Osric, but there will be no one out and about in the storm to overhear us. You need to know, Osric, that there are men in this kingdom who would slice off their mother's head for the chance to dine with the King. Most noblemen know His Majesty sometimes takes his supper with his dwarfs, but that does not mean they like it. Nay, Osric, they do not like it at all. They're powerful jealous of anyone who gets an audience with the King, even the dwarfs. The noblemen have little choice but to tolerate it, but they do not like it. Not even a little."

The momentous day, combined with what Jarin was telling him, took Osric's spirits to a new depth. "What do I do, Jarin? I did not seek this. I would be most happy to go back to the candle shop, and never see the bloody King again!"

"Osric!" hissed the carter, just above a whisper. Jarin leaned close and continued with quiet intensity, "Thee must never again refer to His Majesty as *the bloody King!*' I pray we're safe from prying ears at the moment, but if certain people overheard you sayin' that, it would at least cost you a trip to the whippin' post, and mayhaps your very life!" Jarin paused to let his words sink in, then continued with urgency, "You must always be very humble about any time ya spend with the King, Osric. Never speak of it to anyone, for any reason, if you can avoid doing so. If pressed, let people think you've been forced to dine with the King against your will. If any nobleman gets wind of you tryin' to turn your time with the King to your advantage, they will find a way to have you killed, they will!" Jarin used another flash of lightening to move close to Osric's ear, and whisper, "And there is no one you should fear more than the Lord Chamberlain."

"He's a hateful bastard, he is," said Osric, too loudly.

"Osric! I canna' say it too strongly! You simply mustn't say things like that! Not unless you want your head in a basket, instead of on your shoulders where it belongs!"

Though the carter did not raise his voice above a whisper, the effect of his words hit Osric like icy water and left him humble. He whispered, "I had no thought that life around the King could be so bloody dangerous, Jarin."

"I'm only glad it was me you were talkin' to, and not someone who would run straight to the Lord Chamberlain. Osric, I've no desire to be seein' you or anyone whipped, hung, or beheaded, I don't." The carter paused a moment, "I think the storm has passed on. The thunder sounds more distant now. We best be gettin' some rest. We've at least one more night of bivouac, and probably two, before we reach the castle. Good night, Osric."

Good night, Jarin," whispered Osric.

Overwhelmed by fatigue and sadness, Osric fell into a deep and dreamless sleep that lasted until he was awakened by the herald's horns the following morning. As he stirred, Osric was amazed to find his back, all but free of pain. Evidently, sleeping on sacks of grain was a thing that agreed with him. Osric sat up and looked around. Jarin was missing, but only a moment later, the carter lifted the tarp and said, "Good mornin' to ya, Osric. You was sleepin' like a baby, you was. I didn't even disturb you when I got up to go and fetch the horses. Come along, and I'll wheel you to the latrine."

Jarin helped Osric down from the cart, and he climbed aboard the wheelbarrow. A short ride later, Jarin lowered the handles in front of a roofless tent. "Come along, Osric." Jarin led Osric inside the area designated for the men and told him to use the trench to relieve himself, then to wash his hands in the bowl of water by the doorway. "This is somethin' His Majesty learned from an old book about the Roman soldiers of long ago, Osric. He has made the troops do it ever since. I don't know why it works, but we has a lot fewer people fallin' sick and dyin' on us than we once did."

"Bloody strange, it is. I always just emptied me chamber pot in the alleyway behind the candle shop, I did."

"Aye, Osric, that's what most people do, but not His Majesty. He's right particular about keepin' things clean, he is."

"Bloody strange."

The carter chuckled and said, "It takes a bit of gettin' used to for sure, but once you get on to it, you'll think it quite normal, Osric."

Osric said no more but quickly went about his business, as he was in great need of relieving himself. When he finished, he dutifully washed his hands as Jarin had instructed, then stepped outside to wait for the carter. "Bloody strange," thought Osric, "Bloody, bloody strange." He looked around the camp, and as it had been the day before, he saw no possibility of escape.

Jarin returned and wheeled Osric back to the cart. "Would ya mind givin' me a hand, Osric? We'll lay the tarp out flat and get it rolled up and stored away, then I'll go and fetch our breakfast."

"Yes, of course, Jarin." Osric took the edge of the tarp the carter handed him. They shook off all the water, then together they spread it on the ground.

"Take that corner and we'll fold it in half, Osric." Osric was quick to understand what the carter was doing and they soon had the tarp folded, rolled up, and stored in the box beneath the cart's seat. "Thank you, Osric, it's a might easier with an extra set of hands, it is. Let me give ya a boost up, and I'll run to the cook wagon."

The Carter hurried away while Osric sat on the edge of the cart bed, watching the hum of activity around him. Everywhere he looked horses were being harnessed, tents were being struck, gear was being stowed away, and people were hurrying to and from the cook wagon. A new wave of fear shot through him as he remembered the King's parting words from the night before. Would the Lord Chamberlain be coming for him again? An icy knot formed in his stomach as visions of the terrifying man in black filled his mind. Not until Jarin returned with their morning meal did his tension begin to ease.

"Here ya go, Osric," said Jarin, handing Osric a stein of ale. The carter then tore off a large chunk of dark bread and handed it to Osric. "We need to be quick about it. The next blast from the horns will mean to make ready. If the bleedin' horns blow before you're done eatin', you're out of luck."

Osric quickly devoured the bread and drank half his ale. He took Jarin's teaching to heart and took a careful look around before saying in a low voice, "His Majesty said he might send for me this morning, Jarin. Mayhaps he forgot about me."

Jarin gave Osric a knowing look and said, with a wink, "You're learnin', Osric. Be cautious always. It will be safer once we're on the move, then we can speak freely as long as we're quiet about it. I don't know why you haven't been sent for. There's no tellin' with His Majesty. You may not see him again for weeks, or you may see him every day. He makes up his own mind, he does." They drank the last of their ale, then Jarin returned the steins and basket to the cook wagon. The moment Jarin left, the fear of the Lord Chamberlain began welling up in Osric, again.

In spite of Osric's fears, they were able to use the latrine and complete their preparations for departure without incident. After he had harnessed the horses, Jarin told Osric he preferred to stand by the cart and stretch his legs right up to the time the heralds blew their horns and recommended Osric do the same. "Your arse will appreciate it, Osric. The seat can get mighty hard before the day is done, it can." Though Osric's legs were still feeling the effects of the forced march to the King's tent, he took Jarin's advice and stretched alongside the carter. It was a sparkling clear morning, and the activities of the King's troupe as they broke camp again reminded Osric of a market-Thursday. "We will have to see how the travelin' goes this mornin', Osric. The rain may have muddied up the track to the point where the carts and wagons have difficulty. Bein' near the end, we'll have the most trouble if it's bad."

Osric did not know what to make of the carter's remarks as he had no experience with the business of travel. "Does it ever get so muddy, ye canna' move at all, Jarin?"

"Aye, it's happened. His Majesty likes to push on if we can, but the commander of the guard will argue for makin' bivouac if the mud becomes too bad. He does not like to see the kings party mired down, as it could leave us open to attack, and the King will likely listen to him." As Osric pondered the complexity of travel with the King, the herald's bugle sounded, and Jarin said, "Time to mount up." The carter gave Osric a boost up to the seat then climbed up beside him, and took the reins. "We will be makin' our way out of the forest soon, Osric. The track becomes rockier as we near the mountains, and mud becomes less of a worry. It's just a matter of gettin' across this last bit of the flat lands."

Another blast from the horns set the troupe in motion. The mounted cavalry led the way out of the meadow and back onto the track with the infantry, and the King's carriage following close behind. As he watched the party moving out, Osric was thankful he had not been called to a royal audience and thus spared contact with the Lord Chamberlain and the King's butler. When it came their turn, Jarin shook the reins to urge the big horses into motion, and they took their place near the end of the procession. Although they did encounter mud when they gained the track, it did not prove to be a serious problem, and the travelers were slowed little. Jarin said, "T'was a fast movin' storm so the mud isn't too bad. The real problems come with two or three days of slow steady rain. Then, ya can be dealin' with a real mess, ya can. His Majesty never travels during the autumn rains if he can avoid it."

After the procession settled into its rhythm, and he was certain there was no one within earshot, Jarin once again went over the things Osric must avoid saying and the people he should never trust, giving special emphasis to the Lord Chamberlain.

"Why doesn't the King just send him packin' if he's so bloody dangerous, Jarin?"

"You will find, Osric, that our King is no fool. He believes in keepin' his enemies where he can have his eye on them, he does. Favian is sometimes called the Grand Duke because he was once a prince, and would have become King had his elder brother, Destrian, died without an heir. He could yet become King if His Majesty does not soon produce his own heir. It was only because of his father's actions that our Urloch lived to see his majority. Destrian was on his death bed when he gathered all seven Dukes around him and made them swear in the presence of the Archbishop to depose Favian should the Duke of Bruno attempt to seize the throne during his regency." Though he did not say anything to Osric, Jarin shuddered inwardly at the thought of what life might be like, should the Lord Chamberlain ever ascend the throne. Those unpleasant thoughts drove the carter to a quiet place, deep inside himself. They rode on in silence for several minutes, until Jarin felt compelled to smile down at his passenger and say, "Forgive me, Osric. I'm used to spending me days alone, and I soon run out of things to talk about."

"Think naught of it, Jarin. I too have spent most of me life alone, I have." Having little to discuss was not something Osric viewed as a heavy burden at the moment, as he was absorbed by the passing countryside. The track was flanked on both sides by dense forest, punctuated on occasion by meadows and streams. The party crossed straight through the small rivulets while larger streams were spanned by stone bridges. Osric thought they had traveled longer, without a break for the foot soldiers than they had the previous day, and he soon learned why. Two hours after breaking camp, the travelers emerged from the forest, and onto a broad plain sloping toward the mountains. Osric had never seen such an open place.

When the procession was far enough away from the trees to give the King's guard a clear field of vision, the herald's bugles sounded, and the party came to a halt. Jarin hopped to the ground, then helped Osric down. They stretched, shared water from a stone jug the carter kept below his seat then relieved themselves behind the cart. Perhaps to make up for not having taken a respite earlier, the break lasted longer than the ones of the previous day. As he gazed across the plain, Osric asked, "We'll soon be in the mountains, eh Jarin?"

The carter laughed and replied, "Nay, Osric. Though it looks as if you could reach out and touch them, we won't get to the mountains before nightfall at the earliest, and only then if we stay on the march all day."

"Why wouldn't we be on the march all day, Jarin?"

"One never knows with His Majesty, Osric. If he should decide to spend the rest of the day on this spot, that is what we'll do."

Osric and Jarin stood by the cart, stretching their legs and took a short walk around the cart and horses. After another few minutes, the herald's horn sounded, and the travelers took their seats again and prepared to resume the trip. The troupe moved off down the track and continued making their way toward the distant mountains. Then, no more than a half hour later, the heralds sounded their bugles again. This time, instead of stopping, the vanguard left the track and headed out on to the plain. They continued across the grassland until the horns sounded, and the party came to a halt at the base of the only defining feature for some distance around. The knoll was not large in terms of its circumference but stood nearly as tall as it was wide, making it resemble a grassy dome

"What do you make of this, Jarin?"

"I'm not certain, Osric, but I suspect His Majesty is perchance wanting to hunt his birds."

"Hunt his birds?"

"Aye, Osric. His falcons. Yon hill would be a fine place to hunt from."

"I don't understand, Jarin."

"Tis an old tradition amongst noblemen, Osric. Small game, hares and the like, are hunted with trained birds. Tis quite an amazing thing to watch, it is."

There came three sharp blasts from the trumpets, and Jarin said, "Well Osric, there's our answer, we'll be makin' bivouac right here." They watched as the King's tent was erected, then Jarin said, "I'm going to go speak with the stable master to see if he wants to wait till evening to feed the horses."

"I hope you find me waiting for you when you return, Jarin." Osric gave Jarin a sardonic smile, but the moment the carter departed, his fear of the Lord Chamberlain returned. Those fears soon proved to be warranted when Osric looked up and saw the Duke of Bruno striding toward him, again flanked by two soldiers. Icy fear flooded over Osric as he lowered his head and awaited his fate.

Not bothering to advance all the way to the cart, the Lord Chamberlain halted and pointed his long finger at Osric, saying sharply, "You there! Dwarf! Come with me, immediately!"

"Yes, M'Lord," said Osric. He kept his eyes on the ground and hobbled as quickly as he could to where the Lord Chamberlain and the soldiers were waiting.

"To the King's tent, Dwarf!" The Lord Chamberlain's voice reminded Osric of the cracking of a whip.

"Yes, M'Lord." Osric was grateful to see the King's tent standing a good deal closer than it had been the day before and to have his stick to aid him. He began trudging in its direction as fast has he could. The Lord Chamberlain and the soldiers were right behind him, but only once was Osric admonished to walk faster, and on this trip there was no jab to his back with the butt-end of a lance. Even though he had a shorter distance to cover, Osric was short of breath and his legs were nearing exhaustion when he halted in front of the King's tent. He lifted his eyes just enough to see the feet of the King's butler in front of the tent.

"Thank you, M'Lord," said the butler, bowing to the Lord Chamberlain.

"Get the little bastard ready, Goran, and do not take all day doing it."

"Yes, M'Lord."

Osric kept his head lowered, and trembled in fear as he listened to the Lord Chamberlain and the soldiers marching away.

"Come inside, and do not forget to remove your hat, Dwarf!" hissed the old butler, turning his attention to Osric.

Osric removed his hat as he stepped forward into the tent, not knowing what to expect.

"Stand upon that stool, Dwarf."

"Yes, Goran." Osric used his stick to steady himself as he stepped up on a stool that rose to his knees. As he steadied himself on the stool, Osric experienced an unpleasant flashback of the mound of baskets collapsing beneath him.

"Lay your stick down, and remove your jersey!"

"My jersey?"

"Make me repeat myself again, Dwarf, and you will regret it! Now remove your jersey at once!"

Osric did as he was asked, as anger and humiliation boiled up inside him. It took remembering the King's warning to prevent him from bringing his stick down on the butler's skull. Though Osric did not realize it, the bulging muscles of his upper body did much to soften Goran's tone.

"What is your name, Dwarf?"

"Osric."

"Very well, Osric. Please stand still while you are fitted with the Hunt Master's coat."

Osric was on the verge of asking what in bloody hell the Hunt Master's coat was, but held his tongue. The things Jarin had been teaching him were having their effect. Osric felt a new wave of embarrassment as two female servants entered the tent. One of them was carrying a bright red coat and a large leather glove, while the other carried a broad-brimmed green hat with a long white feather trailing from its brim.

"Here we go, Love," said the woman, as she held the coat up before Osric. "Just stick your arm in the sleeve, Dearie, and we'll be gettin' it adjusted to fit you."

The woman's kind tone helped quiet Osric's anger, and he grudgingly submitted to her request. He inserted one arm into the coat, and then the other. The sleeves were much too long, and the coat hung down to his ankles. The two women went straight to work adjusting it. "Angmar, I think if we just blouse up the sleeves a bit, we can get a decent enough fit on the arms," said the woman who had been carrying the coat.

The other woman sat the hat she was carrying aside and studied the hang of the coat with a practiced eye. "Aye, Juliana, I think that will work, I do, and we can do an inside tuck on the length, I'm thinkin'."

The two women set to work altering the fit of the coat while continuing to address Osric as *'Love'*, and *'Dearie'*. When the seamstress, Angmar, commented to her coworker she thought Osric to be right handsome, he found himself blushing for one of the few times in his life, and not knowing why. Osric was as baffled as he'd ever been, but the friendliness of the two women did much to ease his earlier humiliation. With their stitching completed, the women stepped back to assess their work. They pronounced themselves satisfied, then Angmar leered at Osric and said with a saucy wink, "I'm thinkin' of invitin' this handsome devil to spend the night in me tent, Juliana." What Osric felt went beyond embarrassment, and his feelings were not buoyed when both women roared with laughter.

"That is quite enough, Angmar!" interjected Goran. "You two finish your work and be quick about it. The King is waiting, and I will tolerate no more of your lewdness!"

"Yes, Goran," said the women in unison.

Juliana retrieved the wide green hat she had set aside earlier and placed it on Osric's head to test the fit. The hat came down to the top of his eyes, so the seamstress secured the hat to Osric's head by tying it on with a green ribbon under his chin. She adjusted the long white feather then stood back to inspect her work.

"Aye," said Angmar, "it fits him right nicely, it does. Just one more thing, Dearie," said the woman as she held the large leather glove up to Osric. "Just be slippin' your hand in here, Luv."

Osric hated the hat and struggled to control his rising anger as he slipped his hand inside a glove that came up past his elbow. "I look bloody ridiculous. I should take my stick to these bleedin' wenches," fumed Osric in silence.

"Come along, Osric," hissed the old butler. "You have kept the King waiting long enough."

Osric was relieved when Goran did not order him to leave his stick behind. He had never felt such humiliation as he followed the butler out the back side of the tent to where they found the King relaxing with a stein of ale in the shade of an awning.

"The Master of the Hunt, has arrived, Your Majesty," said Goran in a very formal voice, while executing a deep bow to the King.

"Good morning, Osric. You look very smart, indeed." The King spoke in a pleasant voice, then paused a moment to inspect Osric. "Fredrich, the bird."

"Yes, Sire." A man, also wearing a heavy leather glove, stepped toward Osric, and on his glove perched a large falcon. Fredrich told Osric to stand still and hold up his glove arm in front of him, keeping it parallel to the ground. When Osric lifted his arm, Fredrich tapped his fingers on Osric's glove and clicked to the bird. The falcon then hopped off the man's glove and onto Osric's.

He was stupefied. During his long hours in the bell tower, he had seen many hawks, falcons, and even a few eagles on the wing, but never this close. Given the size of the bird, Osric had expected it to be much heavier than it was. He could only stand and stare in wide-eyed astonishment at the bird he now realized had a hood covering its head.

Come along, Osric," said the King. "Let us go and see what game Red Arrow can find." The King rose and began ascending the knoll.

Goran bent down and whispered in Osric's ear that he must always walk behind the King and always on his sword side. Osric set off and began laboring up the hill, always positioned as Goran instructed, while keeping the King's falcon perched on his arm.

The King's traveling party watched as Urloch II made his royal way up the knoll in the company of the Master of the Hunt, who on this day happened to be a dwarf wearing a bright red coat, and a wide green hat with a large white feather trailing behind it. If the sight struck anyone in the troupe as ludicrous, no one was brave enough to say it out loud.

As the people watched their sovereign prepare to hunt his bird, there were those who suppressed their laughter at the sight of the King's choice of companion, and there were those who had very different thoughts. The King's butler viewed the spectacle with dismay and considered the matter to be a shocking breach of the royal dignity. In another part of the camp, the Lord Chamberlain seethed with silent, impotent rage at being compelled to observe such a sight. Well away from the rest of the people, Jarin stood beside his cart muttering softly, "Oh dear God, Osric. He seems to have taken a bloody likin' to ya, and that may be the worst piece o' luck ya ever had."

Chapter Eight

Osric's Journey Continues

"What does it bloody mean, Jarin?" Osric's voice was at the same time, plaintive, desperate, and quiet. "He forces me to dress in that ridiculous costume, then carry his bloody bird up that stinkin' hill, makin' a total fool of meself in front of everyone! Is this to be my life from now on? I'd rather kiss Brother Benedict's fat arse, I would!"

Jarin whispered, "I wish I had words o' comfort for ya, Osric, but the truth is, I just don't know the answer to your questions. You're the only dwarf in the king's travelin' party, but once we're back at the castle there will be others, and he may well pay less attention to ya."

"Bloody hell, Jarin! Bloody, bloody hell!" cried Osric in quiet exasperation. "I don't want this, Jarin! I didn't bloody ask for it! I want to go back to the candle shop! I want to go back to The Dancing Pig, and drink with me friend, Fendrel!" Osric's anxiety was near to boiling over.

What he was witnessing filled Jarin with fear of what might happen if the muscular dwarf's anger exploded into violence. "The best advice I can give ya, Osric, is to keep doin' as I've told ya. Never give any of the noblemen, especially the Lord Chamberlain, any cause to be jealous of ya. Let them be angry, but never jealous, because their jealousy is what can bloody well get ya killed. With a bit of luck, His Majesty will find someone else to give his attention to once we're back at the castle." Jarin tried to be as reassuring as he could, but in his heart he had little confidence in what he was saying. The carter knew full well, once the King began directing his attention to a particular dwarf, he tended to keep it there for a long time before moving on. "Why don't ya try gettin' some sleep, Man. I'm sure we'll be early on the march in the mornin', and it will likely be a long day to make up for the time the King spent huntin'."

"Aye, Jarin. I'll try. I'm bloody tired, I am."

"Good night to ya, Osric."

"Good night Jarin." Osric drew his blanket around him and tried to make himself comfortable. Though the events of the day had left him exhausted, there was a war raging in his mind, and he was filled with bitter indignation at what the King had subjected him to. "He has his bloody Master of the Birds to take care of his god-rotting hunters, why did he have to dress me up in that stinkin' coat and put me out in front of everyone?" He kept repeating the question with ever more bitterness.

Had he been able to overlook his own participation in the hunt, Osric would have admitted that watching the falcon sweep over the wide plain and return three times with fat hares in its talons had been an amazing thing to behold. Even had he been dismissed, and allowed to return to Jarin's cart after the King ended the hunt, the day would have been better than it was. As it turned out, he had been ordered to dine with the King again, while continuing to be dressed as The Master of the Hunt. They feasted on the hares Red Arrow had killed along with black bread, and brown ale. Osric enjoyed the food well enough, but he did not enjoy the experience of being ordered to sing along with the musicians, even a little.

When Osric returned after dining with the king, he complained, "I canna' sing a bloody note, Jarin! Brother Benedict banned me from the children's choir after but a week, and the god-rotting King makes me sing!" Osric's anger at what he had been subjected to filled him with rage and brought him close to tears.

"The god-rotting bastard just sat there laughin' his royal arse off! I should try to escape and just let the bleedin' knights run me through."

Morning did not find Osric in an improved state of mind. If anything, his mood had grown even more foul. As if being made to dress up in a garish costume and then be paraded in front of the King's party had not been enough, Osric suffered the added misfortune of reliving the experience again and again in his dreams. When the trumpets sounded, well before sunrise, it was a very unhappy man who was roused from a shallow, sleep.

"Good mornin' to ya Osric."

"What's so bloody good about it, Jarin?"

"Aye, Osric, I can well understand your question, I can. Tis a glorious mornin', though. A fine day to be alive, it is. Come along. I'll be gettin' ya to the latrine, and then I'll go and fetch our breakfast."

Osric knew Jarin was trying to make him feel better, and though a part of him appreciated the carter's efforts, it was doing very little to improve his mood. New fuel was added to the inferno of his bad temper when he tried to raise himself from his makeshift bed. Hot pain, much worse than usual, shot up and down his spine, leaving him gritting his teeth, and unable to move for several seconds.

"Osric, are ya alright, Man?"

When the pain eased enough for him to speak, Osric replied, bitterly, "No, I'm bloody *not*, alright!"

Jarin was immobile in the face of Osric's misery. At last, he asked, "Is there anything I can do to help, Osric?"

"Nay, Jarin. This is how I greet most every day of me miserable life." Osric gritted his teeth again as a new wave of pain ran down his spine. At last, he took a deep breath, and asked, "Jarin, could you move the tarp back a bit, so I can stand up?"

"Aye, Osric. That I can do." The carter hurried to roll back the makeshift tent covering the cart bed.

With the tarp pulled back, Osric was able to roll over on to his knees, then use his stick and the side of the cart to get to his feet. As he stood and slowly stretched out his aching back, Osric looked up and to his horror saw the Lord Chamberlain advancing toward him. The fear he felt, when combined with his pain, left him near to fainting. He lowered his head and tried to prepare himself for what ever was in store. When nothing happened after a few seconds, Osric cautiously lifted his eyes, and to his indescribable relief, found the Lord Chamberlain was nowhere to be seen. The man was evidently on some other mission and had turned and gone elsewhere. Still shaking, Osric shuffled to the end of the cart, and with Jarin's help, got to the ground and into the wheelbarrow.

As he was being wheeled in the direction of the latrine, Osric cast a cautious glance around, then said, in a very low voice, "I came near to pissin' myself when I saw the Lord Chamberlain comin' in my direction, Jarin."

"I wasn't far behind ya, Osric. I don't know what business the man was about, but it bloody well looked like he was coming for ya, it did. I'm glad he had other things to attend to."

"Aye, Jarin." Though Osric's mood was far from jovial, being spared another encounter with the Lord Chamberlain left him feeling at least a trifle better. As miserable as he was, Osric had just received an object lesson in how things could be even worse. The carter and the dwarf completed their visit to the latrine, then returned to the cart without incident. Jarin secured their breakfast, and as the carter predicted, they were mounted, and on the march by the time the sun cleared the horizon. They rolled on through the day, stopping only for food at midday and to allow the foot soldiers the occasional respite. The troupe maintained a steady pace across the broad plain with little to break the monotony or interfere with their progress. Not until hours later did the mountains appeared to be getting nearer.

During a rest period late in the afternoon, Jarin waved his arm at the land ahead of them and said, "Can ya see how the slope of the land is gettin' a bit steeper all the time, Osric?"

"Aye, Jarin. I can. Will we be in the mountains tonight?"

"I'm doubtin' that we advance into the pass tonight, Osric. It wouldn't be safe. It only takes a few hours gettin' to the other side, but it's best done in daylight, it is."

"Is it dangerous, Jarin?"

"It can be, but mainly there is no good place for this many people to make bivouac. There are brigands about, though they would never confront the soldiers. The biggest danger comes from the mountain tribes who've never been fully brought under the King's control. They're fearless and fight like demons if challenged. They will steal anything they can, including people. Most likely, Rowan, the high chieftain, will present himself and demand parlance with His Majesty. I've seen it happen a dozen times before, I have. The King's tent will be put up, and Rowan will be received."

"This Rowan chap can make demands of the King?"

"Rowan features himself to be something of a King in his own right. It's a peculiar thing, Osric, but I think they bloody *like* each other, I do. They will spend an hour together, perhaps two or three. They share some ale and His Majesty will give Rowan a few gold talents as a gift, and thank him for his friendship. They clasp hands in full view of everyone, then we all go our own ways." Jarin took a careful look around, then continued just above a whisper, "Me pa told me that when the Lord Chamberlain was servin' as regent, he always chose to fight rather than speak to any of the tribal chieftains. It cost a lot o' men their lives, it did. I think His Majesty has gotten Rowan used to havin' a bit o' money in his purse, and the man likes it, he does. There's men walkin' around today who would be under the soil if the Lord Chamberlain had gotten his way, Osric."

"It's all bloody confusing, Jarin."

"As I said before, Osric, His Majesty is no fool. Just because he would rather hoist a stein of ale with a man than fight him doesn't mean he won't fight if he has to. Never make the mistake of thinkin' the King's weak. He's just bloody smart, he is. His troops love him, and when he asks them to fight, then by God, fight they will! No one in this kingdom has ever challenged His Majesty twice."

The effect of Jarin's words passed through Osric like a cold wind. The magnitude of what had happened to him, and what might lie in store, was now registering with full force. This was not a child's game that would soon be over. Everything he had ever known was gone and had been replaced by things beyond his control and understanding. He came close to offering up an actual prayer of thanks for the good fortune of having met Jarin and the advice the carter had given him. He could now see with stark clarity that following his instincts might well land him at the whipping post, if not the gallows or the chopping block. If he could not control the events around him, he could at least control himself. Osric resolved to learn how to survive in the royal presence and vowed to repay Jarin for his friendship, if ever he could.

The sun was nearing the mountain tops when the trumpets sounded, and the King's troupe again drew itself into a circle. The party halted atop a small rise, about a half hour's march from the first trees of the foothills. The location afforded the troops a clear field of vision, and a position that could be defended should the need arise. Osric watched the King's tent go up and stood stretching by the cart as Jarin departed with his loaded wheelbarrow to feed the horses. He felt an evening chill he would not have experienced back in his garret. They were very near the mountains now, and the patches of snow on the high peaks were clearly defined. Osric thought it all very beautiful.

With Jarin gone, Osric's anxiety level began rising again. He scanned the camp, watching for the approach of the Lord Chamberlain. He considered finding a place to hide, but then dismissed the idea, thinking, "The bloody Lord Chamberlain would have the god-rotting guards searchin' for me." After awhile, his tensions eased, but did not go away completely until after he and Jarin had eaten their supper, and were settling themselves for the night. "I'm bloody glad to have escaped havin' me supper with His Majesty, Jarin," whispered Osric.

Jarin smiled and said, "Aye, be of stout heart, Osric. His Majesty might well turn his attention to other things now."

"I hope he forgets me completely."

"I wouldn't go placin' a wager on that happenin', Osric. As I've said before, His Majesty is right fond of his dwarfs, he is. He does have a great many interests, though, and once we're back at the castle, he could well decide it's his horses or his hounds what needs payin' attention to. You canna' predict His Majesty, Osric."

Perhaps it was the cool mountain air, or perhaps it was not having been subjected to the anxiety of dining with the King. Perhaps it was some combination of the two, but regardless of the reason, Osric slept very well and awoke the next morning much refreshed and in a far better frame of mind. After completing their visit to the latrine, Osric was sitting on the edge of the cart bed, waiting for Jarin to return with their breakfast, when he was again gripped by cold fear as he looked up and saw the Lord Chamberlain striding toward him. Osric lowered himself to the ground and awaited his fate.

This time the Lord Chamberlain did not have other business and continued to march toward Osric. The fearsome man in black did not extend a greeting but merely halted, pointed his finger, and said, sharply, "Come with me, Dwarf, and be quick about it! You are to take your breakfast with the King!"

"Yes, M'Lord." Osric kept his eyes lowered, and began yet another torturous trek to the King's tent. He arrived before the butler with his legs near exhaustion.

"See to it the wretch is made presentable, Goran!" To Osric's ears, the Lord Chamberlain's voice sounded like death itself.

"Yes, M'Lord."

As The Lord Chamberlain turned and went on his way, the King's butler said, in a surprisingly mild tone, "Come along, Osric. You are to have a visit with the barber before having breakfast with His Majesty."

"Yes, Goran."

The old butler did not escort Osric into the King's tent but led him instead into a much smaller tent nearby. Goran pointed to a tall stool. "Sit down, Osric. Henry will be along directly to groom your hair and beard."

Osric climbed up on the stool, with some difficulty, and was soon joined in the tent by a stout, middle-aged man. The barber was carefully dressed, and as well groomed as the King himself.

"Henry, this is the King's dwarf, Osric."

"Good morning, Osric. Please remove your hat, and I will get to work."

Osric did as he was asked, and Henry began trimming his hair and beard. When he was finished, the barber carefully brushed Osric's jersey. It did not take the barber long to pronounce himself satisfied with Osric's appearance. Osric was still wearing his best clothes, and after having spent a lifetime without the services of a barber, he had now visited one twice in the space of a week.

"Come along Osric," said Goran. Osric climbed down from the stool and followed the old butler back outside, and to the King's tent. "Remove your hat and remember what you've been taught." Goran motioned for Osric to stay where he was, then stepped inside the tent, and announced, "Your dwarf has arrived, Sire."

"Excellent, Goran. Please show him in."

Osric entered the King's tent, hat-in-hand, and bowed his head.

"Good morning, Osric. Did you sleep well?"

"Yes, Your Majesty, I slept very well."

"Excellent! The mountain air does wonders for a man's sleep. Be seated Osric, our breakfast will be here directly."

"Yes, Your Majesty." Osric seated himself at the dwarf-sized table and felt a little less of the stress he had experienced during his other audiences with the King. His instincts, and Jarin's teachings, were helping him cope with being in the royal presence.

"Have you a fondness for quail eggs, Osric?"

Osric had neither eaten a quail egg nor had any idea what a quail was. "I've ne'er eaten a quail egg, Sire."

"Well then, we must address that deficiency. Goran, serve the food!"

"At once, Your Majesty." The King's butler signaled to a servant standing at the back entrance of the tent, who then held the tent flap open. Two other servants entered carrying trays, one of which was placed before the King, and the other in front of Osric. He was learning. Osric made no move until after Goran removed the cover from the King's tray and the King had tasted his food. When the cover was removed from Osric's tray, he saw four small eggs in a bowl and a plate containing a fish. There was fresh bread, and of course, brown ale.

Osric found he was very hungry, and devoured the meal while taking care not to eat too quickly, and thus draw a rebuke from the butler. The breakfast was a far cry from the stale bread and rank water he had so often endured in his garret. As a servant was refilling the King's ale stein, Urloch asked Osric if he found his morning meal agreeable.

"Yes indeed, Your Majesty. Thank you, Sire, for allowing me to dine with you."

Osric's response drew a knowing smile from the King who realized his new dwarf was a quick study in the ways of court life. Urloch II then focused his eyes on Osric, who lowered his eyes in fear. After a moment, the King said, "Osric, I have decided to appoint you to be a royal minister."

Osric was bewildered and blinked his eyes before responding. "A royal minister, Sire? I don't know what that means, Your Majesty."

"A King rules through his ministers, Osric. Every department of the government is headed by a royal minister appointed by me."

"You want me to be a part of the government, Sire?" Osric was stunned to the very core of his being.

"Yes I do, Osric. As of this moment, I am appointing you to be my Minister of Tribal Affairs. You shall ride in my carriage today, as befits a royal minister."

Osric was dumbstruck and could only stare at the king in confusion until at last his nerves calmed to the point he could ask, "What is it I am to do, Sire?"

"We shall likely be encountering a tribal chieftain named Rowan sometime before midday. I expect he will want to have parlance with me, and you are to be a part of it. You will sit at my right hand and say nothing, unless I ask for your opinion. When I do ask, your opinion will always be, 'We have been giving this matter serious study for some time, Sire.' You are to deliver your opinion in the most serious manner you can manage. After you finish speaking to me, you are to face Rowan and return him a hard stare. Can you manage this, Osric?"

Osric returned the King a serious look then replied, with perfect timing, "We have been giving this matter serious study for some time, Sire."

Urloch II roared with laughter, slammed his fist on the arm of his chair, pointed at Osric, and exclaimed, "By God, you've damned well got it, Osric!" The King turned to his butler and said, loudly, "Fill his cup, Goran! The Minister of Tribal Affairs must not thirst!"

The next few hours were the strangest of Osric's life, to that point. At the conclusion of their breakfast, the King ordered his tent struck, and sent word to the heralds to alert the people to make ready for departure. Osric left the royal tent in the King's company and followed Urloch II to where his carriage stood waiting. The handsome coach was trimmed with polished brass, and the wheels stood higher than Osric's head. The carriage was pulled by four massive, and nearly identical, gray horses. The driver sat on a high seat at the front of the carriage, and the heralds stood on a platform at the back of the vehicle. The King's footman held the door open for the King, and when Urloch II was seated, the servant indicated it was then acceptable for Osric to board. The seats were well padded and upholstered in red velvet. There was a carpet on the floor and vases attached to the carriage walls held fresh wild flowers. Urloch II sat facing forward, while Osric was seated across from the King, facing backward.

As Osric and the King waited for the royal tent to be stored for travel, the King opened the flap of a leather case and removed a sheaf of papers. He raised his eyes to Osric for a moment, smiled and said, "The King's work is never finished, Osric." The King did not appear to be expecting a reply, and Osric remained silent. A few minutes later, the footman knocked lightly on the carriage door.

"Yes, Rulf?"

"Your Majesty, the troupe is assembled, and ready for travel."

"Very well, Rulf, take your seat, then tell the heralds to sound departure."

"Yes, Your Majesty." Osric heard the footman climb up beside the driver, and a moment later call out, "Heralds! Sound the advance!" The two trumpets sounded as one, and in the distance, Osric heard the commander of the guard order the troops to commence marching. Had Osric not been enclosed in the King's carriage he would have seen that half of the foot soldiers and cavalry were now deployed at the trailing end of the procession. As the carriage began to move, Osric felt it sway gently side-to-side, and then front-to-back. The riding was much smoother than Jarin's cart.

Seeing the surprise on Osric's face, the King smiled again. "The body of the carriage hangs from the axles on chains, Osric. It makes for smoother going, and allows me to get some work done." As before, the King did not expect a response, and he returned to his reading. This was just as well, as Osric continued to be baffled by the morning's events and had no idea how to respond. The carriage rolled on, and soon Osric began seeing evergreen trees as the track took a noticeable upward slant. A little farther along, he saw large rocks and cliff faces outside the window. The King paid little attention to the passing scenery, but after an hour passed, he put his reading down and looked out the window. "I expect we will be meeting Rowan before long, Osric. Do you remember what it is you are to say when asked for your opinion?"

Osric looked at the King, then deadpanned, "We have been giving this matter serious study for some time, Sire."

The King slapped his knee and exclaimed, "Damned good, Osric! Damned Good! You learn faster than my real ministers!"

Osric had no reply, but was left to wonder what the King meant by 'real ministers'. After they had ridden for another quarter hour, Osric heard a commotion coming from the front of the procession, followed by three sharp blasts from the trumpets. The carriage came to a halt, and Osric shot the King an anxious look.

Urloch II appeared unperturbed by what ever was happening and continued to gaze out the window for a moment before turning to Osric. The King smiled, then said in a calm voice, "I suspect we are being paid a visit by a man who thinks himself a King, Osric."

"Is it this Rowan chap you spoke of, Sire?"

Before the King could respond, the Lord Chamberlain rode up, then lowered his head to the carriage window and addressed the King. "Rowan's men have blocked the track, Your Majesty. He is demanding parlance with you."

Urloch II showed no alarm. He exhaled softly, and said, "Very well Favian, have my tent erected in front of the carriage, and I shall receive Rowan."

"Yes, Sire." Before executing the King's orders, the Duke of Bruno delivered the Minister of Tribal Affairs a withering look that would remain embedded in Osric's mind for the rest of his life. His exposure to court life had been brief, but Osric had come to understand that his continued well-being depended entirely upon the King's good will.

The King smiled at Osric with a mildness opposite in measure to the Lord Chamberlain's hostility. "Now remember, Osric, you are to repeat what you have been taught, and when you've finished speaking, turn to Rowan, and stare at him intently."

"Yes, Sire."

The King looked out the carriage window again. He displayed no emotion and appeared to be admiring the view as he awaited his meeting with the tribal chieftain. The Lord Chamberlain returned on foot a few minutes later and knocked on the carriage door. "Yes, Favian?"

"Your tent is ready, Your Majesty."

"Very well then. Come along, Osric. Let us go and have parlance with Rowan."

The footman opened the door and motioned to Osric, signaling that he was to exit the carriage ahead of the King. Osric alit, then stood beyond the Lord Chamberlain, where the footman directed. When the King emerged from the carriage, Osric followed the lead of the others and bowed deeply. Urloch II stood up straight, stretched, then said, "Come along, Osric. Favian, position yourself outside the entrance as protocol demands."

"Yes, Your Majesty." The Lord Chamberlain's rigid, court manners could not completely hide the quaver in his voice that belied his anger.

Goran held the tent flap open, and Osric followed the King inside. The King's armchair was resting on a slightly raised platform, and the dwarf-sized chair had been placed at the King's right, at ground level. Osric could not recall if the King's chair had always been elevated, as his nerves were always too tightly wound during his time in the royal presence to remember small details. The King seated himself and bade Osric do likewise. "When Rowan is announced, we will stand to greet him, Osric."

"Yes, Sire."

The King turned to his butler and said, "Goran, please show Rowan in."

"Yes, Your Majesty." Goran held the tent flap open, bowed slightly, and said to someone beyond Osric's field of vision, "His Majesty, King Urloch II, will now receive you, Sir."

Goran stepped aside as a very large man with red hair, and fierce blue eyes took a step inside the King's tent, then planted his feet. The tribal chieftain wore a very old looking iron helmet and a bearskin vest that left his arms uncovered. A frightening broadsword hung from the man's waist. Rowan crossed his massive arms and struck an aggressive pose, then did a double take when he found himself coming under the intense stare of the dwarf standing beside the King.

"Your Majesty, Rowan, chief of the Ardonians, is presented before the throne of Urloch II to make parlance."

"Good morning, Rowan, I trust you're well," said the King with a pleasant smile as he took his seat.

"Good morning to you, Urloch. I hope that you are enjoying good health, as well." Osric thought Rowan's rumbling voice, was bubbling up from the very bowels of the earth.

"I am, Rowan. I am indeed." The King paused, as if assessing the tribal chieftain, then asked, "What is it you would like to speak with me about, Rowan?"

"As we have discussed many times before, Urloch, I want to know why you are trespassing on the land of the Ardonians." He spoke with boldness, though Osric thought the man's words lacked conviction.

"This is the land of the Ardonians, only as long as I permit it to be so, Rowan." The King spoke with easy confidence, betraying no fear.

"Permit it, Urloch?" replied Rowan, in a sarcastic tone.

The King ignored Rowan's tone, and continued in a pleasant vein "I would much prefer to see your people peacefully prospering than to remove them from this land by force, Rowan." The King paused a moment and eyed the Chieftain with cool detachment. "Rowan, please allow me to introduce Sir Osric, my Minister of Tribal Affairs."

"Who? What in bloody hell is a Minster of Tribal Affairs, Urloch? A dwarf no less!"

"This dwarf has the brain of a much larger man, Rowan, and I trust his counsel implicitly. He is my expert on the tribal peoples. He and I have discussed the possibility of stationing much of the army here permanently and placing this land firmly under the crown's control. Is this not so, Osric?"

Osric gave the King a solemn look and nodded his head. "We have been giving this matter serious study for some time, Sire."

Osric turned back to the Chieftain and stared intently at the man, who did not appear to relish the experience.

Rowan returned Osric's stare for an uncomfortable moment, then attempted to regain control of the conversation when he turned back to the King, and asked, aggressively, "You would do this to my people, Urloch?"

The King looked his guest in the eye and said evenly, "I would prefer not to, Rowan. I would much rather have you as my friend, and see your people living in peace, but if it must be demonstrated that I need no man's permission to travel this pass, then that demonstration can be arranged." He paused to allow his words to sink in then, turning to Osric, he asked, "Is this not so, Osric?"

"We have been giving this matter serious study for some time, Sire." Once again, Osric focused his attention on Rowan and began staring at him even more intently, never blinking his eyes. The Chieftain who had postured before the King now found himself struggling to speak.

Before Rowan could respond, the King brightened, "Where on earth are my manners? Goran! Ale for my guest, and be quick about it!" Urloch turned back to Rowan and said, "Please be seated Rowan, how rude of me to have kept you standing." A servant stepped forward with an armless chair and placed it before the King's dais. The chieftain took his seat and the King asked, "Your family is well, Rowan? I believe your wife had just given birth to another son the last we spoke. I hope the young lad is thriving."

Rowan sputtered, "Yes, Urloch, he is full of life and growing quickly." The Chieftain glanced at Osric again, whose unblinking stare had not wavered.

"Rowan, you must give serious consideration to entrusting your eldest son to me, in order that he receive a proper education. It will equip him to be a great leader when his time comes. What do you say to this Osric?"

"We have been giving this matter serious study for some time, Sire."

"Indeed we have! Indeed we have! Cedric, Barda, and Tybalt have all agreed to send their sons to me to be educated, Rowan. Do not let yourself and the Ardonian people be left behind."

Rowan was now completely off balance. He nodded to the servant who handed him an ale stein. He took a long drink, belched, then said, "If the other tribal chiefs are sending you their sons to educate, then I have little choice, Urloch." Rowan took another quick glance at Osric whose eyes continued to bore into him.

The King slapped the arm of his chair and said, "A damned good decision, Rowan! Damned Good! You're doing what's best for both you and your people. You will not regret it."

The parlance between the King, the Chieftain, and the Minister of Tribal Affairs, continued for another hour, with a considerable quantity of ale being consumed by all in attendance. Rowan departed with the King's best wishes for his continued good health, and with ten silver swans in his purse. The money he had been given was a far cry from the dozen or more gold talents he usually extracted from the King. In addition to having received far less money, the chief of the Ardonians now found himself in the awkward position of having agreed to surrender his son to the King to be educated.

The Chieftain rode back to his village besotted and struggling to understand everything that had just happened. The extent of Rowan's confusion was due, in no small measure to his having been subjected to the unrelenting stare of the King's Minster of Tribal Affairs.

When the King's tent had been stored for travel, and the troupe was again ready to march, Osric's appointment as a minister of the crown came to an end. The King presented him with a Silver Swan and thanked him for his service to the realm. Osric then rejoined Jarin on his cart. The procession spent the rest of the day, winding its way through the mountains and then out on to another wide plain. As night was falling, the carter and the candle maker's assistant rolled across the drawbridge and into the courtyard of the castle.

Chapter Nine

Osric Begins A New Life

After arriving at the castle, Osric helped Jarin feed the horses, then transfer the remaining sacks of grain from the cart to the granary. They pushed the cart to the back of the stable, and when it was stored in its proper place, Jarin reached for Osric's hand. "Well Osric, I'll be leavin' ya now. I've not seen me wife for nigh on to fortnight, and she's likely wonderin' if I'm still alive, she is."

"You have a wife, Jarin?" asked Osric with surprise.

"Aye, a wife and a wee son, as well. I didn't tell you this, Osric?"

"Nay, Jarin. I didn't know this."

Jarin could see the confusion on the Osric's face and moved to apologize for his omission. "Ah, damn it all, Osric. I'm right truly sorry, I am. I had no intent to deceive ya', I didn't. As I said, I'm quite unused to havin' a travelin' companion, and I tend to be a man of few words." Jarin peered at Osric, for a few seconds then continued in a hopeful tone, "Perhaps, after you're settled here, you will be able to come visit us on Sunday. Our cottage lies just beyond the castle walls, just a few minutes' walk away. Me wife and I often stroll by the river on Sunday in nice weather as well, and you could join us there."

"Aye, Jarin. I would like that, I would." Osric paused a moment, "Jarin, what do I do now? Do I sleep in the cart again?"

"Nay, Osric. I've no doubt they will be givin' you a billet in the castle. I'm surprised Walter hasn't yet come to fetch you."

"Who in bloody hell is Walter? I would rather stay with you, Jarin."

"You'd be a welcome guest, Osric, but His Majesty would never allow it. Walter oversees the dwarf community. He answers to Goran, and often directly to His Majesty."

"Oh, bloody hell, Jarin! Someone else to make me life miserable, I expect."

"Don't be too hasty, Osric. I think you'll find Walter to be quite a decent fellow." Jarin took a look around, then whispered, "Osric, what I said about not makin' the noblemen jealous, goes for the dwarfs as well. They're a good lot, mostly, but some can get powerful jealous if they get to thinkin' some other dwarf is gettin' too much of the King's attention, then there's no tellin' what might happen."

Osric felt trapped and helpless. "Oh, bloody hell, Jarin! I don't want *any* of the King's attention!"

Jarin was about to respond when he looked up and saw Walter approaching. "Oh, hold on Osric, here comes Walter, now. I'll make your introductions." When the leader of the dwarf community drew near, Jarin called out, "Hello, Walter. Good evenin' to ya."

"Good evening to you, Jarin. Welcome home. I trust you've had a safe journey?"

"Aye, indeed, Walter. It was a fine journey, it was." Jarin shook Walter's hand, then said, "Walter, I would like you to meet, Osric. He's been travelin' with me these past few days, and a right sound man he is. Osric, this is Walter. He'll take good care of ya, he will."

Osric stared, uneasily at Walter for a moment. The well-dressed man before him stood no taller than he. However, unlike Osric, Walter stood erect and walked without the aid of a stick. He did not appear to suffer from the infirmities that plagued so many dwarfs. Walter appeared to be a good deal older, as the hair peeking out from below his hat was snowy white. The master of the dwarf community had the saddest eyes Osric had ever seen and a deeply lined face that spoke of having seen much of life. Walter extended his hand, "Hello, Osric. I came as soon as Goran sent word of your arrival." Walter spoke in a calm, and measured voice that surprised Osric. Though small in stature, Walter's bearing radiated leadership.

Osric shook Walter's hand, "Hello, Walter." He found the experience of shaking a hand the size of his own, rather strange, and not unpleasant.

Walter turned back to the carter, "Good night to you, Jarin. I must go now and get Osric settled. Please give my best to Gwendolyn, and young Leo."

"Good night, Walter." Jarin reached for Osric's hand again, "It was a real pleasure travelin' with ya, Osric. I hope I can see ya again, regular-like."

"Good night, Jarin." Though Osric had only known the carter a few days, he felt as if something vital was being torn away, not unlike the feelings he experienced when being captured by the King's men.

"Please gather your things, and come with me, Osric."

"All I have is me stick, the clothes on me back, and the hat on me head, Walter."

"You have no change of clothing? No cloak?"

"Nay, Walter. I was taken from the square in front of the candle shop, just as I am."

Walter arched his eyebrows, and said, quietly, "Most irregular, Osric. Most irregular."

Osric did not know what 'irregular' meant but proceeded to tell Walter the story of his capture.

"You *killed* one of the King's horses, and lived to tell the tale?" gasped Walter.

"That is what His Majesty told me, but I think it was one of the bloody knights what actually killed it. I think I only crippled the beast when its damned fool of a rider blocked me escape."

"You are incredibly fortunate to have survived. The King does not take kindly to people killing his horses."

"His Majesty bloody well laughed about it, he did. The soldiers fell upon me. They trussed me up and pitched me into the back of Jarin's cart. Then, that very night, the King ordered me to join him at his supper, he did." Osric then went on to tell Walter of being made Master of the Hunt, and later being appointed, Minister of Tribal Affairs, all of which left Walter staring back at him in stunned silence.

At last the elderly dwarf managed, "Extraordinary!" Walter fixed his eyes on Osric for a few more seconds, then continued, "Well then, come with me, Osric. My wife began preparing a room for you when we learned of your arrival."

Though Jarin had told him there were married dwarf couples living with the King, Osric was startled by Walter's casual mention of his 'wife'. He had known only one other dwarf over the course of his sheltered life, and Godfrey had not been married. He found the concept difficult to accept. As he accompanied Walter, Osric ventured, "Have you been a captive for a long while, Walter?"

Walter turned his large, sad eyes to Osric, and smiled, "I came here of my own free will, Osric, as did everyone else living in the community. No one here is a captive, which makes your situation all the more unusual. Dwarfs have been living with the royal family for generations. I came as a guest of Urloch I, when I was but a young man, shortly after completing my studies at university."

"You know how to read?"

A trace of a smile crossed Walter's lips, "Yes, Osric. I can read, and a good deal more. You see, I was the third son of a Count, and though I was never in a position to inherit the title, I am of noble birth and a distant cousin of both the King and the Lord Chamberlain. My only inheritance was the fine education my father provided me." Walter halted and turned to face Osric, "I have found this to be a place where people of our . . . special circumstances. . . can lead a normal, and useful life. I look after the needs of the dwarf community, but most of my time is spent as headmaster of the Royal Academy where I help prepare sons of the nobility, and other deserving young men, for university. I served as a tutor to His Majesty, his father, the current Lord Chamberlain, and many other noblemen." Walter glanced around to ensure they were not being overheard then continued in a low voice: "I do not know what to make of His Majesty's behavior toward you, Osric, but he appears to have seen something of value in you. I urge you to be very cautious. Keep quiet and learn the ways of the castle. Give the King your loyalty, but never try to be his friend. Kings are only friends with other kings, and very rarely, then."

The events of the past week, combined with Walter's words, left Osric numb with confusion once again. He could think of nothing to say, other than to murmur, "Yes, Walter."

"Very well then, let's get you settled. Have you eaten, Osric?"

"Nay, Walter. The troupe marched on through the supper hour so as to reach the castle before full dark."

"I will have Arabella send word to the kitchen, and your supper will be brought up. I expect there are many others who will be eating a late supper tonight as well."

"Thank you, Walter." Before Osric could continue, they were greeted by a small, cheery-faced woman, waiting for them at the castle door. The woman bore a striking resemblance to Sister Adele, though much smaller, older, and minus the nun's habit.

"Walter, is this our new man?"

"Yes, my Dear. Please meet, Osric. As I understand it, Osric comes to us from the far end of the country. Osric, this is my wife, Arabella."

The small woman reached out and seized Osric's hand in both of hers, then shook his hand warmly. "Welcome, Dearie. We're most pleased to have you with us, we are." Arabella spoke in the manner Osric was accustomed to hearing, and her speech stood in marked contrast to her husband's cultured voice. "Come along, Luv. I've got a nice room all ready for ya, I do. I'm sure you're right tired from your arse bouncin' 'round on that bloody cart all day."

A look of mild exasperation crossed Walter's face, *"My Dear . . ."*

Arabella laughed with glee, "Walter's a stiff old bird, Osric. He's been tryin' to make a proper lady out of me for over thirty years now, and I keep frustratin' him, I do." Arabella laughed again, sighed, then said, "I love him dearly though, and there's not a man on earth I'd trade him for."

Walter glanced down at his feet, then lifted his head, and said with a bemused smile, "Let us get Osric, fed and settled, Arabella. You will have plenty of time to visit with him tomorrow."

"Yes, Luv. Of course."

Walter and Arabella led the way inside the castle, then up a spiral stairway. Though they were both a good deal older than Osric, they were far more mobile and had to pause periodically to allow the newcomer to catch up. When they reached the top of the stair, the couple led Osric out into a large, well furnished, room. The space was well lit by many candles all around outside walls, and by a chandelier hanging above the center of the room. "This is our common room, Osric. This is where we take our meals, and where we gather to socialize in our free time. On Sunday morning, it serves as our church." From across the room, a pair of dwarfs looked up from a board game they were playing and extended Walter a quizzical look.

Walter called out to the pair, "Good evening Clive. Bartholomew. This is our new guest, Osric. It's late, and I will make proper introductions on the morrow."

"Yes, of course, Walter. Welcome, Osric."

Osric found himself speechless. Every piece of the handsome furniture was scaled to dwarf size, save two; the throne and table resting upon a raised dais at the far end of the room. Walter saw the throne seize Osric's attention, and said, "Yes, Osric. That is for His Majesty. He takes a meal with us now and then." Walter turned to Arabella, and said, "My dear, would you send word to the kitchen and have some supper brought up for Osric?"

"Yes, Luv."

Arabella hurried away and Walter said, "Come with me Osric, and I will show you to your room."

Osric followed Walter across the common room, then down a long hallway lined with doors. When they reached an open door, Walter removed a burning candle from a sconce in the hallway, then led the way into the room. "This will be your room, Osric. I think you will find it comfortable." Water lit two additional candles as he spoke.

If he was nothing else, Osric was a man who knew his candles, and he recognized the bright clean flame of a beeswax candle when he saw it. As he looked around the room, he was stunned once again. Though the room was only a little larger than his garret, it contained an actual bed with a feather mattress, a small table with two chairs, and even a colorful carpet on the floor. There was a small fireplace built into the outside wall, a wardrobe cabinet, and wonder of wonders, a window unobstructed by shutters.

"I think you will be comfortable here Osric. His Majesty may choose to move you to a different room in time, but this is quite decent. We will get you to the tailor tomorrow and have you outfitted with some proper clothing." Walter then spent a few minutes explaining the basic rules of the dwarf community and told Osric that in the coming days he would be assigned a job. "Even as the King's guest, a man must earn his keep, Osric," said Walter, with a smile.

"Walter?"

"Yes, Osric?"

"If no one here is a captive, then why do people stay?"

"They stay because they choose to, Osric. You may very well make that decision yourself, once you come to know us. I urge you to give our community a fair test, and not be too hasty to depart. People also stay because the King has a simple rule: if a dwarf chooses to leave, they may never return. Few of our people have ever known better lives than the ones they lead here." As Walter was speaking, there came a tap at the door, and Arabella entered carrying a tray.

"I've brought your supper, Dearie." Arabella gave Osric a warm smile as she placed the tray on the table. "I brought you a nightshirt as well. Walter said you came with but the clothes on your back. We'll be setting that to rights, straight away, we will." Arabella smiled at Osric again, then said, "Come along, Walter. We must let Osric enjoy his supper in peace. Just leave the tray 'til mornin', Dearie. We'll send it back to the kitchen with the breakfast things. Go ahead and turn in when you're ready. No one will be botherin' ya."

Osric was overwhelmed by the kindness being shown him. "Yes, Mistress. Thank you."

"Oh, bosh! None of that 'Mistress' nonsense," laughed Arabella. "It's Arabella, Dearie, just Arabella."

The exchange brought another bemused smile to Walter's lips. "Osric, just snuff your candles when you are ready to retire. If you have the need to relight them, there are always a few candles left burning in the hall. We will leave you now. There is water in the pitchers and a sink for your use. Good night, Osric."

"Good night, Walter." Relight the candles? Was he free to burn candles as he pleased? Bee's wax candles no less? Such a thing would have been unimaginable in the candle maker's garret.

"Sweet dreams, Dearie."

"Good night, Arabella."

After the couple departed, Osric sat down to a supper of dark bread that was both aromatic and delicious, an apple, and a stein of ale. Though he continued to long for the brown ale of The Dancing Pig, the King's ale had grown on him through sheer exposure, and he found it a bit more palatable with each new encounter. With his meal complete, Osric washed his hands and face, then donned the night shirt Arabella had given him. He had never lain on a feather bed before, and he found the experience quite odd after a life spent sleeping on mean pallets of old straw, and lately, bags of grain. Though the feather bed was a new experience, it was an agreeable one, and he was soon in a deep sleep.

Osric's vivid dreams found him revisiting the candle shop and the bell tower. Although, in his dream they had become softer, gentler, places, and instead of being tormented by Brother Benedict, he found himself enjoying brown ale with the man as they sat in The Dancing Pig discussing Fendrel's upcoming wedding. Osric did not find the idea of Fendrel getting married to be at all strange, but never thought to ask Brother Benedict who the rat catcher's bride might be.

He was awakened by a rapping on his door, followed by Walter's voice. "Good morning, Osric. Please dress, and come join us in the commons for breakfast." It took Osric a moment to gather himself and remember where he was. He sat up on the edge of the bed and stared at the window for a moment. As Osric reveled in his lack of back pain, Walter's voice came again, "Are you rising, Osric?"

"Y-yes, Walter. I was a bit confused, I was."

"Very well. Please dress, then join us in the commons. Breakfast will be arriving shortly."

"Yes, Walter." Osric hobbled to the table where he poured some water in the bowl, then splashed some of it over his face. He took a long drink, dressed, then spent another moment gazing out the window, preparing himself to face the unknown. He brushed back his unruly hair with his hands, then stepped out into the hall where he heard many voices coming from the common room. He was not afraid in the physical sense because he had been in many fights in addition to having stared down a menacing tribal chieftain and killing one of the King's horses. What he was feeling as he made his way to the common room was an altogether new sensation. When he reached the end of the hallway, he took a deep breath, then rounded the corner. Before him were more dwarfs than he knew existed. The room became very quiet as all eyes fell upon him. The silence lasted only a moment as the murmur of voices soon rose again as all the people turned their attention to the newcomer.

From his table in front of the King's dais, Walter stood, then rang a small silver bell. When the room quieted, he addressed those gathered. "This morning, I want everyone to welcome a new man to our community. I would like to introduce you all to Osric. Osric comes to us from the far end of the kingdom and has been traveling in Jarin's company for the past few days. Let us all do everything we can to make him feel at home and welcomed."

To Osric's immense relief, Walter made no mention of his having killed the King's horse, serving as Master of the Hunt, or of his brief appointment as a royal minister. Walter simply introduced him as 'the new man'. Never had the word *man* resonated with Osric the way it did on this morning.

From all around the room came voices calling out their welcome. Though Osric had yet to hear any of them, all the dwarfs had their stories and most had memories of facing the community for the first time. He would also come to realize, the warm welcome he was being afforded was a product of Walter's leadership.

"There is a seat here, Osric," said Walter, pointing him to a table near the front of the room.

Osric most always carried his stick in his right hand but was forced to transfer it to his left in order to accommodate the many handshakes he was extended as he made his way to the table. During his trek across the room, he was given more names than he could ever hope to remember. When he seated himself at last, Osric had gone from grave apprehension to a wide smile. The three people at his table introduced themselves as Bryce, Cedric, and Alexa.

Bryce told Osric that he worked in the castle's harness shop, and was well acquainted with Jarin as they both answered to the stable master. Cedric proved to be the second educated dwarf he had met since his arrival and worked in the King's counting house. Alexa was a baker, and as the flaxen-haired woman introduced herself, Osric was overtaken by the most baffling sensation of his life.

Walter rang the small bell again, and when there was quiet, he led the dwarfs in prayer. As the blessing concluded, four dwarfs guided a large rolling table into the room. "Come along, Osric," said Bryce, rising to his feet. "They sends the food up from the kitchen, but we waits on ourselves, we do."

Osric nodded his acknowledgment, then rose and followed Bryce and the others to the table. As they made their way to the food, Osric glanced to his side and saw Alexa smile back at him. His hands were trembling a bit as he followed Bryce's lead and picked up a tray that contained black bread, porridge, and a stein of ale. Osric was mystified by the feelings that swept over him each time Alexa smiled at him.

When they were seated again, Bryce asked, "Tell me Osric, what trade have you pursued?"

"I worked for a candle maker, and on Sundays I was a bell ringer at the cathedral."

"Candle makin' is a fine trade, it is. I expect they will find work for you with our man, Quinn." Bryce paused a moment, shaking his head in a knowing manner, then continued, "Bell ringin' can be bloody hard work, it can. I did a bit of it meself, back in me younger days. Bloody hard work."

"Aye, it can be, for sure." Osric then proceeded to tell of the awful Sunday he spent in the bell tower ahead of the King's visit, and the extraordinary number of pulls that had been required of him. He told of how he had done it all while being given almost nothing to eat, and of his subsequent collapse and rescue by Fendrel.

"That's damned rotten, it is!" said Bryce, with rising heat. "His Majesty would be right upset if he had known of it!" Cedric and Alexa nodded their heads in agreement. "I wouldn't want to be the miserable sod who mistreated a dwarf that way, if His Majesty ever got wind of it! The King would be havin' someone's guts for garters, he would!"

Osric was humbled by the support he was receiving from those at the table. Other than Fendrel confronting the candle maker, and Kurtz chasing away trouble makers at the Harvest Festival, he could think of no other times in his life when anyone had come to his defense. When he saw Alexa smiling at him again, he felt is if he might melt into his chair.

As they completed their meals, the people returned the trays to the rolling table, then began bidding one another good day as they departed to their various places of work. Walter said goodbye to Osric and Arabella, then departed as well, leaving just Osric and his hostess remaining in the common room. "We've a busy morning ahead, Dearie. First I need to get you to the tailor shop and have you measured for some proper clothing. Then, we will visit the cobblers, and get them started on new boots for you. If there's time, I'll start showing you around the castle, and introducing you to the people you should know."

Osric was wearing his best clothes and was rather upset by people saying they were not proper. However, enough time had passed since his capture, that he now reacted more slowly to events. If his clothes were not proper, then he was prepared to let Arabella address that issue. Arabella led the way down a spiral staircase, other than the one leading to the courtyard. After arriving at the bottom, she set off down the longest hallway Osric had ever seen. Candles spaced every few paces lit their way while additional light filtered in through large windows, set high in the stone walls. Osric's legs were beginning to tire when Arabella knocked on a door bearing the image of a needle and thread then entered without waiting for a response.

"Good morning, Angmar. It's good to have ya back home with us, it is." Osric was coming to enjoy the cheerfulness in Arabella's voice.

"Good morning to you, Arabella. Tis a rare treat to travel with the King, it is. And Osric, . . . ya handsome devil, good mornin' to you as well!"

Osric found himself paralyzed with embarrassment as memories of his afternoon spent as The Master of the Hunt came rushing back, along with Angmar's leering invitation to spend the night in her tent. He could only lower his eyes and respond with a weak, "Good morning."

"Come along, Luv. Stand yourself up on this box, and I'll be gettin' your measurements taken. Is he to get the usual assortment of clothing, Arabella?"

"Yes, Angmar. You don't have any special needs do ya', Osric?" asked Arabella.

He found himself as confused as he had ever been, and could only answer, "I think not. I've ne'er owned much in the way of clothes. Just me work clothes, and me Sunday clothes."

"I take it you're wearin' your work clothes, Dearie?" asked Angmar.

"They are me Sunday clothes," replied Osric, with a degree of irritation. "They would become me work clothes at the new year." He had never thought of himself as poorly dressed. The clothes he wore were no different than those of anyone else of his station. In the world Osric had known, only noblemen, the bishop, and prosperous merchants wore fine clothing.

Osric submitted to Angmar's measuring with some reluctance and was grateful when the seamstress refrained from making suggestive comments. As he stood upon the box, the other seamstress who had been on the King's journey looked up from her work, and called out from across the room, "Hello, Osric. So nice to see you, Luv."

Osric had to admit that other than the Lord Chamberlain, a few of the soldiers, and his initial meeting with Goran, everyone he had met thus far, had treated him with kindness. He realized even Goran's hostility had softened a great deal after their initial encounter. Only the Lord Chamberlain continued to stick in his mind like an inflamed boil. "I hope that hateful bastard forgets I'm alive, I do," thought Osric. He sensed he could trust Arabella and resolved to question her about the Duke of Bruno, if and when the appropriate moment arose.

It did not take Angmar long to complete her work, and when she finished, the seamstress drew another flash of embarrassment from Osric when she gave him a suggestive smile, then said, "I'm all done, come back and see me if e'er you're feelin' lonely, Osric."

Arabella laughed and said, "Oh, Angmar, you're a caution, you are." Both women laughed, then Arabella continued, "Thank you, Angmar, I expect it will be a week or so before they're ready?"

"Yes, Luv, a week give or take a day. Are you off to the cobbler, now?"

"Aye, we are indeed. Let's be on our way, Osric. Good day to you Angmar."

"Good day to you Arabella, . . . and don't be forgettin' what I said, Osric."

Yet another hot wave of embarrassment broke over Osric as he mumbled his goodbye. Back in the hallway, he struggled to organize his thoughts, then asked, "Is that wench always so bloody bold?"

Arabella laughed, "Oh, as I said, Angmar is a caution, she is. She's ne'er made any secret of her fondness for male companionship, but she's ne'er caused harm to anyone that I know of, either. She talks that way to pretty much everyone but the King himself." Arabella paused, then added mischievously, "I wouldn't put it past her to talk that way to a priest!" Arabella laughed again, then added in an encouraging tone, "Don't take her too seriously, Dearie. She has a big heart, and she'd do anything for ya, she would."

Before Osric could summon up more questions, Arabella knocked on a door with the image of a boot painted on it, and as before entered without waiting for a response. Once inside, they were greeted by another dwarf. "Good mornin' to ya Arabella." The stocky, middle-aged man looked at Osric, extended his hand, and said, "Ah, it's Osric I think, if my memory is correct."

"Aye, I'm Osric."

"Bertram here. Most folks just calls me Bert, they do. I tossed me name at ya this mornin' at breakfast, but I'm not surprised if ya don't remember me. You heard a lot of names in short order, you did. Welcome to the cobbler's shop, Osric. I expect you're here for new boots, and I'm your man. Step right this way, and I'll get started makin' your pattern."

Osric was measured for new boots and was astonished to learn he would be receiving two new pairs. Arabella then accompanied him to the stable where he was introduced to the stable master, and they were able to say hello to Bryce in the harness shop. Osric had hoped to see Jarin, but was informed by the harness maker, the carter was out in the countryside collecting a supply fodder for the King's stables. Arabella showed the kitchen to Osric, and he was amazed by the beehive of activity there. Before returning to the common room, they stopped briefly at the castle bakery. Alexa looked up from kneading bread, smiled, and Osric's heart skipped a beat.

All through the rest of the day, and the following morning, Osric accompanied Arabella through the maze that was the royal palace. Though he found the building to be confusing beyond words, Arabella always knew what lay behind every door. They had just completed the climb back up to the common room for their midday meal when they found Walter waiting for them at the top of the stairs. "Hello, Luv. You're early."

Walter had a serious expression on his face and did not respond at once. He gathered himself, then said in a low voice, "I've been sent by Goran to deliver a message to Osric from His Majesty. Osric, you are to dine with the King tonight, in the royal chambers."

Chapter Ten

A Royal Invitation

Arabella gasped, and stared at her husband in disbelief until asking in a very quiet voice, "Walter, what does this mean?"

Walter hesitated, he looked at his wife, then turned his attention to Osric. "To my knowledge, no dwarf has ever been invited to dine in the royal chambers. I have visited the royal chambers on many occasions as part of my duties but have never dined there. This is unknown territory, and I do not know what advice to give beyond what I've already told you." Walter glanced around the room then continued, just above a whisper: "I will make every effort to ensure the people in our community know this is something you are doing against your will, Osric. You must never allow anyone to think otherwise."

Osric found himself filled with genuine fear at what was developing before him and had no need to pretend. "It *is* against my will, Walter! I want no part of it! I would be happy to take my supper here in this hall with everyone else! I've no love for spending time with the King."

Walter eyed Osric, "You appear to have seen a barber recently, so I think your hair and beard will be acceptable." He turned back to his wife and said, "After luncheon, you must escort Osric back to the tailor shop and have him fitted for a vest he can wear over his jersey. Then, return him to the cobbler, and have his boots blackened."

"Yes, Luv. I'll see to it, I will." Arabella glanced over Walter's shoulder then waved hello to a pair of men returning for their midday meal, thus alerting her husband they were no longer alone in the room. She turned to Osric: "Go ahead and find a place to sit, Dearie. It doesn't matter where. We encourage people never to sit in the same place two meals in a row. Our dinner will be along shortly."

He looked around the room and decided to sit with the two dwarfs who had just arrived. When the two men saw Osric approaching, they raised their arms and welcomed him to join them.

"Osric, isn't it?" asked a husky and nearly bald man as he extended his hand. "Carac, here. I'm the smithy's helper, I am."

"Aye, my name is Osric."

Before Osric could speak again, the second man at the table extended his hand, "Hello, Osric, I'm Henry. I'm a groom in the stable, though not the stable where Jarin keeps his cart. I help tend to the King's racing horses, on the far side of the castle grounds, I do."

"Hello, Henry."

Henry gave Osric a mischievous smile, and asked, "So, are ya learnin' your way 'round the castle, Osric?"

He responded with his own bemused expression, "It's all bloody confusin', it is. I have no idea where I'm goin' but for Arabella showin' the way." Both of the men at the table laughed and agreed with his assessment.

"Aye, it is confusin' indeed," laughed Carac. "I was bleedin' born here, and I still get confused by it all. I doubt there's anyone who knows the place completely."

"You were born here?"

"Aye. Me old pa was a smithy's helper like I am, and me ma worked in the bakery. They're sleepin' in the churchyard now, God rest their souls. And how did you come to join us, Osric? Most all our people were born here, or within a day's walk. We've ne'er been joined by someone from so far away."

He told his story to Walter because Walter was the leader of the community, and he felt there was little choice but to tell the full truth of his journey. Now he chose his words carefully, not wanting to reveal any more of his story than necessary. "The King was passin' through the town square, he took note of me, and I was asked to join him."

"That's a common enough story," said Carac, nodding. "His Majesty is always on the lookout for dwarfs who might like to come and live here, he is. How was your journey, Osric?"

"It was the first time in me life I e'er traveled beyond sight of the place where I was born. It left me with much to remember, it did."

"What was it like passin' through the mountains?" asked Henry, with an eager smile. "Many's the time I've wondered what bein' in the mountains would be like, I have."

Again, Osric chose his words with care and decided to tell the truth, just not the whole truth. "The mountains are bleedin' beautiful, they are. I'd only e'er seen them at a great distance, from the top o' the bell tower."

"Tell me," interjected, Carac, "Did that Rowan chap they tell of put in an appearance? I've heard he always tries makin' parlance any time His Majesty crosses the mountains."

Osric hoped the sharp electrical pulse that shot through his body at the mention of the tribal chieftain was not evident to the other men at his table. He calmed himself, and replied, "We stopped for somethin' on our way through the mountains. I was with Jarin, well back of the King's carriage, and I ne'er heard what it was all about." Osric resolved to speak to the carter at his earliest opportunity and tell him of his deception, so the story of his appointment as Minister of Tribal Affairs did not become known to the dwarf community.

As the three men chatted, the room filled with dwarfs returning for their dinner. Upon the arrival of the rolling table, Walter stood and rang the small silver bell. As he did at every meal, Walter led the room in prayer before the people made their way to the food. Osric collected his tray and to his amazement found a slice of roasted pork in addition to cooked vegetables, black bread, and a stein of ale. He could not remember ever having eaten meat on a day other than a Sunday.

Soon after the three men returned to the table, they were joined by a woman Osric did not recognize. He was very surprised when she bent down and kissed Carac on his bald head before taking her seat. Seeing the surprise on Osric's face, the smithy's helper laughed, and said, "Osric, this is me wife, Winifred. Winnie, this is our new man, Osric."

"Hello, Osric. I heard we had a new resident. I haven't been here for a meal since Sunday supper. Is Arabella getting you settled?"

He returned Winifred a wry smile, "Well, we've begun. It's all very confusin' it is, Winifred."

She laughed and said, "Oh, yes, it will take a bit of gettin' used to, and please call me Winnie, Osric. Everyone calls me Winnie."

"Winnie works in the nursery, Osric. She helps take care of all the castle's children while their parents are workin'. She doesn't always get to take her meals here."

"There are children here?" Osric was on guard at the thought of potential tormentors.

"Oh, goodness yes, Osric. There are the children of the dwarf families of course, as well as the children of others who work in the castle. Our own sons were raised here, they were."

"Aye, Osric. You may have seen two of our sons on your journey, though you wouldn't have known it. They both serve in the household guard, they do." Carac and Winifred were beaming with pride.

"That's very surprisin'. I ne'er saw any dwarfs with the King's guard."

The others at the table tipped their heads back in laughter. "Dwarfs often give birth to non-dwarf children, Osric," said Winifred, smiling. "None of our four sons are dwarfs."

"Before I met Walter and Arabella, I had only e'er met one other dwarf, and he wasn't married. This is all very new to me, it is."

Winifred reached across the table and squeezed Osric's hand, "We're going to make you feel at home here, Osric. In no time at all, this will seem very normal to you. You will find that dwarfs fall in love, get married, and have families just like anyone else."

Osric lost interest in dwarf families when it hit him that the couple's sons would know all about his journey, as would every other member of the King's traveling party. It would only be a matter of time before the whole story would become known to the community, and Carac and Winifred might already know. "Oh bloody hell," thought Osric, in despair.

Not since the day Father Gregory threatened him with exorcism had Osric been more subdued. In his brief time at the castle he had been given a glimpse of a life immeasurably better than the one he had known. Then, in short order, he had been extended an invitation no other dwarf had ever received, which was followed almost at once by the knowledge the truth of his journey to the castle would soon be common knowledge. The community was now something he very much wanted to be a part of, and Osric felt certain he would be shunned once the story of his time with the

King became known. He would be forced out of the community, and he would have to try finding his way back to the candle shop. Osric grew even more depressed when he realized it was far from certain the candle maker would reemploy him, even if he could manage to get there.

Following the completion of their midday meal, Arabella escorted Osric back to the tailor shop. As they made their way down the stairs and hallway, his mind was in turmoil as he struggled to come to grips with all that was happening to him. Angmar became all business when told of Osric's order to appear before the King. The seamstress displayed a piece of black velvet left over from another project, and Arabella agreed it would make a fine vest. Osric made no comment and left the matter to the two women. His faraway look only increased Arabella's own fears and her concern for Osric. Angmar said she would enlist Juliana's help and assured Arabella the vest could be completed in no more than two hours. In the cobbler's shop, Bertram blackened Osric's boots, then shook Osric's hand, and wished him well. Osric and Arabella, climbed the spiral stairway back to the dwarf quarters, and when they reached the common room, he asked, "What am I to do now, Arabella?"

"There are more places I want to show you, but they can wait. Let's have a nice sit-down, Osric. We can visit and get to know each other better while they make your vest." They sat at a table in front of one of the large windows, and she asked, "Tell me of your life, Osric. I want to know all about you."

In spite of all that was happening, Osric was experiencing an inner warmth he had never known. Arabella had shown him great kindness and now seemed genuinely interested in him. She did not appear to find his appearance disturbing, and for a man who had been called a monster from the day of his birth, this was no small thing. He returned Arabella a weak smile, shrugged, and said, "There is little to tell, I'm afraid. I was a foundling, and I've no idea who me parents might have been. I lived in the orphanage until me sixteenth year, when they found work for me with the candle maker after I failed as a grave digger. I stayed in the candle shop until I was brought here. I started spendin' me Sundays in the bell tower long before I was strong enough to pull the ropes. I've not led much of a life, I haven't." He gave Arabella a mischievous smile, then added, "I've a great fondness for brown ale, I do." He hoped his hostess would be satisfied with his brief biography because he now realized he was powerless to resist answering any question this kind woman might ask.

Osric's hopes were short lived. Arabella smiled at his ale comment then asked, "Tell me of your life in the orphanage, Osric. Was life hard for you there, Dearie? I fear that it was."

He felt a tidal wave of emotion flooding over him as he struggled to maintain control. A small tear appeared in the corner of his eye and his voice was unsteady when he answered, "Aye, it was hard for me there. It was hard for everyone. It was the worst when I was a wee child because I walked so poorly, and I received many beatings because of it. I still walk poorly. I've ne'er met anyone with any love for the orphanage, I haven't." He then related his many encounters with Brother Benedict and the times he had been beaten then locked in the child's coffin for hours at a time. Sensing he could trust Arabella, Osric looked her in the eye and added with quiet ferocity, "It all left me with little love for the bastards in black robes, it did."

Arabella gasped, and checked her surroundings before whispering, "Osric, there's no danger of me repeatin' what you just said about the church, not even to Walter, but I beg you not to be sayin' things like that where you might be overheard by someone who would do you harm." She continued to look at Osric with intensity then continued, "Always assume the walls in this castle have ears, Dearie. Be very careful what you say, and be even more careful who hears ya say it." Arabella's words were reinforcing Jarin's earlier warnings.

He looked at her with sad eyes, "Yes, Arabella. Jarin and Walter have both warned me about me loose tongue. I'll be right careful, I will."

"Please do, Dearie. I'd hate to see any harm befall ya, I would."

Osric only now realized Arabella was holding his hand. For the first time in his life, he had some inkling of what it might have been like to have had a mother. He looked at her, then asked, "What do you make of this business of dining with the King, Arabella? I want no bleedin' part of it, I don't."

Arabella paused and considered her response. "I know you don't, Osric. Walter and I will do all we can to make sure everyone knows that. I hope ya' don't think unkindly of me husband for tellin' me of your experiences with the King. He trusts me, and I trusts him. Our trust has kept us bound together for many years." She looked into Osric's watery eyes and squeezed his hand. "The best I can determine, Dearie, is that the King saw something in you during that journey that sets you apart in his mind. Be this good, or be this bad, I canna' say. The only advice I can give ye is to be very humble, and do not try to become the King's friend. Our community has many good people, but they will not hold with someone seekin' special privilege."

"I seek no privilege! Walter said dwarfs are free to leave, and mayhaps that is what I should be doin'."

She sighed deeply, then said, "From what Walter has told me, you would not be allowed to leave, Osric. Not for the time being, at least. Perhaps things will be different after you meet with the King this evening."

"Oh bloody hell," said Osric, to no one in particular.

They continued to talk and Arabella told Osric of her life in the castle, and how she met and fell in love with Walter. At last she stood, then looked across the courtyard to a clock tower much like the one Osric was so familiar with. "It's been nearly two hours, Dearie. Let's go see if Angmar has your vest ready."

Osric's body went through the motions of returning to the tailor shop, but his mind was in another place. What, he wondered, would he need to make the trek back to the candle shop? Could he even find his way to the track leading to the mountains? What would he eat? What would he drink? Where would he find shelter along the way? How could his weak legs carry him that far? What if he encountered Rowan again? "I would never get there. It's bloody hopeless," concluded Osric.

So great was Osric's anxiety, he would have been unable to recall any part of that afternoon, even if pressed for an answer at sword point. He was fitted with his new vest, then allowed to return to his room where he tried, with little success, to rest ahead of his upcoming supper with the King. The mental torment he experienced that afternoon was equal to the worst Brother Benedict and the orphanage had ever dealt him. Though he had already dined with the King three times, he knew what he was facing would be very different, even if he could not understand why. If nothing else, the other occasions came when the dwarf community was no more than an abstract idea, and he could not have cared less. In but two days, the abstract had become a reality that held the promise of a much better life, if he could only avoid being shunned.

Much too soon, he heard a tapping at his door, followed by Walter's voice. "Osric, I've come to escort you to your audience with the King."

"Yes, Walter. I'm coming." Against his will, Osric rose from his bed, then brushed his hair back. He put on his new vest, took a deep breath, then joined Walter in the hallway.

Walter looked Osric over, then said, "The tailors did a fine job on your vest, and I see Bertram got your boots to looking presentable as well. Come with me, and I will deliver you to Goran."

Osric felt as if his legs were made of lead as he followed Walter down the hall and through the common room. Several members of the community had already gathered in the common room ahead of the evening meal, and as the two men passed through, only the tapping of Osric's stick punctuated the silence. Walter said nothing as they made their way to the spiral stairway, then along the corridor leading to the tailor and cobbler shops. Before reaching either of those doors, Walter stopped and unlocked a different heavy door. He removed a candle from a hallway sconce and used it to light a lantern hanging inside the door. They closed the door behind them, then descended a flight of stairs by candle light to where another hallway stretched into the inky distance. Walter halted and used the privacy of the setting to reiterate his intention to do his utmost to prevent problems with the community.

"Thank you, Walter," said Osric, with great humility. "I fear I will be shunned, and driven away to live as a vagabond."

"I pray it does not come to that. The people in our community may not be so quick to judge as you fear, Osric. Though no dwarf has ever been summoned to dine in the royal chambers, many have been singled out by the King for attention, and I trust our people will remember that. Come now, we must not keep His Majesty waiting."

The hallway was not only very dark, it was also noticeably cooler and damper than the one they had just left. As they walked, Walter explained, "We're in a tunnel that runs under the main courtyard. It connects the Royal Wing to the shops and factories that keep the place running. It can also be used to safely move soldiers in the event of a siege." Walter's voice, and the tapping of Osric's stick, echoed eerily in the dark, damp, place.

"The Royal Wing is where the King lives?"

"Yes, Osric. Only the King's immediate family, the household staff, and invited guests are allowed to be there. Not even the Lord Chamberlain or the Arch-Bishop may enter without His Majesty's permission."

This knowledge did nothing to bolster Osric's mood and had the effect of adding even more distance to the forbidding tunnel. His legs were weary by the time they topped another flight of stairs and emerged into a room with large double doors. After the blackness of the tunnel, the many candles burning there, made the space seem bright as day. The two large doors were painted a deep red, and trimmed in brass, with the royal coat of arms gracing each of them. Walter pointed Osric to a spot in the middle of the room, and said, "Wait here, and do not forget to remove your hat, before passing through these doors."

"Yes, Walter."

Walter stepped forward, then reached up and tapped on the knocker, before stepping back and standing beside Osric.

A small window within a large door opened, and the helmeted head of a soldier appeared. The window closed, and there came the sound of a heavy bolt sliding back. One of the large doors opened, and Osric felt a sharp jolt of fear as he recognized the knight who had held him at lance point while he relieved himself in the woods. "Good evening, Sir Brom," said Walter, bowing to the knight. Osric followed Walter's lead and bowed as well.

"Good evening, Walter." Without waiting for a response, Sir Brom pointed to Osric, and said, "You there! Step forward!"

Fearing his legs might fail him at any moment, Osric removed his hat, and passed through the doorway. Before the door closed, Walter asked, "Will he be given an escort back to the community, or do I need to return for him, Sir Brom?"

"We will see to it he is returned safely, Walter. Good night to you, now."

"Good night, Sir Brom."

The knight gave Osric a quick inspection, then said, "Come with me." Osric was led up yet another flight of stairs, then down a whitewashed hallway decorated with tapestries, and illuminated by many candles. When they came to a set of ornate doors, the knight said, tersely, "Wait here, and be silent." The guards stood aside, and Sir Brom tapped on the knocker. A moment later, the door opened and the King's butler appeared. "His Majesty's guest has arrived, Goran."

Goran bowed to the knight, "Thank you Sir Brom." Goran looked to Osric, then motioned for him to enter. After the door closed, the King's butler gave Osric yet another inspection, then asked, in a low voice, "Do you remember all you've been taught about being in the royal presence, Osric?"

"Yes, Goran."

The old butler eyed Osric for another moment, then said, "Very well then. Come with me. His Majesty is expecting you."

Osric followed Goran across a well-furnished room to where a pair of soldiers clad in chain mail stood guarding another set of imposing doors. The butler halted before the soldiers. "His Majesty's guest has arrived." The guards said nothing, but stepped aside, and allowed Goran to pull on an embroidered cord, hanging alongside the door.

From within, came the King's voice: "Enter."

Goran motioned for Osric to wait, then stepped inside the door, bowed, and said, "Your guest has arrived, Sire."

"Excellent, Goran! Please show him in."

"Yes, Sire." Goran stepped backward out of the door, then turned to Osric, and motioned him forward. Trembling in fear, Osric entered the room and bowed before the King. The butler then addressed the King in a very formal voice, "The dwarf, Osric, appears before His Majesty, King Urloch II, as commanded, Sire."

"Hello, Osric," said the King, with a smile.

"Hello, Your Majesty."

"Goran, please seat my guest."

"Yes, Your Majesty. Come this way, Osric." Goran escorted Osric to a table and chair, similar in size, than the one employed on the journey to the castle, but far more ornate. Osric had no more than taken his seat when a servant stepped forward and presented him with a stein of ale.

From behind his table, the King lifted his own stein, and said, "To your health, Osric!"

He returned the toast, "And, to yours, Sire!" Thus began the most stupefying evening of Osric's life. In addition to the musicians who had accompanied the King on his journey, there were acrobats, jugglers, and storytellers. The entertainment was accompanied by more good food than Osric could have ever imagined and many steins of brown ale. His years attending the Harvest Festival had taught Osric how to pace his drinking, but he had become rather besotted when the King brought the evening to a close. The entertainers departed, and Osric found himself alone with Urloch II.

The King fixed Osric in his gaze, and in a voice far more sober than Osric thought possible under the circumstances, asked, "Do you have any idea why you were invited here tonight, Osric?"

Struggling not to slur his words and embarrass himself, Osric replied, "Nay, Sire."

"I received an envoy from Rowan, the morning after we returned to the castle. Rowan has offered to withdraw all his people from the vicinity of the mountain pass and see to it that travelers are not attacked and robbed. He made this offer in exchange for being released from his promise to send his son to me to be educated. Osric, a good thing has happened without the loss of life, and it has saved me a great deal of money, as well. You played an important part in it. You served your King well, and your King wanted to show his gratitude."

"Thank you, Sire."

"Is there anything else I can do for you, Osric?"

"Sire, you have already done far more for this poor workin' man than he ever dreamed of." For once, there was not a trace of false humility in Osric's voice.

"Oh, come now, man!" boomed the King, with a broad smile. "Surely there is some small thing a King can do for a subject who has served the realm so well."

Osric's life flashed before his eyes, and his mind raced ahead of the avalanche of memories rolling over him. Fighting against the effects of the ale he had consumed, Osric calmed himself, then put all caution aside, and said in a small voice, "Well Sire, perhaps there is one small thing, but it wouldn't be for me."

"What is it, Man?"

"Sire, I have a dear friend who has long dreamed of livin' in one of those places where the monks and brothers never speak. They eat little, and they spend all their days in prayer. I've heard of 'em, but I don't know what they're called."

"A monastery?"

"Aye, I think that's it, Sire."

"What is your friend's name, Osric?"

"Brother Benedict, Sire."

Chapter Eleven

The Day After

sric was escorted back through the dark tunnel, then up to the dwarf quarters by a member of the household guard. He found himself in a condition, not unlike the many times he had staggered back to the garret following a day of drinking at the Harvest Festival. Thoughts of the festival naturally led him to think of Fendrel and the memory filled him with melancholy. He hoped his friend the rat catcher was faring well. How, he wondered, could he get a message to Fendrel and let him know he was safe? Perhaps Arabella would know a way.

His escort said little until they reached the dwarf quarters, but once they topped the spiral stairway the young man appeared very familiar with his surroundings, and Osric soon learned why. As the guard bade Osric goodnight in the common room, he extended his hand and said, "I'm Peter, son of Carac and Winifred. You may have met them already. I serve in the household guard, and I accompanied His Majesty on his recent journey."

"Aye, I have met them. They made me feel most welcome, they did."

The young man smiled, and said, "I would knock on their door, but I'm sure they've retired. Good night to you, Osric."

"Good night, Peter."

As Osric went about the business of getting ready for bed, his mind was in turmoil. "Oh bloody hell. He knows everything about the journey and me supper with the King as well. Now everyone will know of it before the day is over tomorrow. Oh bloody, bloody hell."

The anxiety Osric felt was offset to a degree by his hopes for what might lie in store for Brother Benedict, and he even managed a round of silent laughter before drifting off to sleep. He slept well and was slow to respond to the knocking on his door the following morning. Against his will, and longing for more sleep, Osric responded to the persistent knocking, "Yes?"

"Good morning, Osric," said Walter. "Church begins in an hour, please dress and join us in the commons."

"Yes, Walter."

Osric realized he had lost track of the days since his capture. "Is it Sunday?" he wondered. "It must be, or Walter wouldn't be sayin' it." He tried to recall everything that had happened to him of late, then asked himself, "Has it really only been a fortnight since Fendrel saved me life?" He concluded that it had indeed only been just two weeks since his collapse in the square that might have ended in his death had he not been rescued by the rat catcher. His amazement at all that had happened during this short period of time was soon displaced with his thirst and the pounding in his head. In his garret he would not hesitate to drink from his pitcher, but here in the castle he gave more consideration to his actions. He pondered the situation for a few seconds, then drank his fill.

Osric dressed but did not don the velvet vest. He brushed his hair back and steeled himself against the reception that might await him. When he entered the commons, he found the furniture had all been rearranged. The tables had been moved to one side, and the chairs were arranged in front of the King's table, which had been transformed into an altar. There was a noticeable drop in the murmur of voices as Osric entered the room. He looked around, not knowing what to do next. Being the center of attention left him remembering all of the worst events of his life. He had made the decision to sit by himself when, to his relief, he saw Carac motioning to him. He hobbled across the room and took a seat next to the smithy's helper.

Carac looked over his shoulder with a bemused smile, then whispered, "Me son tells me you had quite an evening, Osric."

Carac's words were spoken with humor rather than hostility, and though Osric was embarrassed, he was also relieved. "Aye, I expect I did." He looked at Carac and Winifred, then said in a beseeching tone, "I ne'er asked for it, I didn't. None of it!"

The couple smiled, and Carac said, "We know you did not seek this, Osric. Everyone in this community knows we are here at the King's pleasure, and we have no choice but to obey his orders. Do not beset yourself with worry." As Carac spoke, they were joined by Peter, who sat down on one of the dwarf-sized chairs. The strapping young man did not appear to find the small chair uncomfortable, and he nodded his greeting to Osric.

As he sat with Carac and his family, Osric continued to sense he was the subject of much curiosity in the room. Though the mood of the community as a whole did not appear hostile, he observed a very small dwarf giving him a cold stare. The person fixated on him looked more female than male, and was no larger than a child. Osric only determined the sex of the individual when the man rose and made his way to the confessional booth. Osric whispered to Carac, asking who the man might be.

"That's Hadrian. He's long been a favorite of the King and has played the fool at court a number of times. He's likely upset about you having supper with His Majesty. He's all bluster, Osric. Do not trouble yourself."

"I hope he knows I did not invite myself to dine with the King."

"I'm sure he knows, Osric. Walter spoke to everyone, but it's unlikely to matter. Hadrian can be powerful jealous, he can."

"Bloody hell," thought Osric.

Carac nudged Osric to let him know he was being summoned to come and confess. Osric made his way to the confessional and once inside engaged in a moment's silent laughter at the memory of his many false confessions, in particular those he made to young Father Stephan. Given his change of circumstances, Osric calmed himself and decided he would take no risk. Though everything he told the priest was complete fiction, it was believable enough not to arouse suspicion. Later, he realized it was the first time since he was a child he had attended church without viewing the proceedings through a small window in the bell tower.

As the congregation rose at the conclusion of the service, Osric caught a glimpse of Alexa smiling at him from across the room, and once again he was gripped by feelings he could not explain. The congregation lingered for a while, exchanging greetings and chatting in low voices. Then Carac touched Osric on the arm and said, "Come along Osric, it's the men's job to move the furniture, before and after mass. Walter knew you were very late last night through no fault of your own, so he allowed you to sleep a bit longer this morning."

Osric proceeded to assist Carac in rearranging the furniture. The two muscular dwarfs were able to carry one of the heavy oaken tables by themselves, while other tables were being moved by three and four people. As they were in the middle of moving their second table, Osric glanced across the room and saw Hadrian staring at him again. The tiny man was standing in one spot with his eyes riveted on Osric and making no effort to assist in the work. "I should give the little bastard a taste of me stick and teach him to keep his bloody eyes to himself, I should," thought Osric. At another time in his life he would not have hesitated to confront Hadrian, but he knew making such a scene now would be a very foolish act, so he let the urge pass.

As they were returning to get another table, Osric found Bertram walking beside him. "It seems you've come to Hadrian's attention, Osric."

Osric returned the cobbler's mischievous grin. "Aye, it seems so, Bert."

"Ignore the little ankle-biter. Walter told us the truth, and if Hadrian thinks poorly of ya, then he's the only one. We're all here to serve the King, Osric. You've done naught but what you were told to do, and no one can criticize ya for that."

Osric felt very relieved. "Thank you, Bert."

After the furniture had been returned to the proper places, the people relaxed and conversed until the rolling table appeared, laden with food. Walter rose, rang the small bell, then said a blessing. Osric thought the room seemed fuller than it had at any time since his arrival, and Carac explained how some members of the community lived and worked out on the King's estates, and did not take their meals in the commons during the week. Sunday dinner, however, was something that drew almost every member of the extended community together.

When it came his turn, Osric collected his tray and was preparing to rejoin Carac's family, when Hadrian spoke up from behind him. "I expect this is bloody poor fare, compared to the King's table." The tiny man's nasal voice was dipped in acid.

Osric waited until the initial flash of anger passed, then turned to Hadrian and responded in a calm voice, "You will be most welcome to take my place, should I ever be invited again." He then began eying his tiny antagonist with the same intensity he had given the tribal chieftain. If Hadrian had hoped to provoke a response that would have ended with Osric's expulsion from the community, his effort was a dismal failure. The calm words and Osric's intense gaze, stopped the tiny man, cold. Hadrian returned Osric's stare for a moment, then pivoted and stomped away without speaking. Though he was feeling rather satisfied by his handling of the situation, Osric continued to taste the anger on his tongue for several seconds.

He returned to the large, round table where Carac and his family had gathered. In addition to Peter, two of the couple's other sons had joined them as well. "Osric, these are me sons, Thomas, and Gavin. Boys, this is our new man, Osric. Make your old pa proud, and extend him your welcome." The two young men reached across the table and shook Osric's hand. "Our eldest son, Francis, is seldom able to join us for Sunday dinner. He serves as steward on one of the King's more distant estates. When we see him, it's most often at mid-week when he comes to report to The Minister of Crown Lands."

Osric's mind was a mix of confusion and wonder. Not only had he recently met the first married dwarfs he had ever known; Carac and Winifred had a substantial family. Their sons were not dwarfs, and all held important positions. As Osric pondered the situation, the last empty chair at the table was filled by Alexa, thus adding to his confusion.

Winifred asked, "Osric, have you met my niece, Alexa?"

"Y-yes I have. Hello, Alexa."

"Hello, Osric," said Alexa, with a smile. She turned to the three boys and said, brightly, "Hello cousins."

"Hello, Lexie," said the boys, in unison.

"What a wonderful thing, havin' a family must be," thought Osric, as he looked back at his life. His first Sunday dinner in the dwarf quarters exceeded even the best fare Sister Adele had provided him in the bell tower and was not far removed from what he had been served at his supper with the King. Carac told him the meal was not out of the ordinary for a Sunday dinner, and it was a tradition that kept the dwarf community bound together. All around him, at his table, and at the others, happy conversation swirled, while Osric's emotions ranged from awe to envy.

As the people at Carac's table enjoyed their Sunday dinner, Alexa asked, "Tell us how you came to join us, Osric."

Osric thought he now understood how a rat felt when viewing its world from the inside of one of Fendrel's traps. He paused a moment, gathered himself, then decided to tell the group the whole story, hoping they would understand. Osric told them how he had killed one of the King's horses in the melee leading to his capture and how he had been bound, then pitched into the back of Jarin's cart, drawing gasps from many at the table.

"He's tellin' the truth," said Peter, fighting back his laughter. "I wouldn't go spoilin' for a fight with this man, I wouldn't." Thomas grinned and nodded his agreement.

Osric then related his other experiences with the King during the journey to the castle, leaving his dining companions wide-eyed. When he finished, Osric looked to every face at the table, then said in a beseeching tone, "I ne'er asked for any of it, I didn't. I only held back the truth out of fear you would send me away, which you will likely do now."

From everyone at the table came laughter, and cries of, "Nay, never, you've done nothin' wrong!"

Carac spoke up, "Peter and Thomas told me your story, Osric, and I understand why you feared sharing it with us. But, do not worry, Man! You're amongst friends here, you are! You've no more freedom to disobey the King, than anyone else!" Everyone at the table murmured their assent, leaving Osric overwhelmed with relief. As he basked in the glow of the good will being afforded him, he saw Hadrian sitting with a pair of rather unpleasant looking dwarfs, and all of them were glaring at him with malevolence. The disconcerting moment passed when Alexa spoke up, "Who's ready for a game of Fox and Geese?"

Everyone at the table, save Osric, voiced the affirmative, prompting Winifred to ask, "You don't care to play Fox and Geese, Osric?"

He returned her a shy smile, shrugged, and said, "I've no idea what it is, Winnie."

Everyone at the table laughed, and Winifred said, "Well, there's nothin' to fear, and it doesn't take long to learn."

Alexa hurried to a cabinet along the wall, then returned with a board with many divots carved in its surface, along with a tray containing the game pieces. "First, we take turns rollin' the dice, to see who is going to be the fox. The rest of us will become the geese. The fox tries to gobble up the geese, and the geese try to trap the fox in a circle. It's good fun, it is."

Osric took his turn rolling the dice, and his total of three meant he would be one of the geese. Thomas rolled double sixes and became the fox. Around and around the table, the dice were passed and rolled. The fox pursued the geese, while the geese tried their best to elude or entrap the fox. In the end, all the geese were eaten amidst much laughter and promises of vengeance to be taken against the fox.

At the game's conclusion, Alexa did not sit down when she returned from putting the game away. "It's a lovely day, and I'm thinkin' a walk by the river is in order, I do."

Everyone at the table voiced their agreement with the exception of Peter and Thomas who explained they were to report for duty within the hour. Osric told the group he would be happy to join them, provided they could abide his slow pace. Everyone laughed, and assured him, speed was never the goal of a Sunday stroll by the river.

As they were making their way to the stairs, Osric quietly asked Carac about the two rough looking men sitting with Hadrian. Carac glanced over his shoulder, then whispered, "Oh, bloody hell, it's Leofrick and Barda. They muck out the pig sheds, the lowest job there is. The swine they clean up after are smarter than they are. They work on one of the more distant estates and seldom put in an appearance here, which is fortunate for them. If His Majesty knew them any better, he would have them sent away, and if they're listenin' to Hadrian, then they're up to no good." Carac's words did little to reassure Osric.

Alexa was not the only one who thought a stroll in the spring sunshine was a good idea, and there were many people making their way down the stairs to the outdoors. As the group stepped into the courtyard, Osric realized he was out-of-doors for the first time since arriving at the castle. They made their way across the courtyard, then out through the castle gate. As they walked toward the river, Osric realized Alexa was walking beside him. As it always did, her presence unsettled him in ways he did not begin to understand. As the group strolled in the shade of the large trees lining the river, Osric looked up and spotted Jarin sitting with his wife and child. He was nearly as happy to see the carter as he was to see Fendrel on the night the rat catcher saved his life.

"Jarin!" cried Osric as he hurried forward, extending his hand to the carter.

"Osric! It's good to see ya' man!" Jarin jumped up and began pumping Osric's hand. "So how is life in the castle treatin' ya? Is Walter gettin' ya all settled?"

"It's been bloody interestin', it has."

"Osric, this is me wife, Gwendolyn, and me son, Leo. Gwenny, this is the chap what traveled with me, I told you of."

The plump, blonde woman shifted the baby to her other arm and extended a hand to Osric. "I'm most pleased to meet ya, I am. Jarin told me of your adventures with the King on your journey."

The tinge of embarrassment Osric felt at being reminded of his exploits with the King was soon overcome by his happiness at seeing the carter again. They were joined moments later by Alexa, who also called out her greeting to Jarin and Gwendolyn.

"Hello to you Lexie, are ya takin' good care of me friend, Osric?

"He seems to be right capable of takin' care of himself, he does," laughed Alexa. As she spoke, they were joined by Carac, Winifred, and Gavin.

"Sit with us, sit with us," said Jarin smiling, and spreading his arm. "Winnie, Carac, it's good to see ya." Jarin eyed Gavin a moment, then continued, "Your lads are grown to be quite strappin' young men, Winnie, and I expect you will be a granny soon." Though Jarin had tended toward silence when traveling, the words were fairly flowing out of him on the banks of the river, and his rapid speech reminded Osric of Fendrel.

Winifred responded with a laugh and said she would be only too happy to see her sons marry and make her a grandmother. The group chatted amiably for the next hour, while young Leo was passed from lap to lap. At last, Carac and Winifred announced they were returning to their quarters, and Gavin elected to accompany his parents.

After Carac's family departed, Jarin repeated the story of Osric's adventures with the King, for Alexa. The carter embellished a bit and went into more detail, and the second telling of the story left her no less fascinated, leading her to chime in, "Osric had supper with the King last night, Jarin."

"Bloody hell! You didn't!" cried the carter, in astonishment.

"Aye, Jarin. It's true, though I wish it wasn't." Osric wished he could be alone with the carter, so he could tell him of the trap he had set for Brother Benedict, but thought better of doing so in a place where he might be overheard.

They visited until Gwendolyn announced it was time to get Leo home and feed him. Jarin said he would go with them, and bade Osric and Alexa good day. After the carter and his family departed, Osric found himself sitting alone with a woman, who was not a nun or the candle maker's foul wench, for the first time in life. His mind was in turmoil. He found himself wanting to speak to her but struggled to find words. At last, Osric managed to ask how she had come to live in the castle.

After a moment's thoughtful silence, she began, "As you may have guessed, Osric, dwarfs are not uncommon in our family. My mother was aunt Winifred's sister. Though I was not born in the castle, I remember no other place. My parents were not dwarfs and neither are my brothers and sisters. When I was but three years old, I was given over to the care of my aunt and uncle, and in every way that matters they are my true parents. Though their sons are my cousins, they are more like brothers to me than my own brothers ever were. I rarely saw my mother and father while I was growing up, and now that they're gone, I canna' honestly say I miss them much." Everything Alexa said was delivered with a quiet honesty. She betrayed not the hint of a tear, and Osric sensed a great inner strength residing within this person who continued to unsettle him in ways no one ever had.

Once they began talking, Osric found the conversation came easily. "Alexa, what do you know of this Hadrian chap, who is so upset with me?"

"Oh dear," said Alexa, shaking her head and sighing. "I hadn't realized he was upset with you, but if he is, then it's apt to get worse." She paused a moment before continuing, "He courted me once, and I rejected him. Even though I made it very clear that I would never want anything to do with the little worm, he has never gotten over it. He continues to get powerful jealous of anyone showing me any attention. Uncle has warned him to mind his behavior, but it does little to deter him."

"Oh, bloody hell," said Osric.

"Oh bloody hell, indeed," said Alexa, smiling at him. In the distance, the clock tower chimed and she said, "We should be getting back, Osric. We dine an hour early on Sunday evenings."

As they walked, side by side, back to the castle and up the stairs to the common room, Osric was taken with the sensation that he was now much lighter, and his shuffling walk became almost effortless. He thought walking beside Alexa to be almost as wonderful as the brown ale of The Dancing Pig. As they entered the commons, they found Walter and Arabella sitting at one of the tables in the room, rather than at the one the two of them usually occupied in front of the King's dais. Walter waved and invited Osric and Alexa to join them.

"Come sit with us, you two," said Arabella, smiling and waving. "We're never terribly formal, but we're quite informal for Sunday supper, Osric. This is a time when Walter and I like to sit and visit with people, and we wanted to ask how you enjoyed your first Sunday in the community."

The response of the dwarf community following his supper with the King, combined with spending the afternoon in Alexa's company had left Osric as happy as he had ever been. He felt much of the anger and bitterness that had defined his life, melting away. He told Walter and Arabella he had enjoyed his Sunday, and even though he had much to learn about the castle, he had come to see the community as a place where he wanted to stay. As he answered their questions, Hadrian, Leofrick, and Barda caught Osric's attention. The momentary distraction was enough for Walter to direct his attention to the three men, who were glaring at Osric.

That Walter was the leader of the dwarf community, was not a matter of chance. He sized up the situation in an instant, then said, in a muted voice, "This matter will be dealt with."

Well after the other dwarfs had returned to their chambers, Walter performed a duty required of him every evening before he retired. He opened the shutters of a window in his small sitting room, then looked across the courtyard to the Royal Wing. The task normally required but a few seconds to accomplish, but on this night Walter drew a sharp breath when he saw the red lantern glowing in a window of the keep. He was being summoned to attend the King. Walter pursed his lips for a moment, then closed the shutter.

He entered his bedchamber and sat on the bed next to Arabella. He bent and softly kissed his wife's forehead.

Walter and Arabella exercised caution, even in the privacy of their bedchamber, and spoke in whispers. "What is it, Luv?"

"I have been summoned, my dear."

Arabella's eyes went wide, "What do you think it means?"

Walter smiled, then kissed her forehead again. "I have my suspicions, but I will keep my own council for the moment. You know I will tell you the whole truth, once I know what it is, my dear."

Arabella smiled back as she squeezed his hand, "Yes Luv. I know that. You mustn't keep the King waiting. Go now."

Walter was silent as he passed through the deserted common room, then down the stairs. He unlocked the door to the tunnel, lit a lantern, then hurried down the stairs and under the courtyard. He appeared at the doors of the Royal Wing, less than ten minutes after seeing the red lantern. He tapped at the knocker and stood back. The small window opened for a moment, and Walter was admitted. He was not escorted to the large receiving room where the King had entertained Osric, but to a much smaller sitting room, used only by the royal family. Goran greeted him at the door with an expression that bespoke a comradeship, born of the duties and responsibilities the two men shared.

"Good evening, Walter."

"Good evening, Goran."

"He is expecting you." The butler pulled on a cord, and there came the faint tinkling of a bell on the other side of the door.

"Enter."

"Your Majesty, Walter has arrived."

"Show him in, then give us our privacy, Goran."

"Yes, Your Majesty."

Given the setting, and that Walter was the King's cousin, Goran made no formal announcement but simply motioned for the leader of the dwarf community to enter the room.

"Your Majesty," said Walter, bowing.

"Come in, and be seated, Walter." The King flashed a smile, then as he always did, asked, "And how is my old school master faring?"

"He is faring very well, Sire, and he trusts his old pupil is as well."

"He is indeed." The King smiled again, and as he had many times before, thanked Walter for having helped prepare him so well for leadership. Urloch II paused a moment, then said in a more serious tone, "Walter, I've summoned you to inquire how the new man, Osric, is adjusting."

Walter considered his words, then said, "It is, indeed, an adjustment for him, Sire. I have reason to think Osric led a most difficult life before he came to us, but he appears to be quite intelligent and has displayed a decent concern for others. I think he will become a valued member of the community."

The King told Walter of Osric's performance during the encounter with Rowan and how impressed he had been by it. He then related the subsequent developments regarding the tribal chieftain. "I think this man is well out of the ordinary Walter, and I want you to make every effort to ensure he finds a home here. I want to know if anyone interferes with that happening." The King paused again, letting eyes rest on Walter for a moment before continuing. "Is there anyone I should know about, Walter?"

Walter had no doubt the King already had the answer to the question. He knew his were not the only eyes and ears Urloch II had in the dwarf community. Ordinarily, Walter would not have raised the issue of Hadrian, and would have dealt with the man himself. However, he knew better than to be evasive when the King asked such a direct question. "It's Hadrian, Sire. He appears to find

Osric's presence most upsetting. I intend to call him aside upon the morrow and counsel him in the strongest possible terms not to be causing trouble."

"Do you think counseling him will dissuade him from further misbehavior?"

Walter paused . . ."One can never be certain with Hadrian, Sire. He can be very willful. If counseling fails to change his behavior, I will be forced to take stronger measures."

The King was silent for several seconds, then said, "I prefer not to wait on this matter, Walter. I want Hadrian sent away."

"How soon do you wish this done, Sire?"

"Do it tonight." The King tossed a bag of coins to Walter. "Give this to Hadrian. This will enable him to live decently for a few weeks. Encourage him to seek employment with traveling minstrels, and tell him he will forfeit his freedom should he ever attempt a return to the castle."

"Very well, Sire. Is there anything else, Your Majesty?"

"See to it, Osric is protected, Walter. You will be accompanied back to the dwarf quarters by guards who will attend to Hadrian's removal. He will be driven to an inn on the outskirts of the city, and be given his freedom in the morning. Good night, Walter."

"Good night, Sire.

In its youth, Castle Tyrion stood as a grand palace, and home to a vibrant court life at the heart of the city. The castle was the home of kings for many generations but became the official residence of the Lord Chamberlain following the construction of the current royal residence. Though Castle Tyrion has not moved, the center of the city shifted well to the east over the hundred years since the construction of the new palace. The Lord Chamberlain's residence was slowly reduced to a crumbling outpost, nearly an hour's walk from the home of Urloch II.

Castle Tyrion is a forbidding place, looking more like a prison than a palace, and has little to recommend it in the way of beauty. The common citizens of the city began referring to it as 'The Black Anvil', long ago. The meandering pile was built of a dark stone that has only grown darker with the passage of time. The darkening of the stone marked the slow decay of Castle Tyrion to where the habitable portion of the building had been reduced to the Lord Chamberlain's personal quarters, a barracks room for his guards, a stable, and a kitchen.

Alfred the cook found Castle Tyrion intimidating during daylight and much more so at night. He had been summoned to attend the Lord Chamberlain following Osric's supper with the King, and he trembled in fear as he waited to be received. The cook had no love for the Lord Chamberlain but did his bidding because he lived in constant fear of his parents being evicted from the farm they occupied on the Duke's estate. Alfred was escorted into the Lord Chamberlain's receiving room after midnight and found the Duke of Bruno sitting before the fire, drinking brandy.

The Lord Chamberlain continued to stare into the flames, as he asked in his hard, challenging, voice, "Tell me what happened tonight."

"Walter escorted that new dwarf, Osric, to supper with His Majesty in the royal chambers, M'Lord."

"I already know that, you damned fool! I want to know why!"

"From what I have been able to learn, M'Lord, the King was well pleased with something the dwarf did for him regarding some tribal chieftain. His Majesty appears to be right fond of the little bastard, he does. That's all I know M'Lord."

The Lord Chamberlain was silent for a few seconds, then slammed his fist against the arm of his chair, "Bah! . . . Keep your eyes and ears open, and let me know at once if you learn something new. You are dismissed!" The Lord Chamberlain turned and looked at Alfred for the first time, then tossed some coppers in his direction, forcing the cook to pick them up from the floor.

Chapter Twelve

An Uneasy Life

Walter returned to the dwarf quarters accompanied by two soldiers that he led straight to Hadrian's room. Walter pointed out the door, and one of the soldiers pounded on it with his fist, then entered without waiting for a response.

Hadrian stirred on his bed, then looked up in confusion. He could make out little in the dim light of Walter's lantern. "W-what is the meaning of this?"

This was not the first time Walter had been compelled to send a dwarf away, and experience had taught him not to waste words or time. "Get out of bed and dress yourself, Hadrian!"

"W-what is happening, Walter?"

"Hadrian, you are being sent away, by order of the King! If you force me to repeat my order, these men will assist you. If you attempt to call out, it will go very badly for you. Now, rise, and dress yourself at once!" Walter managed to convey a sharp sense of urgency while raising his voice very little.

Walter lit a candle in addition to the lantern he was carrying. When Hadrian's eyes focused, he saw the two soldiers resting their hands on the grips of their swords. He began to protest, but Walter had only to raise his finger, and Hadrian was silenced. Hadrian got out of bed, and as he dressed, the soldiers began stuffing his belongings into a leather bag. Hadrian found himself being marched down the spiral stairway leading to the courtyard less than ten minutes after Walter's arrival.

Jarin was waiting for them with his cart when they entered the courtyard. Before allowing the soldiers to lift Hadrian up to the seat, Walter handed over the bag of coins, and told the bewildered man the money was from the King. He then repeated the King's instructions regarding future employment and warned Hadrian against ever returning to the castle. The small man listened to it all in icy, venomous, silence. When Walter finished speaking, he nodded to the soldiers who then boosted Hadrian up to the seat alongside Jarin. The guards climbed into the back of the cart and stood behind the driver and his passenger. Jarin shook the reins and began driving away. Walter watched and did not return inside until the main gate closed behind the departing cart. The whole business left him very uneasy, and he could only hope he had seen the last of Hadrian.

Walter returned to his chambers, then bolted his door. Only the married dwarf's had doors that could be bolted from the inside. He removed a decanter from a cabinet, then poured a generous measure of brandy. Walter well understood his duty to the King and the necessity of Hadrian's removal, though neither of these things had made the evening's task any less odious to him. In his heart, he would have preferred dedicating his life to his books and students. However, short of removing himself from the King's protection in his old age, he saw little choice but to execute his sovereign's orders.

Walter was sitting in his arm chair, sipping brandy by the light of a single candle, when Arabella emerged from their bed chamber. She paused a moment, knowing her husband would not be drinking brandy at this late hour unless his mind was troubled. She smiled, but said nothing as she went to him. Walter made room for her on his lap, and as he had countless times before, held his wife as one might hold a child. She covered them with the shawl she had been wearing, as decades of their devotion passed between them. She turned her head, kissed his cheek, then reached for his brandy. She took a sip, then smiled at him, and he smiled back.

"What was it, Luv?"

"I've just sent Hadrian away, my dear."

Arabella sighed, as she nestled closer to Walter, "Oh, dear. I feared this would happen one day, I did. I've long worried that Hadrian's jealousy would be his downfall." She paused a moment, then lifted her face to Walter's, "Did something happen that moved the King to make this decision?"

"It's Osric, my dear. The King knew Hadrian was attempting to cause trouble for him. I don't know who else in the community reports to His Majesty, but as we've always known, there is someone. It seems our new man has gained the King's special favor, though I do not believe he ever sought it. We must exercise great caution in the days ahead."

"I fear Osric led a dreadful life before coming to us, but he seems decent enough in spite of it."

"That has been my impression as well. However, I fear events are beyond his control. We must do what we can to serve the King and the community, but we must always consider our own positions, my dear. We've grown too old to go out into the world, and begin a new life."

Arabella said nothing. She pressed her cheek to Walter's chest, and held him close.

Osric awoke the following morning to the knock on his door. He was now familiar enough with the community's routine to know what was expected of him. He dressed, then brushed his hair back with his hands. On this morning, he felt almost relaxed as he entered the common room. He spied Bertram sitting alone, and joined him. "Good mornin', Bert."

"Good mornin' to ya, Osric. What do they have you doin' today?"

Osric extended Bertram a dry smile, shrugged, and said, "That will be up to Arabella, I'm still learnin' me way around, I am."

"It takes some time, it does."

Osric and the cobbler were soon joined by two dwarfs Osric had not yet met. Their conversation was similar to his other mealtime discussions. Names were exchanged along with the jobs performed by his new acquaintances. The stories of Osric's journey to the castle and his supper with the King were now common knowledge in the dwarf community, and the two men assured Osric they bore him no ill will, as he had done nothing but obey the King's orders. Osric found the kind words comforting, but his relief proved to be short-lived as the people in the room became aware of Hadrian's absence. The mood shift within the room was noticeable, and as the murmuring voices grew louder, individuals began approaching Walter and whispering questions.

At last the leader of the dwarf community rose, and rang the small bell. When he had the room's attention, Walter said, "It is my duty to inform you that Hadrian has chosen to leave the community. He expressed his desire to seek a new life and departed the castle last night."

The volume of the voices rose, and Osric heard people near him asking, "Why would Hadrian leave without sayin' goodbye? Bloody strange! I'm thinkin' he was sent away, I do." As the people mulled over Hadrian's departure, many curious looks were cast in Osric's direction.

"Oh bloody hell," thought Osric.

Over the next week, Arabella continued escorting Osric around what he learned was called the domestic wing of the castle. Everywhere they visited, Osric found at least some of the workers to be dwarfs. There was nothing about any of the jobs that made them especially suitable for people of small stature, and it led Osric to ask Arabella why the castle employed so many dwarfs. Arabella told him the royal family had viewed it as a matter of Christian charity for generations. Dwarfs were often left with few opportunities in the wider world, and made to suffer through no fault of their own. Arabella told him Urloch II had been especially generous to the dwarf community, and he was the only King she knew of, to have ever taken meals in the common room.

As the week progressed, mealtimes grew more uncomfortable for Osric, as it came to be generally accepted, Hadrian had not left of his own accord. Though no one made any direct comment to him, he was left with the clear sense that at least some people were holding him responsible. He found the community's concern for the man puzzling, as Hadrian did not appear to have been well liked. Though Osric would not have characterized Carac and Winifred's behavior as unfriendly, he felt they too had put a certain distance between him and themselves. Things did not improve when word filtered back that Leofrick and Barda had also been dismissed from the King's service.

On Saturday morning Arabella escorted Osric to the tailor and cobbler shops where he was given his new clothes and boots. Two sets of his new clothing were comparable to what he was wearing when he arrived at the castle, while one set was much nicer. To his surprise, his new clothing also included a warm cloak for winter. Arabella explained the nice clothes were for church, Sunday dinner, and other special occasions that arose during the year such as Christmas and the King's birthday celebration. Bertram encouraged Osric to keep back one pair of boots to be worn with his good clothing as well, and to come by and get his boots blackened any time they were in need of it.

Osric struggled to make sense of it all. His old life, and his old anger now, seemed to belong to someone else. While in most ways, his life had improved beyond his wildest dreams, the persistent undercurrent of tension in the community in the wake of Hadrian's removal, kept him on edge. At times, Osric found himself close to actual prayer as he hoped the community would come to see that he had nothing to do with the three men being sent away.

Throughout the difficult week, Walter and Arabella continued to give Osric their support, as did Alexa who engaged him in friendly conversation when the opportunity arose. However, when Sunday came again, Osric found himself sitting with unfamiliar people, both at church and at dinner. Though there was no overt unkindness directed toward him, people seemed reluctant to engage him in conversation. He was not invited to join in a table game after dinner, and questions began stirring in his mind. He wondered just how much his life had improved if he was to be outcast within the community.

He was alone when he stepped out into the courtyard that Sunday afternoon. He explored around the outskirts of the castle grounds for a bit, then crossed the broad square and entered the shady cool of the large trees lining the river. As he hobbled along, trying to understand all that was happening to him, his melancholy evaporated when he spied Jarin and his family taking their leisure by the water's edge. When he was within hailing distance, Osric called, "Jarin!"

"Osric, me friend! Come join us."

Osric enjoyed the company of Jarin and his wife until Gwendolyn again announced it was time to take Leo home to feed and change him. As Jarin made to leave with his wife and child, Osric touched the carter on the arm, and asked if he might stay a bit longer so they might have a private word.

"Aye, Osric, of course." Jarin turned to his wife and said, "Run along, Gwenny, and I'll be home directly." Gwendolyn extended her husband a curious look, but said nothing. As she was leaving, Jarin asked, "What's on your mind, Osric?"

Osric surveyed the immediate area for curious ears, then said, "It's this business with Hadrian, Jarin. I don't know what to bloody make of it, I don't. People seem to think I had somethin' to do with him bein' sent away, but I ne'er did a thing to the man, and I ne'er spoke a bleedin' word to the other two what got sent away. No one seems to have had much love for any of 'em, and it seems bloody strange, it does. You're the only one I feel safe in askin' about it."

Jarin too, checked his surroundings before responding in a low, but intense voice. "I'm here to tell ya, Osric, it was a bloody long night for all of us when we took Hadrian away, it was. The little bastard refused to go to sleep, and the soldiers had to guard him all night long. I just hope the damned fool doesn't try comin' back to the castle or he might bloody well find his neck on the block." Jarin paused, before continuing in a more thoughtful tone, "As I told you, durin' the journey, the dwarfs are a good lot, mostly, but some can get powerful jealous, they can. I know that few people cared much for Hadrian, but he had been a part of the community for a long while, and that seems to matter a great deal to the dwarfs. As for the other two sods, they never lived in the castle, and no one seems to know much about 'em. They'll soon be forgotten." Jarin smiled at Osric for a moment, then clapped him on the shoulder, saying "Be of stout heart, me friend. Do as you're told, and do nothing that might reflect poorly on ya. Give it a bit of time, and it will get better. I'm sure of it, I am."

Though Osric had grave doubts Hadrian's removal would be forgotten any time soon, Jarin's words did have a calming effect, and he felt some relief for having heard them. He thanked Jarin and felt enough better to extend the carter a mischievous smile and ask, "Do you remember when we were travelin', and me tellin' ya of me troubles with Brother Benedict?"

"Aye, indeed, Osric. He sounds like a right miserable sod, he does."

Osric spoke in a conspiratorial voice, and told Jarin of the trap he had set for his life-long tormenter, whereupon Jarin dissolved into hysterical laughter. After several seconds, the carter managed to sputter, "Bloody hell, Osric!" before being seized by another round of convulsive laughter. When Jarin regained his composure at last, he clasped Osric's hand, "I best be gettin' back to me cottage, Osric, or Gwenny will go to frettin'. I hope to see ya again next Sunday, if not sooner."

"Goodbye, Jarin." Osric heard the bell tower chime, then got to his feet and began making his way back to the castle. Though he had lived the great bulk of his life in isolation, the loneliness he was feeling now had an altogether different quality, as it was coming when he found himself surrounded by people for the first time since leaving the orphanage. His anxiety eased a bit, when he was invited to join Carac's family for Sunday supper, and he found Alexa sitting next to him.

After breakfast on Monday morning, Osric was surprised when Walter came to him and announced he would be escorting him instead of Arabella. "My wife has completed the first part of your introduction to life in the castle, Osric. This morning, I am going to accompany you to meet Quinn, the royal candle maker. Given your experience in the candle making trade, I thought it best to begin with the candle shop as we find employment for you. Should he decline to take you on, we will explore other possibilities. Is there anything you would rather do, than work in a candle shop, Osric?"

"Candle makin' and bell ringin' are the only things I know, Walter, and I've little love for bell ringin'."

"Very well then, let us go and speak with Quinn."

It had not occurred to Osric that the candle maker would have a choice in whether or not to employ him, but as Walter explained, anyone entitled to use the world *Royal* ahead their job title had considerable latitude in how they chose to run their particular enterprise. Walter led Osric down the spiral stairway to the long hall leading to the tailor and cobbler shops. They walked past those places to the very end of the corridor, then turned a corner and proceeded down another long hallway Osric had not known existed until this moment. Osric's legs had grown weary by the time Walter entered a door bearing the image of a burning candle.

A tall man with curly gray hair looked up from his desk and seemed to sniff the air before speaking. "Oh, hello Walter. Good morning to you."

"Good morning to you, Quinn. . . . I would like to introduce you to Osric, who has recently come to live in our community. He has considerable experience in the candle making trade, and I wanted to speak to you about the possibility of him finding employment with you."

Quinn eyed Osric for a moment, sniffed the air again, then asked, "You've worked for a candle maker?"

"Aye, Sir."

"How long?"

Osric thought a moment, "I don't know exactly, Sir, but since I left the orphanage in my sixteenth year."

"Were you a guild member?"

"Nay, I was not a member of the guild, but my master was, Sir. I was just his helper."

Quinn fixed his eyes on Osric with a stare nearly as unnerving as Father Gregory's. "I expect you made tallow candles?"

"Aye, Sir. Mostly tallow candles. They are what the common people use. We made bee's wax candles ahead of Christmas each year, for the cathedral and the Count. We made soap four times a year, at the turnin' of each new season."

"I dislike the smell of tallow candles, as does His Majesty," sniffed Quinn. "They're sooty, and the King does not allow their use, anywhere in the castle. This shop does not make them at all." Quinn continued making Osric uncomfortable as he stared at him, coolly. "You do know beeswax candles are more difficult to make but are superior in every way, do you not?"

"Aye, Sir."

"We do make soap in this shop, but we serve far more people than your provincial candle maker, and we make it on the first week of each month. It is the only time we use any tallow. Do you know how to pump a bellows?"

"Aye, Sir. I've spent much time pumping the bellows, I have."

"You can keep the fire in the melting oven where it needs to be so the wax does not burn?"

"Aye Sir, I've done much of that, I have."

"Do you know how to make wick?"

"Aye, Sir I've made a great deal of wick, I have."

Quinn turned back to Walter, sniffed, then said, "I will give him a trial, Walter. I will grant him a month to prove himself. If he fails, I will return him to you."

"That is very fair, Quinn." Walter looked to Osric, and said, "I will leave you here Osric. Do you think you can find your way back to the commons for the midday meal?"

"Yes, Walter."

"Very well then. I will be on my way. Good day, Osric. Good day to you, Quinn, and thank you."

"Good day, Walter."

Everything about the royal candle shop was far from what Osric's idea of a candle shop should be. While his old employer had but one vat and oven in his melting room, the royal candle shop had six of each. Ash was not collected with each new season but was removed from one oven each Monday after the fire had been allowed to die and the ashes cool from the preceding Friday. All of the candle shop's ash removal now fell to Osric, beginning with his first day in the shop, and there would be no additional coppers for climbing inside the ovens. In fact, he learned there were to be no wages at all during his trial month with Quinn. There were other men who pumped the bellows, made wick, and dipped the candles. Osric was to become a regular Monday evening visitor at the bath house.

When he was not cleaning ash from an oven, Osric was put to work shaving down the large cakes of hard bee's wax into pieces more suitable for the melting vats, sweeping the floors, and any other disagreeable task that needed doing. Unlike his old shop, wood arrived at the royal candle shop as logs that first had to be cut to length, then split into pieces suitable for the ovens. Sawing and splitting wood came to occupy much of Osric's work day. The only good moments came if Jarin happened to be the carter delivering the logs, and he was able to exchange a few words with his friend. A very few words, to be sure, as Quinn hovered over the shop like a hawk, ready to pounce on any worker engaging in conversation lasting longer than the minimum necessary to get the work done. It did not take long for Osric to conclude, his new master was no brighter than his old one, and he had to resist the urge to wish all God's blessings on Quinn. The warnings he had been issued by Walter and Jarin, and his lingering fear of being subjected to an exorcism, kept his tongue in check.

In addition to the all hard work that went along with his new job, Osric was also faced with a considerable walk to and from the common room, where before he had only to climb the stairs to his garret. The distance and his slow pace left him with time to do little more than eat his midday meal before he had to begin trudging back to the candle shop. The weariness Osric felt at the end of the day, combined with the community's continuing coolness toward him, drove him to the solitude of his room soon after supper. However, if there was anything Osric knew how to cope with, it was being alone, and unlike the garret, his room in the castle had a window that afforded him a fine view of the courtyard and all of the activities there.

Though he always received a stein of ale with each meal, the stein in the common room was half the size of those Kurtz served up in The Dancing Pig, and there was never more than one of them. There was no ale house to visit that he knew of, and he had never heard anyone in the community speak of one. He resolved to question Jarin about alehouses at his first opportunity. Though Walter, Arabella, and Alexa were friendly to him, Osric's sense of isolation continued to grow, and the memories of his old life began to soften. More than anything, he missed Fendrel's company at The Dancing Pig, and Kurtz's wonderful brown ale. It led Osric to grumble under his breath, "A bleedin' thimble full of poor ale at the end of the day is almost worse than no ale at all."

Osric's third week in the candle shop saw no improvement, and it led to more questions about his new life. Though his days were filled with hard work and melancholy, a smile from Alexa in the common room was enough to quash any thoughts of running away. By the end of his first month in the royal candle shop, Osric had come to a grim acceptance of his new reality. Though the work was hard, and there was too much walking to suit him, he had a decent place to lay his head, he was well fed, and people were beginning to warm up to him, again.

The castle's work week ended on Saturday afternoon, when the bell tower announced three o'clock. Osric was resting in his room before supper when there came a knock on his door. He opened his door and was surprised to find Walter returning him an odd smile. "H-hello, Walter."

"Hello, Osric. May I come in?"

"Yes, of course." Osric stood aside, and then closed the door behind his unexpected guest. Being visited by the leader of the dwarf community made him very uneasy. "What is it, Walter?"

"Osric, I have just received word that you are to join the King for supper tonight."

Osric stared in wide-eyed disbelief for a moment, then cried, "What? No! Oh, bloody hell, Walter! I don't want to go!"

"I'm afraid you haven't a choice, Osric. To disobey the King will be far worse for you than anything that can come from dining with him."

"Why is this happenin', Walter? People have only just begun speakin' to me again after that damned business with Hadrian."

"I have no good answer for you, Osric. I know only that your appearance before the King has been ordered, and disobeying could put your freedom, or even your very life, at risk." Walter paused for a moment, taken aback by the stricken look on Osric's face. "Osric, be assured, Arabella and I will do everything possible to ensure the community knows this is not a matter of your choosing. On this, you have my word of honor."

"After the business with Hadrian, I don't think they'll listen to you, Walter."

Walter felt his own emotions rising and wished he could do more than offer his assurances the community would be told the truth. Until very recently, no dwarf had ever dined in the royal chambers, and now Osric was being ordered to do so for the second time in a bit over a month. Walter gave Osric his assurances again, then said, "For now, you must get to the bath house, then dress in your best clothes. I will return for you in an hour."

It was as if someone else had been ordered to dine with the King. Osric began experiencing an odd sensation of detachment and felt as if he were floating outside his body. When he failed to respond, Walter repeated his instructions. Like a man being roused from sleep, Osric managed to reply in a child-like voice, "Yes, Walter. A bath, then me Sunday clothes. One hour."

"Very good, Osric. Go now, and get thee ready. I shall return at the appointed time, and escort you to your audience with the King."

Osric complied with Walter's instructions. He went to the bath house, then donned his best clothing and was waiting in his room when Walter called for him. Though he accomplished these things, the sense of being outside his own body persisted until he found himself standing at Walter's side before the heavy doors of the Royal Wing.

The guards admitted Osric, and Walter was informed the King's guest would be escorted back to the dwarf community at the end of the evening. The guards then delivered Osric to Goran, who was waiting for him outside the doors of what proved to be a receiving room of modest proportions.

Goran gave Osric a brief inspection, then said, "I see you have received your new clothing, and you are at last properly attired for a royal audience. Come with me, and do not forget to remove your hat."

"Yes, Goran."

The King's butler pulled on a cord, and a moment later Osric heard the King's voice: "Enter."

Goran stepped inside the door, bowed, and said, "Your guest has arrived, Your Majesty."

"Excellent! Show him in, Goran."

Osric entered the room, and as he bowed before the King, Goran made his formal announcement. "The dwarf, Osric, appears before His Majesty, King Urloch II, as commanded."

"Hello, Osric."

"Hello, Your Majesty."

"Please seat my guest, Goran."

As it had been at his other audiences with the King, Osric was seated at a table scaled to suit a person of his stature, then presented with a stein of ale.

The King lifted his stein to his guest, and said, "To your health, Osric."

Osric returned the toast, "And to yours, Sire."

The King took a long drink, then let his eyes rest on Osric. "Do you know why you have been summoned Osric?"

"No, Sire." Something in the King's voice put Osric on guard.

The King paused a moment before continuing in a rather mocking tone, "Did you really think I would have your 'dear friend' sent away to a monastery without first investigating the matter, Osric?"

Visions of being tied to the whipping post danced before Osric's eyes, and his fear turned to raw terror. His nerves were on fire as he struggled in vain to answer the King's question, but the words would not come.

"Your King has asked you a question, Osric, and he wants an answer!"

With his eyes cast down, and his heart pounding, Osric managed to respond in the weakest of voices, "I had hopes you would, Sire." The King's eyes continued to bore into him for a very uncomfortable interval, and Osric feared he might wet himself as the tension became almost unbearable.

Osric's heart was near to exploding when the King raised his arm and pointed his finger at him. Another painful moment elapsed before the King exploded into laughter while banging his fist on the arm of his chair, and thundering, "WELL PLAYED, OSRIC! . . . BLOODY WELL PLAYED!"

Chapter Thirteen

Osric Decides To Run Away

The supper Osric was treated to was replete with much good food, and many steins of ale. The musicians performed for the King and his guest, but on the whole, the affair was a bit more subdued than Osric's earlier visit to the royal chambers. At various times during the evening, the King laughed, and expressed his admiration for the way Osric had settled his old score with Brother Benedict. It took Osric over an hour, and three steins of ale for his nerves to calm and his breathing to return to normal.

It wasn't until after the musicians had been dismissed and the King had consumed a considerable quantity of ale and brandy himself that he told Osric the story. "When my agent reported back to me, and I learned of how this Brother Benedict had mistreated you and other dwarfs, I was tempted to have him put in irons and flogged. After I considered the matter, I decided honoring your request to be the most appropriate course of action. I presented the Arch-Bishop with several bottles of fine wine, and at my suggestion he arranged to have your 'dear friend' removed to an island monastery in the Adriatic. It's an inhospitable place, well beyond the sight of land, and seldom visited by anyone. Barring divine intervention, your 'dear friend' will be buried there."

When the King completed his story, it took all of Osric's will power to keep from breaking into laughter, and shedding tears of joy, but he expressed his thanks with only a small smile and a bow of his head. As the evening was drawing to a close, the King extended Osric a bemused smile and asked, "Do you have any other 'dear friends', you would like to reward Osric? I caution you in advance never to repeat what you did for Brother Benedict."

The King did not enunciate his words with his usual clarity, and Osric proceeded with a boldness born of his own ale consumption. He paused a moment, then said with deep sincerity, "There is one man, Sire. A truly dear friend, who saved me life only a few days before your visit to my town."

"You would not be so foolish as to attempt deceiving your King, would you Osric?"

"Nay, Sire."

"Very well then, tell me of your friend."

"His name is Fendrel, Your Majesty. Fendrel, the rat catcher. He is the dearest friend I e'er had, and I sorely miss his company."

"What would you like me to do, Osric?"

"Fendrel would be a most excellent royal rat catcher, Sire, if e'er you had need of one."

The King considered Osric's words a moment, then turned to his butler and asked, "Goran? To your knowledge, has there ever been a royal rat catcher?"

"Rat catchers from the city have been employed from time-to-time, as we had need of them Sire, but there has never been a royal rat catcher in residence in the castle during my time of service, and I have never heard of one being employed in the past."

The King looked to Osric and deadpanned, "Goran supervised construction of the castle, when work was begun over a hundred years ago, and he would know if anyone would." The King's remark caused a flicker of embarrassment to cross the old butler's face, while Osric released an involuntary guffaw. The moment of levity soon passed, and the King returned to his normal countenance.

"Find someone to escort Osric back to the dwarf quarters, Goran. I bid the both of you a good night."

Osric rose when the King did and kept his head bowed until Urloch II passed through a set of doors at the back of the room. Though his eyes were cast down, he could see just enough to notice the King was rather unsteady on his feet. Osric found that he too had some difficulty walking straight, as a member of the household guard escorted him back to the domestic wing. When they reached the long hallway at the top of the tunnel stairs, Osric was asked if he could complete the walk back to the dwarf quarters on his own, and he was only too happy to do so. He was grateful to be alone with the wild thoughts racing through his mind, "Oh, what a bleedin' night this has been! I was near to pissin' meself when the sod started laughin', I was. But if it means I'll be seein' Fendrel again, then it was bloody well worth it." Osric paused a moment, then muttered, "Bah! I'm only foolin' meself. I'll ne'er see Fendrel again."

Early on Sunday morning as most members of the royal household staff were preparing for church, Alfred spotted the red pennant flying on the distant rampart of Castle Tyrion. Following an hour's walk, he found himself in the entrance hall of The Black Anvil, awaiting an audience with the Lord Chamberlain.

Alfred knew the King had again dined with the dwarf, Osric, in the royal chambers. He had been diligent in gathering as much information as he could, though he feared the Lord Chamberlain would be disappointed. Hadrian's removal had badly compromised his ability to keep abreast of events in the dwarf community. Alfred was now in the business of scouting for someone to replace Hadrian as the Lord Chamberlain's eyes and ears among the dwarfs.

The Lord Chamberlain's butler frightened Alfred nearly as much as the Duke himself. When he appeared in the hall, Alfred braced himself against the upcoming meeting. The butler escorted Alfred into the room, then said in a very formal voice, "My Lord, your guest has arrived as ordered."

The Lord Chamberlain was being assisted by his valet in dressing for a hunt, and did not look at Alfred, but said, tersely, "Speak!"

"M'Lord, as I'm sure you know, His Majesty once again received the dwarf named Osric, in the royal chambers. I have made several inquiries regarding the purpose of this visit but have learned nothing definite. One of the servers I questioned said he had the impression the King simply enjoys this dwarf's company."

"You've no idea what was said?"

"The King was greatly amused by the dwarf having arranged to have someone sent away to a monastery. Then, at the end of the evening, he asked if there was anyone else he would like to help."

"He's doing royal favors for a dwarf?"

"So it seems, M'Lord."

"If you want your family to remain on my farm, then you had best not withhold anything from me, Alfred! Dismissed!"

Osric awoke the next morning to the knock on his door, sharp pain in his back, and a grinding headache. He rose, then went to his window and looked across the courtyard to the clock tower. He saw that Walter was not allowing him to sleep in the way he had following his first supper with the King. Osric donned the Sunday clothes he had worn the night before and hoped they did not reek of ale. He drank from his pitcher even though he was forbidden to do so, then made his way to the commons. Carac appeared to have entered the room only a moment earlier, and Osric went to assist him in converting the space into a church.

Though the smithy's helper was not rude, it soon became evident he was maintaining his distance, and they exchanged few words while they moved furniture. All through church, and Sunday dinner, everyone in the community, save Walter and Arabella, were very cool to him. It seemed that all the good will that had been restored since the removal of Hadrian had been undone. "Oh bloody hell," thought Osric, as his spirits sank to new depths, "Oh, bloody, bloody hell."

There was to be no walk by the river that Sunday. The skies were the color of lead, and the sound of the wind penetrated the stone walls and heavy windows of the common room. Torrents of rain arrived before Sunday dinner was complete, accompanied by great flashes of lightning and crashing thunder. A few members of the community gathered by the windows and watched the storm, while most people played games and socialized. Osric returned to his room alone and pulled one of his chairs near the window. The storm brought back vivid memories of that terrible afternoon in the bell tower ahead of the King's visit, and his subsequent collapse in the square. He watched the storm until there came a lull in the thunder, then got into his bed, and closed his eyes. Osric was possessed by a fatigue that went beyond the physical. In the space of a day, he had grown weary of life. He could have never imagined such loneliness to be possible when surrounded by other dwarfs. As he drifted into slumber, all the familiar things of his old life became softer and gentler in his mind, and he was filled with longing.

He fell into a deep sleep the storm's return did not disturb. Wild dreams took him back to The Dancing Pig, and Fendrel. He drank brown ale with the rat catcher in a place that was both his garret and The Dancing Pig, while they shared bout after bout of silent laughter, reveling in delight at the thought of Brother Benedict living out his life in a bleak, island monastery. He was roused by a rapping at the door, and he crossed the room to answer it. Osric found, to his astonishment, the rat catcher standing before him with the strap of his leather bag over his shoulder, grinning from ear-to-ear.

"Osric, me friend! Are ya gonna invite me in?"

Osric was too stunned to speak and leaped forward to seize Fendrel's hand. The hand disintegrated beneath his touch, then Osric awoke with a jolt to find himself on the floor beside his bed with his arms wrapped around his pillow. It took a few seconds for the reality of the stormy afternoon to return, and when it did, he was filled with melancholy. "I feel like a bleedin' child, I do," muttered Osric, as he climbed back into bed. He buried his face in his blanket, as he tried in vain to stem the flow of tears. He drifted into a strange state of being neither fully awake nor asleep. His mind was a wild collage of the people and places that had shaped his life. Brother Benedict locked him in the child's coffin, but he was soon rescued by Fendrel. They were pursued by the tribal chieftain, and the Lord Chamberlain as Jarin drove them all to the safety of The Dancing Pig. Once inside, they enjoyed a fine meal served up by Sister Adele, who was now a tavern wench. Later, the candle maker aided him in ringing the bells in the alleyway behind the alehouse, while his foul wench danced with Father Stephan to the music of the King's minstrels.

A persistent knocking at his door finally roused Osric from the strange dream state. He sat up and blinked his eyes as he returned to consciousness. From outside the door, he heard Walter calling between knocks, "Osric? . . . Osric?"

He got to his feet, then shuffled across the room without the aid of his stick, and opened the door, "Y-yes Walter?"

"Are you quite alright, Osric?"

Though he was far from alright, he responded, "Y-yes Walter. Is something the matter?"

"I was told there were strange noises coming from your room, as if you were in pain."

Osric was an accomplished liar and quickly moved to hide the truth from the leader of the dwarf community. He laughed a little, shrugged, then said with a small smile, "I feel like a damn fool, I do. I fell asleep, and me dreams caused me to tumble out of bed. I've ne'er done that since I was a wee child."

Walter did not appear to find the explanation convincing, and fixed his eyes on Osric for a few seconds before asking, "Are you sure that's all it was, Osric?"

He had come to respect Walter, and it pained him a bit to expand upon the lie he had already told. "Oh yes, Walter. I'm quite sure, I am." As Walter continued to rest his eyes on him, Osric's survival instincts took over, and his true feelings were kept well hidden.

"What on earth were you dreaming about, Osric?"

Though, in fact, he remembered the strange dream in great detail, Osric responded, "Oh, I ne'er remember me dreams, Walter. I forgets 'em as soon as I wakes up."

Walter stared at Osric a few more seconds, then let the matter drop. "Very well then, Osric. We will be dining in a few minutes, and I wouldn't want you to miss your supper."

"Yes, Walter. I will be down directly." Osric closed the door, then went to his sink and poured water into the basin. He splashed water on his face, then waited until the water became still. He spent several seconds looking at his reflection, then whispered softly, "It canna' be any worse than dealin' with Brother Benedict in the bleedin' bell tower." Osric took a deep breath and braced himself for a return to the common room.

Not many people had left the commons on that stormy afternoon, and there were few empty chairs when Osric returned for supper. To his regret, Carac and Winifred were surrounded by their family, and there were no openings at their table. Osric decided to join two men, whom he knew little of, at their small table. A moment after he sat his tray down, one of the men rose and went to sit elsewhere. Though Osric found this action hurtful, he did not respond to the provocation. He nodded to the remaining man, and said, "I'm Osric. I work in the candle shop."

The man hesitated a moment before speaking, "I know who ya are. I'm John, I work in the cooperage." Little more was said as they ate their meal. Osric was preparing to return his tray to the rolling table when John ventured to ask, "How did it come to be that you're takin' supper with the King? Are ya some kind of bloody nobleman?" There was neither kindness nor humor in the man's voice.

Osric clenched his jaw, and said through his teeth, "I'm no bloody nobleman! I was raised in a stinkin' orphanage and put to work with a candle maker when I was but a lad of sixteen. I've no bleedin' idea why the King has invited me to supper, and it was never a matter of my choosin'."

John eyed Osric for a few seconds, then arched his eyes and responded with a trace of sarcasm, "I'm thinkin' ya know more than you're lettin' on, I do. Everyone knows you've become the King's special favorite." John appeared to be on the verge of taking the accusation further, but Osric's bulging arms and the fingers that were tightening around his oaken stick ended the discussion.

Osric returned to his room after Sunday supper, as depressed as he had been since coming to live in the castle. He went to the window and gazed out at the courtyard until the last of the gray afternoon faded to black. A vague plan began taking shape in his mind, as he considered ways he might escape the castle. He thought he could probably steal enough bread to last him three or four days, but what would he do then? If he could not find work, he would be reduced to beggary, and he had never begged for anything. Then, in a flash, he remembered the Silver Swan he had hidden away since receiving it from the King as payment for his services as a royal minister, and his thoughts of running away took on a new urgency. "A Silver Swan will buy bread and ale for a bleedin' month or more," thought Osric, with rising excitement. He fell asleep filled with thoughts of escape, but his sleep was plagued by troubling dreams, and he slept poorly. When the knock came on his door the following morning, he found it very difficult to rouse himself.

Over the next few weeks it became apparent Quinn was also harboring resentment over Osric's access to the King, and this did not make life in the candle shop any easier. He continued experiencing fitful sleep, and the stresses in his life led to an even deeper sense of isolation. Walter spoke to him on several occasions and assured him all the members of the community had been made aware of the truth. Though Osric always thanked him for his efforts, it was evident the leader of the dwarf community had been unable to influence the situation in Osric's favor. This difficult period continued until after the Mid-Summer Night's Eve festival. The only bright spots during this dismal time came on Sunday afternoons when he was able to escape the community and meet Jarin by the river for a few hours. Then, for two long weeks, Osric saw nothing of the carter, either on Sundays or delivering logs to the candle shop during the week.

Osric's Sunday routine had become set. He had no expectation of being invited to join anyone for games and conversation after dinner, and as soon as he returned his tray to the rolling table, he made straight for the spiral stairway that led down to the courtyard. After two weeks without seeing Jarin, his spirits were very low as he passed through the castle gate and made his way across the square. He came close to actual prayer as he began searching for Jarin in the crowd of people enjoying the summer afternoon by the riverside. He trudged along, venturing farther down the stream than he ever had. He was nearly out of hope and was resigning himself to spending yet another Sunday alone when, to his joy, he spotted the carter sitting with Gwendolyn and Leo.

He hobbled forward, exceeding even the pace he had been forced to walk with a lance at his back, ahead of his first meeting with the King. "Jarin!" called Osric, his voice cracking with emotion.

"Osric, me friend! I was hopin' to see ya today. Come and join us, I've news to tell ya."

Osric hurried forward and seized Jarin's hand. "I've missed ya' Jarin. Have ya' been away?"

"Aye, indeed I have Osric. I was travelin' with the King again, I was."

"Bloody hell! No one told me. I had no idea you were away."

"Seems a bit odd, it does. I would have thought Walter would have mentioned it to ya."

"Nay, Jarin. No one said a thing to me. Where ever have you been, and what news do you have for me?"

"I've been back to your town, Osric. It seems the Count extended the King an invitation to return for hunting during the time when you came to join us. We were there for a whole week, while His Majesty, the Count, and several other noblemen hunted wild boar and stags. It seems the hunting thereabouts is quite good, and His Majesty had never hunted there. When the weather was right, they took their birds out and hunted small game with them as well."

Talk of his town filled Osric with homesickness. "Did ye get the chance to walk about the town a bit, Jarin?"

"Aye, indeed, Osric. The stable master gave me leave to go into your town on market day, and have a look-see. I went to the candle shop where you once lived and saw that the window, what the horse broke, had been replaced. I sought out folk in the square I thought I might trust, and I asked after you. It seems you've become quite famous in your town, after killin' the King's horse and all." Jarin paused, and shook his head, smiling and laughing softly at the memory of Osric's battle in the square, before continuing, "One lad I spoke with, I forget his name, said he had often delivered tallow to your candle shop, and remembered you well. He was the one what told me I should visit The Dancing Pig and inquire after a chap named Fendrel. Well, I did just that, and I met up with him, I did. Quite a fine fellow, he is too."

"You met Fendrel?" Osric stared wide-eyed at the carter, as he was overcome with emotion.

"Aye. We shared some ale, and toasted ya, we did." Jarin grinned at Osric, then added, "That man Kurtz brews some damned fine ale too, by God! Damned fine ale!"

Osric continued to be gripped by emotion as he listened to Jarin tell his story. At last he asked, in a small voice, "And, is Fendrel faring well?"

"He's well, and misses ya' greatly, Osric. Fendrel said he is quite busy with his rat catchin', as he always is in summer. He sends ya his best regards and hopes you are well and happy in your new life. He said the Harvest Festival won't be the same without ya." Jarin paused a moment, "I ne'er let on anything about you havin' supper with the King and all, and the troubles it caused ya. Oh, and I nearly forgot, Fendrel told me your old master has employed a new dwarf, and he's now livin' in the garret."

"Oh, bloody hell," said Osric, out of pure reflex. Though he did not miss either the candle maker or the garret, the thought of another person living in the place that had been his home for so long, left him feeling very peculiar.

The afternoon passed too quickly, and long before Osric was ready to say goodbye, the clock tower informed him he must return, or miss his supper. The thought of another person living in the garret drove home the reality, that a chapter of his life had now closed forever, and there could be no returning to his old master. These thoughts weighed on his mind after he bade Jarin good day, and began trudging back to the castle. He could not make himself believe the King would actually bring Fendrel to the castle, and he became so focused on running away, he would have been hard pressed to recall any detail of his supper that evening.

The next afternoon, as Osric was brushing himself off after cleaning ash from the smallest melting oven, he noticed a bag made of heavy cloth lying on the wood pile and wondered what it might be doing there. He spent the rest of his Monday cutting wood, and when he returned with an arm load, he moved the bag to one side before adding his wood to the pile. "What bloody good luck! I could never leave without something to carry me things in." He kept his eye on the bag and found himself a little happier with each return trip when no one reclaimed it. As he stacked the last piece of wood of the day, he glanced around the room, and when no one was watching, he slipped the bag under his jersey and pressed it flat against his chest.

Later, in the privacy of his room, he examined the bag and discovered a tear in its bottom. "I canna' believe someone threw this away, because of this tear. People in the castle dunno how easy their lives are, and they've never had to do without. This can bloody well be mended, it can." He knew exactly the person to speak to. Angmar had, after all, invited him to come and see her. Osric resolved to stop by the tailor shop on his way to work the following morning and ask for her assistance. Though he was still leery of the woman's lewd advances, Osric thought it was an acceptable risk because he was now more determined than ever to run away, and did not plan to be in the castle much longer.

The next morning at breakfast, Osric was greeted with the same coolness he had experienced over the past several weeks, though it now bothered him a good deal less, as he thought, "I'll be kissin' this lot goodbye in a few days, and they can go hang themselves." After breakfast, he returned to his room long enough to hide the bag under his jersey, then departed a bit early for the candle shop as to allow him time to pay a call on Angmar. When he reached the tailor shop, Osric took a deep breath, then knocked. As he had seen Arabella do, he entered without waiting for a response.

"Osric! Ya handsome devil! You've come to see me at last!" laughed Angmar, the moment he entered the shop.

Osric had always thought of Angmar as being rather old but was startled by the sudden realization that she was probably younger than he. Struggling against his flash of embarrassment, he did his best to smile, then said, "Good mornin' to ya Angmar. I was wonderin' if ya might could help me with a wee job of mendin'?"

"Of course I can, Luv. What is it that needs mendin'? Did you tear your new trousers?"

"Nay, me trousers are fine." He withdrew the bag from beneath his jersey and showed it to the seamstress. "Someone pitched this away, and I'm thinkin' it would be easy enough to mend. It would be right useful to keep me things in, it would."

Angmar inspected the bag and shook her head as she responded, "Aye, easy enough to fix for sure, Osric. Some folks can be right wasteful, can't they? I'll sew a piece of material over the tear on the inside, and it will be better than new." She looked back to Osric, and asked, "Are ya needin' it straight away, Luv?"

"Nay, I was thinkin' I would leave it with ya, and fetch it back at day's end, or even tomorrow."

"I'll have if for you this evenin', Luv." She paused a moment, then asked, "How is life in the castle treatin' ya, Dearie? I heard about ya havin' supper with the King. What in bloody hell was that like?"

He responded in a very low voice. "I ne'er want to do it again, I don't. It was not a matter of my own choosin', and I've told everyone who would listen, they're welcome to take me place, should he invite me back."

"I do not envy you, Luv. I'm satisfied with what I have, I am. I've no desire to be rubbin' shoulders with the high and mighty."

"Nor, do I, Angmar. I must be goin' now. Thank ye, for helpin' me."

"Think naught of it, Dearie."

He continued on to the candle shop, with a higher opinion of Angmar, thinking, "She jests a bit, but like Arabella said, she has a right good heart, she does." His work day was no better, or worse than his others. Quinn said little to him, and Osric spent most of his day in the small courtyard outside the candle shop, sawing and splitting wood. Though he interacted with his coworkers very little, he kept his ears open for any comments regarding the missing bag and was pleased when no one mentioned it. "I guess someone really was throwing the bleedin' thing away. That's their loss, it is." Now that he had a definite plan in mind for escaping the castle, he came to see his isolation in the community as an advantage that would help him slip away.

Osric stopped at the tailor shop on his return to the common room, and Angmar greeted him with a cheery smile, "Hello, Dearie. I've got your bag all mended, I do. I covered the tear with a scrap piece of strong material and stitched it good. It'll last ya a long time, Luv."

"Thank you, Angmar. I have a few coppers, and I can pay ya."

"Nay, Luv. I'm not allowed to take any payment from folk livin' in the castle. I'm paid me wages from the King's purse, just as you are." Angmar paused a moment, then extended Osric a saucy smile, "Ya could come *pay* me a visit after Sunday dinner, if you've a mind to. Me room is right in back of the shop. No one ever comes by on a Sunday. You'll be glad ya did."

"Oh bloody hell," thought Osric, as he felt his chest tightening. "I-I, dunno what to say, Angmar."

"No need to say anything Dearie, but think it over." Angmar paused, then added with a soft smile, "It's a real invitation, Luv."

Oh bloody hell were the only words that came to his mind, until he was at last able to sputter, "I-I'll think about it, Angmar. Thank you again for mendin' me bag."

"You're welcome, Luv, and don't be forgettin' what I told ya."

Having the means to carry his things sped up Osric's plans for leaving, and all through the rest of the week, he pilfered what food he could. He calculated that by week's end, he could collect enough to sustain him for at least three days. He even managed to get one of the small pewter ale steins back to his room. The stein would make it much easier to drink from the streams he hoped to encounter on the road to the unknown. He stored it all in the bag. His initial plan was to simply walk out of the common room after Sunday dinner with his bag in hand and hope no one noticed. Then, it occurred to him to look out his window. Osric stood on a chair, then pulled himself up over the sill. When he looked below, he saw a bushy shrub growing near the castle wall. "That's bleedin' perfect!" he said, rather too loudly. "I can just drop the bag into the bush, and walk out with nothin' but me stick in me hand, like any other Sunday."

When he began packing on Saturday night, it soon became obvious the bag would not hold all of his belongings. He opted to leave the Sunday clothes behind, as well as what he was wearing when he arrived at the castle. Osric decided it was essential to pack the cloak as it could double as a blanket, and his spare boots were too valuable to leave behind. He packed carefully and put the food inside his boots. Satisfied with his efforts, he hid the bag under his bed and donned his night shirt. As he drifted off to sleep, he was struck by the thought that he might be spending his last night in an actual bed, for a long time to come.

Though Osric took little notice of those around him the following morning at church, and then at Sunday dinner, several members of the community commented to one another that Osric looked happier than he had of late. Not knowing when, or if, he might enjoy a good meal again, Osric ate everything he could, then returned to his room and changed into his best set of work clothes. He pushed a chair to the window, then climbed up and unlatched it. He took a careful look around. If anyone saw him drop the bag, his escape could be foiled before it began. However, most people were still enjoying their dinner, and the guards always faced away from the castle. Osric decided not to hesitate, as activity in the courtyard would only increase as people left to go walking. He took another careful look. When he did not see anyone looking in his direction, he dropped the bag into the bush. The bag's trip took less than two seconds, and Osric hoped with all his heart no one had seen it fall.

He continued to observe the courtyard for a few more seconds, and when no one made a move to where the bag landed, he closed the window. Osric took a last look at the little room. So clean, so comfortable, so warm and dry. It was, by far, the nicest place he had ever lain his head. That he was prepared to trade such comfort for the unknown, was a measure of the alienation he had come to feel in the dwarf community. The moment of introspection did not last long, because he wanted to put the greatest possible distance between himself and the castle in the event anyone went looking for him. Osric braced himself, then closed the door behind him. He strode down the hall, and through the commons to the stairway. He kept his eyes pointed straight ahead acknowledging no one as he marched out of the dwarf community.

Osric gained the courtyard, then scuttled around to the bush, and retrieved his bag. Now, if he could just make it out of the castle without being questioned, he would be on his way. He hoisted the bag to his shoulder and began walking with a purpose. Osric's heart was pounding as he passed through the gate then on to the drawbridge without being challenged. Then, he was over the bridge and into the square. There were more people around him now, and dwarfs being a common sight in the vicinity of the castle, no one paid any attention to him. He hoped being among people would make him less conspicuous, and this proved to be the case as he was able to reach the far side of the square without being stopped. Instead of entering the trees, Osric stuck to the cobblestone street that paralleled the river, as it would make for faster walking, and he believed it to be the route leading out of the city.

After nearly an hour of heavy exertion, he knew he had forced his weak legs far beyond their normal limit and he must stop to rest. He moved off the track, then sat down and concealed himself in the shrubbery. His heart was beating rapidly, and he was perspiring. He looked around and saw no place to drink, other than the river which was now some distance away. Osric thought about it for a while, then decided he could go a bit longer without water. He would rest then put more distance between himself and the castle. He would turn toward the river for the night, then rest as long as he wanted. As Osric's legs were recovering, he heard the sound of horses approaching, and shifted himself to deeper cover, muttering, "Bloody hell, are they looking for me already?" Then, to his relief, he realized the horsemen were moving toward the castle, not away from it. He was still free!

Exercising caution, Osric peered through the bushes and watched the riders as they cantered past. What he saw stunned him as nothing ever had. There, surrounded by four soldiers and looking none too steady on his mount, rode Fendrel.

Chapter Fourteen

Osric Has New Hope

sric crawled out of the bushes, then struggled to his feet as hot pain flooded his legs. His hard march away from the castle had taken a heavy toll. He hobbled out to the middle of the road and watched as the horsemen continued on their way to the castle. Osric leaned against his stick and remained transfixed until the riders disappeared over a hillock. Though he wanted nothing so much as to crawl back into the bushes and rest, he muttered, "I canna' bloody run away now. I must start back before I find meself locked out, and banished from the community." Osric's pain was being offset to a degree by his joy at having seen Fendrel. Once he began walking he felt rather light on his feet, in spite of his fatigue. As he trudged toward the castle, he heard the bell tower chiming in the distance, and he knew there was no chance his slow pace would get him back in time for supper. His only hope now was getting there ahead of the closing of the gate.

His euphoria was short lived. With his legs growing ever weaker and needing frequent rest, Osric's journey back to the castle lasted far longer than his march away from it. He hobbled into the courtyard, only minutes ahead of the gates being sealed for the night. Never had the spiral stairway been longer or steeper. His pain was intense, and he feared his legs might fail before he reached the top and send him tumbling back to the bottom. He was unable to climb more than three steps without resting and was twice forced to sit down to keep himself from falling. Sitting eased his pain but proved to be a mixed blessing as getting back to his feet became more difficult each time he rose. All through the arduous climb, Osric prayed he would not encounter anyone and be called upon to explain himself. He was as relieved as he had ever been when he topped the final step and emerged into the common room.

The commons usually cleared out soon after Sunday supper, and Osric was grateful to find the room deserted. Just a few more agonizing steps and he would be back in his room without having been questioned. He hobbled across the large room and was a step away from his hallway when Walter appeared from his own hallway. Osric felt a wave of humiliation sweep over him but said nothing and continued on. In spite of everything, he felt remorse at the thought of having failed Walter. When he closed his door at last, he made straight for his pitcher and drank it all. He was grateful to be alone and for the opportunity to rest his burning legs. Osric opened his bag and retrieved the bread he had hidden in his boots. He had just begun eating when there came a knocking at his door. Fearing the worst, and too weary to move, Osric took a deep breath, then called out, "Come in."

Walter stuck his head inside the door. "Hello, Osric. May I come in?"

"Y-yes of course, Walter." To his relief, Walter displayed no anger, and his tone was that of a concerned father.

Walter closed the door behind him, then asked, "May I sit down, Osric?"

"Yes, of course, Walter." Osric felt as if he was about to be judged by God himself.

Walter sat down at the table and rested his sad eyes on Osric before he spoke. "My wife and I noticed your absence at supper, so I checked your room, and you were not here. I made some inquiries, and Alexa told me she had seen you leaving the common room soon after dinner this afternoon, well before most people had finished eating. When you did not return for supper, I began keeping a watch for you. I saw you from my window when you entered the courtyard carrying a bag. Is there anything you would like to talk about, Osric?"

Osric was physically and mentally exhausted, humbled, and humiliated. He knew this was not a time to be evasive. "I ran away, Walter, but I changed me mind and came back."

Walter extended Osric an understanding smile, then said just above a whisper, "I feared that might be the case. You're fortunate to have made it back before the gate closed, or you would not have been allowed to return. That is His Majesty's firm rule." There was a heavy silence before Walter continued, in a soft voice, "I'm very sorry things became so uncomfortable for you here that you felt it necessary to leave us, but I am glad you changed your mind and returned before it was too late. Arabella and I have been very worried about you."

Walter's kind words and lack of anger filled Osric with gratitude. He hung his head, shame- faced, and said, "I'm sorry to have caused you worry Walter. You and Arabella have shown me more kindness than anyone ever has."

Walter took his time before asking, in a gentle tone, "What made you change your mind about leaving, Osric?"

Osric struggled to organize his thoughts, then began, "When I had supper with His Majesty, he asked if there was anything he might do for me. I told him of me friend Fendrel who saved me life a few days before His Majesty came to visit my town. I told him Fendrel would be a most excellent royal rat catcher, if e'er he had need of one. I ne'er dreamed he would really order Fendrel to the castle, but this afternoon when I was well away from here, I saw Fendrel ridin' past with some soldiers. I knew then, I must return."

Though Walter had spent a lifetime dealing with kings, and royal politics, he was still astonished that Urloch II had made such an offer, and very impressed that Osric was quick witted enough to seize upon the opportunity. "Most remarkable, Osric . . . most remarkable indeed." Walter smiled at him and said, "My instincts tell me the castle will soon be served by a royal rat catcher."

"Will Fendrel be livin' in the castle, if he becomes the royal rat catcher, Walter?"

"Unlikely. Few people other than dwarfs and the household guard are billeted in the castle, Osric. If it proves true that your friend is the new royal rat catcher, then he will likely be assigned a King's cottage outside the castle walls."

"How is it that Angmar lives in the castle?"

"Angmar once lived in this community. She was married to a dwarf named Richard, who was a tailor, like herself. She was also the mother of a dwarf, named William. Both her husband and her son were taken by sickness when young William was but three years old. That was nearly five years ago. It was a very difficult time for her. Though Angmar no longer resides in the community, His Majesty allowed her to remain in the castle."

He did not know what to say, but once again his opinion of Angmar rose. At last, Osric said in a humble voice, "I'm grateful you are not angry with me, Walter. I'm feelin' much better about things, I am."

As Walter rose to take his leave, he shook Osric's hand, and again welcomed him back to the dwarf community. "Be of stout heart Osric. Things are improving, even if it isn't apparent. I know of no reason why you would not be allowed to visit your friend on Sundays, and that should make your life better." Walter paused and looked into Osric's eyes, "I keep my ear very close to the ground in this community, and please trust me when I tell you the mood is shifting in your favor."

When he was roused the next morning, his state of mind was much improved, though his legs were still feeling the effects of his escape attempt. Walter's words combined with a good night's rest and having seen Fendrel, left Osric almost giddy with happiness. He dressed after splashing some water on his face, giving little thought to what might await him in the common room. When he arrived at breakfast the clamor of voices quieted, and he found many eyes upon him. The stares were not hostile, and most faces seemed to be expressing remorse. Osric did not know how to respond and betrayed little emotion as he collected his tray then took a seat at an empty table. He was not alone for long, as he was soon joined by Bertram and Bryce the harness maker.

Bertram did not hesitate and extended his hand to Osric upon sitting down. "Osric, I fear the folk here have treated you very poorly, they have. I want to extend to you my regrets at any part I may have played in it. No one should be forced to run away over matters they had no control over."

Before Osric could respond, Bryce interjected, "Aye, Osric. People here, meself included, have behaved like childish fools. You ne'er sought the King's attention. We always knew that, but for some reason people started treatin' ya poorly, then just kept up with it. I'm damned sorry it happened that way, I am."

"I hope it's not too late for us to be friends," said Bertram.

After he recovered from his surprise, Osric smiled at the two men, and said, "Nay, Bert, it's not too late. I ne'er had any ill will toward ya, nor you Bryce."

"Damned glad to hear that!" said Bertram, with a smile. "I don't need to tell ya life can be hard for a dwarf, and the thought of you bein' forced away and havin' to live rough because of how we treated one of our own, got a lot of people to thinkin', it did."

"Aye," said Bryce. "There is no excuse for us not lookin' out for our own, there ain't."

Osric was so overcome he could barely speak. He feared a tear might rise in his eye, but he spared himself that embarrassment through sheer willpower. It was obvious the story of his running away was now common knowledge in the community, and before Osric returned his tray to the rolling table that morning, more than a dozen people, including Carac and Winifred, came by and expressed their regrets at the way he had been treated. Being welcomed back into the community, and the likelihood he would soon be reunited with Fendrel, left Osric far from the despair he was feeling only a day earlier.

In spite of the weakness in his legs, Osric made it to the candle shop on time that morning with his heart as light and happy as it had been in a long while. He was in a state of wonder at the way his life had turned around in so short a time. Osric even experienced a momentary flirtation with the idea of taking Angmar up on her invitation, but soon dismissed the thought. His spirits dimmed a bit when he remembered it was a Monday, and he had hours of crawling in and out of a melting oven ahead of him, which was the last thing his aching legs needed. Osric's spirits took another blow when he realized he would be dealing with oven number one, the oldest, largest, and most difficult of the ovens to clean. However, not even the prospect of that dreaded task could undo the happiness he felt at the prospect of again sharing some ale with Fendrel.

Osric entered the candle shop and nodded his greetings to his coworkers. Quinn forbade all talking that did not pertain to getting the work done. Thus, it had taken a long time for Osric to get acquainted with the people in the candle shop. He collected the ash bucket and small shovel from their pegs on the wall, then proceeded to oven number one. He unlatched the oven door then reached inside, feeling for any glowing embers that might be lurking in the ashes. He had been burned on more than one occasion, and he thought the ovens should be allowed to cool from Thursday, rather than Friday, but it was a matter Quinn would not even consider.

The first part of the cleaning job was easy, as he was able to reach the ash from a standing position outside the oven, and he soon had the bucket filled. He carried the ashes across the room and emptied them into the ash box, then climbed up on a small ladder and used the tamper to pack the ash down before returning to the oven. As Osric crawled out of the oven with his fourth bucket of the morning, intense pain shot through his back and down his legs as he tried to stand. The pain was so great he lost his grip on the bucket and it went clattering to the floor. "Oh, bloody hell!" cried Osric, as he clenched his teeth and waited for the pain to ease.

The worst of the pain passed before Quinn reprimanded him, and he was able to continue with his work. Though he did not drop the ash bucket again, the pain was relentless, and all through the morning his pace became ever slower. The walk back to the common room at midday left Osric close to tears, and he feared he might vomit when he began eating.

Alexa sat down at his table, smiled, and when she saw the pain written in his face, asked with alarm, "Osric? Are you unwell?"

Had it been anyone else, Osric would have snarled, but after he calmed himself for a moment he replied in a low voice, "It's the pain in me bloody legs and back. I've had a damned difficult mornin' cleanin' the oven, I have."

"Oh dear." After a brief pause, she asked, just above a whisper, "Why did you want to leave us Osric? Has it been that bad for you here?"

In spite of the effect Alexa had on him, Osric felt his temper rising and responded with more than a trace of petulance, "People have hardly spoken to me since His Majesty summoned me to supper! I didna ask to break bread with the man, but it looked to me that the people here wanted me gone because of it! What was I to think?"

"You're quite right, Osric. Things got out of hand, and that should never have happened. Walter told everyone the truth, but for reasons I do not understand, the community chose not to heed his words." Alexa looked at Osric a moment, "I'm dreadful sorry things happened the way they did Osric. I, for one, want to see you living here in this community for many years to come."

"Th-thank you, Alexa. I ne'er sought the King's favor, I didn't. I ne'er wanted to be taken prisoner and brought here against me will in the first place. I ne'er asked for any of this, but now that I'm here, I want only to be treated as everyone else."

Alexa reached across the table and took Osric's hand, and an electric shock shot up his arm. She looked at him with a tear in the corner of her eye, "Of course you do, Osric. That is only your due. You've been badly mistreated, and there's no excusing it." He would have been content to hold Alexa's hand indefinitely, but she soon released her grip and dried her eyes on the corner of her baker's apron. She smiled at him, "I hope the community can manage to put this unpleasantness behind us, Osric."

"Thank you, Alexa." Osric heard the bell tower announce three-quarters of the hour. "I must be startin' back to the candle shop now or I will be late, and bloody old Quinn will bark at me."

"Goodbye, Osric. I hope the second half of your day is better than your first."

Osric was not far into his return to the candle shop when he knew the afternoon would be no better than the morning. He had badly overtaxed his weak legs and he knew it could be days before they returned to normal. "What was I bloody thinkin'?" he muttered to himself. "I can barely bleedin' walk. What made me think I could run away?" He was now willing to forgo his supper and go straight to the bath house when his day was done, where he would soak in hot water for as long as they let him.

He was greeted by Quinn's sharp words the moment he entered the candle shop, "Osric, I inspected number one, and you are well behind where you need to be! You must put forward a greater effort! We begin making soap upon the morrow, and you must complete your work!"

Osric felt his fingers tightening around his stick, then drew himself back from something he would be certain to regret. "Yes, Quinn. I will do my best to finish the oven today."

"You *will* get that oven cleaned today, if it takes you 'til midnight!"

"Bloody hell," thought Osric, as he returned to his task. His pain was unrelenting as he struggled through the afternoon. Quitting time came, and the other workers departed to their supper while Osric labored on. There was still ash remaining when it occurred to him that he might be able to leave some of it behind. Quinn was far too large to fit through the oven door, and neither of the other dwarfs working in the shop were likely to climb inside and inspect his work. As the pain in his body became almost unbearable, Osric decided to take the chance. He filled the bucket a last time, then shoveled the remaining ash to where it could not be seen from the door. He carried the bucket to the ash box, emptied it, tamped the ashes down, then put the bucket and shovel away. He was making his way to the door, with visions of the bath house dancing before his eyes, when he was confronted by a very angry Quinn.

"You have taken far too long to complete your work, Osric, and your sloth has caused me to be late to my supper! Your wages this week will be reduced by one-half."

Osric glared at Quinn, thinking, "It wouldn't kill ya to miss a bloody meal, ye fat arsed swine!"

The venomous look on the muscular dwarf's dirty face, and the stick in his hand, turned Quinn's anger to fear in an instant. He said in a more even tone, "Get thee to a bath, and do not be late in the morning or ye shall have no wages at all."

Osric's eyes burned into Quinn as he clenched his teeth, and snarled, "May God bless and keep you, Master." The blasphemous remark left Quinn dumbstruck. Osric said no more as he pivoted and made for the door. For the time being, his great pain was being overridden by his greater anger. His burning rage left him wanting to beat Quinn senseless, "I should do to that bastard's god-rotting skull, what I did to the King's horse!" Not until he reached the stairway leading to the dwarf quarters, did his awareness of the pain return with a vengeance. The climb proved to be even more difficult than the one he had experienced the night before, and this time he was unable to complete the climb without encountering other people. He was halfway to the top when he was overtaken by two men returning from the bath house.

Both men were shocked by the combination of Osric's grimy appearance, and the agony writ upon his face. "Good god, Osric!" cried Derrick, the potter. "Let us be givin' ya a helpin' hand up the stairs!"

Under normal circumstances Osric hated being touched, but he was too spent, and in too much pain, to protest. The two men positioned themselves, one under each arm. Derrick gently took Osric's stick from him and carried it in his free hand as the two men assisted him to the top of the stairs.

"Will ya be all right now?" asked Derrick, as he returned Osric's stick.

Osric grimaced and said, "I'm not bloody all right, but I think I can manage me way to me room now. I thank ye both for helpin' me." As he hobbled across the commons he saw the rolling table had been returned to the kitchen, and he knew he had missed his supper. "Bloody hell, but I've gone hungry before." He struggled to his room, collected clean clothes, then made his way back to the stairs. He would have to climb the stairs again, but he hoped soaking in hot water would ease his pain enough that he could do so unassisted.

As Osric was crossing the common room, he encountered Walter who was shocked by his appearance. "My word, Osric! You look terrible!"

"I feel bloody terrible, Walter."

"What happened?"

Osric related all the misfortunes of his day, including having his wages docked.

"I shall speak to Quinn, Osric. I may not be able to get your wages restored, but I will see to it you are given the day off tomorrow to recover."

"T-thank you, Walter."

"Did you miss your supper?"

"Yes, Walter."

"Go take your bath and clean your clothes. I will have Arabella send to the kitchen and your supper will be waiting in your room when you return."

"Thank you, Walter. I'm most grateful, I am." Osric wondered how he could have ever thought of turning his back on this kind, and decent man.

Osric made his way to the bath house, stripped, then settled into a tub of hot water. He soaked a long while before soaping himself and then washing his clothes. He lingered in the tub until the attendant told him the bath house was closing for the night. Soaking in the tub had its desired effect, and his pain was eased enough to allow him to climb the stairs without assistance. As he ate the meal Arabella had left for him, he sighed, "Oh, what a bleedin' day this has been."

Early the next morning, Walter appeared in the candle shop and confronted Quinn. "Quinn, I am here to inform you Osric will not be reporting for work today, by my approval."

Quinn was still smarting from Osric's blasphemy and eyed Walter with suspicion. The royal candle maker arched his eyes and sniffed, "And for what reason?"

"Osric's weak legs are no fault of his own, and you badly overworked him. He needs a day to recover." Walter did not mention Osric's escape attempt, as he thought Quinn to be a rather stupid man, unworthy of either long explanations or confidences.

Quinn was not fond of dwarfs generally and only employed them out of fear of offending the King, and for their usefulness when cleaning the ovens. Though he resented the leader of the dwarf community in particular, it was not lost on Quinn that Walter was the King's cousin, and he gave his reluctant approval for Osric's absence.

A day of rest that included another long soak in hot water did much to restore Osric's legs, as well as his spirits. The absence of pain allowed him to again focus his mind on reuniting with Fendrel. Walter's great kindness left him regretting his decision to run away even more. "I should have just listened to him and waited for things to get better. What a damned fool, I was."

Later that evening, as he was preparing to retire, Walter performed his daily duty and looked across the courtyard. To his chagrin, he saw the red lantern burning. He changed into clothing appropriate for a royal audience, then made his way through the tunnel and presented himself before the doors of the Royal Wing. Goran ushered Walter into the small sitting room, where he was most often received by Urloch II.

The King wasted little time with pleasantries. "I read your report regarding Osric's attempt to run away, Walter. How is it that things got so out of hand he saw no choice but to flee?"

Walter considered his words, then began, "You know me well, Sire. I trust you will take me at my word when I tell you, both Arabella and I did all we could to ease the way for Osric in the community. As you know, jealousy has always been an issue with my people."

The King weighed Walter's statement, then sighed, "Alas, I fear the fault may lie more with me than anyone, Walter. The fact is, I've come to enjoy the man's company a great deal. Given a proper education, an able-bodied man with Osric's intelligence and tenacity might well be one of my generals. . . . Has the climate in the community improved at all?"

"I believe it has, Sire. A number of our most influential people have gone to Osric and expressed their regrets over what he has been made to suffer. I took it upon myself to grant him a day away from his work today, as to allow his legs time to recover. I do not believe it made Quinn very happy, but I felt it necessary given your earlier instructions regarding Osric."

The King scoffed, "Quinn had best mind his manners or he'll find himself mucking out stables on my most distant estate. I'm in full agreement with your decision, Walter." The King paused to think a moment, then said, "That will be all, Walter. Keep me informed. We may need to make other arrangements for Osric."

"Yes, Sire." As Walter made his way back to the dwarf quarters, he wondered what 'other arrangements' might mean.

It was past midnight when Alfred was escorted through the gloomy corridors of The Black Anvil and announced to the Lord Chamberlain. After the butler departed, Alfred struggled to keep his knees from knocking as he waited for the Duke of Bruno to acknowledge his presence.

At last, the Lord Chamberlain turned to Alfred, and asked in a hard voice, "What is this nonsense of the King's favorite dwarf running away, and then returning to the castle, all about?"

Alfred had anticipated the question and was prepared. "As I said at our last meeting, M'Lord, the King offered to do the dwarf a favor, and it appears he has made good on it. He sent members of the household guard to the provinces with orders to return someone named Fendrel to the castle, in order that he could be appointed the royal rat catcher. . . . M'Lord."

The Lord Chamberlain had trouble containing his anger as he received the news and slammed his fist against the arm of his chair.

"A King doing royal favors for a bloody dwarf cannot be tolerated, Alfred! This must be stopped, and you will be the one to stop it! You are to poison the little bastard, at your first opportunity!"

"C-commit murder, M'Lord?"

"Would you prefer to see your family put off the farm?"

"N-no, M'Lord."

"Then take that," said the Duke, pointing to a small vial sitting on a table. "It's essence of belladonna. Put ten drops in his ale, and that wretched little beast will trouble us no more."

"Y-yes, M'Lord. . . . At my first opportunity."

"Your 'first opportunity' had damned well better fall within the next week, or your family will find themselves without a home! Do you understand me?"

"Y-yes, M'Lord."

"You are dismissed!"

Alfred made his way back to the palace through the dark streets, deep in torment over what the Lord Chamberlain had ordered him to do. He did not want to see his family put off the land on which they had labored so hard, but neither did he want to commit a murder. Many unpleasant thoughts troubled his mind. "I wonder if I could give him just a few drops that it might make him sick, and I could tell the Lord Chamberlain, he survived in spite of me best efforts? . . . Bah! The hateful bastard can see through walls, then he'd be havin' me flogged or worse, and me Ma and Pa would become beggars in their old age. I'll take servin' duty and poison the little sod at Saturday supper, then confess me sins on Sunday mornin'."

Osric reported to the candle shop on Wednesday, feeling much better. Quinn said little to him, and the man's demeanor led Osric to think the royal candle maker may have been warned about his behavior. Given a choice, he would have preferred having nothing to do with the King, but if the man wished to intervene and prevent Quinn from abusing him, he would accept the help with gratitude.

He spent his morning performing a variety of chores, including his first turn at pumping the bellows since coming to the royal candle shop. Though he had no great love for the bellows, it felt good to once again perform a familiar task. His old skills soon returned, and he kept the thickening ash water simmering at just the right temperature until another man took over when the tallow was added to begin the soap making process. Upon his return from the midday meal, Quinn ordered Osric out to the courtyard where a load of wood was being delivered. Osric broke into a smile when he found Jarin preparing to drag a log from the bed of his cart, and hurried to assist him.

Jarin knew of Quinn's prohibition against unnecessary speech and whispered, "Osric, me friend. Guess who me new neighbor is."

"Fendrel?" gasped Osric.

"Aye, indeed," whispered Jarin with a grin. "He begins his duties as the royal rat catcher on Monday. I'm thinkin' we should all gather at my cottage on Sunday afternoon. Gwenny can bake some tarts, I'll procure a bloody big bucket of ale, and we'll have a fine time of it, we will."

Osric did not hesitate to agree, and the afternoon flew by as he cut and split the logs. His joy at the prospect of the grand reunion on Sunday, combined with the improved climate in the dwarf community left him the happiest he had been in a long while. Osric was resting on his bed before going to Saturday supper, giddy with excitement for the next day's reunion, when he rose to answer a knock at his door. He opened the door to find Walter, accompanied by two soldiers. An ice cold shock surged through Osric as he assessed the situation in a heartbeat. He struggled for words, "W-Walter, am I bein' sent away?"

"No, Osric. You are not being sent away. Far from it. His Majesty has ordered that you be removed to new chambers, in the Royal Wing."

Chapter Fifteen

The King's Fool

sric's exit from the dwarf community was accompanied by none of the drama surrounding Hadrian's removal. Osric sat in stunned silence as the two soldiers respectfully packed his belongings, until he managed to stammer, "W-why Walter? Why is this happenin'?"

Walter extended a kind smile, "I've no good answer for you, Osric. I wish I did. This is something that has never happened in all my years, here. The only thing of which I'm certain is that neither of us has any choice but to obey His Majesty's orders."

"But, what am I to do in the Royal Wing, Walter? Will I be goin' to the candle shop as I have been? Will I be able to go to visit me friend Fendrel tomorrow?"

Walter was touched by the pain in Osric's voice, and the desperate, heartbroken look on his face. Like the King, he had come to enjoy Osric's company, and it saddened him that he had so little to offer in the way of an explanation. "As I said, Osric, I haven't any answers. You are to join the King for supper this very evening, and I'm certain all your questions will be answered at that time."

Osric felt like a drowning man, floundering and helpless, just beyond reach of safety. His instincts were telling him the reunion with Fendrel would not take place the next day, and that his life was taking an even more momentous turn than it had when he was captured in the square. Every nerve in Osric's body was shrieking in rebellion at the injustice of it all.

It did not take long for the soldiers to complete their work, and well before he was ready to leave his room, Osric found himself being escorted out of the dwarf community. Everyone who had gathered in the common room ahead of Saturday supper, understood in an instant what was happening, and watched in frozen silence as the little procession passed by. Alfred the cook had just helped roll the food table from the dumbwaiter to the serving area, and the sight of Osric being led away shocked him even more than it did the dwarfs. Alfred's enormous relief at not having to commit a murder was balanced by his fear of the Lord Chamberlain's reaction to the news.

At the large table where Carac's family had gathered, Alexa reached out and grasped Winifred's hand, and asked in a hoarse whisper, "My god, Aunt Winnie, what does this mean?"

"I don't know, Lexie. I don't know."

Saturday supper was always one of the most pleasant times in the weekly cycle of events in the dwarf community, but on this Saturday the evening meal began in gloomy silence as the people struggled to make sense of the situation. The dark mood in the room was offset by the jubilant smile on Alfred's face as he filled the trays. Walter was not present to address the community, and as the murmur of voices grew ever louder, Arabella rose and rang the small bell. When the room quieted, she began, "If I may be so bold as to speak in my husband's stead, I can tell you this much, Osric has not been sent away from the castle. He is being sent to live in the Royal Wing, by orders of His Majesty. This is *not* a matter of Osric's choosing! That is all I know. I do not know why this is happening. I trust Walter will have more to say on this matter when he returns. I implore all of you to remain calm, and do not let anger cloud your judgment."

If Osric had felt as if he were floating outside his body prior to his second supper with the King, what he was experiencing now left him in an even more detached frame of mind. He was escorted down the spiral stairway, through the tunnel, then admitted past the large red doors of the Royal Wing. Through it all, Osric felt like a tiny bird, struggling to fly in the face of a raging storm.

The doors to the anteroom opened, and Goran instructed the party to follow him. The King's butler led the way up another flight of stairs, then through a series of hallways to a door that had been left standing open. Goran entered the room, then indicated the others were to follow. Once the party was in the room, Goran said, "These are to be your quarters, Osric. I trust you will find them agreeable." Goran turned to the soldiers, "You men, put Osric's things in the wardrobe, then return to your duties. Walter, please remain here."

Though his senses were still reeling, Osric calmed himself enough to venture a cautious glance around the room, and what he saw left him wide eyed. Instead of the gray stone of his room in the dwarf community, this room was paneled in dark oak. There were tapestries hanging on the walls, and there were carpets on the floor. A large window, with many panes of leaded glass, added to the sense of space. The room was well appointed with furniture scaled for a dwarf, and a half dozen bee's wax candles made the chamber feel very warm and welcoming. It took Osric a moment to realize Goran was speaking to him and had just repeated himself.

"What do you think of your new quarters, Osric?"

"I canna' believe it, Goran. . . . Why is this happenin' to me?"

"His Majesty will explain it all in due time, Osric. The barber will be along soon to groom your hair and beard. When he has completed his work, Henry will guide you to the bathhouse. You are to have a bath, then change into your best clothing and ready yourself to dine with the King. Do you understand?"

"Yes, Goran," Osric's inner self cursed the King, the palace, and the universe in general.

The royal barber entered the room carrying a tall stool. Walter, Goran, and Henry exchanged greetings, then the barber addressed Osric, "I'm Henry, I believe we met during the King's journey from the provinces. Please have a seat on the stool, and I will get thee looking presentable."

As Henry set about his work, Goran said, "Walter, please come with me, so I might have a word with you."

Walter followed as Goran led the way down the corridor, then into a vacant room. The butler closed the door, and Walter asked, "What is the meaning of all this, Goran?"

Goran took a deep breath, then began, "Walter, Osric is soon to learn he is being appointed The King's Fool. As you know, His Majesty has appointed fools in the past, but only on a temporary basis for a court function. Osric's appointment is to be in the old tradition, and he is to be presented at court, on Monday. After his appointment, he will become the King's near-constant companion. You are not to discuss this matter with anyone, until after His Majesty has made the formal announcement on Monday."

"Oh, my word," gasped Walter. The leader of the dwarf community knew full well that to be appointed The King's Fool, meant a man was anything but a fool, as the holder of that title had the absolute right to say anything he wished to the King, without fear of punishment. As The King's Fool, Osric would enjoy an access to the King, any nobleman in the realm would kill his own mother to attain. This latter fact filled Walter with cold fear.

"There is more, Walter. I do not know the details, but His Majesty learned of a threat against Osric's life and made this move to protect him. Perhaps he will tell you of it in his own time, but it goes without saying you are never to discuss the matter with anyone. Not even your wife."

"I understand, Goran. His Majesty can, of course, rely on my absolute discretion." Though Walter was far too wise to voice a comment, his suspicions immediately fell on the Lord Chamberlain. Osric's murder would not be the first to be carried out on the orders of the Duke of Bruno. When the conversation ended, Walter said good day to Goran but did not return to the community. After he locked the door to the tunnel, Walter turned away from the dwarf quarters and proceeded in the direction of the cobbler shop. He unlocked an unmarked door, then used a candle from the corridor to light a lantern. He bolted the door from the inside, then climbed a long flight of stairs and entered his private study in the Royal Academy.

Walter placed the lantern on a table but did not extinguish it. He intended to spend some time thinking, and he would need it when he returned to his chambers. Walter removed a flask of brandy from a cabinet, poured out a measure, then settled himself at his desk. He turned to gaze out the window and began contemplating the extraordinary turn of events.

To the extent Walter owned anything beyond the clothes on his back, this room was his. Arabella knew of it but had never visited, as women were not permitted to enter the Royal Academy. No one other than the King himself could enter this room without Walter's permission. He sipped his brandy and pondered how Osric's new situation might affect the dwarf community.

The present King's grandfather, Urloch I, had as his fool a dwarf named Myron. Walter remembered Myron from the time in his youth he had been allowed to observe his father being received at court. Myron was an intelligent, quick-witted man, not unlike Osric, and the thing that troubled Walter most about Myron's memory was the manner of the man's death. Myron served as The King's Fool for a bit over two years before he was poisoned, then run through with a sword as he lay dying. Though the assailants were soon captured, not even torture could get them to betray their employers, and they took their secrets to the grave. It could have been any of the kingdom's seven Dukes, or some combination of them. To this day, Walter was in a state of wonder that Urloch II had survived to maturity. He suspected there was more to the story than Destrian VII swearing the other six Dukes to depose his brother, the Duke of Bruno, in the event he attempted to usurp the throne during the period of his regency. If jealousy was a problem in the dwarf community, it paled in comparison to the rivalry among the country's high ranking nobles. Walter did not envy his older brother who had inherited their father's title, and a lifetime of court intrigue to go with it.

Walter spent the rest of the long summer evening deep in thought. As the shadows made their slow march across the window, he contemplated all the possible outcomes of the King's decision. When the last daylight faded, Walter stood and stretched, then picked up the lantern and spent several minutes strolling through the deserted rooms of the Royal Academy. All students and faculty were away on summer holiday, and would not return until after the Harvest Festival. The academy consisted of only four lecture halls, a library, and the student living quarters. It was rare to have more than thirty students enrolled at any time, but the small size of the institution was not a measure of its importance. It was here the sons of the nobility, diplomats, generals, and the selected sons of wealthy merchants, were prepared for university, and the foundations laid down that would equip them to inherit the reins of power. It was a source of great satisfaction for Walter that he had been able to touch the lives of so many of the country's most important men. Now, he could only hope he had touched those lives deeply enough that he might avert a tragedy for Osric.

Henry finished barbering Osric, then said, "Gather your best clothes, and come with me. I will show you to the bathhouse used by the household staff. Take good note of your room's location when we leave, and remember the path back to it." As Henry led the way, he began pointing out what the various rooms were. "The doors we have just passed are the barracks rooms of the rank and file guardsmen. This is the dining hall you will use. The latrines are down there." He gestured to the far end of the hall and said, "The guard commanders reside in those rooms while on duty, though most also have a King's cottage in the city where their families live." Henry opened an unlocked door and led Osric into a large room containing several partitioned bathtubs. "You are free to use any of these, and I suggest you do so a minimum of once per week if you are to be living near the King, as he expects his staff to be clean. My own rooms are just over there, as is my cutting shop. Make a point of visiting me once each month. I do not normally come to anyone's room to groom them, but I came to you today because Goran requested it. A request by Goran should always be viewed as coming from the King himself, and you would do well to remember that."

Osric had never been more bewildered. His life in the candle shop and the bell tower had been harsh and dull, but at least his old life had followed a predictable pattern, and he had been able to soften the hard edges of that life with Kurtz's wonderful brown ale, and Fendrel's company. Now, nothing made any sense, and his life was growing more baffling by the hour. Henry told Osric not to tarry in his bath, but to take care of matters, dress, then return to his room, and be ready when Goran called for him. Osric did as he was instructed, and was making his way out of the bath house when he encountered Carac's son, Peter.

"Good Lord, Osric! What on earth are ya doin' here?"

"H-hello, Peter. I've just been told that I'm livin' here now, but I don't bloody well know why."

"The hell, you say! When did this come about? I've ne'er heard of a dwarf livin' in the Royal Wing, I haven't."

"I've not been here an hour, Peter. I was given a room near where the guards live. Henry cut me hair, then brought me here to have a bath. It's all bloody puzzlin', it is."

Peter glanced around, then whispered, "Are ya havin' supper with His Majesty again?"

"Aye, that's what they told me."

"I wish ya the best of luck. I need to get me own bath taken before Sunday dinner tomorrow." Peter paused, then asked in a very quiet voice, "Is there anything you'd like me to tell the folk in the community, Osric?"

"Aye, Peter, there is. Tell them I ne'er, bleedin' asked for this. None of it, and I wish I was back livin' in the community, I do."

"Aye, Osric, I can be doin' that for ya, I can."

Osric began making his way back to his new room, wondering if it might be possible to escape the castle again, but he soon realized the maze that was the Royal Wing left him not knowing how to so much as get outdoors. He passed a balcony railing on his left where an opening in the wall afforded a view of a large room lit by windows in the ceiling. The room was ringed by balconies on all sides, and three stories below an indoor fountain bubbled. Osric wondered how he could have failed to notice this place on his way to the bathhouse. He took his bearings and decided he was certain this is the way he had come from his room. Osric thought a moment, then muttered, "Henry must have been pointin' out the barracks rooms when we passed this way." He spent a moment peering over the railing at the pleasant atrium, then continued on his way.

Given the extent of his confusion, Osric was relieved when he found his door. He was alone for the moment, so he began inspecting his new quarters. It was a good deal larger than his room in the dwarf quarters, much larger than his garret, and infinitely nicer than the orphanage. The room had a fireplace against the outside wall of adequate size to heat the room in winter. Osric carried a stool over to the large window, then stood upon it and looked outside. He saw a courtyard below him, though not the one he had become familiar with. He saw the magnificent gray horses that had pulled the King's carriage, standing in a stable against the far wall. He was still standing on the stool looking out the window when Goren entered the room without knocking. "Let me have a look at you, Osric."

He stepped down from the stool and faced the King's butler.

Goran gave Osric a careful inspection, then said, "Very well, Osric. You are acceptable." The butler paused, then continued, "You will soon be given additional clothing Osric, and you will be expected to make yourself as presentable as you are at this moment, at all times."

Osric did not respond, but thought, "Bloody hell! Am I to be some kind of bleedin' dandy?"

"Do you understand what I'm saying, Osric?"

"Yes Goran, I understand."

"Very well then, follow me." Goran led the way down the corridor, with Osric laboring to keep up the pace. After making several turns, and descending a long stairway, they came to a set of gilded doors, bearing the royal coat of arms. "Wait here, while you are announced, Osric." Goran tugged on a red velvet chord, hanging alongside the door, and a bell could be heard on the other side.

From within, came the King's voice, "Enter." Goran stepped into the room and made a formal announcement of the King's guest. Goran turned to Osric and bade him enter. Osric did so and bowed before the King.

"Good evening, Osric."

"Good evening, Your Majesty."

Goran seated Osric as another servant stepped forward and presented him with a stein of ale. The King raised a toast, "To your health, Osric."

"And to yours, Sire."

"I'm famished! Serve the food, Goran." At the butler's signal, servants emerged from behind a curtain and placed large trays before both Osric and the King. Osric was now familiar enough with court protocol that he knew to wait until the King had begun eating, before touching his own plate. A servant uncovered the tray, and Osric saw a wonderful assortment of breads, meats, and vegetables before him. Though he had eaten well since coming to the castle, moments like this brought back vivid memories of the stale bread and rank water he had been served in the candle maker's garret. The King attacked his food with relish, pausing only to tell Osric he had spent the day hunting, and had acquired a great appetite.

Osric found he too was hungry, and enjoyed the fine meal as a servant refilled his ale stein twice before he consumed the last morsel on his plate. After the dishes had been cleared away, and more ale poured, the musicians made their appearance. The routine of a royal supper was becoming familiar to Osric. He enjoyed the music, though it seemed to him the King cut the performance a bit short when he dismissed the musicians. When they were alone, the King focused on Osric, smiled, and said, "Do you find your new quarters agreeable, Osric?"

"Aye, indeed I do, Your Majesty, I canna' believe it, I can't."

"Believe it, Osric." The King smiled again, then continued, "Osric, when the court assembles in the throne room on Monday, I will be announcing to all the kingdom's nobles, that I am appointing you to be The King's Fool. Do you know what that means?"

He had no idea what it meant, but he didn't like the sound of it, and answered with caution, "I was often called a fool by Brother Benedict, and me old master, I was, Sire."

The King tossed his head back in laughter, "I've appreciated your honesty from the day I met you, Osric, and honesty is what being The King's Fool is all about." The King's laughter subsided, then he continued in a more serious tone, "Osric, if you were a genuine fool, you would not be receiving this appointment."

"I'm afraid I don't understand, Your Majesty."

The King smiled again, "I know not from whence the title comes, Osric. It has been ever thus, as far as I know. The King's Fool is not a true fool, but is the one man in the realm granted the right to speak his mind to the King, at all times, without fear of punishment. Osric, it will be your duty to keep me honest. The position has most often been left vacant during my reign, and that of my father's as well. However, I believe you are the ideal person to fill the role. . . . Do you accept?"

Osric found himself speechless. At long last, he stammered, "H-have I a choice, Your Majesty?"

"You do, but if you refuse me, I shall have you sent away, and I will see to it you never again set eyes on your friend, the rat catcher."

A silent scream reverberated through every corner of Osric's being, "OH BLOODY HELL, YOU GOD-ROTTING PIG'S ARSEHOLE! THIS IS NOT FAIR! IT IS NOT FAIR!" There were a thousand angry images flashing through Osric's mind, and it took all his willpower to calm himself, and say, "I accept, Your Majesty."

"Excellent, Osric. You have made a wise decision. In addition to your new chambers, you shall be receiving a Silver Swan every Saturday and a Gold Talent at Christmas. All your needs will be provided for, and you will be able to save most all your money. Serve me faithfully, Osric, and I will see to it, you become a wealthy man."

Osric listened to the King's words in stony silence, thinking, "Keep your bleedin' silver, let me see Fendrel, and kiss me hairy arse while you're at it!"

Osric was awakened early on Sunday morning, then directed to a chapel. After mass, a member of the household guard escorted him to the dining hall, and instructed him to be quick with his breakfast, then return to his room and await further orders. Thus it was, Osric was standing on the stool observing the activity in the courtyard below when there came a knocking at his door. He made no move to answer it, but simply called out, "Enter," as he had heard the King do.

The door opened, and Angmar poked her head inside, smiled, and said, "Osric, ya handsome devil! I ne'er thought I'd be seein' ya here in the Royal Wing, I didn't."

Though his opinion of Angmar had risen a great deal since their first meeting, Osric was still wary of the woman's tendency to make lewd remarks. However, at that moment, his reservations were more than offset by his relief at seeing a friendly face. "H-hello, Angmar."

She closed the door behind her then strode across the room. She put her arms around Osric, and held him close, and he returned her embrace. Though no one had ever held him like this before, the experience was doing much to ease his troubled mind. Angmar pulled away and looked into his face. There was a tear in the corner of her eye, and her voice was breaking as she spoke in an intense whisper. "I cried meself to sleep last night after I heard of ya bein' removed to the Royal Wing, Osric. . . . Be very careful here, Luv. Be very careful, and be afraid."

Though he had been baffled since arriving in the Royal Wing, Osric had not experienced real fear, until this moment. "W-why should I be afraid, Angmar? What is it I have to fear?"

Angmar's voice continued to be low and intense. "Maybe I'm being a worryin' fool, but I don't like this one bit, Osric. The Royal Wing is filled with treachery from tail to snout, and no good ever comes from this place, it doesn't." She paused, then turned her head and took stock of Osric's new quarters. "This is a very fine room, it is. Much nicer than me own, but I'd rather see ya livin' in a bloody stable if it meant ya havin' a long life to go with it." She looked into Osric's eyes, "I greatly fear that you're here because you've made an enemy of the Lord Chamberlain, Luv, and short of the King himself, there's no worse enemy ye could have."

"Oh bloody hell," murmured Osric.

"Aye, Dearie, bloody hell to be sure." Angmar released her embrace, then said in a normal tone, "I canna' be wastin' time, Osric. I need to check your measurements, then busy myself with the clothes you will need when you are presented at court tomorrow. I've a very long day ahead of me." It only took Angmar a few minutes to check Osric's measurements, and when she was finished, she held him close once again. She was fighting tears as she whispered in his ear, "Don't be forgettin' what I told ya, Luv. Do all ye can to keep yourself safe. I'll be back first thing in the mornin' with the clothes you will need at court." She released him, then turned, and fled the room.

Osric began to tremble. Not even being locked in the child's coffin by Brother Benedict had left him feeling as vulnerable as he was at this moment. Every nerve in his body was on fire, and he could not make his mind focus on anything but Angmar's warning, and how alone he was. He was surrounded by people who were not his friends, and he could not trust. He was trapped in a situation he did not begin to understand, and he had no idea how to cope with any of it. He could see no way to escape, and as if Angmar's warning had not frightened him enough, Walter's words from their first meeting came echoing back, "Give the King your loyalty, but never try to be his friend, Osric. Kings are only friends with other kings, and then, very rarely."

The only remarkable thing about the remainder of Osric's Sunday was just how little happened. After Angmar's departure, the morning was uneventful until a member of the household guard tapped on his door to inform him Sunday dinner was being served. During the meal, the soldiers and other members of the household staff regarded him with mild curiosity, but otherwise ignored him. He found Sunday dinner for the household staff to be a quiet affair, involving none of the noisy socializing of the dwarf community. When he finished eating, Osric returned to his room where he remained undisturbed until he was called to supper.

During the course of the long afternoon, his boredom overcame his nerves to the extent he was able to doze. He slept until he awoke with a jolt, to the certain knowledge he was missing the reunion with Fendrel. "Oh, bloody hell! What must they be thinkin'? Surely Jarin has heard the news of what happened to me and passed it on to Fendrel." Osric's loneliness was now being compounded by the profound sadness of having been denied his reunion with the rat catcher.

When he returned to his room after supper, Osric stood on the stool and gazed out the window until darkness fell, and his legs and back grew weary. He visited the latrine, changed into his nightshirt, blew out the candles, then settled himself for the night. He did not sleep well and woke often between a series of confusing and frightening dreams. When sleep became impossible, he rose and carried a candle to the hallway, lit it, then returned it to his room. Osric had lived much of his life in the dark, and had never feared it, but this night was like no other he had ever experienced. Having some light in his room eased his tension enough to allow him to sleep a bit, before being awakened by a rapping at his door.

Osric informed the person knocking on his door that he had risen, and the voice told him he was to waste no time eating his breakfast, then return to his room. Not knowing what was required of him, Osric stood and stretched his aching back, then dressed in the clothes he had worn to dine with the King. Breakfast in the dwarf community had always been a lively time, with all the members extending their greetings, and mixing bright conversation with their morning meal. Breakfast in the staff dining hall was much quieter, and Osric thought the atmosphere rather chilly. It was as if the people in the Royal Wing neither liked nor trusted one another very much. He saw it as no great burden to hurry through his porridge and ale, then return to his chamber.

Back in his room, Osric lit another candle. He could not see the bell tower from this room, but it was still dark, so he knew it was quite early. He seated himself at his table and waited for what ever was to come next. The heavy silence added to his tension, and when the knock came on his door at last, it startled him a great deal more than it would have in his garret.

"C-come in."

Angmar opened the door, and called, "It's just me, dearie."

Osric thought Angmar's natural good cheer seemed rather forced, and this added to his anxiety. "Good morning, Angmar."

She placed a bundle on the table, then said, "I need you to try all this on, Luv. I hope they won't take much fittin' because we've little time."

Osric watched as the seamstress unpacked the bundle, and was horrified by what he saw. Both the trousers and the jersey Angmar delivered had bright blue and orange stripes! "What in bloody hell is this?" gasped Osric.

A humorless smile crossed Angmar's face, and there was sadness in her voice, "These are your clothes, Luv. Please do not resent me for them. They are not of my choosin'."

"I won't wear them!"

She gave Osric a pained smile, then said in a very soft voice, "I'm afraid ya haven't a choice, Luv. This is what The King's Fool wears at court."

"I'd rather be sent away to muck out pig barns!"

Angmar was taken aback by the ferocity in Osric's voice. She calmed herself, and spoke in a consoling tone, "Oh Dearie, I'm afraid it's much too late for that, it is. You've agreed to this, and now ya canna' change your mind." Their eyes met as they both fought against their anger. "Ya must make the best of it Luv. Take his silver. Hide it away, then flee when ya get the chance. That is your best choice, Dearie."

"I didn't know what I was bloody agreeing to!"

"Aye, Luv, I believe that, I do, but I'm doubtin' it will make a difference to His Majesty." She returned Osric what she hoped was an encouraging smile, "Come along, Luv. I'll step out of the room while you try on the clothes." When Osric gave no sign he was going to cooperate, she said in a soft, pleading, tone, "If nothin' else, Luv, please do it for me. I don't want to find meself cast out of the castle."

Angmar's plea broke the stalemate. Osric had little concern for what happened to him, but he would not let his personal outrage put Angmar in jeopardy. He took a deep breath and resigned himself to his fate. "Alright, Angmar. I will don the clothes and do me best."

"God bless you, Osric. Just call for me when you're changed, I'll be waitin' outside your door."

The seamstress stepped out into the corridor while Osric donned the clothes. Though he had no way to inspect himself, he had no doubt about how ridiculous he must look. As if the absurd clothing was not enough, he saw that Angmar had also brought him a hat made of the same striped material. The hat had three arms extending out from its crown, and at the end of each arm dangled a small brass bell. Every fiber of Osric's being shrieked in rebellion, and he cursed the day he met the King. At last, he took a deep breath and called out for Angmar to return.

The seamstress reentered the room and asked him to stand on the stool while she inspected the fit of the new clothing. Angmar's emotions were running as high as Osric's, and she struggled to keep her voice from breaking. "I believe this will do nicely, Osric. I don't see anything I need to alter."

Osric attempted to make light of the situation and said, with false gaiety, "If I didn't look so bleedin' ridiculous, I would say 'tis quite the nicest set of clothing I've e'er owned, it is."

She seized Osric's hands, looked into his eyes, then said in a dry whisper, "Ye must be braver than you've ever been, Osric. Do not try to run away from this, or the people at court will eat ya alive, they will. Play the harlequin with a smile on your face, and never let 'em know they're hurtin' ya. Never! That will be your best defense. I don't know when I might be seein' ya again, Luv. May God be with ya, Osric." Angmar said no more. She embraced Osric, kissed his cheek, and hurried from the room.

Chapter Sixteen

Life At Court

After Angmar's departure, Osric's anxiety continued to grow until Goran called for him two hours later. "Stand up and let me have a look at you Osric . . . and put your hat on."

Osric suppressed his anger, steeled himself, then complied with Goran's orders. He remained as impassive as he could while the old butler inspected him.

"That will do. Now, come with me." It infuriated Osric when he heard the bells on his hat tinkling as he walked, so he removed it and carried it in his hands until Goran ordered him to put it back on. Osric followed the King's butler through a confusing series of hallways, then down a spiral stairway he had not seen before. Though he had been living in the castle for some months, not even his current anxiety could quite displace his amazement at the size and complexity of the building. At last, they arrived in a room where several people were sitting on high backed benches lining the walls. Goran pointed Osric to a seat. "Wait here Osric, and I will return when His Majesty is ready to receive you."

The room went quiet when they entered and remained so until after Goran departed. Then, a rather poorly dressed man spoke up, "So, it's true then? You're the one who is to be appointed The King's Fool?"

Osric attempted to answer but his dry throat caused him to stammer, "A-aye, that is what they have been tellin' me, it is, M'Lord." The state of the man's clothing led Osric to think he was speaking to a very low ranking noble, and only the sword on the man's belt said he was anything other than a common tradesman.

The man responded with a sarcastic laugh, "I've heard a rumor such a thing might take place."

The man's voice was as cold and impersonal as the Lord Chamberlain's, which only added to Osric's distress. He could think of no response, so he remained silent. If it came to a fight, he doubted his stick would prevail unless the man was a poor swordsman, not that he wouldn't defend himself with all he had. Osric's state of mind led to desperate, fatalistic, thoughts, "He may run me though in the end, but I'll bloody well cripple the bastard if he gives me half a chance! What do I care if I'm dead? At least I'd be well done with the bleedin' King, I would." The minor noble's eyes remained locked on Osric until Goran returned and summoned him to follow.

Grateful to be out of the room, Osric accompanied the butler down a short hallway to yet another set of ornate doors displaying the royal coat of arms. Goran rang the bell, and Urloch II bade them enter. "The King's Fool, has arrived at court!" laughed the King, upon seeing Osric.

He had heard the King laugh enough times to recognize a difference in the man's tone. This was not the King's normal laugh, but a laugh with a biting edge directed at him. He was also instantly aware of the elegantly dressed, but unattractive, woman sitting next to the King. Though Osric had never seen the Queen, he had little doubt as to whom the woman was. He bowed before the royal couple. "G-good morning, Your Majesty."

"Osric, I present to you, Queen Jacquelyn. My dear, this is Osric, who is very soon to become The King's Fool. Osric, you will address the Queen as Your Majesty, or Your Highness, just as you do me."

"Yes, Sire." Osric was struck by the woman's long face, large teeth, and prominent nose. It did not escape his notice that the Queen was also somewhat larger than the King, who was not a small man. Osric held his tongue, as his thoughts regarding the Queen were best left unspoken. "It's no bloody wonder he keeps company with the dwarfs!"

"Are you ready to be presented to the court, Osric?"

Though he would rather kiss Brother Benedict's backside, and wanted only to be far away from the King and castle, Osric responded, "Aye, Your Majesty. As ready as I will ever be."

"Very well, Osric. Goran, instruct The King's Fool as to what will be expected of him."

"Yes, Sire. . . . Osric, when the King and Queen enter the throne room, you are to follow them down the aisle, then wait at the base of the dais until they are seated. After the Lord Chamberlain has been seated, you will then be directed to your own chair. Remember, Osric, walk two paces behind the King, and always on his sword side."

"Y-yes, Goran."

"Goran, alert the heralds."

"Yes, Sire." Goran slid open a small panel, then signaled to someone on the other side.

The King and Queen took up positions just inside the door, and a moment later, the herald's played a fanfare. Osric stood behind the royal couple and trembled as the double doors swung wide. Then, as if he needed additional stress, the first person he saw when the doors opened was the Lord Chamberlain who was, as always, dressed in menacing black from head to toe. The Lord Chamberlain turned to face the assembly, then called out in his hard, metallic, voice, "All rise! All rise! All rise, for the King honors us with his royal presence!"

Osric heard much shuffling of feet, followed by a moment of silence before the trumpets sounded again. The Queen took her husband's arm, and the royal couple swept forward with easy grace, as Osric did his best to keep pace. They entered a room resembling the nave of the cathedral where he had rung the bells for so many years, but of an even grander scale. From behind the royal procession, the Lord Chamberlain called out, "All hail the King and Queen! All hail His Majesty, King Urloch II, our sovereign ruler, lord of the seven duchies, he to whom we owe our all! All hail Her Majesty, Queen Jacqueline, the royal consort!" The nobles responded with tumultuous cheering, and Osric's mind flashed back to the day he was captured in the square. He trailed the King and Queen as they marched the length of the great room, thankful the din was drowning out the bells on his hat. They made their way down an aisle strewn with rose petals until they reached the base of a dais supporting twin thrones. Osric halted as he had been instructed, while the royal couple ascended the seven steps. One step for each duchy.

The King and Queen turned to face the great room, then stood before their thrones acknowledging the cheering crowd for what seemed a long time to Osric. At last Urloch II looked to the Queen, and at some unspoken signal, they sat down together. The Lord Chamberlain then ascended the dais and took a seat to the King's right, one level lower. The King looked to Osric, then pointed him to his seat at the far left end of the platform, two steps below the royal couple. The King and Queen sat in gilded chairs, adorned with precious gems. The Lord Chamberlain's seat was only a little less ornate. Osric's chair was bright red, and decorated with peacock feathers, rendering it altogether absurd. The room quieted as Osric began laboring up the steps, but the bells on his hat provoked much laughter. When he reached his chair, Angmar's words echoed in his ears, and instead of surrendering to the rage inside him, Osric turned to face the room. He removed his hat, then swept it down in front of him, as he executed a deep bow to the assembly, thus provoking even more raucous laughter. He had just won the opening skirmish, while thinking, "I will kill that bastard King if I e'er get the chance!"

Osric put his hat back on, and as he began to sit down, his chair shot out from under him, causing him to fall flat on his back. As the room exploded in new laughter, Osric was filled with white-hot fury in an instant, then just as quickly gained control of himself. He lay spread out on his back for a moment, planted the end of his stick against the floor, and reached as high as he could. Then, using nothing but his arm strength, Osric vaulted upwards into a standing position without first getting to his knees, and the court emitted a collective gasp. He again removed his hat, bowed to the court, then pivoted on his heel and bowed to the King and Queen. He replaced his hat, then marched around to the back of his chair. Osric gripped the heavy cord that had been used to pull the chair out from under him, then looked straight into the eyes of the member of the household guard who had executed the prank. He snapped the cord between his hands, like a blade of grass, eliciting yet another gasp from the court. After bowing once more to the royal couple, Osric took his seat. He had just won again. He had silenced the court, and now everyone knew The King's Fool possessed the strongest arms in the room. Osric might be the shortest man at court, but much larger men would think twice before challenging him to unarmed combat.

Even though Osric had first come to his attention when he battled, then killed, his horse in a town square, the King too had been reduced to awed silence by the display of strength he had just witnessed. Urloch II soon recovered his composure, then tapped his scepter against the floor for silence. The King raised his right hand, and spoke in a loud, clear voice, "I, King Urloch II, do hereby decree from the throne, to all the realm's nobility, that from this day forward, the dwarf Osric is officially declared The King's Fool. Furthermore, the appointment is to be permanent. By ancient tradition, The King's Fool may only be stripped of his office with the consent of four of the seven Dukes." After a moment's quiet, all the nobles rose to their feet and began applauding.

Osric did not know what he should do, so he stood and bowed to the court. To call the moment extraordinary in his life would not do justice to the moment. After a lifetime of abuse at the hands of Brother Benedict, the candle maker, and many others, the realm's assembled nobility had risen to their feet to salute him. To what degree their applause was sincere, Osric could not say as he very quickly surmised the nobles would do as they were expected when in the presence of the King.

When the applause ended, the members of the court took their seats. The Lord Chamberlain remained standing and announced the first person to be received by the court. It turned out to be the man who had questioned Osric earlier. Just as he thought, the man proved to be a minor noble; a Baron, who ranked below a Count, and far below a Duke. A Baron, as Goran would later explain, was often little more than a land owner with some distant connection to the royal family, often possessing far less wealth than a merchant. Though Osric was baffled by the workings of the court, he suspected this might be the one and only time the man would ever be received by the King. As the Baron stepped forward to receive a medal recognizing him for some service to the realm, he made a quick glance in Osric's direction. The Baron's eyes bespoke a hatred for the idea of a low-born dwarf enjoying access to the King he could only dream of.

The Baron cast Osric another ugly glance as he backed away from the royal couple. As the man retreated, the King asked, in a laughing voice, "And what does The King's Fool think of the first royal recipient of the day?"

Osric was now beyond caring what happened to him, and, after a moment's hesitation, decided to test the limits of his new office. He responded in a firm voice, "I believe the sod is havin' the best day of his bleedin' life, he is." The King and the entire court, with the notable exception of the Baron, burst into laughter and clapped their approval. Osric breathed a sigh of relief, as it appeared he had filled his intended role. The King's Fool was twice more asked to render his opinion of those being received by the King before the morning's meeting of the court adjourned, and both responses were met with laughter and approval.

After the morning session of the court drew to a close, all the noblemen and their ladies made their way out onto a broad terrace overlooking the river while the great hall was being made over for dining. Osric was instructed to remain at the King's side, always standing with Goran, two paces away. On the terrace, only the Dukes enjoyed the privilege of approaching the King. Urloch and the Dukes engaged in bantering conversation about hunting, and the upcoming race meet to be held on the grounds of the royal estate during the Harvest Festival. Several wagers were made, and recorded by Goran in a ledger. On another section of the terrace, the Queen and her ladies-in-waiting conversed with the women of the court, beneath an awning bearing the Queen's standard.

The Queen rejoined the King when the court luncheon was announced, and the members of the nobility waited respectfully as the royal couple led the way back inside the throne room. Osric followed, as he was ordered to do, never having felt more ridiculous. The only positive aspect of the moment was the absence of laughter directed at him and his tinkling hat. The royal couple took their seats, and Osric was directed to a chair at the far end of the long table. Because the King and Queen were already seated, all the nobles sat down as they reached their assigned places. Although it was not apparent to Osric, the seating was carefully arranged by rank throughout the great hall. The Lord Chamberlain sat to the immediate right of the King, and a woman Osric took to be the Lord Chamberlain's wife was seated next to him. The other six Dukes, their ladies, and the Arch-Bishop completed the head table, their proximity to the King determined by their length of time they had held their titles. The twelve Counts and their wives, along with several foreign ambassadors, were seated at smaller tables in front of the head table, with the many Barons and Knights filling out the back of the hall The guests of the nobility looked down upon the feast from balconies on three sides of the great room.

When all the nobles had been seated, the Lord Chamberlain stood, and raised his hand. When the room fell silent, he turned to the Arch-Bishop, who was seated to the King's left, bowed slightly, and said, "Your Grace, if you please. . . ."

The Arch-Bishop stood, and made the sign of the cross to the King and Queen, then turned and did the same to the room. "Please bow your heads . . ." The bishop preceded to give what Osric thought to be an overly long blessing. In addition to the royal couple, he mentioned the Lord Chamberlain, and all the Dukes, Counts, and ambassadors by name. Osric was grateful when he blessed the Barons and Knights as a group.

After the bishop took his seat, a steady stream of servants bearing large pitchers appeared from behind a curtain and began filling wine glasses and ale steins. Next, came servants delivering what proved to be an elegant meal for everyone in attendance, with the exception of Osric. No one at the head table, including the King and Queen, touched their food until all the Dukes and Counts had been served. Servants removed the tray covers beginning with the King and Queen then by rank. Osric could see generous cuts of roasted meats, cooked vegetables, and sweet cakes on the other trays, and his appetite was whetted. His was the last tray at the head table to be uncovered, and as the servant stepped back, four pigeons exploded out from under the cover, and the room dissolved into hysteria, with no one laughing louder than the King.

Osric sat in stunned silence for a moment, then bellowed, "BLOODY HELL!" and this resulted in a new round of raucous laughter at his expense.

"Is The King's Fool having a problem with his dinner?" boomed the King, laughing with his whole body.

"I NEAR SOILED ME BLEEDIN' TROUSERS!" bellowed Osric, and the laughter in the room rose to a new level.

The King slapped the table and called out, "Who among the seven Dukes believes The King's Fool should be removed from his post?"

"Not I, not I," echoed the reply down the table, as the court continued to roar with laughter.

"Goran! A brandy for The King's Fool, and a proper meal! It seems the man has little taste for pigeon."

"Yes, Sire."

It soon became obvious the moment had been planned because as soon as the King finished speaking, a servant stepped forward and presented Osric with a large goblet of brandy.

"To The King's Fool, boomed Urloch II, lifting his stein to Osric."

Osric lifted the goblet and returned the King's toast. The others at the head table took hearty drinks of wine or ale, while Osric took a sip of the fiery brandy.

"What's this?" cried the King. "A sip will not do, Osric! Show your sovereign proper respect, and empty your cup down your gullet!"

"OH BLOODY, BLOODY HELL!" thought Osric, in desperation. He contemplated the huge measure of brandy in his hands, steadied himself, then toasted the King once more. He lifted the goblet to his lips and drank it off at a single pull. Osric's heart was racing, and he felt as if he had swallowed molten wax. He gripped the edge of the table and braced himself against what was soon to hit his stomach. When the initial shock of swallowing the brandy passed, Osric took up his stein of ale and drained it in an effort to cool the fire in his mouth. He soon realized water would have been the better choice, as he was already beginning to feel the effects of the brandy. "OH BLOODY HELL!" cried Osric, as the court roared with laughter once again.

Osric's afternoon soon dissolved into a bewildering kaleidoscope of images. How long the banquet lasted, and what ever came later was lost in a drunken haze. He did not have another coherent thought until he opened his eyes in his room, the following morning. He did not know the time of day, but the light streaming in through his windows told him the morning was well advanced. He saw a tray of food and a pitcher of water waiting on his table. Osric struggled to his feet, and upon standing, he was hit with the full force of a blinding hangover. His temples throbbed, and his eyes felt as if they might explode out of his skull. He likened the taste in his mouth to the inside of Fendrel's rat traps. Osric used his stick to steady himself and struggled to bring the spinning room under control. It was a long time before he was able to make his way to the table, and drink all the water in the pitcher.

The water cleared his head to a degree, and he plopped down on a chair. His legs felt weaker than usual, and he blinked his eyes again and again in an unsuccessful attempt to get them to focus. At last, he tore off a chunk of black bread and ate it. His system was calmed a bit by the bread on his stomach, and he ate the rest of the loaf. He was in need of more water but did not know where to get it. Osric had no idea what this day might have in store for him, he only knew he must make his way to the latrine, and soon. Leaning on his stick more than usual, he hobbled out to the corridor, and on toward the latrine. He was still wearing the suit of striped clothing Angmar had given him the day before, but had misplaced his hat. "Sod that bloody hat," mumbled Osric, as he hobbled, and staggered to the latrine door.

He relieved himself then noticed water bubbling up from what appeared to be a fountain for drinking purposes. He sampled the water, and when he found nothing peculiar about the taste, drank his fill. Osric felt somewhat better as he made his way back to his room with the idea of lying down again, but when he arrived he found a man he did not recognize waiting for him.

"Where have you been?" The man's tone of voice reminded Osric of Goran at their first meeting.

"I've been to use the latrine."

The man seemed reluctant to accept Osric's explanation, but after a moment's hesitation, said, "Very well then. Wash your face, and come with me."

Osric's mental and physical state left him in no mood to be ordered around, and he snapped, "Who in bloody hell are you?"

The man took an aggressive step towards Osric, who immediately brought his stick up in fighting position. The stranger had witnessed Osric's display of strength in the throne room and froze in his tracks. With some considerable effort, the man calmed himself, cleared his throat, then said, "I am, James, the under butler. It is surprising we have not met. Goran would not normally deal with you directly." James felt genuine fear in Osric's presence and had to calm himself again before continuing. "You will most likely be dealing with me, rather than Goran, in the future. I have been sent to escort you to the King. Please come with me. . . . Where is your hat?"

"I don't bloody know."

"You must find it at once."

Osric took his eyes off the servant, and surveyed the room. He spotted his hat resting atop a bed post and hobbled over to retrieve it. He held the hat in his hand and made no move to put it on until James told him he must. Osric donned the tinkling hat while vowing a terrible vengeance against everyone who had ever forced him to wear the cursed thing. With great reluctance, he followed James out of the room and through yet another bewildering series of hallways and staircases. They arrived at a door that was ordinary in every way except for the royal coat of arms. James rang the bell, and Urloch II bade him enter. A moment later, Osric was admitted to the King's presence.

"You look bloody terrible, Osric!" laughed the King, upon seeing Osric's bloodshot eyes, and haggard expression.

"I feel bloody terrible, Your Majesty."

"Perhaps you should not drink so much."

If he was, in fact, free to speak his mind to the King, he meant to test it. "I did what you bloody well told me to, Sire!"

The King roared with laughter. "That you did, Osric! That you did! . . . Be seated," said the King, pointing Osric to a dwarf-sized table. "This is the room where I do most of the realm's business. It is my working chamber, and where you will be reporting most mornings. I only sit in the throne room when the full court meets twice a year, and that is more than enough. Make yourself comfortable, luncheon will be served directly."

Osric appeared to vanish from the King's thoughts as Urloch returned to the papers on his desk. As the King read from the papers and made notations with a pen, Osric took stock of the room. There were more books than he had ever seen lining the walls, including some very large volumes. Multiple candles burned in addition to the ample sunlight being admitted through the large window. He soon understood that this room was a place of work. It was not ostentatious, and it was not meant to impress anyone with the trappings of royalty. However, it did not take Osric long to become bored, and he was on the verge of nodding off when the bell rang.

"Enter."

Goran entered the room and bowed to the King. "Luncheon has arrived, Sire."

"Excellent, Goran! I'm famished." The King used his forearm to unceremoniously clear an area on his desk as a servant placed a tray in front of him. A moment later, a second servant placed a tray in front of Osric, who listened carefully for the sound of pigeons. He breathed a sigh of relief when he heard nothing. Osric was rather surprised when no priest appeared to give a blessing, and the King simply started eating. It was a simple but substantial meal, much like what would be served in the dwarf community on a work day. There was a piece of roast chicken, bread, some cooked vegetables, and a pair of hard boiled eggs. Like every meal he had been served in the castle, there was a stein of the King's inferior ale, which tasted especially unpleasant to Osric in his current condition.

The King did not speak until after he had finished eating. He pushed his chair back a bit from the table, then took a drink of his ale. The King smiled at Osric and said, "You had a grand time at the banquet yesterday, Osric."

"Did I, Sire?" Osric returned the King a blank expression, having only the blurriest memory of the previous afternoon.

The King laughed, "Aye, indeed you did. You danced with all of the Queen's ladies-in-waiting, then you performed a dance of your own invention for the entire court. Later, you honored us all with a song, though none of us could quite understand the words."

"Oh, bloody hell," thought Osric. "I am afraid I've no memory of it, Sire."

The King laughed, and said, "All's well, Osric. Everything you did was well received by the court. We will be leaving soon for a hunt. Have you hunted before, Osric? Other than the time you assisted with my birds?"

"Nay, Sire."

"It will be a large hunting party today. Nearly all the men of the court will be riding. I've sent word for the seamstresses to bring your Master of the Hunt costume, and they should be waiting for you now. Once you are properly attired, we can be on our way. I am going to step into my wardrobe and don my hunting kit. I shan't be a moment." The King paused, then as an afterthought, asked, "You do ride, do you not, Osric?"

"Oh bloody hell," thought Osric. "Nay Sire. I've ne'er ridden a horse before."

The King pondered Osric's response a moment, then said, "That should not be a problem. It is a simple skill, easily mastered."

Osric's mind was filled with curses. After the King departed, he was escorted to a small room a short distance from the King's work chamber, where he found Angmar and Juliana waiting for him.

"Hello, Dearie," said Angmar, with a gayety Osric did not find convincing. "We've been given to understand you're going hunting with His Majesty this afternoon."

"Aye, I was just told as much."

"Hello, Osric."

"Hello, Juliana."

When the servant departed, Angmar put her lips to Osric's ear and whispered, "How bad was it at court yesterday, Luv?"

"It was bloody awful," whispered Osric.

She stepped back and extended Osric a sad smile. "Come along then, Dearie. The costume should fit without any alteration. It's not been touched since you wore it last."

"It canna' make me look any more ridiculous. At least I can shed this bloody hat for a bit."

Angmar gave Osric a sly wink, leaned close, and whispered, "Be brave, Luv. Be brave and ne'er forget what I told ya."

The two seamstresses unpacked the Master of the Hunt costume, then stepped out of the room to allow Osric to change. He did so while feeling as defeated as he ever had. His head continued to throb and his eyes felt only a little less like they might explode than they had when he awoke. The prospect of riding a horse terrified him, and thoughts of another afternoon spent in the company of the King and the nobility filled him with the darkest despair. At that moment, Osric would have willingly exchanged what ever remained of his life for a few hours in The Dancing Pig, drinking

Kurtz's brown ale with Fendrel. When he finished changing, Osric called for the seamstresses to return.

"Let me have a look, Dearie." Angmar inspected the fit of the bright red jacket and green trousers, then declared herself satisfied. She bent low and hugged Osric, whispering, "Be brave Luv. Keep yourself safe."

Osric had grown rather fond of being hugged by Angmar, and no longer resented it in the least. To his great surprise, Juliana also hugged him and wished him well during what ever was to come. The two women escorted Osric back to the King's office and rang the bell. Angmar whispered, "We won't be comin' in Luv." Osric cast sad eyes to Angmar and nodded his acknowledgment.

He was admitted back into the King's work chamber while a guard escorted the two women back to the domestic wing of the castle. The King was dressed in black leather armor, and Osric thought the man's appearance to be quite striking. "You look very smart, Osric. Let us be off."

Accompanied by Goran and other servants, the party made their way out to a courtyard where two carriages stood waiting for them. Osric and the King boarded the royal carriage, while Goran and the other servants climbed into a smaller, unadorned, coach. As the carriages made their way through an archway and into the courtyard Osric was familiar with, they were joined by several mounted members of the household guard. The procession was nearing the drawbridge when Osric chanced to look out the carriage window, and his heart skipped a beat. There, not five paces away stood Fendrel with his head bowed, and the strap of his leather bag over his shoulder. It took all of Osric's will power to resist calling out to his friend.

Following a journey lasting perhaps half an hour, the King's party arrived on a wide plain where a number of carriages and many horses were gathered. Several colorful tents and awnings had been erected where the nobles and their ladies were taking their ease as they awaited the arrival of their King. As the royal carriage drew to a halt, the Lord Chamberlain called for silence. The heralds sounded their trumpets, and the King was announced. Urloch II stepped down from the carriage, waved to the crowd, then climbed into the saddle of a magnificent black horse. Once the King was mounted, all the other nobles followed suit until everyone was in the saddle, with the exception of Osric.

"This way, Osric," said Goran.

Osric's fear of riding a horse turned to outrage when he realized he was expected to ride, not a horse, but a donkey. He looked at Goran with pleading eyes, and the old butler nodded his head. "I am supposed to ride a bleedin' donkey?" whispered Osric.

"Yes, Osric. Do not fear. The beast has been trained to follow the horses. Just take the reins in one hand, and hold on to the saddle with the other. Carry your stick across your lap."

"Bloody hell," muttered Osric, as he was helped into the saddle. To his further embarrassment, Goran tied the cloth under Osric's chin to secure the bright green hat to his head, then straightened out the flowing white feathers that trailed behind. A groom took the side of the donkey's bridle and led Osric to where the King and the rest of the noblemen awaited The Master of the Hunt. Such was Osric's rage, he did not realize the entire assembly was laughing at him until the donkey halted alongside the King's hunter. As the laughter subsided, a hunting horn sounded, and the King's hounds were released. The dogs were given time to find a scent and when they bounded away in search of their prey, the mounted men rode off in pursuit. The horsemen soon left Osric far behind, as he did his best to goad the donkey into motion. The donkey would sometimes trot a bit, but most often walked, and sometimes refused to move at all. As the hunting party raced across the plain, Osric and his donkey followed in their general direction, urged on by shrieks of laughter coming from the women under the awnings. "I will kill that bastard King, if e'er I can," said Osric aloud, not caring who heard him.

Thus, the tone was set for Osric's life as The King's Fool. In the months that followed, he was ever present at the King's side and was the butt of endless jokes. Osric learned to defend himself verbally, much to the King's delight, but a rage built inside him that was ever more difficult to suppress. Only Angmar's advice and the growing number of Silver Swans in his purse kept his anger from exploding. Osric now possessed more wealth than he ever dreamed of, and there would be a gold talent presented to him on Christmas morning. If he could ever manage to escape the King and castle, he now had the ability to buy his way into the guild, and acquire his own candle shop, as well.

Four days ahead of Christmas, The King's Fool rode atop a huge log as a dozen servants used ropes to drag it into the largest of the royal sitting rooms. This was the yule log, and as long as it burned, the servants and staff of the Royal Wing were largely exempt from the strict rules of decorum that applied the rest of the year. Late that evening, as the first winter storm of the season beat its fury against the windows, Osric sat sipping brandy with the King as they warmed themselves before the fire. As Osric contemplated the contrast between his present condition and his life in the garret only a year ago, Urloch broke the pleasant silence when he asked, "How old are you, Osric?"

He thought for a moment, then replied, "I think I am about forty years of age, but I don't know exactly, Sire."

"As old as that? I thought you to be a much younger man, Osric." The King was quiet for a minute, then continued, "Osric, it is most unseemly for a man to be forty years of age and still a bachelor. It is high time you were married."

Chapter Seventeen

The Marriage of The King's Fool

An electric shock flashed through Osric. The King's words reverberated in his ears, leaving him too stunned to respond. It took several seconds for him to stammer, "M-married, Sire? M-me?"

"Yes certainly, Osric. Why shouldn't you be married? It is the natural state of a man to be married.."

"I-I've ne'er considered the possibility, Sire."

"It's high time you did. . . . Have you anyone in mind who might make a suitable wife, Osric?"

"Nay, Sire." Osric regretted his words the instant he said them because once he recovered from the initial shock, he realized there were two women he thought would make acceptable wives. No woman had ever filled him with the warm and confusing feelings Alexa left him with, and he had grown quite fond of Angmar as well, once he had come to know her.

"Do not concern yourself, Osric. I will have the Lord Chamberlain search out an acceptable wife for you."

A silent scream echoed through every corner of Osric's being. "Oh bloody hell!" His mind raced, and he made a desperate attempt to recover the moment. "I-I do know of someone, I might take as a wife, Sire."

The King waved his hand, dismissing Osric before he could explain himself. "This is a matter best left to the Lord Chamberlain, Osric. He has had three wives and has much experience in the business of matrimony. He can be relied upon to find you a suitable mate."

"But, Sire . . ."

"Enough, Osric! The matter is settled!"

Though The King's Fool enjoyed considerable latitude when speaking to the King, it was not without limit. When Urloch II pronounced a matter closed, then all discussion was ended. Osric felt as if his skin was on fire, and in spite of the King's pronouncement, he made one more futile attempt to mention the possibility of marriage to either Alexa or Angmar, only to be cut off. At last, a defeated Osric lifted his goblet to his lips and swallowed the brandy in a single gulp. He sat with his eyes closed as the fiery liquor burned its way to his stomach. "Oh bloody hell!" thought Osric. "Oh bloody, bloody hell! Why the god-rotting Lord Chamberlain of all people? My God, what kind of woman will that hateful bastard find for me? Oh, bloody hell."

On the far side of the city, Alfred the cook trembled as he waited outside the Lord Chamberlain's sitting room. It was just before midnight and would soon be the morning of Christmas eve. Alfred had never found The Black Anvil more intimidating. After he failed in his attempt to kill Osric, he had been forced to his knees, begging the Lord Chamberlain not to cast his parents out of their farm. He had succeeded, but at great personal cost. Fearing not just for his parents, but for his very life, Alfred had been compelled to create an even more extensive network of informants within the dwarf community and the kitchen. All his spies made their reports to the Lord Chamberlain through him. Alfred was faithful in his duty because he suspected the Lord Chamberlain had many sources of information, and he knew the costs of misleading the man would be dire if he was ever found out. When the butler admitted him at last, Alfred felt as if he was being led to his own execution.

The Lord Chamberlain sat facing the fire and did not acknowledge Alfred when he was announced. Time stopped as he waited for the man to speak. When words came at last, the man's voice cut like an icy knife, "Will you be visiting your parents for Christmas, Alfred?"

"I've no plans to do so, M'Lord. It is a long way to travel on foot, in winter, and my duties in the castle would not allow me enough time."

The Lord Chamberlain responded with a long silence and the knot in Alfred's stomach was as taut as a bowstring. "You will be given the use of one of my horses. Ride to the estate and visit your family. His Majesty will know you are on a mission for me, and your absence in the kitchen will be excused. You are to make the rounds of the Christmas day gatherings and identify the tallest woman of an age to marry. She need not be a beauty." The Lord Chamberlain turned to Alfred for the first time since he entered the room, then pointed to two leather pouches lying on a table. "Give one pouch to her father, and the other to the girl. Return her here to Castle Tyrion before the new year, and your family will be assured of at least one more season on the farm. Do you have any questions?"

"No, M'Lord."

"Do not return to the palace tonight. You will be given a billet in the guard's quarters. Leave at first light, and you should arrive by early afternoon. Fail me Alfred, and you will not be the only one to bear the consequences of your failure."

Alfred was quaking at the prospect of the task before him. "Y-yes M'Lord."

"Dismissed."

As the Christmas eve festivities began winding down in the dwarf community, Arabella took Walter's arm, and together they bade the remaining revelers a good night. After Walter bolted the door to their chambers, Arabella embraced her husband and whispered in his ear, "I think it's a pity that poor Osric was not allowed to enjoy Christmas with us here in the community. It's always such a happy time. I so hope he's faring well in the Royal Wing, I do."

Ever cautious of being overheard, Walter responded in a very soft voice. "His Majesty assures me Osric is flourishing, but one must take everything the King says with a grain of salt, I'm afraid. I suspect the King and Osric may have very different points of view on the matter."

"I canna' help but think Osric is feelin' very lost and lonely. Who would he have to talk to? Who could he trust? The Royal Wing is filled with every manner of treachery, it is."

"It is indeed, My Dear. . . . It is indeed."

"I think things are changin' for our people, Walter. Maybe I've lived in the castle too long, and grown too suspicious in me old age, but I have the nagging fear that some of the trust has gone out of the community. It's as if people are fearful and watchin' each other for no good reason."

"I've felt the same thing, My Dear. . . . That cook, Alfred, has shown an interest in our community these past months that goes well beyond normal curiosity."

"I've ne'er trusted that man, I haven't. I'm very careful what I say around him."

Walter released Arabella from his embrace to where he could see her face. "I suspect Alfred works for the Lord Chamberlain. That young man is ambitious and too clever by half. I've seen to it that the people he speaks to tell him things that are believable, but not quite the truth."

Arabella covered her mouth as she stifled a gasp. "Walter, really?"

Walter returned his wife a sly smile, then said, "Aye. The Royal Wing does not harbor all the castle's wit and guile, my dear."

Outside the castle walls, Jarin and Fendrel sat before the hearth in the carter's cottage, enjoying the last of the ale they had acquired for the occasion. Jarin's wife and child were sleeping peacefully, and the two new friends kept their voices low as they took their ease before the fire.

"Oh, how I wish our friend, Osric could be here with us tonight, Jarin."

"Aye, Fendrel. I sorely miss his company, I do."

"It's thanks to him I have me new position, a fine cottage to live in, and the best income of me life. He's the dearest friend I e'er had, he is."

"Aye, he's a good man, Fendrel. A damned good man." Jarin paused for a quiet laugh. "After the strangeness of our first meetin', it's a wonder the two of us e'er became friends at all, it is. What with him bein' all trussed up like a pig on market day and gettin' pitched into the back of me cart and all. I was just damn glad he didn't have his stick when I untied him, or he might have used it on me." Though he had often told Fendrel of the first day he had spent with Osric, it was a tale that improved with each retelling.

As he had come to know and trust Jarin, Fendrel shared the stories of the weapon he and Osric had created in the garret, the night he saved Osric's life in the town square and of their mutual hatred for Brother Benedict. The rat catcher could reduce the carter to helpless hysteria each time he told the story of Osric's wooden tube in the bell tower. "It was as if God himself let go a bloody great fart straight from heaven, Jarin! The damnedest thing I e'er heard, it was!"

When their laughter subsided, Fendrel asked, "What do you suppose he's doin' right now, up there in the Royal Wing of the castle, Jarin?"

"From what people who work there have told me, he's likely sittin' before the fire drinkin' brandy with the King himself. I've been told His Majesty is right fond of staying up to all hours of the night, and Osric only leaves his side to sleep."

"Osric is right fond of his drink, he is, but I canna' help but think he isn't much enjoyin' himself."

"I only hope he can manage to keep a sword out of his belly, I do."

"Aye, Jarin. I hope for the same thing, to be sure."

After they finished the last of the ale, they shook hands and clapped each other on their shoulders. "Good night to ya, Fendrel, and a merry Christmas to ya."

"And the same to you, Jarin." They agreed to walk to church together in the morning, and then attend the Christmas feast that would be provided by the King for all the royal retainers living beyond the castle walls. Fendrel stepped outside and wrapped himself in his cloak against the bitter wind. The combination of bright moonlight and new snow allowed him to snuff out the candle lantern he was carrying. Fendrel did not hurry to his bed, but walked to where he was clear of the cottages and had a good view of the ghostly hulk of the castle. He sheltered in the lee of a large tree as his eyes adjusted to the moonlight.

After awhile, Fendrel spoke in a soft voice that was soon lost in the wind. "Where are ya, Osric? What in hell are ya doin' up there in that bloody castle? It's not where ya belong, Man. We should be drinkin' good ale in The Dancing Pig, wishin' Kurtz a merry Christmas, and wishin' Brother Benedict a bloody great boil on his arse." He paused for a few seconds as he gazed at the dark castle, then lifted an imaginary ale stein. "A merry Christmas to ya, me friend, where ever ya are in there." Fendrel was about to turn back towards his cottage when he glimpsed a silhouette in an upper story window of the palace. The person appeared to be looking out into the moonlit night. Was it Osric? He could not tell, but the silhouette seemed the right size. Fendrel watched the window until it went dark, then turned toward the shelter of his cottage.

Alexis and Winifred shared a cup of wine in the common room before retiring. "Is something the matter, Lexie? You've seemed very far away this evenin'. Christmas eve is always such a happy time in the community. What troubles your mind, Dear?"

Alexis dabbed a tear in the corner of her eye, then looked at her aunt. "I fear I have made a grave mistake, Aunt Winnie."

"What kind of mistake?"

"It's Osric, Aunt Winnie. I could ne'er quite understand the feelings I had for him. . . . I know he's far from handsome, and he's lame of foot as well, but there was always something that drew me to him. Now he's been taken away, and I fear I will ne'er see him again." Alexis paused and gathered herself before continuing, "I know he led a dreadful life before coming to us, and I should have been bolder. I should have realized he would ne'er have it in him to approach me, and now there is little chance of it ever happenin'." She was silent for a moment, then looked into her aunt's eyes and added with quiet intensity, "I will ne'er marry a man I do not love, Aunt Winnie. I would rather die alone a hundred times over than do that."

On a rocky, windswept speck of land in the Adriatic, Brother Benedict paused as he returned to his monk's cell after midnight mass. He gazed out at the moonlit sea for a moment, as he contemplated the bewildering changes that had come to his life. He was bone weary, as he had been since arriving in this place, and he would be back up in two hours for prayer. It was very early on Christmas morning, and yet the air was not terribly cold. It was supposed to be cold on Christmas. It always had been so in his homeland, before he had been ordered to this island monastery. His addled mind could make no sense of it.

Why had this happened to him? What had he ever done to deserve such a fate? He had never been given an explanation, only the choice of facing the inquisition or exile to this island. The mere thought of the inquisition terrified him, and he chose banishment to this place where he received little to eat and had only a hard pallet to sleep on. Now, his life was defined by endless prayer, toil in the gardens, and a silence broken only by the wind and the sea birds. The only spoken words he ever heard were in Latin, a language he had never mastered. As he was being sent away his superior told him with grave certainty, this monastery would be the last place he would ever know in this life, and he should consider himself fortunate. For reasons he could not fathom, some part of him wanted to blame his predicament on the wretched dwarf who once rang the bells in the cathedral, but try as he might, he could imagine no scenario where Osric might be responsible for his woes.

Alfred reined in his horse outside the cottage of Stone Gate Farm. It was the house he had been born in, and where his parents still lived. The farm was the only place having any sense of home for him, and yet his family owned not a square inch of it. His parents had toiled here from the first days of their marriage to keep themselves fed and housed, but their endless labor had enriched no one but the Duke of Bruno.

"Ma! Pa! It's me!"

A moment later, the door opened and his mother appeared, wiping her hands on her apron. "Freddie!" she cried. "What in heaven's name are ya doin' here, son? We weren't expectin' ya!"

Alfred swung down from the horse and embraced his mother. "It is me Christmas gift from the Lord Chamberlain, Ma.

He lent me a horse and gave me leave to come for a short visit. I must be back at the capital by the new year. . . . Where's Pa?"

"He's down in lower pasture, seein' to a ewe what's gone lame. I expect he'll be back soon. Have ya eaten' son? I can make ya' somethin' straight away, I can."

"Aye, Mother, please. I've been ridin' since before dawn. I'm hungry as a wolf and half frozen, I am." Alfred reached for a pouch hanging from the saddle and handed it to his mother. "Mayhaps this can be a part of our Christmas dinner."

She looked inside, and cried, "Oh, my word, Freddie! It's a great fat goose! Where ever did ya get it?"

Alfred gave his mother a conspiratorial wink, and replied, "Have ya any idea of the number of geese what gets roasted for Christmas dinner in the palace, Ma? They won't miss one, trust me."

"Freddie! You stole this from the King?" His mother asked the question with wide eyes and a sly smile of her own. The crofters who eked out their livings on the great estates never viewed theft from the nobility as a crime or sin.

His father returned while Alfred was eating, and they exchanged warm greetings. His parents were grateful for everything their only son had done to keep them on the farm. When he finished his dinner, Alfred put the Lord Chamberlain's horse up in the stable, then helped his father tidy up the farm chores. They retired to the warmth of the hearth several hours earlier than they would have on a day other than Christmas eve. Over the rest of the afternoon, and into the evening, they consumed several cups of his father's hard cider before trekking to midnight mass, leaving themselves just sober enough as not to attract the unwelcome attention of a priest.

It was after Christmas dinner the following day that Alfred's real mission began. He set off with his parents to attend the round of gatherings hosted by the independent farmers and merchants of the surrounding community. Christmas afternoon parties were a tradition of long standing, and people might attend as many as a half-dozen of them, exchanging good cheer with all the hosts while adding to, and subtracting from, the trove of cakes and tarts at each stop. By the time they visited the fourth party of the afternoon, Alfred had yet to spot any marriageable girl meeting the Lord Chamberlain's criteria, and he was worried. At the home of Cedric the miller, fortune smiled on him at last when he saw the miller's daughter filling steins, with a resigned expression on her face that said she would rather be elsewhere.

The storage room of the mill had been given a good cleaning and given over to the business of dancing and drinking. Two casks, one of cider and the other of ale, were flowing freely while musicians played, and people danced. A large table was laden with tarts of all descriptions. At any other time, Alfred would have been more than happy to immerse himself in the festivities, but he was on an urgent mission, and time was running short.

Alfred had not had regular contact with the community of his birth for some time, and he did not immediately recognize Hildegard. He remembered her only as a girl a few years younger than himself. Now, she stood nearly a head taller than her father and resembled the stocky miller in every way but his beard. Hildegard wore no wedding band and seemed to fit the Lord Chamberlain's requirements perfectly. Alfred wasted no time in reintroducing himself and was rewarded with a shy smile when he invited her to dance. Alfred attended no more parties that day. He spent the rest of the afternoon talking to, and dancing with, the miller's daughter. The last thing he did before departing was to go to Cedric and ask permission to call on Hildegard the following day.

The week between Christmas and the new year found Alfred calling at the mill-house every afternoon, as he pursued Hildegard with vigor. They took long walks, as weather permitted, and talked for hours. Two days before he was due to return to the castle, Alfred spoke to her father and assured him his daughter would be wed within a month, if she would be allowed to accompany him back to the castle. "I know it is a most unusual request Sir, but there is not time to have the banns of marriage properly read here before I must return to the King's service. It's doubtful I will be able to return before Mayfair at the soonest, and more likely it would be at Mid Summer's Eve, a half year from now."

The miller greeted the request with mixed feelings. On the one hand, he was grateful a suitor had stepped forward to seek the hand of his unnaturally tall daughter, a thing he feared might never happen. On the other hand, he found the whole business more than a little strange. Why, he wondered, would a strapping lad like Alfred seek the hand of his daughter, when so many other marriageable young women must surely be available in the capital? Alfred played his hand with care, and when the miller appeared to be wavering, he spoke up, "I seek no dowry, Sir. In fact, I am prepared to present you with a sum of money as a token of my sincerity, should you honor me with your blessing."

The miller opened the leather pouch Alfred handed him, and released a quiet gasp at the six Silver Swans it contained. "Oh, my word! H-however can you afford this, Alfred?"

"I have a good position at the castle, Sir. This is but a trifle compared to the worth of me having found a suitable wife, it is."

"I must say, I'm astonished by this, Alfred."

"I returned home, with the hope of finding a proper wife. I am most reluctant to take as a wife, anyone used to the ways of the city. I know the people here, and I know Hildegard is the kind of wife I seek, Sir."

The money in Cedric's hands soon displaced his questions. After a few minutes spent conferring with his wife, the miller extended his hand and gave the couple their blessing.

Thus it was, that very early on the frosty morning of New Year's Day, with both sets of parents looking on, Hildegard departed the mill-house with Alfred. Hildegard's mother shed many tears as she watched her daughter ride away, though she had been assured they would return as often as was possible. Money had changed hands and promises of marriage were made; yet, through it all Alfred managed to avoid making any direct statement that he would be the one marrying the miller's daughter.

Because the horse had to carry the weight of two riders plus Hildegard's bag, the return to the castle took longer than the journey to the estate. The travelers did not arrive in the capital until late in the afternoon. Prior to setting off with Alfred, Hildegard had journeyed little farther than an hour's walk from the house where she was born, so it came as no surprise the provincial girl was overwhelmed by the sights and sounds of the city. As wide-eyed as she was, it did not escape her notice that they rode on past the city center. Alfred laughed and assured Hildegard there was nothing to worry about, as arrangements had been made for her lodgings, ahead of the wedding. Hildegard learned she would be living in Castle Tyrion, home of the Lord Chamberlain, until her nuptials.

After Queen Jacquelyn excused herself for the evening, Osric was left alone with the King and Goran. He sat with Urloch II before the fire in the modest sitting room where the royal couple took their meals on those evenings they did not entertain guests. The King drank the last of his ale, then waved off his butler when he moved to refill his stein. "A glass of wine, Goran, and pour one for The King's Fool as well."

Osric did his best to avoid letting the King see any sign of his inward cringe. Though he found some wines more tolerable than others, he cared little for the stuff and hoped he would not be required to consume more than a single glass. When compelled to drink wine, Osric was possessed with a longing for the brown ale of The Dancing Pig that went beyond words.

When their glasses were in hand, the King made a toast. "To the success of your wedding, Osric."

The King had said nothing more of marriage since first mentioning it, and Osric had dared to let himself think the idea was but a passing whim and had been forgotten. Now, he felt invisible fingers tightening around his throat, as the room filled with stifling heat. "W-wedding, Sire?"

"We discussed the matter not a month ago, Osric. Don't tell me you've forgotten? The Lord Chamberlain was successful in searching out a bride for you. You are to be married in the morning, by the Arch-Bishop, himself."

"B-but Sire…" Osric was cut short and not allowed to protest. Sweat began trickling down his back, his heart was pounding, and his breathing was difficult.

"Do not disrespect your King, Osric. Lift your glass, and join me in the toast."

"Y-yes, Sire." Osric complied, then emptied the glass while wishing he had a barrel of brown ale to drown himself in.

"Off with you now. Back to your chambers. You've a full day ahead of you tomorrow. You will be awakened early, so the seamstresses can fit you with the wedding suit they have been preparing."

He felt sick, and dead inside. It took a great effort to acknowledge the King. "Y-yes, Sire."

Osric was escorted back to his chambers by two guards. The moment the door closed he changed out of the striped suit, and into his good clothing from the dwarf community. Osric removed his bag of coins from its hiding place and tucked it inside his jersey. He intended to flee the castle or die in the process. Osric eased the door open, and his first cautious step into the hallway was met by the two men who had escorted him back to his room.

"And where might you be off to, Dwarf? If you're needin' to use the latrine, we'll take ya there, otherwise get to thy bed and stay there."

"Oh, bloody hell," thought Osric, as he closed the door. "I guess I'm not ready to die, after all." He got undressed and climbed into his bed. He was filled with indescribable fear and rage. His whole body was trembling, and he could not make his mind focus. Should he go back out to the hallway and engage the guards? What would death by a sword be like? Would it matter? It would be over quickly. Members of the household guard were much more than common soldiers; they were all exceptional fighters, and he knew he could never hope to defeat them. If they didn't kill him, he could well find himself bleeding, and chained in a dungeon. "Oh bloody, bloody hell!"

In time, Osric fell into a shallow, tormented sleep, and when he was awakened well before dawn, he felt as if he had not slept in days. The first people to visit his chambers were Angmar and Juliana, who brought him a new suit of clothing, identical in cut to The King's Fool costume, but of a red-and-white checked pattern. The suit of clothes included another hat with even larger bells dangling from its arms. Before they departed, both seamstresses hugged Osric and through their tears wished him Godspeed through what ever lay ahead.

After the women left, the guards who had prevented Osric from escaping during the night escorted him to a richly paneled chamber where the King, the Lord Chamberlain, and several other noblemen awaited him. They welcomed him as the guest of honor to the all-male 'groom's breakfast'. The breakfast included the largest sausage Osric had ever seen, a plate of oysters, several steins of ale, a goblet of brandy, and some odd looking mushrooms. Osric sat stone-faced through the meal, while the King and the others roared with constant laughter as they made ribald comments about his impending nuptials, his duties as a groom, and the symbolism of the foods.

Though he enjoyed no part of the breakfast, the alcohol dulled his mind enough to prevent him from exploding in rage. Then, something other than the alcohol began making him feel very strange. Voices were being amplified, and every sound reverberated. The room began pulsating with the most vivid colors he had ever seen. There were no musicians present, yet Osric heard strange music in his head, and he was mesmerized by the golden snowflakes settling on all the furniture in the room.

When he was escorted back to his chambers, Osric found the barber waiting for him. Henry did his best to trim his hair and beard while Osric kept trying to sing. He was unable to explain to Henry what it was he kept laughing about between songs, and why he could not sit still. The barber gave up on grooming Osric and returned to his quarters leaving the befuddled bridegroom alone in his room until a little before ten o'clock when two guards entered without knocking. "Come with us, Dwarf. You've a wedding to attend."

His first instinct was to fight, but the two guards were large and well armed, and two more men were waiting in the hallway. One of the men outside his door held a leash attached to the neck of a small dragon that was poised to attack. Osric was not so besotted he could not recognize the utter futility of resistance, so he returned the men the same lop-sided grin that had always driven Brother Benedict to distraction. As he was being marched away in the middle of the four men, the world around him began melting. The castle was now a bewildering crazy-quilt of sounds and vibrant color. Strange music filled his head, and he thought he could fly if the guards would only let him try. The bewildering experience continued until, in a flash of clarity, he found himself standing at the foot of an altar in a small chapel that was slowly rotating. The King and Queen were present, as were the Lord Chamberlain and other nobles whom he recognized, but could not name. The pipe organ played, the people stood, and the tallest woman Osric had ever seen, began making her way down the aisle toward him. As the ghostly, white, apparition approached, his knees grew weak and he wanted to flee, but someone had nailed his feet to the floor. From the choir loft a chorus of demons chanted, "Oh bloody, bloody hell."

No one could have said which of the bridal pair was the more aghast. Both Hildegard and Osric were dumbstruck by the sight of the other. Osric's tenuous grip on reality began deserting him again as the rotational speed of the room increased. His next conscious thought came when he heard the Arch Bishop repeating a question to the tall woman. She seemed confused and slow to respond, whereupon the King answered the question for her, "SHE DOES!" The Arch Bishop stared at the King in wide-eyed disbelief for a moment, before turning his attention to Osric. The Bishop began to speak, but before he could complete the question, the King boomed, "HE DOES!"

The Bishop was dumbstruck, and returned the King a stare that would have gotten another man put in irons. He took a half step backward, then raised his trembling hand and made the sign of the cross before the couple. "I-I now pronounce you man and wife."

Chapter Eighteen

It All Goes Wrong

The wedding feast following the nuptials reduced Osric to a giggling, shadow of the man who killed the King's horse in the town square. He consumed much more ale and brandy, along with another serving of mushrooms. He had been served the mushrooms at the suggestion of the Lord Chamberlain who recommended them to the King as a means of keeping a reluctant bridegroom, with a predisposition to violence, docile during his wedding.

Among the many people within the Lord Chamberlain's web of intrigue, was an old woman around whom many dark rumors circulated. She attended the Lord Chamberlain when summoned, and it was only through his protection that she was able to keep the inquisition at bay. The woman had supplied the mushrooms, as well as the poison in the failed attempt to kill Osric in the common room. She had cautioned the Lord Chamberlain against feeding Osric more than a few of the mushrooms, as eating too many could result in madness. The mushrooms were delicious, and Osric had consumed two large servings.

Osric opened his eyes, then squeezed them shut in a futile attempt to cope with his blinding headache. No candles were burning in his room, and only the faintest trace of predawn light fell upon his window. He struggled to regain consciousness with agonizing slowness. His first coherent thought was the jarring knowledge he was not alone in his bed. Then, like a flash of lightening on a dark night, he realized the other person in his bed was the tall woman who had attacked him again and again, in his nightmare. Then, a moment later, he knew it had not been a nightmare, it was a memory. Osric had only the most confused picture of all that had happened to him since the groom's breakfast the day before, but enough of it came back for him to grasp the fact the woman snoring in his bed was his wife.

His struggle to regain control of his senses began to falter, and his grip on reality began slipping away again. He retained just enough of his faculties to understand that his quarrel did not lie with the woman sleeping in his bed. At some primal level, his instincts told him she had no more desire to be his wife than he had to be her husband.

The pulsating lights he had experienced the day before returned, this time minus the colors but accompanied by the scent of burnt tallow. A wave of nausea swept over him as he fought for control of his mind and body. When he got to his feet he found, to his horror, that he wore no night shirt. He was hot with embarrassment, and grateful the woman continued to sleep. Moving as silently as he could, he found his good clothes from the dwarf community and dressed himself. He gathered up his stick, put on his cloak, and tucked his bag of coins under his jersey. Some part of him hoped he would find guards waiting outside his door and the matter could be ended here and now. Today, he would fight without hesitation, regardless of the odds.

He eased the door open and brought his stick up in fighting position. There was no response from the hallway. If he was not being guarded, then there was at least the possibility of escape. He took a half step outside his door and saw no one. Osric made a futile attempt to remember the way back to the domestic wing. If he could only find the common room, or the candle shop, then he could get outside, and flee the castle. The thought occurred to him that he might even seek refuge in Angmar's room if he could only find the tailor shop. His plan was more of an assortment of random thoughts than any viable plan of escape because he did not know where he was going. His only goal was to be very far away from the King and castle.

Osric's freedom of movement in the Royal Wing was restricted to the dining hall, the latrine, and the bath house. He was always escorted everywhere else he went, and guards posted inside the building prevented people from roaming the Royal Wing at will. He sat off in the direction of the bath house because it was the most distant place he could go without being confronted by a guard. As he neared the atrium, Osric slowed when he heard the unmistakable sound of the King's voice. He crept up to the railing, never letting his stick touch the stone floor. He peeked around a pillar, and there far below, stood Urloch II, speaking with a nobleman he did not recognize.

"You bastard!" thought Osric. "I wish I had a bloody great stone I could drop on your bleedin' skull you god-rotting, swine!" He looked around for something he could use in lieu of a stone. He saw nothing in the hallway in either direction, and he began testing doors. The first two he tried were locked but the third was not. He opened the door and was greeted with a powerful stench. The room appeared to be a latrine, as the only thing in the room was a large earthenware chamber pot, that was near to overflowing. "I'll empty the bloody thing, I will," muttered Osric, grinning with excitement.

On a normal day the smell would have repulsed Osric, but this was far from a normal day. He was now functioning on some other plane and did not hesitate. He left his stick lying on the floor, then picked up the reeking vessel and started back toward the atrium. The large chamber pot was well within what his arms were capable of lifting, but his legs were being tested to their limit. On any other day, he would have sat his burden down and rested along the way, but now his weak legs were being bolstered by adrenalin, hate, and the lingering effect of the mushrooms he had eaten. He carried the chamber pot back to the railing, locked his knees, then hoisted it above his head. He took a moment to steady himself, then launched the vessel and its contents downward with all his strength, while letting go a guttural scream. "SIRE!"

Urloch jerked his head in the direction of Osric's voice, only to see the chamber pot, and its trailing arc of excrement, inches from his head. There was no time to react, and his facial expression never changed. The King's life ended in an instant as he, the shattered chamber pot, and its contents all went crashing, and sloshing to the floor. Urloch II lay in a spreading puddle of excrement, mixed with his own blood. There was still a trace of the smile on his face he had extended the nobleman only a moment earlier.

Osric was wild with jubilation. "I did it! I did it! I killed the bloody King! I did! I did!" Osric hugged himself with glee and spun in a little circle as the nobleman who had been speaking with the King recoiled in horror.

A brief, heavy, silence ended when the nobleman pointed to Osric and screamed, "SEIZE HIM!" Members of the household guard came running from the shadows in the corners of the room, looking up toward the railing high above, where Osric stood. Somewhere, a horn sounded, and the guards went running for a stairway.

Osric surveyed the scene for a moment then hugged himself again. "Well, I best be off. Kurtz will have The Dancing Pig open soon, and with this bag of money I can drink brown ale till I'm bloody well pickled, I can." He was in no particular hurry as he hobbled back to the room where he had left his stick. "I must have me stick if I'm to walk all the way to The Dancing Pig. . . . It will be good to see Kurtz again, it will. Mayhaps Fendrel can join me, too." He picked up his stick and was about to return out the door he had just entered when he noticed a second door. "I wonder where that leads?"

He tried the door and was elated to find it opened to the outdoors. "This is bleedin' wonderful, it is! A door to the outside was right here all along. So bloody close, and I never even knew of it!" He stepped outside and closed the door behind him. He had not been outdoors since his last outing with the King several days earlier, and the cold, fresh, air smelled wonderful. He hugged himself once again, then set off for The Dancing Pig. He walked a short distance then encountered a wall and was faced with turning either left or right. He shrugged his shoulders, "What do I bloody care?" He opted to turn right, and when he reached a notch in the wall, he paused a moment to peer through it. "Bloody hell! I'm as high off the ground as the bleedin' belfry! No matter. Me arms are strong. I'll find a place to climb down, and I'll be on me way." Though chaos was raging throughout the Royal Wing, it was not enough to penetrate the warm, happy, bubble surrounding Osric.

He continued on until he saw armed men racing toward him from a door at the far end of the catwalk. He did not panic, but simply turned around and started back the way he came. He saw another group of men charging toward him from the opposite direction. Osric took a quick step, then used his stick to vault up into the notch. "I'll just wait here until these damned fools have gone on their way, I will."

As he waited in the notch, Osric's mind began returning to the moment, and time began slowing down. He now understood the men meant to kill him, or even worse they would haul him away to be tortured, and then killed. The guards were bounding toward him from two directions, though they seemed to be running through heavy mud, and their voices were drawn out and distorted. A calmness settled over Osric. "I won't be tied to the whippin' post, I won't. . . . I will make my own choice. . . . I will not be taken." He spent a moment surveying the countryside. In the distance he saw the mountains where he had faced down the tribal chieftain, and the memory brought a smile to his face. Then he turned back to face his pursuers. The soldiers were very close now but moving even more slowly, and their voices sounded as if they were coming from deep inside a well. Then, the cold, hard, reality of his situation came into sharp focus. Osric looked to the sky, and just as a hand was about to seize his ankle, he let himself fell backward off the parapet. "Oh bloody hell!"

Angmar and Juliana were being escorted to the Queen's chambers for a fitting when pandemonium erupted in the Royal Wing. All around came shouts, "The King has been murdered! He was killed by his damned dwarf!" Bells rang, and horns sounded. Running feet, and angry voices could be heard everywhere. The guard escorting the seamstresses hesitated a moment, then abandoned the two women and raced away.

They looked at each other wide eyed, then Angmar cried, "Juliana! We must get to Osric's chambers at once! We must get to that poor girl before the Lord Chamberlain has her put to the sword!" The women were just familiar enough with the Royal Wing that they were able to find Osric's chamber in short order. They burst into the room without knocking, and Angmar ran to the bed and shook Hildegard. "Wake up Girl! You must wake up! Your life is in danger! Wake up Girl!"

It took Hildegard a moment to fathom what was happening. She drew the blanket up to cover herself. "W-who are you? What is the meaning of this?"

"We're friends of Osric. Your husband. We've no time to explain! Dress yourself as quickly as you can, Girl! There is not a second to waste! You are in grave danger!" When Hildegard hesitated, Angmar screamed, "Now girl!"

The terror in Angmar's voice was all the convincing Hildegard needed. She sprang out of bed without regard to her nakedness. She pulled on her clothing and her shoes. As frightened as she was, she did not forget the bag of Silver Swans Alfred had given her and stuffed it inside her bodice.

Juliana took a cautious look outside the door, then motioned for the others to follow. All around them were the sounds of chaos. It proved to be their good fortune that the guards were searching for a dwarf, and they all ignored the three women. They were not halted until they reached the anteroom at the top of the tunnel.

"And where do you think you're going? No one is to enter or leave the Royal Wing!"

Angmar summoned up all her courage and invoked the Queen's name. "We were attending Her Majesty, and she ordered us back to the domestic wing at once! Now step aside and let us pass, or answer to the Queen!" The guard hesitated a moment, then unbolted the door, and allowed the women to leave. Juliana lit a candle lantern, then the women descended the stairs and ran the length of the tunnel. When they reached the domestic wing, they found madness running rampant there as well. Angmar knew how to bypass the common room, and she led Hildegard through a series of hallways to a door opening onto the courtyard. Before they stepped outdoors, Angmar gave Hildegard directions to Jarin's cottage. "Here, take my cloak. Ye must get yourself to the carter's cottage, Girl. He's a friend of your husband. Tell Gwendolyn who you are, and who sent you. My name is Angmar. Remember that! Gwenny knows me, and she will take ya in. Do not show your face outside again until things are calm! Ye must get through the gate before it closes! Go now, Girl! Do not run, but make haste, and do not look back toward the castle!"

Jarin had just crossed the drawbridge on his way to one of the King's estates to collect a load of grain when he heard alarm bells ringing. The bells were followed in short order by a great deal of shouting. From somewhere within the din of voices he heard someone cry 'The King is dead!' He did not know what he should do, but his instincts were telling him to keep his cart moving forward, and he urged his horses to a faster pace. Jarin turned away from the square, then drove down a deserted street running parallel to the western wall of the palace. From high on the parapet he heard loud voices, and then he saw Osric standing in an archer's notch. Jarin halted his cart and sat staring in disbelief at what he was playing out before his eyes. He could see the heads of two groups of men racing toward the notch, and as they converged, Jarin watched in horror as Osric stepped backward off the wall.

As Osric's life was ending, time slowed to a crawl for Jarin. It seemed to take hours for Osric to make the journey from life on the parapet to death on the rocky ledge separating the moat and castle. A silence penetrating every corner of the world ensued, and Jarin heard nothing. Neither the shouting of the men on the wall nor anything else reached his ears. Everything was moving at the pace of a glacier.

Jarin saw the men peering down at Osric's body; then someone must have given an order because all the men turned and went running back the way they had come. There was no activity on the parapet, and there was no one on the street. "They must be plannin' to deal with his body later," muttered Jarin. "I'll have none of that, I won't." He drove as close to Osric's body as he could. "I hope the bloody moat is well frozen, I do." Casting aside all fear of what might happen to him if caught, Jarin jumped down from the seat and raced across the frozen moat without first testing the ice. It held. He paused a moment to look at Osric's face. His eyes were open, and there was the faintest trace of a smile on his lips. He looked as if a great peace had fallen over him.

His moment of reflection was very brief. Jarin gathered up Osric's body and ran back to the cart. He lowered the body into the back, then covered it with the bags that were meant to be filled with grain. Jarin took a quick look in all directions, then said a silent prayer of thanks when he saw no one watching. He turned the cart around and began driving as fast as he dared without attracting attention. As he was turning into the lane leading to the King's cottages, he encountered Fendrel on his way to his work in the palace.

"A good mornin' to ya' Jarin." Something in the carter's face evoked instant fear in Fendrel, and his bright smile evaporated. "What's wrong, Jarin?"

"Get thee up on the seat Fendrel, and make haste!"

Fendrel knew nothing of what had happened in the palace, but the tension in Jarin's voice told him something was very wrong. He wasted no time in complying with the request. "What is happenin' Jarin?"

"Everyone at the palace is shoutin' the King is dead, and I think Osric may have killed him! Osric is dead as well! I saw him die. His body is covered by the bags in the back of the cart. Don't look! Keep your eyes straight ahead!"

"Bloody hell!" said Fendrel, rather too loudly. "What are we to do, Jarin?"

"If the King is dead, that means the Lord Chamberlain will take the throne. From what everyone has told me of his time as Regent, I'm wantin' no part of a King Favian. He will likely cast out all the retainers from their cottages anyway, and replace us with people of his own choosin'. So I'm thinkin' we go before we're thrown out. I've got the King's horses and cart, and with all the confusion, it'll be days before they know they're missin', if they ever do."

"I will follow your lead, Jarin. You know far more about the ways of the palace than does this poor rat catcher."

Jarin reined the horses in front of his cottage, then jumped down from the seat. He removed three of the large bags from the back while making certain Osric's body remained covered. "Fendrel, I think it best you not look at Osric now," whispered Jarin. We'll give him a proper burial later. It will be certain death for us if the soldiers learn that we have his body."

"Aye Jarin, you're right." Fendrel had led a life nearly as sad as Osric's, but what he felt at the moment went beyond words. He got down from the cart seat and fought back tears as he followed Jarin into his cottage.

When they opened the door, they found that Gwendolyn had a guest. Jarin faced his wife and asked, "And who is this?"

"This is Hildegard, Jarin. She is Osric's wife, or perhaps by now, his widow."

"Osric is dead, Gwenny, but we haven't the luxury of mournin' him now. Quickly! Start fillin' these bags with our belongings and all the food stuff we have. We must flee while there is still time. Fendrel, I suggest you run to your cottage and collect your things as well. We must make our way out of the city as fast as e'er as we can!"

No one seemed to notice them in the mad confusion sweeping the city, and in well under an hour, Jarin's family, Hildegard, and Fendrel were beyond the city walls and traveling toward the mountains as fast as they dared. Gwendolyn sat beside her husband on the cart seat, holding Leo in her arms. The young boy was bundled against the cold to the point he was hardly recognizable as a child. They rode on past midday without incident, and their tensions eased with every mile they put behind them. Jarin and Fendrel began to talk of their affection for Osric while Hildegard listened stone-faced.

"It's a bleedin' miracle how all this came together, Fendrel. We could have just as easy been all on our own, and we would have never escaped."

"Aye, Jarin, a miracle indeed, for everyone but Osric."

"Thank God we have his body, and that it will not be made a spectacle of in the square."

"Indeed so, Jarin."

The travelers entered the mountains by late afternoon, and Jarin was relieved beyond words that the air was warming. The sun was shining and there was little wind. The branches of the passing trees were dripping water, but Jarin knew they could not traverse the pass before dark. As night was beginning to fall, he headed the cart into an area free of snow and began following a stream bed away from the track. The ground was frozen to the point the cart and horses left few traces, though a skillful tracker could have followed them. Jarin could only pray they were not being pursued. When they were well removed from the track, Jarin halted the horses, and they made camp. They would eat cold bread this night, as they dare not risk making a fire.

Jarin rigged the cover over the back of the cart, as he had so many times before on his travels with the King. Fendrel and Jarin uncovered Osric's body and removed it from the back of the cart. They spent several minutes looking upon their dead friend with solemn respect. "Do ya think we should say a prayer for him, Fendrel? You knew him best. What would he want?"

Fendrel thought for a moment. "Let's all say our own silent prayer. Truth be told, Osric didn't hold much with priests and the like. The church dealt him naught but misery."

Two tumultuous days had reduced Hildegard to a state of numbness. She had said little during the journey, but as the group looked down at Osric's broken body, she spoke up in a clear voice. "I thought I was to marry Alfred, but he deceived me. Osric was me husband for less than a day. I didn't even know him. I ne'er dreamed I'd e'er be marryin' a dwarf, but I can tell that you good people loved him dear. Mayhaps I could have as well, had I been given the chance."

Hildegard brushed a tear from the corner of her eye, and as she did, Fendrel took her in his arms and held her close. He had never held a woman in his arms before, and yet it seemed the most natural thing he had ever done. Hildegard offered up no resistance and returned Fendrel's embrace. That night as the travelers sheltered beneath the tarp, Jarin and Gwendolyn kept Leo between them in a cocoon of warmth, while Hildegard slept wrapped in Fendrel's arms.

After a cold breakfast, Jarin and Fendrel surveyed the area around their campsite. "This is really quite a beautiful spot, Fendrel. Do ya think Osric would object to this as his final restin' place?

Fendrel considered the idea for a moment, then responded, "I think he would like this place very much, Jarin, but how ever will we dig a grave in this frozen ground? We haven't even a spade."

Jarin pointed out the many large flat stones lining the stream bed. "I noticed those stones last night, Fendrel. I think we can use them to build a tomb. We will build it thick enough that no wolf can e'er dig it open." The four adults set to work, and by mid-morning Osric was ready to be laid to rest. As they were positioning the body for the final time, Fendrel noticed an odd bulge under Osric's jersey just above his belt. When he opened the belt and lifted the jersey, the bag of money fell out. Fendrel opened the leather pouch and was dumbstruck by what it contained. There was a Gold Talent, twenty Silver Swans, and at least thirty coppers. This was more money than anyone in the group had ever seen.

After staring at the money for several seconds, Fendrel handed the pouch to Hildegard. "You are his widow. This is rightfully yours."

Hildegard accepted the pouch, then withdrew her own pouch from inside her bodice. She held up her six Silver Swans for all to see, then added them to Osric's money. After a moment of thoughtful silence, she began, "I am a stranger to you, yet you have risked your lives to save mine, and cast yourselves out of your homes as well. We will share in this. There is more than enough here to buy a free held farm, far from the capital, and large enough to support all of us. We have horses to work the land, and a good cart. I know the millin' trade, and mayhaps we could build a mill as well." She looked at Gwendolyn for a moment, then smiled, "Nothin' would be better for your Leo than for him to grow up breathin' fresh country air, far from the stench of the city, Gwenny." The four adults found themselves overwhelmed by the events of the past day, and they all came together and held one another.

Fendrel and Jarin completed the task of enclosing Osric in his tomb, then they said another silent prayer. As a final gesture, the two men laid down a circle of the flat stones around the outside of the makeshift crypt. "An 'O' for Osric," said Jarin with a smile. "The only marker he will e'er have."

After a last look at Osric's grave, the travelers climbed back aboard the cart. Jarin knew they dare not tarry any longer, because the mild weather would not last. If a storm hit before they crossed over the pass they could find themselves trapped, and facing almost certain death.

In spite of their fears the weather did hold, and they were able to cross over the pass and down the other side without incident. As they sat by a fire that evening, they could see storm clouds gathering over the mountains, and Jarin knew they had been very fortunate. A big storm could block the pass for weeks, but such a storm would also prevent anyone from pursuing them.

The rider was bent low over his horse's neck and had his mount in a dead run. He brought the horse to a partial halt, vaulted from the saddle, then sprinted toward the guard post at the gate of Castle Tyrion. The guards instantly brought their weapons into fighting position and halted the runner. They only stopped the man for the moment it took to identify him as Sir William of Bern, commander of the household guard.

"What is the almighty rush, Sir William?"

"The King is dead! Now step aside you damned fools!"

"Dead? The King is dead? When? How?"

"Minutes ago! Now step aside and let me pass! I must see the Lord Chamberlain at once!

When Sir William was informed by the Lord Chamberlain's butler, that his master was not yet available, he drew his sword and put the tip to the man's throat. "I will see the Lord Chamberlain at once, you insolent bastard!"

"H-he is still dressing. I will get him."

"I will go with you. Now, make haste!"

Sir William pushed the butler aside when they reached the Lord Chamberlain's dressing room. He swung the door wide to find the Duke being dressed by his valet. The shock of being intruded upon was followed by instant outrage. "What in God's name is the meaning of this, William? I shall have you flogged!"

The knight returned his sword to its scabbard, then went to one knee, and bowed his head. Sir William lifted his head, faced the Lord Chamberlain, and said. "The King is dead! Long live the King! Long live King Favian!"

"What? Dead? . . . Urloch is dead?"

"Yes, Your Majesty. Less than a half-hour ago."

"How in God's name did he die?"

"He was murdered by The King's Fool, Sire."

"The King's Fool? How could that wretched dwarf manage to murder the King? Where were his guards?"

Sir William paused a moment, then proceeded with caution. "The King was in the atrium, chatting with Count Dorian, of Bishop's Bridge. The dwarf threw a chamber pot at His Majesty, from an upper story balcony, Sire."

The Duke of Bruno was a hardened cynic but responded with profound incredulity. "He murdered the King with a chamber pot?"

"Yes, Sire. A very large one, used by the guards when on duty."

"Where is the dwarf now? Is he in chains?"

"The dwarf is dead, Sire."

"Did the guards kill him?"

"No, Sire. He took his own life. He leapt from the parapet before he could be captured. He perished in the fall."

"Where is the body? The murderer must be drawn and quartered, then burned in the square, before the eyes of every citizen in the city!"

Sir William paused and cleared his throat. "When I saw the dwarf was dead, Sire, I directed my men to finish securing the castle, thinking the body could be dealt with later. When matters were in hand, I accompanied a party to recover the body, but it was nowhere to be found."

"He escaped?" bellowed Favian.

"I cannot believe he is alive, Sire. I do not believe anyone could survive a fall from that height. Even had he lived, he would have been too badly injured to move. I think his body was spirited away by some unknown person. There were footprints in the snow."

Favian paused and calmed himself. His mind was working very fast. He had more important matters to consider than the body of a dead dwarf. "William, assign twenty of your most reliable men to guard the Queen around the clock. They are never to let her out of their sight. Not even for even a moment. She is not to be allowed contact with anyone. Not her ladies in waiting, not the clergy. No one! Do you understand?"

"Yes, Sire."

"After Urloch's funeral, she will be held under constant guard, until such time it is determined that she not be with child. If she is not, then she will be dispatched to a nunnery."

"And if she is, Sire?"

"Then other measures will be taken. I've no intention of ever serving as regent again."

The funeral of Urloch II was carried out with all the pomp due a murdered monarch. He was laid to rest next to his father in the royal tomb with every noble in the kingdom looking on. The royal funeral was followed by thirty days of official mourning when all the citizens of the realm were required, on pain of flogging, to attend mass daily and pray for the soul of their departed king.

When the appearance of the Queen's menstrual blood revealed she was not with child, selected members of the household guard were sworn to secrecy on pain of death. The chosen men then escorted Jacquelyn to a convent far from the capital. Her place of exile was as bleak and forbidding as the monastery housing Brother Benedict. She would never be seen in public again.

Favian VII used the mourning period to consolidate his grip on power. As Jarin had predicted, all the royal retainers were dismissed from their positions. Though some were later reinstated, most were not. In recognition of his service to the new King, Alfred the cook was given title to Stone Gate Farm and made a Baron of the realm. In the confusion surrounding the death of Urloch II, no one ever noticed Jarin's theft of the King's cart and horses.

Though Walter feared the worst, Favian seemed to forget about the dwarf community completely. Though he would continue to serve as headmaster of the Royal Academy until his death, Walter had little contact with the new King. The dwarf community that had survived for so long began melting away under Favian's neglect, and within a decade there were no more dwarfs living in the palace.

Two months after the death of Urloch II, King Favian VII called all his ministers, and the Dukes, to council. After all those in attendance were sworn to secrecy, the King began to speak. "Gentlemen, I am sure all of you have heard the revolting stories regarding manner in which our late Sovereign met his death. They are most unseemly, and cannot be allowed to persist. It simply cannot become accepted knowledge that a mad dwarf killed his king with a barrel of shit!" The King paused while his eyes burned into each man in the room, then he continued: "If the nobility allows itself to become the laughing stock of the common people, then we may all find our heads on spikes atop the city walls." The intensity in Favian's voice warned everyone who might have had a private laugh over the nature of Urloch's demise, never to do so again. The attendees became very sober, as the King again let his eyes rest on every man in the room, one by one.

"I have had my private secretary prepare a history detailing the many crimes committed by our late King. A copy of this history will be passed to every schoolmaster in the kingdom, as well as every professor at the university. They will, in turn, transmit the story to everyone in their charge. The history will be read from every pulpit in the land, every year, for as long as it takes. . . . Gentlemen, beginning today, the dwarf Osric will be known as the greatest hero in the history of the realm. Osric shall be known to one and all as a man who sacrificed himself in order that the country might escape the cruel yoke of Urloch's tyranny. From this day forward, it is documented, and sworn by all of you that after vanquishing Urloch II in a sword fight, Osric met a hero's death, battling the few guards still loyal to the King. You will all affix your names to this history. Make no mistake, if this history does not take root, you are all facing the loss of your lands, titles, and mayhaps your heads. Therefore, gentlemen, it is incumbent upon you to ensure its success. This story costs us nothing, and protects us all against the rabble."

Every man in the room knew the history contained not a kernel of truth, yet every man swore an oath to its authenticity and affixed his signature to the document. In the months and years that followed, swift and brutal punishment was meted out to anyone found spreading the lie that King Urloch II had perished in any manner other than by Osric's sword. By the time Favian VII passed the throne to his son, Asher IV, Osric's heroism was being celebrated every spring at the equinox, in every corner of the kingdom.

Epilogue

Fendrel's letter to the future.

My name is Fendrel. I was a rat catcher in my younger days, and later in my life I was a farmer and a miller. I am being helped in this writing by my daughter, Freida. She is writing my words for me, as I never learned to read. She is the one who devised the code this story is written in. I am an old man at the time of this writing. I do not know my true age, but I expect I am not long for this world.

Much has been made of the story of Osric in my country in the years since his death, all of it told by people who never met him. I knew Osric very well. He was my dear friend. I want to tell the true story of his death, as far as I know it, so the story does not die with me.

Though Freida is my daughter in every way that matters, she is the product of Osric's loins, not my own. I married Osric's widow, Hildegard, some weeks after Osric's death. Osric and Hildegard were forced into marriage by King Urloch II. They had never met until the day they were wed. They were married less than one full day when Osric perished after having slain the king.

Hildegard was with child at the time we were wed, and Osric was the only man she had ever known. Osric was a dwarf, and my Hildegard was an unnaturally tall woman. Our Freida was born beautiful and perfect in every way. She brightened our lives beyond measure. Hildegard and I were wed for more than twenty years when my dear wife was taken from me, and we never had another child. Today my Freida is the wife of Leo, son of Jarin the carter, and Gwendolyn. She is the mother of Charles, Peter, and Magdalene.

They are the grandchildren of Osric by blood. They are all of normal stature. They are the joy of my old age.

The story of Osric that is told to every child today, says he killed King Urloch II with a sword. I do not believe the truth of this. I never saw a sword in Osric's hands, and I knew him as well as anyone ever did. Nor do I believe he had any knowledge of swordsmanship, and he could never have prevailed against a trained swordsman, as was the King. Dark rumors abounded following the death of Urloch II, saying Osric killed the king with a chamber pot. I do not know if this is true, but I think it more believable than the story of swordplay.

Today it is taught that Urloch II was a cruel man, but that was not what I saw during his reign. I was for a time the royal rat catcher, a position secured for me by my dear friend, Osric. Though Urloch II could laugh at another man's expense, I thought him for the most part to be a decent and generous king. He treated all his retainers well and was a far better ruler than the two kings who have come after him.

On the day that both Urloch II and Osric met their deaths, I fled the capital in the company of Hildegard, Jarin the carter, his wife Gwendolyn, and their son Leo. In our flight, we carried with us the body of Osric. Osric was not killed by the King's soldiers as the story is told today. He took his own life, to avoid capture, by jumping from the castle wall. I know this to be true because Jarin the carter witnessed this act with his own eyes, then retrieved the body of Osric and carried it away.

The tomb dedicated to Osric in the capital is empty or holds the body of some other person. Jarin the carter and I buried Osric in a tomb of flat stones, midway into the western side of the great pass, near the bed of a stream. The grave is marked by a circle of flat stones. Jarin the carter and I last visited the grave ten years ago and found it undisturbed. The land has taken Osric into its bosom, and the tomb we made for him is not now easily observed. I pray he will remain at peace.

We have led a prosperous life of farming and milling since fleeing the capital many years ago. Money paid to Osric and Hildegard by the king made our good fortune possible. To preserve the true memory of Osric, my son-in-law, Leo, will carry these pages to the salt mine below the capital. He has not visited that place, but his father knew it well. The mine is never heavily guarded, but Leo will go there on Christmas eve next, when the guards are certain to be asleep or drunken. Jarin the carter observed many years ago, in the course of his duties, that the King's ministers stored documents and other things in a worked out section of the salt mine, as things were well kept there, and did not rot away. Leo will distribute these coded pages amongst the other document kept in the mine. He will also take with him, the old leather bag I used to ply the rat catching trade. In the bottom of the bag will be hidden the key to reading these pages.

Perhaps no one will ever find the pieces to this puzzle, but such is the love of the false story of Osric in my country today, I am of a great certainty that it is far too dangerous to life and limb to tell the truth of his death in my own time. Though the story of Osric that is told today is false, let no one doubt that he was a real person. At this writing, his daughter, and three of his grandchildren live and thrive. Of those who fled the castle that day so long ago, only Leo and I remain among the living.